MISSED THE MURDER WENT TO YOGA

D.B. ELROGG

A MILO RATHKEY MYSTERY

Missed the Murder Went to Yoga
A Milo Rathkey Mystery

ISBN 9780999820049 (paperback)
ISBN 9780999820032 (eBook)

If you wish to contact the authors, you may email them at: authors@dbelrogg.com

This is a work of fiction. All characters and incidents are totally from the minds of the authors and any resemblance to actual persons, living or dead, or incidents past and present are purely coincidental.

Cover Art by Jason Orr

#3

Dedicated to Jack Archer Goldberger
Who Delightfully Delayed This Book

SPECIAL THANKS TO

STAN JOHNSON
JODY EVANS
DR. ELENA CABB
DOUG OSELL
NICK GOLDBERG
PIPER GOLDBERGER

1

Four inch stilettos, ponte pencil skirt, hot pink blouse, black shorty jacket with ruffles, and platinum blond hair sashayed into the Black Bear Restaurant. Patsy Rand scanned the north-woods themed chop house for her quarry. After collaring the maître d', she zeroed in on the baby-faced, thirty-something, with a receding hairline sipping his cocktail. *Drink up sonny boy, your world is about to come crashing down,* she thought as she arranged herself on the chair opposite him. "Mr. Gain? Peter Gain?"

The photoshopped version of Patsy Rand on the dust cover of her book did not prepare Peter Gain for the garish woman who seated herself across from him. He nodded. "Ms. Rand?"

Noticing his hand covering her book, she charged ahead. "Great read, don't you think?"

Gain's temples began to throb, and his shoulders stiffened. "What's your game?"

"Game?" she smirked. "This is not a game. Rethink your attitude, Junior, while I visit the powder room. I'll have a brandy old fashioned sweet."

Gain caught the waiter's attention and ordered Rand's drink.

Rand returned, took several healthy gulps of her cocktail, snapped her fingers at the waiter, and declared it unacceptable. "A proper old fashioned should have more bitters. A restaurant with your reputation should know how to make a classic cocktail."

The waiter apologized and removed the drink.

Gain sat back in his chair folding his arms. "Are we here so you can abuse the wait staff?"

Rand's face hardened. "I demand proper service. You clearly don't. You're a sniveling little man like your father."

The waiter returned with a second old fashioned. Rand sipped it and sent it back with a wave of her hand. Her well-manicured fingernails tapped on the table as she continued, "My book exposes your daddy for what he was—a murderer. You, the spawn of a killer, will lose everything. It's time for justice, my boy. It should have happened thirty years ago."

The waiter returned for the third time with another brandy old fashioned which Rand declared acceptable. She proceeded to order a rare ribeye, baked potato, and julienne vegetables as if she called people the 'spawn of a killer' every day and expected them to remain and break bread with her. The waiter turned to Gain. "Sir?"

"You'd better order," Patsy Rand baited. "If you stomp out of here like the privileged putz you are, you'll never know how I plan to kill your deal to sell your daddy's company."

Gain blanched.

Rand smiled, "Yeah, I know all about your deal."

The deal was not public knowledge and fragile. Rand would be a complication. "Give me another drink, and the check," Gain said handing his menu back to the waiter. He gritted his teeth, inhaled, and proceeded in a calm and measured tone. "If you try to publish this pack of lies, you will be stopped."

Rand drained her drink, her eyes never leaving Peter Gain's face. "Honey, years ago when I first tried to tell the world about your murderous father, I didn't have the money to fight." She leaned into the table. "This time I have friends, friends with money."

"Friends?" Gain sneered. "Who are these supposed friends?" Gain knew his late father had enemies who would love nothing better than to destroy his reputation. He worried that the book could not only destroy everything his father built, but, as Rand threatened, it could stall the sale of his company.

"I have an army," Rand said smugly. "Your father's enemies, rich enemies, are eager to back my book." She thought she saw him wince as her salad arrived.

Is she bluffing? Gain wondered. He shoved the book to her side of the table, hoping it and Patsy Rand would disappear.

"Keep it," Rand said. "I have a warehouse full of them." She flipped the book, exposing the title, *Empire Built on Blood: The Real Story of Harper Gain.* "Catchy title, doncha think?" His look of panic exhilarated her.

"If you have so many books, why do you need backers?" Gain asked.

3

"Don't you listen? The money's not for printing, but to fight you in court. It's all about justice."

Meeting Patsy Rand face-to-face was a mistake. Peter Gain stood and left his nemesis sitting alone.

Still smiling, Patsy stroked her picture on the back of the dust jacket before depositing the book into her purse. The waiter delivered her steak. She devoured it without further abusing the staff. She had another event this evening.

§

Sutherland McKnight pulled into the expansive garage, parking his Porsche next to the Bentley. McKnight, co-owner of the sprawling Lakesong Estate along with Milo Rathkey, noticed the gap between his car and the Rolls where Milo's Honda usually took up space, a reminder Milo was not at home. Sutherland also had plans for this evening—a quick virtual ride on his stationary bike, a shower, and then out to a new brewery with a loose group of school and business friends. Not his usual Thursday evening, but he was looking forward to it.

As he walked down the hall past the kitchen, he heard his chef, Martha Gibbson, call his name which surprised him as she had the night off. "Mr. McKnight, Jamal is here and would like to ask you a question."

Martha lived in the caretaker's cottage with her younger sister and two brothers, whom she had been raising since the death of their parents five years ago. Fourteen-year old Jamal was the oldest of the two brothers. On cue, the tall high school freshman stood up and shook Sutherland's hand as coached by Martha

"Mr. McKnight, I was wondering if it would be ok if I bought a new rim for the basketball court behind the maintenance shed—it's a little droopy. I have birthday money to buy a new one." He glanced at Martha who nodded her approval. "I made the first cut on the freshman team."

"Congratulations on making the cut!" Sutherland said giving Jamal a high five. "That's great! I can get the new…"

"…Jamal wants the new rim, and he has money for a new rim," Martha said cutting off Sutherland's offer to pay for it.

Martha's eyes told Sutherland that this was about parenting not basketball rims, so he moved to the installation. "Sure, go ahead. The ladder and tools are in the shed, and I'd be glad to help you install it. I loved playing basketball in high school."

"I know. I was looking at the trophy case by the gym and saw an old plaque with your name on it," Jamal blurted.

Sutherland smiled at the memory. "Is that still there? We were state runners-up when I was a junior."

"What position?" Jamal asked.

"Guard. I was the sixth man. What are you? Forward? Center? You're tall enough."

Jamal smiled. "I'm playing center now, but I'd rather be a forward. I need work on my jump shot."

Martha watched the exchange between her brother and Mr. McKnight. Sutherland had his dad's gift of engaging people, taking a real interest in them.

"What's wrong with center?" Sutherland asked.

"It's rough in there. I'm tall, but I have no weight. I get pushed around a lot."

"I did too. No meat on my bones, that's why I played guard."

"Maybe we can play a little one-on-one," Jamal said.

Emphasizing each word, Sutherland said, "You are on."

Martha laughed, "Millennial vs whatever."

"Gen Z," Jamal filled in the blank.

"Okay, Gen-Z, go make sure your brother hasn't burned down the cottage." She waited until he was gone before saying to Sutherland, "Sorry to interrupt you earlier Mr. McKnight, but I could see by the look on your face that you were about to build a full court, and seating for a crowd."

"Full court with parquet floors—don't forget the lighting. Oh, with lighting, we'll need a roof!"

"That would be called a gym, Mr. McKnight."

"Great idea!"

"No! Just no!" Martha sighed.

§

Amy Gramm and Linda Johansson were about the same age, had raised their kids together, and loved reading mysteries. To have some fun and to keep their sanity, they formed a mystery book club. Their kids were now grown; their lives had taken different paths, but the book club kept them connected.

Looking around the living room Amy asked, "How many are we expecting?"

Linda began counting on her fingers. "You, me and Erin—three. Patsy, Charles, Crystal, and Evelyn—seven.

And our guest author, Ron Bello, emailed me this morning to say he's coming—that makes eight that we know of."

"I'm here too." A lean, rugged man with sun-aged skin came in from the front office, "Hi Amy. I'm Liam. My sister is forcing me to be the bartender, gopher, and all-around helper."

"Liam just moved back from California to take a job with the city," Linda explained.

"Really? You left sunny, warm California for Duluth in the fall, soon to be winter?" Amy laughed.

"I know Duluth. There's no bad weather, just bad clothing. A friend from Sweden told me that," Liam proclaimed. "I finished setting up the bar in the front office. What else do you need?"

"We need three chairs from the dining room here in the living room," Linda indicated.

Liam arrived seconds later carrying all three chairs, setting them in front of the fireplace.

"You can join us Liam," Linda said.

Liam shook his head, "No. I'll be across the hall at the bar. That's as close as I'm coming to your murders."

Amy laughed, "We don't commit them. We only read about them."

Linda smiled, but she understood what Liam was not saying.

Amy checked the time on her phone. "People will be arriving soon. I'll get the plates and silverware."

Linda nodded. "I've set them out in the kitchen."

The doorbell buzzed. Erin Cohen, the other book club founding member, let herself in. "Am I the first one here?" she called as she walked into the dining room with her hotdish and was joined by Amy carrying a basket of plates and silverware

"Yes, after me," Amy joked. "Is that a new coat, Erin? The color is great on you!"

"Yes, thank you so much Amy. Boy, I need to hear that today." Erin smiled.

"Put your world famous hotdish down next to the crock pot of Linda's chili," Amy said. "We have food for the soul and body tonight!"

"Come back to the living room, Erin," Linda called. "Tell me what you think about how the room is set up."

"In a minute; it's wine time!" Erin yelled as she walked into the front office bar and folded her coat over the back of a Queen Anne chair. She turned and stared at Liam.

He beamed at the woman he almost married years ago. Her chestnut hair still bounced in curls to her shoulders. She smoothed the curls behind her ear and smiled.

"I'm the bartender tonight—still Chardonnay?" Liam asked.

A million unasked questions rushed in, but only silly words about wine and book clubs came tumbling out. "Bartender at a book club? Fancy," Erin said. "It's good to see you, Liam, but I've moved on to Merlot these days."

Before Liam could respond, the front door swung open. Dr. Charles Carlson arrived with his usual raw vegetables and dip platter from Super One.

"Coats and drink orders in here," Liam instructed.

Erin, hoping to find out why Liam was back in Duluth after twenty-five years, picked up her wine glass and joined Linda who was still rearranging chairs in the living room,.

Carlson dropped his coat on the chair, introduced himself to Liam, and ordered a scotch and water.

Liam pointed to the dining room. "Put your food across the hall, and I'll have the scotch waiting for you."

Carlson nodded at Amy as she straightened out the plates and silverware. He dropped his contribution, still in the grocery bag, onto the table and hustled back to get his drink. Amy, knowing Carlson's habit of doing nothing beyond bringing a store bought, preassembled, not-quite-fresh vegetable tray to these gatherings, removed the plastic wrap and made the veggies presentable on one of Linda's plates.

The featured guest, author Ron Bello, rang the doorbell and was greeted by Dr. Carlson who had collected his scotch and was closest to the door. Linda and Erin came down the hall to shake Ron's hand and invite him into the living room.

Seeing Liam at the bar, Ron smiled. "Liam Johansson? What are you doing here?"

"Ron Bello! One of my favorite people!" Liam said. "What can I get you to drink? It's on the house."

"I'm a dry red wine guy, Liam. Do you have a cab?"

Liam leaned down, pick up a bottle, looked at the label and said, "I've got a 2016 Decoy Sonoma Cabernet, sold at the finer Super Ones."

"Sounds perfect, but you didn't answer my question. Why are you here?"

"Linda there is my sister. She's forcing me on a new career path—bartending at book clubs." Liam handed Bello his wine.

Laughing, Ron said, "I would like to catch up. It's been what, at least a decade."

Ignoring the offer to reminisce, Liam changed the subject, "Read your book—loved it—where Nethercamp is gunned down—nice."

Ron's sly smile betrayed his words, "All my characters are fictional. Any resemblance to persons living or dead is coincidental."

"Right. Coincidental but cathartic."

The conversation was interrupted by a quarrel flowing through the open front door. Still arguing, the tall, lithe Crystal Bowers and diminutive Evelyn Chen took their places at the bar. The entry was getting crowded. Bello allowed himself to be guided down the hall to the living room by Linda and Erin. Dr. Carlson trailed behind,

The squabbling between Crystal and Evelyn subsided for the moment, allowing Liam to introduce himself and take their drink orders. Amy called and waved from the dining room, "Hi Crystal, Evelyn. Bring your goodies over here."

"Evelyn, what tasty weeds did you bring us?" Crystal asked as the two entered the dining room.

Evelyn, an herbalist, looked angry and said, "I have brought my usual steamed vegetable dumplings. I see you have brought your usual—nothing."

"Wrong, as usual, Evelyn!" Crystal said, pulling a plastic grocery bag out of her Louis Vuitton Tote. "Hawaiian rolls. I spent my third-quarter bonus enjoying the islands. These rolls were everywhere. Where did you spend your third-quarter bonus, Evelyn?"

"I spent my time working hard in my shop not for big pharma. Besides those rolls came from Mount Royal Market. It's right there on the bag. A little north of Hawaii isn't it?"

Crystal sighed. "Evelyn, besides being extra crabby tonight, you're so literal. Only the bag came from the Mt. Royal Market."

Continuing their dispute, the duo dropped off their food and joined the main group in the living room where the crowd had gathered around Ron Bello asking questions about his book, *Death Comes To The DA,* as he signed their copies.

The wooden front door slammed open, crashing against the metal umbrella stand, flinging it and several umbrellas against the wall. Evelyn startled at the unexpected bedlam coming from the front entryway. Amy looked at Linda who rolled her eyes as they heard muffled cursing and howling. "Where is everyone? Where am I supposed to go? Somebody get me a strong brandy old fashioned sweet. Immediately!"

Crystal edged her way out of the circle surrounding Bello and walked into the hallway. "We're back here, Patsy. Can you be any louder?"

Ignoring the comment, and the mess she made, Patsy Rand stilettoed through the hall into the living room, surveyed the scene, and plopped herself down in an overstuffed chair ignoring the gathered group.

"Tough day, Patsy?" Amy asked.

"The worst," Patsy crabbed, rummaging through her red Cartier purse. "That Black Bear Restaurant has become a pit! Where's my damn antacids?"

Crystal reached into her purse producing a sample bottle of pills and placed them near Patsy. "Take one. It will help your stomach."

"I took something at dinner. It's not working," Patsy complained.

"These are new—stronger," Crystal persisted.

Evelyn Chen pulled a dark half-filled bottle from her purse. "Here you go Patsy, some of my killer herbs for your stomach."

Patsy waved her off. "Forget it, Evelyn. You've already killed with your potions; I don't plan on going that way."

"Qu si ba," Evelyn spat as she turned and left the room seeking the bathroom.

"Whatever that means," Patsy yelled after her. "Where are you going?"

"Being around you makes me sick," Evelyn said as she disappeared into the hallway.

"Not as sick as that guy you killed!" Patsy yelled after her. "Where's my drink?"

Bemused—and never wanting to miss an opportunity to take notes on possible characters—Ron Bello turned to observe the traveling circus that had crashed the room. All humor drained from his face as he stared at the woman who did not look in his direction.

"Everybody!" Linda announced. "The food is ready." The crowd followed her down the hall to the dining room. Linda joined her brother at the bar. "Is that old fashioned ready yet?"

"I'm on it," he said, muddling the bitters, sugar, and cherries with a splash of soda.

Not joining the others, Patsy whined from the living room, "I've eaten dinner; I need my drink!"

"Oh, come on Liam," Linda rolled her eyes, "you don't have to do it right. Here, let me pour the brandy; I want to shut her up."

Liam watched his sister pour about half a glass of brandy before saying, "You know ice is supposed to go in too."

Linda grabbed a handful of ice cubes and threw them in spilling some of the drink. "There! Just hurry up."

Ron Bello trailed the group heading to the dining room. Seeing Linda and Liam alone in the office-turned-bar, he joined them. "That woman back there, how could you invite her into your house?"

Linda shrugged. "Patsy? She's usually a pain, but I agree, she's on her game tonight."

Bello pointed his finger down the hall. "Don't you know who she is?"

"I didn't see her," Liam said, wiping off the finished drink and setting it on the corner of the bar.

Linda laughed, "She's Patsy Rand." .

"No, she's not!" Bello challenged. "She's Patsy Nethercamp! Nethercamp! The woman who put Liam in prison. The woman I got disbarred!"

Linda gaped in stunned silence.

"Son of a bitch!" Liam swore.

Across the hall in the dining room, the friendly chatter around the food table was broken by a crash and a scream. Linda rushed into the room to find Erin standing over the remains of the thick glass beverage dispenser which had plunged from the table onto the hardwoods. Water, orange slices, and cucumbers littered the flooded floor, drenching some of the food. Blood was flowing down Erin's arm.

"I...I...just touched it and it...look...the stand cracked!" Erin cried.

"You're hurt!" Linda said.

Erin nodded holding her bloody arm away from her clothes. Amy handed her a fist full of paper napkins which Erin applied to her arm. Linda yelled to Liam to get paper towels from the storage shed out front.

Bello crossed the hall to the dining room and leaned against a wall, removing himself from the drama.

"Way to mess up a party, Erin," Crystal blurted. "My rolls are sopped! Why is nobody else's dish ruined?"

Linda countered, glaring at Crystal, "Water spilled. Nothing was done on purpose."

"Get those cucumbers off my rolls!" Crystal continued looking around the room. "Where's Evelyn?"

"I'm so sorry. The stand broke!" Erin whined.

Dr. Carlson looked at Erin's arm. "Run cold water over that cut. I've got some antiseptic samples in my coat."

Erin, holding her arm, rushed to the bathroom. It was locked.

"What the hell is going on?" Patsy Rand asked her from across the hall in the living room.

"I'm bleeding," Erin said as she turned and raced into the kitchen.

"What kind of a meeting is this?" Patsy muttered.

Erin began running cold water from the kitchen sink over her arm when Crystal joined her. "I'm looking for napkins."

"Thank you, I could use some more."

"Not for you! I need them to blot this water off my leggings," Crystal fumed.

"Of course," said Erin sarcastically. "Try the butler's pantry." *Apparently water spots on spandex trumps a bleeding arm,* she thought.

As Crystal left the kitchen, Dr. Carlson arrived with the antiseptic. "This stuff is amazing," he said. "Got a clean napkin?"

Erin pointed to a pile of napkins Crystal left on the counter. He used them to dry her arm.

Holding up the tube, he explained, "This is a wound guard. It not only prevents infection, but it seals the cut."

"Does it sting?" Erin asked.

Dr. Carlson shook his head, not sure if that was true or not.

Evelyn slipped out of the bathroom and drifted down the hall to the dining room. "What happen?" she asked noticing the cleanup effort.

Linda turned to her. "The water jug hit the floor and exploded."

"Oh…I'd help, but I'm not well." Evelyn had unearthed her coat from the pile on the chair in the office. "I think I have a touch of stomach flu. I'm going home."

"Oh really?" Linda asked.

"Feel better, Evelyn," Amy said.

Evelyn did not hear her friends as she had already closed the door and was heading to her car.

Crystal, who had emerged from the kitchen through the butler's pantry in time to hear Evelyn's flu comment, shouted, "Dump those dumplings, or we'll all be sick!"

Thinking it was rude of Crystal to shout about dumping the dumplings, but agreeing it wasn't a bad idea, Linda whispered to Amy, "Too bad. They're always so good."

"Paper towels," Liam announced as he came carrying three rolls.

"What took you so long?" Linda demanded.

"That shed is a mess!" Liam shot back.

"We need a garbage bag too," Linda crabbed. "Get one from the kitchen. We don't have an hour and a half to wait."

Liam left saying nothing.

Ten minutes into the cleanup, Dr. Carlson reentered the dining room from the kitchen thinking he had waited long enough to avoid the pedestrian cleanup. "Ladies, you're doing a fine job, but I'm hungry." He began to fill his plate with Erin's hotdish, bypassed his own crudités, and reached for the steamed dumplings.

"Wouldn't eat those if I were you," Crystal warned.

"And why not?" Dr. Carlson asked.

Crystal explained Evelyn's stomach problems and chided Carlson for not helping.

"I was doing first aid in the kitchen. Now I'm hungry."

"Gotta feed those hair plugs? You got a nice crop of fuzzies coming in on both sides," Crystal joked, knowing he hated any reference to his receding hairline.

Linda continued to pick up the glass from the floor. "I hope we're not in your way, Charles."

The doctor was about to retort when a second loud crash of breaking glass came from the living room. Amy and Linda looked at each other. "Now what?" Linda asked in exasperation.

The crash was followed by two loud thuds and a moan. Everybody froze except Amy who ran to the living room.

Amy found Patsy Rand lying on the floor, face up, blood pouring from a cut on her forehead. The oversized wooden coffee table had been moved back about a foot, and there was blood—lots of blood. Patsy was rasping, hand on her chest. Amy dropped to one knee to check Patsy's pulse.

Dr. Carlson ambled into the living room plate in hand. "Oh Lord! Somebody bring a cold washcloth from the kitchen. Patsy's hit her head."

Amy gestured to Dr. Carlson to come closer whispering that Patsy had a weak pulse, was having trouble breathing, and her skin felt clammy.

"She was also complaining of stomach upset," Crystal said. "Maybe it's flu? Can you faint from stomach flu?"

"She can if she's dehydrated," Dr. Carlson advised.

"Please check her, doctor," Amy demanded. "She's not looking good."

Patsy continued to fight for breath.

With a sigh, the doctor placed his plate on the coffee table, knelt to put his fingers on her throat, checking Patsy's pulse for himself. "It's weak. Somebody call for an ambulance."

Erin came into the room with a cold washcloth and handed it to Amy who placed it on the gash on Patsy's forehead.

Looking at the blood, Erin backed up, leaned against the entry, and whispered, "I'm feeling a little woozy,"

Crystal, made herself comfortable on the corner of the sectional, grabbed her long blond hair smoothing it over her left shoulder, and patted the cushion next to her, "Come, sit down Erin. We don't need another fainter. Let the professionals take care of Madam Rand."

Liam dropped the garbage bags and began sweeping up the ice cubes and shards of glass from Patsy's shattered drink. "Watch your step everyone. I don't know if I got it all," he shouted.

Dr. Carlson said he could hear a siren. Standing up, he added, "I'll direct the EMTs in here."

Patsy's eyes opened with a start, and she grabbed Amy's arm. "Hurt. Yellow."

"Don't talk. The ambulance is coming Patsy," Amy said.

"The book," Patsy whispered. "Why?"

Dr. Carlson was explaining Patsy's symptoms to the EMTs as they came into the house with a stretcher and medical gear. Amy stepped back to let them work.

After a few minutes, Crystal announced, "We think it's stomach flu,"

"What's her BP?" Dr. Carlson asked the EMTs.

"Low," one of the EMTs replied.

"And she's not responding," said the other as they moved Patsy onto the stretcher and wheeled her out of the house. Dr. Carlson and Amy followed.

Almost everyone, even Crystal, went out to the front lawn to watch the ambulance pull away. Liam and Ron Bello were left alone in the dining room.

Bello approached Liam. "You recognized her, right? Nethercamp."

Liam tied the garbage bag in a double knot. "Takin' out the garbage."

An hour later Amy called Linda to say Patsy had died in the ambulance on the way to the hospital.

2

A persistent ringing roused Milo Rathkey from a deep and dreamless sleep. Squinting at the offending phone, he noted an unknown number but answered anyway and was amused to hear a female voice urging him to hire Duncan Construction for any of his home remodeling needs. Chet Duncan was the last errant husband Milo followed when he was a private investigator. He always hated that part of PI work, but it paid the rent.

Making rent was not a problem for Milo anymore; not since he was an unexpected beneficiary in the will of John McKnight—Sutherland McKnight's father—that left him fifteen million dollars and half ownership of Lakesong, John's sprawling estate on the north shore of Lake Superior in Duluth, Minnesota.

Now shaved and showered, Milo made his way to the morning room, walking through Lakesong's park-like two-story gallery—a grand glass domed park-like room complete with trees, cozy seating arrangements, and a spotless white marble floor. Milo gave a quick glance at the Guiana chestnut tree searching the branches for his friend, Annie the cat. Annie usually led the way into the kitchen for bits of his breakfast, but she wasn't hustling this cloudy morning. The calico cat stretched, yawned, and inched her way down the tree, falling in line behind Milo before picking up the pace and darting ahead of him.

"Hi Martha," he waved as he passed the kitchen.

"Good morning, Mr. Rathkey," she returned. "Hello Annie."

Annie gave her a silent meow but continued leading Milo into morning room. The cat never forgot to acknowledged Martha whose family fed her cat food when human food wasn't an option.

Milo tossed two folders on the breakfast table as he made his way to the coffee urn.

"Morning Milo," Sutherland said folding his Wall Street Journal.

"Right," Milo mumbled.

Sutherland, tall and thin with sandy brown hair, sat in contrast to Milo's shorter thicker frame and curly black hair. Martha delivered Milo's usual breakfast—scrambled eggs, bacon, and hash browns. He, in turn, broke off a few small pieces of bacon and dropped them for Annie.

"Morning Annie," Sutherland said in a loud voice. The cat ignored him. "Why doesn't she ever talk to me?" he complained.

"You don't do anything for her," Martha said. "Milo feeds her breakfast treats. The sibs and I feed her cat food and clean her litter box."

"I rescued her! Well, my father rescued her from the shelter, sort of like the way he rescued Milo," Sutherland teased.

"I didn't come from a shelter," Milo complained, "but I have to admit, I purr while in the library."

Sutherland turned to Martha. "Is purr another word for snore?"

"Don't get me in the middle of this. You two argue between yourselves." She returned to the kitchen.

"What's in the folders?" Sutherland asked taking a sip from his blue breakfast smoothie.

Milo looked up from his plate. "Blue? Why blue? What happened to sickly green?"

Sutherland held it up. "It's blueberry season! You didn't notice that my smoothies change color with the seasons?"

"They've always been green up until now."

"But different greens, Mr. Detective, depending on the greens in season."

"But this one's blue; blueberry season ended last month."

"How do you know that?" Sutherland asked.

"Mary Alice and I went blueberry picking last month," Milo said, referring to Mary Alice Bonner, the blue eyed widow of James Bonner who was murdered at his New Year's Eve party. Mary Alice was trying something different, the different being Milo.

Sutherland laughed at the idea of Milo the berry picker. "So, what happened to your blueberries?"

"You're drinking them. I hate blueberries, but I like Mary Alice," Milo admitted.

"Remind me to thank Mary Alice for my breakfast. So, what's in the folders?" .

Milo looked at the two folders in front of him. "They're copies of the police file on my dad's murder."

Sutherland checked Milo's face—he gave nothing away. "You're ready to investigate?" Sutherland asked.

"Yeah, I guess. I got a copy of the file from Ernie Gramm a couple of months ago. I've been sitting on it, but I think I'm ready."

"If I can help, let me know."

"Yes, as a matter of fact, you can. I'm getting kinda used to you being along on these investigations. Besides, the theory you latch onto is always the wrong one, so I can eliminate it early," Milo said with a smile.

Sutherland began to object but had to admit his theory of bodies in a tunnel or buried under the back lawn were not his best moments. Milo slid one file over to Sutherland, gave Annie another piece of bacon, and squeezed ketchup on his hash browns. Sutherland began to read the file.

Milo ate his breakfast, periodically gazing out the morning room's wall of windows as the layers of gray mist swept over Lake Superior. The lake was rough today. Milo thought it looked cold.

Sutherland had stopped reading and was staring at Milo.

"What?" Milo asked.

"It says here your father was shot on a construction site at the Miller Crossing strip mall."

"Yeah?"

"In the late seventies when your dad was killed, The Miller Crossing strip mall belonged to McKnight Realty. It was my father's first and only foray into real estate development."

The creases in Milo's forehead deepened. "How would you know that? You weren't even born yet."

"True, but when I joined McKnight Realty, *after I was born*, I was eager for the company to get into development. After some heated discussions, dad told me about building this strip mall. All I could get out of him was it didn't go well, and he didn't want to do another one. He never told me 'didn't go well' meant a death on the property or that the death was your father. Why would he keep that a secret?"

Milo stopped eating. "That's one question—another question is what my dad, a detective, was doing at a half-built strip mall." Milo's forehead creases became deeper.

§

Amy Gramm zipped up her quilted jacket, tucked a red plaid blanket around her legs, and settled back to watch comings and goings at the Duluth harbor from her deck. Working in an emergency room for twenty-five years, she had seen her share of death but not where she went to relax and socialize. Ever since she and Ernie bought this house on Observation Hill, the busyness around the harbor calmed her. Two ships were being loaded and a tug was guiding a salty into port. She warmed her gloved hands around her coffee mug and took a sip.

Through the sliding glass doors, Ernie spotted Amy's red blanket. Last night she was upset over what had happened at the book club. Finding her on the deck this morning was no surprise. He poured a cup of coffee, threw on his jacket, and joined her. "Brrr! Pretty cold for breakfast on the deck," he said as he sat down.

Amy looked at him and smiled.

After several minutes of silence Gramm pointed to the neighbor's yard. "Sure am glad Tom planted that tree a coupla years ago. It's gorgeous. I think it's on its way to turning red."

"Fifteen," Amy said.

Gramm turned to look at her. "What's fifteen?"

"Tom planted that tree fifteen years ago, not a couple."

"Really? Time flies."

Amy knew this was Ernie's way of checking in—making sure she was okay—without asking a lot of details. Over the last thirty years, they had developed their own code. Neither of them wanted their jobs to come home, but this was different.

"They think it was her heart," Amy said, her gaze still fixed on the harbor. "Strange thing though, none of the drugs worked—not even a little bit. I've never seen that before."

Ernie kept drinking his coffee. He was glad he brought his jacket. This could take a while.

Amy continued, "She said 'hurt'—which makes sense, and 'yellow' before she lost consciousness."

"Yellow?" Ernie asked, not having a clue why that might be important. Amy was thinking out loud.

She shrugged, "They did the best they could, but she failed so quickly—not textbook at all."

Ernie rearranged his cold hands around the fast cooling coffee cup and wished he had worn his gloves.

"Someone's burning leaves. Ernie, go arrest them," Amy teased.

"I like the smell, besides if it isn't homicide, I don't care."

Amy took a deep breath. The cold air filled her lungs, cooling the unease she felt. "Even though the hospital said it was heart and respiratory failure, I don't know."

After thirty years of marriage, he understood that Amy wasn't making idle chit chat. She was smart. She had seen it all. His cop persona came to the surface. "So, she failed quickly. It was not textbook. She said something about yellow, and you have questions."

Amy turned to him and smiled. "For a cop, you listen well."

"I keep telling you, I'm phenomenal."

She reached over and squeezed his arm. "You are. So, what happens next?"

"I call Doc Smith. The body's transferred for autopsy." Ernie got up.

"What if I'm wrong?" Amy asked.

"You, my dear, are never wrong. Can I get you more coffee?"

"I'm good," Amy said, sending her focus back over the harbor. An ore boat was leaving under the Aerial Bridge—life continued.

Gramm went to the kitchen to call Doc Smith, the Medical Examiner.

§

"Work calls," Sutherland said as he slid the police file back to Milo.

"That's your copy. Finish reading it and we'll talk later," Milo said sliding it back.

"Sure, but can you legally copy a police file? I thought they were—you know—classified or something."

"It's a forty year-old unsolved murder. I don't think the CIA cares."

"So, you trotted a police file into Kinkos?"

"No. Agnes copied it for me on my copy machine," Milo boasted.

"We have a copy machine?"

"We do not have a copy machine. I have a copy machine which I purchased for my assistant. If you want to use it, let Agnes know. She'll take it under consideration."

Agnes Larson's tenure as the Lakesong house manager only lasted about six months. She was now Milo's personal assistant, fewer complications for Agnes' growing romantic relationship with Sutherland.

Sutherland wondered if Milo was kidding. "Is it a real copy machine, like for an office?"

Milo made a sweeping gesture with his arms. "It's huge, takes up about three stories. We had to punch through the ceiling to get it in here."

Sutherland sighed, "I don't have time this morning, but I'm checking it out tonight."

"Do I warn the copy machine or Agnes?" Milo yelled after him. He heard the door to the garage close. Sutherland was gone. Martha had left earlier. Besides Annie, Milo was now alone in this rambling house. He spun the police file around a couple of times on the table before getting up for a second cup of coffee.

Standing at the window, Milo watched the white capped waves crash against the basalt boulders that lined a section of

Lakesong's beach. The wind was picking up. Building a fire and reading about a fictional murder would be the perfect remedy for feeling maudlin on this dreary day. On his way to the library—police file in hand—the intercom announced, *Gate Open*. This was electronic genius Ed Patupick's creepy addition to Lakesong—an intercom with a woman's voice. Milo preferred the old buzzer.

Either a forgetful Sutherland was at the front gate—doubtful—or Agnes had arrived at Lakesong. Milo changed his course and headed to Agnes' office.

They arrived at the same time. "Morning, Mr. Rathkey," Agnes greeted him while hanging up her bright red coat. Milo had been noticing that Agnes was not the Agnes he met months ago at the Bonner New Year's Eve Party. She had morphed from plain to pretty and appeared to be younger, her blond hair seemed brighter somehow, and she smiled more often. How it all happened, he had no clue.

"Did you change your hair?" Milo asked.

Agnes laughed, "About three months ago—remember the reunion? If I keep it this way, I need to get it cut again. What do you think? I could grow it out."

"It's all nice," Milo said taking the middle road and changing the subject. "I'm afraid I ratted you out to Sutherland,"

She stopped short not knowing what he meant.

"Our copy machine, I told him about our copy machine. You may get a visit. I told him he needs to make an appointment."

Agnes shrugged, "He's gonna want to get a guy, isn't he?" she said, referring to Sutherland's proclivity for having a 'guy' to maintain everything from cars to chimneys. "By the way, have you seen your old door? I hung it on the wall in your office yesterday."

"Checking it out now," Milo said opening the connect-ing door to his office. There on the wall between the large windows, framed in beautiful dark mahogany, rested the middle panel of his old weathered oak door. It had taken its place among the rare first edition mysteries and original oil paintings John McKnight had collected.

Milo laughed, "It's a Milo Rathkey relic!"

"Modern Realism," Agnes countered.

The partial door was a gift from his former landlord, Ilene, of Ilene's Bakery, where Milo had rented an office and an adjoining room for ten years. Painted red letters read RAT KEY INVESTIGATIONS; the H, fading years ago, was never repainted. Milo took a picture of the door with his phone and sent it to Ilene.

"This is great! Thanks," Milo said. "By the way, I have a new job for you. It doesn't have to be done tomorrow, and if it's too much, tell me."

"I'm intrigued."

"This house is full of books. They're in the attic, the library, my office, the vault and I don't even know where else. There are bedrooms upstairs that may have books. Who knows? Could you..."

"Catalogue them? Of course. I would love to," Agnes said. "In my previous position I computerized all the artwork. I can do something similar for the books. Do you know if any of the books have been cataloged in any way?"

"I asked Sutherland. He found a partial list of first edi-tions in John's papers but nothing else. The list should be on your desk. Winter is coming; since reading is my winter sport, I want to know what my reading choices are."

Looking over the partial list of first editions, Agnes began planning out loud, "I will need to purchase a bar code scanner and library software."

"Yeah right. I was gonna suggest that," Milo said sarcastically.

"Should I use Lakesong's credit card or Rathkey's credit card?"

"I think Lakesong; even though I'm the one that reads them, the books belong to the estate." Milo figured Sutherland could help foot the bill for some of this.

"I have ordering to do," Agnes said opening up her computer as Milo entered his office.

Milo threw down his copy of the police file and watched it glide across John McKnight's polished mahogany desk— now Milo's polished mahogany desk. Milo sat down in the large swivel chair and leaned his head back against the soft leather. He had told Sutherland he was ready, yet his attention wandered, and he found himself swiveling in the chair looking at the first edition books behind him, the artwork on the walls, and the fireplace with the two facing comfortable chairs. Except for the *Rat Key* original, this was still John's office, almost the way he left it. The file remained unopened, locked by the fears of an eight-year-old boy who had lost his father and was told there wasn't enough money to stay in the family's house. After all these years, the fear still made his stomach ache. The irony was not lost on Milo, now a millionaire sitting in a mansion but not being able to shake that age-old fear of being homeless.

Also, learning about his dad dying on John McKnight's property threw him and all his cop-like objectivity for a loop. His father and surrogate father, John McKnight, were connected, both with stories to tell—both dead. Did John's guilt bring Milo and his mom to Lakesong? Did guilt make Milo rich?

"So, John," Milo said, *"is there something you want to tell me? Like why my dad died on your property."* He waited—no answer. Milo opened the first page of the folder. Despite having a state-of-the-art computer, he began jotting facts and reactions on a yellow legal pad—old habits die hard.

— *July 10 1978/11:33PM/ Call comes in, gunshots at the Miller Crossing construction site (Owned by John McKnight)*

— *Karl Rathkey shot three times from behind. DOA*

— *Two shots in the back and one in the back of the head—execution?*

— *Moonlighting as an armed guard nights? (Why? Never mentioned. Rank at time: Detective)*

— *Possible burglary of construction equipment gone bad*

— *Shooting investigated by Sergeant Rod Prepinski and Patrolman Mark Crandell*

— *Responded 11:40*

— *Ambulance called 12:05 (Why so long—25 minutes)*

— *Final conclusion, Rathkey shot by person or persons unknown.*

Agnes had clipped the report to the left-hand side of the folder with pictures on the right. Milo took a deep breath and began studying the pictures of the scene. In the forty-year-old washed-out color photos he saw the half-built strip mall, piles of lumber, cement blocks, spools of wire, and dumpsters overflowing with debris. The second picture of the parking lot showed patches of black asphalt through a sea of brown dried mud. Some tire tracks and footprints were visible. His experiences told him what should be coming next—pictures of the victim.

Milo paused, "You're not eight," he said to himself. Turning to the third picture, he saw a body lying face down, the dark t-shirt and head covered in blood. The smiling man with dark curly hair he remembered was unrecognizable.

Milo turned his focus to the series of yellow forensic numbers around the body marking points of interest. To his mind, the numbers were placed in a random fashion. Milo searched the file for a description of each number, a standard in any investigation. It was missing. This file was incomplete.

Milo returned to the second picture. On closer inspection, he noticed some of the tire tracks were not clear. The same was true for footprints. He pulled a magnifying glass out of his desk drawer and made a closer scan of the pictures. An attempt had been made to obscure those tracks, yet not all the tire tracks and footprints were affected this way. Milo stiffened. His jaw clenched, and he drew in a long breath through his teeth. He knew what he was looking at.

3

"Got anything I can help with Sarge?" Patrolman Kate Preston asked Sgt. Robin White as White was getting settled at her desk. "I'm looking to tag along," Preston added.

White smiled at the brown-eyed, fresh-face patrolman trying to age herself by pulling her hair back into a grandma bun. "Not today. Not this weekend. We have zero cases. After this storm passes, it should be warm and sunny—my last chance for a summer sail," White said, remembering how eager she was for experience when she was a rookie. She slid a note pad over to Preston. "Put your name down so I remember you when we have something."

"Don't hoist that jib yet, partner," Lt. Gramm, the fifty-something-homicide detective shouted from his office. Gramm's bushy-white eyebrows were elevated, a sign that something was brewing.

White's shoulders sagged. Preston jotted her name on the pad and disappeared. White got up and headed into Gramm's office. "Whaddaya got?"

"Before we get into it, do I call tomorrow's warm September weather Indian summer, Native American summer, or First Nation summer?" Gramm asked, referring to White's Ojibway ancestry.

"Let's go with a warm day in the fall," White offered knowing Gramm was working his way through being sensitive.

"I'll note that," Gramm said.

"Why is my warm day in the fall going to be interrupted?" White asked, putting her long black hair into an *it's-time-to-work* ponytail.

Gramm explained the death of Patsy Rand and Amy's doubts about natural causes. He told her about his call to Doc Smith and the fact an autopsy was planned for today. "So, we just wait," he said.

"You're telling me a woman at a mystery book club meeting may have been murdered? Who does that?" White asked.

"I have no idea. I don't know if I can investigate it—Amy is a witness. That's the Deputy Chief's call. Everything is up in the air."

§

Liam Johansson put glasses and plates into the dishwasher. His sister Linda was busy filling a second black garbage bag with the remains of last night's book club fiasco. After the ambulance left with Amy, Dr. Carlson, and the dying Pasty Rand, Linda apologized to Ron Bello, and the night ended.

Linda looked out the kitchen window. "Liam! Hurry! The garbage truck is coming."

Liam picked up the garbage bags and hustled out to the alley as the truck arrived.

§

Milo's late morning swim was long and therapeutic. After doubling his normal laps, he collapsed into one of the chaises scattered around the glass-enclosed indoor pool. *I have to check if either of the investigating cops are still alive,* Milo thought, wishing he had a bottle of water. Of course, he did have a bottle of water at the pool bar only twenty steps away. Reclining on the chaise, he watched the leaves scudding across the glass enclosure and decided he didn't have enough energy to get up.

§

Sutherland's Friday morning was productive and profitable. Several commercial and residential deals that were in the pipeline had closed, and new business leads were almost double. His assistant, Loraine, had a small mountain of paperwork needing his attention which he dealt with in quick order. He had questions about two residential agreements and sent out emails to the agents. The rest of the paperwork he walked back to Loraine for disbursement or filing.

"We are ordering lunch from The Salad King," Loraine said.

"Great. Could you get me their ahi tuna," Sutherland asked, "with a side of broccoli?"

Loraine added that to the list.

"Charge the tab to the office," Sutherland said as he headed back to his office.

Loraine smiled. The Salad King on Fridays usually meant free lunch for the staff. "One last thing, Mr. McKnight, the ovarian cancer event, you know, lighting the bridge in teal, is coming up soon. Should we give the usual? Your father always gave…"

"Double it," Sutherland said. "Business is good."

Loraine nodded, knowing the charity was special to the McKnights.

Sutherland filled his water bottle from the cooler, sat down, and opened the file Milo had given him at breakfast. *Another typical Friday,* he thought, *old business, new business, order lunch, open a police file.* He laughed at his joke and got a few stares from staff passing by his office door.

As Sutherland read the details of Karl Rathkey's death, his humor dissipated. The only other police file he had ever seen was on the hit-and-run death of Agnes Larson's sister, Barbara. That file included pictures of the scene, the street outside city hall, but not of Barbara. Sutherland avoided the picture of Milo's dad.

Flipping through the papers, Sutherland noticed the file itself was about the same size as the hit-and-run file. *Shouldn't the file of a murdered policeman be thicker than the file of a hit-and-run?* He wrote 'thin file' down on a sticky note and put it on the outside cover.

Though he avoided the picture of Karl Rathkey's body, Sutherland noted the placement of the bullets listed in the report, two in the back and one in the back of the head. He had seen enough movies to know what that could be. Another sticky note was pasted onto the outside cover. This one read *assassination?*

§

As Gramm put Doc Smith on speaker, he went to the door and waved White into the office. "I've got Robin here with me, Doc."

Doc Smith began, "What I've got is preliminary."

Gramm rolled his eyes and mouthed, "he always says that."

"The victim suffered respiratory and heart failure, but I am betting against natural causes. Other than an ulcer, she was a healthy sixty-year-old, except, of course, for that gash on her forehead. That was caused by her falling against the coffee table. I surmise she stood up and collapsed."

"So, she was fine until she died," Gramm added.

"She shouldn't have died. I haven't found a legitimate cause for her heart to fail. She ate a big meal about an hour or two before death, and there was a moderate amount of alcohol in her system, but no drugs that I could find. The lab report from Minneapolis might give us more."

"What lab report?" White asked.

"According to your boss, the victim said the word yellow," Smith said. "There are several poisons that can lead a person to seeing yellow, green, or red. One or two of them are detectable only by chromatography. We don't have the equipment. The lab guy I sent it to owes me a favor, so I am hoping for results by Monday morning."

White smiled. "So, we don't have a murder until Monday."

"If at all," Smith said.

The phone went dead.

"What's with you people?" White asked noting that Gramm did it all the time.

"What?"

"You people—old guys who never say goodbye."

§

"Good evening, gentlemen," Martha said as Sutherland and Milo sat down for dinner. "Tonight, you have stuffed chicken breasts with tomato pesto using my homegrown tomatoes, also garlic, pecans, arugula, parmesan cheese, and olive oil. For a side, we have roasted green beans with toasted slivered almonds. Mr. McKnight, I have a mixed green salad with vinaigrette, and Mr. Rathkey, the usual iceberg lettuce with blue cheese. The wine is an '05 pinot noir."

"Sounds great," Milo said.

Sutherland agreed.

Sutherland watched Milo's usual habit of using his fork to cut a slice of his iceberg wedge. "Why do you do that?" he asked.

"Why do I do what?" Milo questioned.

"Use only your fork instead of a knife and fork."

"If you're working on my table manners, you're doomed to failure."

"No, no I was just wondering. Dad did it that way. Did you pick that up from him?"

Milo thought for a minute. "I don't know. I always did it this way."

"Blue cheese on iceberg lettuce was his favorite salad. In fact, it was his only salad," Sutherland mused.

"Where are you going with this?" Milo asked.

I don't know. Maybe it's the police file bringing up thoughts of your dad, my dad, coincidences. Should we compare notes while we eat?"

"Let's wait until after dinner," Milo said. "I'm working on my table manners."

Sutherland changed the subject, "It should be beautiful tomorrow, sunny and warm, the last gasp of summer. How are you going to spend it?"

"I'm buying a car, and Sunday I'm taking it for a spin up the North Shore."

Sutherland choked on his wine. "A new car? Finally!"

"You are assuming facts not in evidence," Milo said.

"But you said…"

"…I'm buying a car. I didn't say *new* car."

"You're buying a used car?" Sutherland couldn't believe it.

"It's an '87 Mercedes 560SL convertible."

"I'm familiar with the Mercedes SL line. It's classic and impractical. I'm so proud," Sutherland joked. "What happens with your Honda?

"It stays," Milo said.

"Of course," Sutherland sighed.

Milo was pleased Sutherland's attention was captured by the shiny object of the car and not his companion on his motoring escapade, Mary Alice Bonner.

After dinner, Sutherland lit the fire pit on the back terrace as he and Milo sat enjoying a drink. The predicted weekend warm front had already arrived giving the two a comfortable evening. Both men watched the lights of an ore boat standing still on the dark lake, only an illusion created by the enormity of Lake Superior.

"So, you looked at the file," Milo said.

"I did," Sutherland said picking up the file from the side table. "I even wrote two sticky notes."

Intrigued, Milo asked, "So whaddaya got?"

"My first note says, *thin file*. Shouldn't the shooting of a policeman be thicker, more thoroughly investigated?"

"Sticky note number two?"

Sutherland was hesitant to proceed. The impersonal in his office became personal on the back terrace. "This note is indelicate."

"Look," Milo said to himself as much as Sutherland, "the hard part of any investigation is to keep emotion out of it. On any murder case, I'm Mr. Indelicate. It's a way to create distance. On this one, the victim is my dad. But if we're going to succeed, we need to try and forget that. So, sticky note number two?"

Sutherland took a sip of his Scotch, looked at his sticky note, and without looking at Milo, said, "Assassination."

"What leads you to that?" Milo questioned.

Turning his attention back to Milo, Sutherland said, "I know I go off on tangents, so let me know if you think this is crazy, but the way your dad..."

"The victim," Milo corrected.

"...the victim was shot in the back and then the head. It was like that movie where Tom Cruise was an assassin."

"Good. Let's give your movie-going-insight another fact. There's no mention of shell casings."

"Shell casings?"

Milo nodded, "This was supposed to be a construction site burglary gone bad. No shell casings. It doesn't fit."

Sutherland was still not getting the connection.

Milo tried to break it down. "Let's say you, Sutherland McKnight, go to steal stuff from a construction site. You're looking for easy in, easy out."

"Okay," Sutherland said.

"Why'd you bring a gun?"

"I...I...have no idea."

"Is the theft of a front loader worth the extra prison time?"

"Not for me," Sutherland declared.

Milo took a sip of his after-dinner gimlet. "Back to the robbery. All is going well. You're doing a great job until this person challenges you. He's facing you. How do you shoot him in the back?"

Sutherland paused trying to think how this could happen. "I can't shoot him in the back."

"So, who does?"

"Oh, I'm not alone. It's me and my pal. There are two of us, but the victim only sees one."

"Good. So, you and your pal are robbing this construction site. You're challenged; your pal shoots twice from behind. The victim falls. Now what do you do?"

"Run like hell!" Sutherland said.

"Exactly. You don't stop, shoot one more time, pick up your shells, and then rub out your shoe and tire tracks."

"If you do, it's…"

"…your second sticky note."

4

J amal, new basketball rim in hand, sat on the edge of
Martha's desk chair in the kitchen bouncing his left
heel in an unconscious keeping of time until Sutherland
arrived for his Saturday morning smoothie. Jamal had been
sitting on the left side of the double-grand entry staircase
until Martha spotted him and insisted he wait, out of sight
in the kitchen, for Mr. McKnight to finish his breakfast.

"Settle down," Martha ordered. "If Mr. McKnight has
plans this morning, you and I will put the rim up later."

"He said he wanted to do it today and play some one-
on-one," Jamal countered.

Martha shot him her 'Martha Look.' "Excuse me?"

Jamal slumped down at Martha's desk and mumbled,
"He wanted to do it. I don't want to leave him out. He's your
boss. He might get mad at me and fire you," Jamal added,
pleased with his creative excuse.

Martha hid a smile. Jamal was bright and funny, but older sister silence was best at this point.

As Sutherland broke the threshold to the hearth room, Jamal shot up. "I bought a rim, Mr. McKnight."

"Great!"

Jamal bounded across the hearth room, followed Sutherland into the morning room. and handed him the orange rim.

Sutherland examined it. "You got a good one. Let's hang it after breakfast."

Jamal beamed.

Martha interrupted, "Good morning Mr. McKnight. If you have plans today, Jamal can…"

Sutherland held up his hand. "Rim hanging is my plan this morning."

"Okay." Martha seemed appeased and pleased.

Sutherland added, "I checked out the backboard. It was awful, so I bought a new one. We can put that up first."

Martha shot Sutherland a look—not the 'Martha Look,' but close.

He shrugged. "The old one was warped, Martha. Putting a good rim on a bad backboard makes no sense."

Martha turned away and rolled her eyes. *There's so much testosterone in this room I could slip on it.*

Sutherland sat down to his blueberry smoothie. Seconds later a loud meow was heard coming from the direction of the gallery. Milo's Morning March was on its way. Annie the cat arrived in the hearth room first, followed by a yawning Milo who immediately poured himself a cup of coffee. Surprised to see Jamal, an infrequent visitor to the morning room, Milo told him to sit down and have some breakfast.

"He had breakfast and hour ago!" Martha called from the kitchen.

"I could eat again," Jamal blurted.

"An hour is a long time between meals when you're a teenager," Milo said as Martha handed Milo the usual eggs, bacon, and hash browns.

"That looks good." Jamal smiled at Martha.

"If you give me another plate, I'll give him some of mine," Milo offered as he fed several bits of bacon to the cat.

"I can whip him up a junior Milo plate," Martha said, "this one time."

"That," said Milo gesturing to the large orange object in the center of the table, "is a basketball rim."

"It is." Jamal beamed.

"We're going to put it up this morning," Sutherland said, "along with a new backboard I have in the garage."

"Do you play basketball, Mr. Rathkey?" Jamal asked.

Milo laughed, "I dribble my coffee, not a basketball."

"With your tennis skills, I would have thought you'd be the monster on the basketball court," Sutherland kidded.

"In what world does playing tennis have anything to do with basketball?"

"They're both played on courts," Jamal offered.

"Jamal, eat your second breakfast," Martha said, handing him his plate.

"What are you doing this morning?" Sutherland asked Milo.

"I told you, I'm getting my car." Milo slogged his hash browns through a pool of ketchup.

"From where?" Sutherland asked.

"Harry Reinakie."

"Of course, but I thought he sold Cadillacs." Sutherland remembered that Harry was a former client of Milo who worried his wife, Heidi, was cheating.

"And classic cars," Milo added.

"What are you buying?" Jamal broke in.

"A 1987 Mercedes 560SL."

"A what?" Jamal asked.

"It's an old sports car."

Jamal squinted. "Why old? Wouldn't you want a new one?"

Milo explained that it was the car he wanted when he was a teenager.

"Do you need a ride to the dealership?" Sutherland asked.

"Harry is delivering it," Milo said. "I've become *his* client."

Agnes Larson waved as she walked into the morning room. "Hello all."

"It's the weekend! Is Milo working you on a Saturday? I hope he's paying you overtime," Sutherland joked.

Agnes poured herself a cup of coffee. "No and no. It's gorgeous out there," she said pointing to the expanse of Lake Superior, "and I'm hoping to avail myself of the chair by the lake and read. There's a puddle in my backyard thanks to the rain yesterday afternoon, but it's not quite the same view."

Jamal snickered.

"Jamal and I are going to avail ourselves of two wrenches and a ladder to restore the basketball court to its former glory," Sutherland boasted. "It's a historic court, having been the home to one of Duluth East's superstar basketball players."

"Let me guess…" Agnes smiled, "you?"

"Varsity sixth man junior and senior year."

"Sixth man? You didn't start?"

"They saved the best for last," Sutherland defended his position.

Agnes turned to Milo. "Did you play?"

"Basketball?" Milo shook his head. "They wouldn't even let me watch."

§

Over breakfast, Gramm filled Amy in on the progress in Patsy Rand's case. She wasn't surprised that the autopsy didn't show anything suspicious but was interested in the extra test Smith had ordered at the Minneapolis lab. "So, does that test have to do with Patsy saying the word yellow?" Amy asked.

"That's what the doc said," Gramm explained

"Oh my! I hope I haven't wasted everyone's time. She just said yellow; she didn't say she *saw* yellow."

"This is on Doc Smith. I told him what you said, and he took it from there," Ernie said putting extra butter on his toast.

Amy gave him a disapproving look.

"What?" Ernie defended his butter.

"One more pat and you'll be seeing yellow," Amy teased.

"If I was seeing yellow, what would I have?"

"It's the side effect of so many things."

"Name one besides extra butter."

"Diabetes. Too much Digitalis, to name two."

"Doc Smith says she was healthy except for an ulcer. Do you know different? Was this Rand woman a diabetic or on digitalis?"

"I don't think so, but I don't really know." Amy took a sip of her coffee. "If the lab finds something, will you be on the case?"

"I doubt it. Normally it would be O'Dell, but he's slammed, so I'm thinking Robin takes the lead."

Amy smiled, "Robin. Yeah, it's about time a woman broke into your boy's club."

§

Agnes put her romance novel down, leaned her head back, closed her eyes, and let the morning sun bake into her bones. Lake Superior was calm and Agnes was content. She knew this would be the last warm fall weekend and hoped the warm feelings she had for Sutherland would continue through the cold winter. She smiled and thought, *How corny! My brain must be swimming in estrogen reading this romance novel.*

Her reverie was interrupted by echoes of a basketball bouncing on a hard court. She opened her eyes. *Sutherland and Jamal must have gotten the backboard and rim up without either going to the hospital.* The sun was now high in the sky, and she was stiff—time to get up and walk. The basketball court was calling.

When John McKnight installed the court for his young son, Sutherland, he had added a three-tiered bleacher. Martha was sitting in the middle of the second tier watching her brother and a grown-up Sutherland play one on one.

Sliding in next to Martha, Agnes asked how it was going.

"They're both shooting fools, but neither can dribble to save their lives," Martha said.

47

"Forwards," Agnes sighed. "Dribbling. Who needs it?"

Martha turned in surprise. "You know basketball?"

Agnes nodded, watching Jamal hit on an outside shot, followed by a little trash talking. "Yeah. I played a little in high school. Volleyball was my main sport, but I made the basketball team. I was a forward. How about you?"

"Guard. I got the dribbling genes in the family," Martha boasted.

"Did you start?"

"Point guard on two Duluth East tournament teams."

"I didn't know I was in the presence of b-ball greatness," Agnes laughed.

Sutherland looked like he was going to drive to the basket, faking out Jamal by pulling up and draining a bucket. More trash talk ensued.

"They have the trash talk down," Agnes laughed.

"I taught Jamal trash talk early. It's part of the game. Can you shoot?"

"Now? Pretty rusty."

"Monday morning, eleven o'clock, we practice," Martha directed.

"The purpose being?"

"Let's say helping my brother improve his game. A little two-on-two."

"Two-on-two? You and me versus Jamal and the sixth man?"

Martha shot Agnes a sly look.

Agnes thought about last summer and the arrogance Sutherland displayed about his tennis game. She wondered if he had gained some humility after the trouncing Mary

Alice and Milo gave him. Continuing to watch the game, Agnes again pointed out, "neither one of them can dribble."

"Exactly," Martha agreed. "Could be fun."

5

After stopping at the front desk for a newspaper, Ron Bello requested a window seat at the hotel restaurant. He couldn't pass up Sunday morning brunch with its views of Duluth's inner harbor. Having checked out the menu on line, he ordered Southwestern Eggs Benedict with avocado sauce, orange juice, and coffee.

The former newspaper reporter leaned back, accepted his coffee, and checked out the Duluth News Tribune. On the front page, below the fold, a picture of Patsy Rand and a headline stared at him: *Police Investigate Suspicious Death*.

Reading on, Bello found the story to contain only two facts: Patsy Rand died, and police had asked for an autopsy—a sign there could have been foul play. The first, predictable. The second, problematic.

§

Dr. Charles Carlson tramped out onto his Congdon Park driveway in search of his Sunday paper. The morning was warm with a slight breeze easing Carlson's foul mood as he stomped down the long, tree-lined driveway. How many times had he requested the newspaper delivery people bring the paper to the porch? Each time they declined.

His second wife, Wendy—in her snug black yoga leotard—was waiting for his return, hands on hips. "What's in the paper, Charles, that's more important than enjoying my breakfast?"

"Nothing is more important to me than you and your scrumptious breakfast, my dear." Charles followed her to the house, admiring the leotard and all that it held.

Charles sat down and was about to open his paper when Wendy snatched the paper away, sat on his lap, and stroked the side of his face. "You're still not enjoying my crepes," she cooed. "They're a new recipe from class."

Charles put his arm around her, lifted his fork and began the well-rehearsed dance of eating and admiring Wendy's new recipes. She rewarded him with nuzzles and kisses to the back of his neck—a great start to a Sunday morning—warm weather and warm Wendy.

If he were honest, Dr. Carlson preferred eggs and toast, but Wendy was boning up on French dishes in advance of their Paris trip. Given his money shortage, the settlement with Peter Gain and Tettegouch Software couldn't come fast enough.

"These crepes are delicious!" Carlson said, thinking to himself, *too thick, and raw batter on the inside.*

"I'm so glad you like them, lovey," Wendy murmured and nuzzled Charles' neck one more time. "We will be so sophisticated when we dine at those overpriced Frenchy places on our trip."

She slid off her husband's lap, grabbed her car keys, and declared, "I'm off to yoga."

Charles sighed, waited for the garage door to close, disposed of the crepes, threw some bread in the toaster, and sat down with the paper. Patsy Rand's picture jumped out at him. His eyes narrowed as he read the headline.

"Suspicious? An autopsy?" he said to himself. "Where the hell does that come from? I told them heart attack!"

§

For a brief second, Milo, in a precaffeinated haze, wondered why Annie hadn't followed him to the kitchen. Then it hit him: this was Sunday, Martha's day off—no bacon. *How does the cat know what day it is and I don't?*

Milo stumbled into the morning room where he stood in line behind Sutherland who was filling his travel mug with coffee. Martha always set up the coffee Saturday night with an automatic timer that started the brew process.

"I hate these long coffee lines," Milo complained. "Don't be ordering one of those soy chai latte teas with a kale stick that take forever to make."

Sutherland finished filling his mug before turning around. "I don't even know what that is. I'm going to brunch."

"Ah, real food. Your smoothies will complain," Milo cracked, knowing *going to brunch* was code for spending the day with Agnes.

As Milo poured his coffee from the carafe he said, "Before you take off, I got ahold of one of the cops that's mentioned in the police report. I was gonna set up a meeting tomorrow. What's a good time for you?"

Sutherland checked the calendar on his phone. "Any time after ten and before two," he said.

"I'll let you know," Milo said taking a sip of coffee.

Sutherland proceeded down the hall, opened the door to the garage, turned around, and yelled, "Great car Milo!"

Milo nodded, "It adds class to the garage."

Sutherland laughed, "Yet, I don't think the Rolls is feeling bad about itself."

§

"Guess who died," said Jay, the college student Evelyn Chen hired part time.

Evelyn, who was busy filling the cash register, said nothing.

Jay repeated himself thinking Evelyn didn't hear him. "It was that Patsy Rand woman who died. You know that woman who kept accusing you of killing customers. I don't know why you didn't sue her. Isn't that slander or something?"

Evelyn, continuing to ignore Jay, went to wait on the first customers of the morning.

Jay, finding only four bottles of turmeric on the shelf, retreated to the backroom to find four more bottles. Evelyn had explained to him that four was an unlucky number. To avoid that, she wanted eight bottles of everything on the shelves.

After the customers left, Evelyn turned to her young, chatty employee. "I avoid thinking or talking about death. It was how I was raised. Please change your topic of conversation."

Jay continued to count and stock bottles.

§

Peter Gain was tied up with the sale of his father's company, Tettegouch Software, and was unable to enjoy the beautiful weekend,. He massaged his shoulders to alleviate the tightness that came with pricey lawyer conference calls. Last week the lawyers disposed of several nuisance claims from distant relatives and former employees. However, Dr. Charles Carlson, cousin of his father's former partner, had a more legitimate claim. He had, at last, been placated with the promise of a healthy payoff when the sale was completed. All complications having been dealt with, Gain could get back to his life as a chemist. The tension eased.

Gain sat back on his patio lounge chair, opened his Sunday morning paper, and was greeted by the face of Patsy Rand. The accompanying article announced her death. He looked pleased—another nuisance disposed of. He neglected to read the entire article which quoted anonymous sources saying her death Thursday night was suspicious and an autopsy had been ordered.

§

Milo maneuvered the phone caddy into the center vent of the Mercedes in case he needed to use it as a GPS today. The

Mercedes—a pre-GPS classic—didn't have built in digital gizmos. He liked that. Milo adjusted the seat and revved up the V-8 engine feeling like he was seventeen again.

He had planned to go to 'fancy but casual'—thanks to N&J Fine Men's Clothiers—for his first drive in the dream car, but Mary Alice warned him to come prepared to hike. He wore a pair of jeans, a new t-shirt, and his old tennis shoes. Milo threw his jacket in the trunk *just in case*, a habit only people who lived in Duluth would understand.

The wind ruffled his dark, curly hair as he drove the convertible toward Mary Alice's London Road estate. Milo wondered if the perfect Mrs. Bonner was someone who could handle windblown—so much to learn.

The classic car dipped as Milo drove in past the open gates. *Were they always open or did she open them for me?* He liked the second idea better.

He parked behind the large black SUV in the circular drive. Mary Alice, clad in khaki pants, aqua t-shirt, and BDry hiking shoes emerged from the tennis courts encircled by three large, excited dogs.

"What is that?" she asked, pointing at Milo's new purchase.

"This," he said with a sweeping gesture, "is a 1987 Mercedes 560SL."

She wove in and around the barking dogs to the front of the car, sliding her fingers over the shiny pale hood. "It's gorgeous," she said walking over to the passenger seat. "This leather feels new. Was this car kept in a cave, or has it been redone?"

"If I can believe Harry Reinakie, it was owned by an older couple in West Palm Beach who didn't drive it much. After they died, it sat in a probate fight for a couple of years."

"So, it's like new," Mary Alice said.

"New old," Milo corrected.

"Oh, I want to ride in this! We will have to plan a day!"

"What's wrong with today?" questioned Milo.

Mary Alice laughed, "There's no room for my friends," she said gesturing to her dogs, "unless Luna, Phoenix, and Flash are going to ride in back like prom queens waving to their adoring subjects."

Flash, the greyhound, heard his name, came over to Mary Alice, and leaned into her leg for pets. Luna and Phoenix continued running around the circular drive, chasing each other, late migrating Monarchs, and a few falling leaves.

Mary Alice raised the back of the SUV and opened the doors to the two personalized dog crates. The crazy clown act stopped. Luna changed course, screeched to a stop, and artfully leapt into the crate with her name on it.

Milo was impressed, "She reads?"

"Oh yes, nothing but the best and brightest."

And yet I'm here. His thoughts were interrupted by copy-cat Phoenix. The two dogs sat in their crates panting with silly grins on their faces. The doors were open—they could run and escape, but neither moved. Mary Alice strolled over to two captured canines, gave them both a treat, closed the crate doors and lowered the back of the SUV.

"What about Flash?" Milo asked.

"In the back seat," Mary Alice said, opening the side door and crate. Flash jumped in, made himself comfortable, and sighed.

"Let's go." Mary Alice called to Milo.

"Do I have a crate?" he asked.

"You're a special case. You sit in the front," Mary Alice laughed.

Milo lingered on the phrase, *special case* and wondered if it was a positive. He took a longing look at his about-to-be-abandoned new old car and, as instructed, slid into the passenger's side of the SUV awaiting his treat.

Mary Alice pulled out of driveway, pushed a button on the rear-view mirror to close the gates of her estate, and headed up the shore.

She does close the gates, Milo thought. *One question answered.*

"We're going up to Castle Danger north of Two Harbors. The dogs can run, and we can have a picnic," Mary Alice explained.

"Castle Danger. That's a tiny place. I've been through there a couple of times, staking out waywards that liked to rendezvous at Gooseberry Falls. Never saw the attraction of a rendezvous in the woods," Milo said.

"Maybe you weren't with the right person," Mary Alice teased, flashing the blue eyes in that special Mary Alice way.

And that's my treat, Milo thought. "Castle Danger—I've never seen a castle."

"There isn't one. My dad said it was because a ship named The Castle went down on the rocks there."

On the way, Milo saw a number of side roads that led to picnic areas, but Mary Alice blew past them. Finally, she turned off onto a rutted, oiled road. Luna and Phoenix complained with single barks.

"You seem to know where you're going," Milo noted as Mary Alice made a sharp turn onto a long, blacktopped, tree-lined drive that led to a log cabin.

"Welcome to my little house in the woods."

The dogs were up and barking, urging Mary Alice to let them out to run. "You get Flash," she said to Milo. "I'll take care of my noisy ones, Luna and Phoenix."

Milo was prepared for Flash to flash out of his crate. Instead, with care, he stepped down from the vehicle, stretched, yawned, and started sniffing the ground and trees. He sat and looked up at Milo as if to say, "If you want to sit here, I'd be only too glad to keep you company."

The other two dogs were running together in the cleared area by the cabin. Luna started heading to the path that led into the red-and-yellow-leafed woods. She was woofed back by Phoenix who, having run into a skunk earlier in the year, was a little more cautious.

"Come on, Milo and Flash. Let's go for a hike," Mary Alice urged.

Milo woofed. Flash followed with less enthusiasm.

Mary Alice strolled down the white-birch lined trail to a much narrower footpath that paralleled a small stream. Phoenix and Luna raced ahead while Flash padded between Milo and Mary Alice, looking up at Milo from time to time as if to question the reason for this forced march.

As the path turned to the west, the stream widened into a pond. Luna and Flash waded in belly high to drink while Phoenix splashed into the water, legs flying, causing Mary Alice to laugh. "He loves this place," she said as she stopped and sat down on a log. Phoenix swam to the other side of the pond, shook off, and dashed in again, swimming back to the other two dogs, barking as if leading them on to the fun. He was ignored as the other two sniffed their way along the shore.

"You better sit down," Mary Alice said, slipping off her nylon drawstring backpack. "Phoenix thinks he's a fish. We'll be here for a while."

Milo did as ordered. Mary Alice handed him a bottle of water out of her backpack.

"Thanks, I was about to join Flash in the water."

"I always hydrate my pets," Mary Alice quipped.

Do I want to be her pet? Milo wondered.

Mary Alice flashed those beautiful blue eyes and shoulder bumped him. "You know I'm kidding."

Milo decided *pet* was fine as he opened the water and looked around. The trees, the still pond, the narrow path along the stream reminded him of a fall-themed painting in the Lakesong's Library "Is all this yours?"

"Yes. It's part of my home. My real home. The place on London Road, as much as I have been trying to change it, is still James'."

Milo had met her deceased husband only once, hours before he was murdered, but in that brief encounter he knew that James Bonner was not a stroll-along-the-lane kind of a guy. "Did you buy this for the dogs?"

Mary Alice looked at him, as she brushed wisps of her breeze-blown blond hair away from her face. "I kinda like that idea, but no. This is for me."

"It's nice."

"It is, isn't it? It all belonged to my family when I was a girl, and now it's mine again."

Phoenix came dashing out of the water toward Milo, shaking and spraying him with streams of water. Mary Alice turned away laughing while Phoenix followed the spraying by laying his wet head against Milo's lap.

"He's a clown," Mary Alice said.

"I guess I looked too dry," Milo cracked as he scritched the dog behind his ears. Phoenix looked up and licked Milo on the face. Flash was having none of that and tried to push Phoenix away from Milo.

"Oh my! They're fighting over you."

"Yeah, me and the guys. I don't seem to have grabbed Luna's heart though."

At the sound of her name, Luna strolled over and laid down by Mary Alice. "We ladies are much harder to attract," Mary Alice sassed. "Here, have a granola bar to sooth your broken heart." The two sat in silence munching on granola. This afternoon, that smile and those eyes were his—his and the dogs, but he didn't mind sharing.

Mary Alice stared at the pond as she explained, "When this belonged to my family, we would come up here all the time—year-round—swimming, skating, cross country skiing. I even learned to shoot up here." She threw him a knowing glance, reminding him of her prowess with a gun. "My mother had to sell it after my father died. When it came back on the market, I picked it up."

Milo remembered Creedence Durant—Milo's recently acquired financial advisor—saying that her father's death was probably a suicide due to money troubles. Milo waited for more information. She didn't offer anything except sticks thrown into the pond which Phoenix dashed after and retrieved until fatigue won out.

Breaking the silence, she asked, "What are you working on these days?"

Milo picked up a stick and threw it down the path. Phoenix and Flash looked at him and put their heads back down into nap mode. Luna didn't bother to look up. "I'm currently investigating the death of my father."

The blue eyes opened wide. "Why? I know he died when you were young, but I thought it was medical or something."

"Sort of, he came down with three bullets in the back."

"Oh my God!" Mary Alice exclaimed. "I didn't know. I'm so sorry."

Milo shrugged. "As a boy, I was told he died on the job, in the line of duty."

"And now?"

Milo drank the last of his water and handed the bottle back to Mary Alice's outstretched hand. "I don't know. Lots of questions," Milo said, scritching a sleeping Flash behind his ear.

Mary Alice stood up. "Let's go back to the cabin for my picnic if we can get my four-legged friends to join us."

Milo and the dogs fell in behind her.

"So, how is Agnes Larson working out as your personal assistant?" she asked as they hiked.

"That idea of yours—hiring her as my assistant—is working out great for both me and Sutherland."

"Agnes Larson and Sutherland McKnight. I have to say, I didn't see that coming, but I like it."

As the path widened, Milo took a shot. "Mary Alice Bonner and that guy Rathkey, didn't see that coming either."

Mary Alice put her arm in his. "I like that too."

6

Setting her coffee down, Robin White once again drew her hair up into her work-mode ponytail while checking the computer for weekend arrests—nothing that needed her attention. As she picked up her cup—thinking she had a few get-it-together minutes—Lt. Gramm bellowed her name. Activity in the bullpen area stopped. Some laughed. One officer asked, "Can't he text you so I don't spill my coffee on my shirt when he shouts?"

White stood up. "We've had the technology conversation. It's all I can do," she explained, picking up her note pad.

"Sergeant! Now!" Gramm yelled again.

"Coming!" she yelled back.

There was more laughter.

"What's up?" she asked as she strolled into Gramm's office.

"I got Doc Smith on speaker. He's got the lab results from Minneapolis."

"Hi, Doc," White said. "What do we have?"

"Murder," Doc Smith said. "Poison."

"So, Amy was right," Gramm said.

"More than right, she deserves a medal. This poison is hard to trace. It causes yellow-green vision distortion, and without Amy's observations, we would have missed this one."

"What's the poison?" White asked.

"Aconite. Back when I was a boy it was called wolfsbane. It's really bad stuff."

"How was it administered?" Gramm asked.

"No puncture marks. We're guessing it was ingested,"

"Wouldn't she have tasted it?" Gramm asked.

"In food, but not in alcohol. The poison is prepared in a tincture using almost pure alcohol, and she had a couple of drinks that night."

White crossed her arms and leaned back in her chair. "Who knows how to do that—a pharmacist?"

Doc Smith gave the Cliff Notes explanation of what chemistry would be involved in making a tincture of aconite, saying that anyone who knows how to use Google could find the recipe. He added that the poison interferes with the lungs and heart. He said if the victim was drinking before she died, all she would know is she had a strong drink. He ended with, "I'll send over all my fancy scientific stuff for your reading enjoyment. I'm calling this murder." The phone went dead.

White shook her head. "And goodbye to you, Doc Smith," she said to no one.

Gramm picked up the in-house phone. "I'm calling the Deputy Chief. I think you're going to take lead on this one. I'll consult. If you want, we can bring in Milo."

White straightened up, took a sip of her coffee, and considered the offer. Milo was easy to work with and saw small details that she could miss. This being her first investigation, she agreed. "Milo would be good."

"Waiting on hold," Gramm said, "Better get forensics over to the victim's house. We need to know who this woman was, and who would benefit from her death."

"We also need to notify next of kin," White added, "Got any idea of who that is?"

"None. That would be your job…now."

"I need an assistant," White muttered.

§

Martha had finished with breakfast, the sibs were off at school, and Agnes was waiting for the UPS truck with her scanner and cataloging software—perfect time for a little test of the new basketball rim. The warm weekend weather had given way to a crisp but sunny morning.

After spending the better part of an hour playing one-on-one with Martha, Agnes was out of breath. "I can't…you're too good," she said as she flopped down on the bleacher. "Are you still playing?"

Martha sat down next to her. "I am. I started playing again when Jamal was in fifth grade," she said, leaning back with her arms resting on the next second tier. "I'm ten years older than the sibs. I was the honeymoon child. When I took over guardianship, I had to figure out how to make a connection with each one. Basketball was the ticket with Jamal."

"You know, I forget you're their sister, not their mother," Agnes said.

Martha laughed. "I'm not that old! Breanna is eighteen!"

"Good point. Are you getting used to Breanna being away at college?"

"Away? She's only up over the hill at UMD."

"Well, she's not here at your cottage," Agnes clarified.

"True, but I'm having a problem with space," Martha said.

"Space? As in too much space?"

"I wish. Not enough space. When we moved in, Darian was five. He and Jamal had shared a bedroom, so I kept it that way. Now Darian is ten and Jamal is a tall fourteen year old. Jamal's feet hang off the bunkbed and the room's too small for two single beds. If I split them up, Breanna will have no place to sleep when she comes home."

"Have you mentioned this to Milo and Sutherland? They might be willing to add on to the cottage."

"I am sure Sutherland would build a mini mansion bedroom; I'm not going there," Martha said.

Agnes smiled, "You know, you're right. Milo might be more sensible."

"I think we'll play musical beds. I'll split them for now, and when Breanna comes home, Jamal will move back in with Darian." Martha stood up. "I think we need a couple of plays before we take on Jamal and Sutherland."

"Oh yeah. Good idea," Agnes said, draining her water bottle.

"With your outside shooting, Ms. Volleyball, I thought I drive the lane and if blocked by both of them…no-look pass to you," Martha said.

"I like it. With your dribbling skills we can also do a give-and-go. Let's run through them a couple of times. When are Jamal and Sutherland practicing next?"

"Tonight, before supper," Martha replied.

"Won't it be getting dark?"

Martha laughed. "You know how Sutherland always takes a simple project and makes the Taj Mahal?"

"Yup."

"He comes by it naturally," Martha explained.

"What does that have to do with playing in the dark?" Agnes asked.

"Sutherland told me he was in fifth grade when his father installed this court," Martha said, walking over to an electrical box on the side of the maintenance shed. She flipped the switch and pointed to each of the four lights, two on the building and two on poles behind the far side of the court.

Agnes gaped in amazement. "I thought they were security lights. Sutherland's father lit the court? Who lights a kid's practice court?"

"The same guy who installs a permanent bleacher."

Agnes looked around. "Where's the concession stand?"

"Behind the broadcast booth," Martha joked.

The two began practicing their plays, running through them until they got their timing down.

§

Milo, driving his old Honda, picked Sutherland up from his office shortly after ten. Sutherland was outside waiting. "Where's the Mercedes?" he asked as he slid into the 2004 Honda.

"I'm working. Do you take the Bentley or the Rolls to the office?"

"I could."

"But you don't. The Mercedes is my fun car. End of discussion."

Sutherland shrugged. "This is my first time in your work car."

Milo said nothing.

"It's clean!" Sutherland exclaimed.

"Why is that a surprise? Mr. Anderson keeps cleaning it for no reason," Milo said. "By the way, we have to do this interview with Crandell fast. I have to meet Ernie and Robin for lunch. There's been a murder."

The idea of another police investigation piqued Sutherland's interest. "I don't have to be back until two, and I eat lunch."

Milo laughed. This was not the same Sutherland he met nine months ago in the law offices of Haney, Jenson, and Hamft. "We're going to Gustafson's on Superior Street."

"I've never been there. I look forward to it."

Milo doubted that eagerness would remain for long. Sutherland at Gustafson's could be humorous. Turning his attention to the case at hand, Milo filled Sutherland in on what he discovered about former policeman Josh Crandell. "He took early retirement and is living in Morgan Park. At first he refused to talk and hung up on me, then called back and wanted to talk."

"Why?" Sutherland asked.

"Don't have a clue."

The Morgan Park area of Duluth was a company town built to support a now defunct steel plant. Modest homes with affordable price tags made the area attractive to new families and retirees. Milo pulled up in front of a narrow, two-story, dirty-white stucco house, complete with matching porch—the kind built before World War Two. A crooked, cement walkway led to the wooden porch steps with flaking white paint and a nail working its way out of the bottom rise. Both men avoided it.

Milo pushed the black doorbell button and was greeted by a weary looking woman with gray hair, thin lips, and no smile. Her face read 'whatever you're selling, I'm not interested.'

"Mrs. Crandell?" Milo asked

"Yeah?"

"I'm Milo Rathkey. I'm here to see your husband. He knows we're coming."

She turned and yelled into the house. "Hey Josh—you expecting people?"

"Yeah! Let em in," a man yelled from somewhere near the door.

She stepped back and let Milo and Sutherland enter. Josh Crandell was sitting in a brown, faux-leather recliner. His almost-crew-cut hair was still brown with patches of gray and white showing at the temples. He was thin—a somewhat remarkable achievement after a lifetime of sitting in patrol cars. One side of his face gave the impression he was a nice guy. The other seemed to be in a permanent smirk. Milo wondered if he had suffered a stroke.

He didn't get out of the recliner as Milo introduced himself and Sutherland.

"I know you're an ex-cop," Crandell said to Milo, "but he isn't."

"He's my associate," Milo explained.

"You pay him too well. He dresses better than you," Crandell mocked.

"Family money," Milo said.

Crandell squirmed in his chair trying to sit straighter. He threw his *Guns and Ammo* magazine on the floor. "So, you're Karl Rathkey's kid. I didn't know him. I was new to the force when he died."

Milo and Sutherland sat down on the couch opposite the recliner. "What can you tell us about the night he died?" Milo asked.

Crandell's half-smiling face stopped smiling. His voice rose and cracked as he lowered the footrest on the recliner and leaned forward. "Don't dredge that up again. Everybody's dead. Keep it up and you'll join 'em."

Sutherland's heart sped up. He was not used to having his life threatened but remained silent. Milo, short on time, took the opposite approach. "Don't threaten me, Crandell!" The two men locked eyes. It was like two stags ready to rear. "I read that pitiful police file. Those pictures scream coverup."

Crandell backed down, leaned back, and lifted the recliner leg rest. "I was a rookie."

"Tell me about that night," Milo pressed.

Sutherland continued his silence.

Crandell rubbed the top of his head with long boney fingers. "It's all in the report. It was forty years ago. Me and Rod Prepinski were in the neighborhood when the call came in. That's all."

"Why were you in that neighborhood? It wasn't your patrol area."

"I dunno. Rod was driving. I think he had a girl up there or somethin'. Rod always had a couple of girls he checked on. I used to have to wait in the car. Now, are we done?"

"What do you remember of the scene?" Milo continued.

Crandell reached down, picked up the *Guns and Ammo* magazine, and began rolling it. "We get there and see a body. Rod says, 'Geez, it's Karl Rathkey.' He sends me into these half-built buildings to see if the perp was hiding inside while he called for an ambulance and backup."

At this point, Sutherland jumped in, "He sent you alone?"

"Yeah, he sent me in alone. I was the rookie. That was Rod. If it was dangerous or disgusting, I had to do it. Of course, give him a few beers, and he took on the world." Crandell's crooked smile grew broader. "Yeah, Mr. Tough Guy…"

Sutherland interrupted, "Where is he now?"

"Dead. He got his pickin' a fight with some guy in a bar. He was always doin' that, and he was a lousy fighter, couldn't punch. Anyways, he stumbles out to the alley to fight this guy. The next day he's found beaten to death. They took baseball bats to him. Now are we done?"

"No. Who's they?" Milo asked.

Crandell twitched and shrugged. "How the hell do I know?"

"Someone beats your partner to death, and you don't know what happened?" Milo wasn't buying it.

"He wasn't my partner anymore. He retired—fifteen years ago. I always figured it was a husband or a boyfriend."

"So, who killed my father?" Milo asked.

Crandell continued to roll up his *Guns and Ammo.* "Okay, you wanna know? I'm gonna tell ya. It's not in the file, but we figured it was two punk brothers, Dwaine and Byron Wills. We busted them a couple a-times for stealing construction stuff. We were building a case against them, but they disappeared."

"Disappeared?" Sutherland asked.

"Yeah—disappeared as in we couldn't find them no more. Like what's gonna happen to you if you keep asking dumb questions. It was forty years ago. I've told you all I know. Let it go!" Crandell threw the magazine onto the floor.

Milo persisted, "You rubbed out the tire tracks and the footprints at the scene? You forgot to remove those pictures."

Crandell ran his tongue over the front of his teeth. "You're full of shit!"

"The pictures show it!" Sutherland blurted.

Crandell shrugged.

Milo stood up. "Look Crandell, you and your partner covered this thing up. Makes you an accessory, if not the murderer."

Crandell's face contorted in anger. "That's a lie. None of that's in the file! Get the hell out of here!" The footrest snapped down—Crandell burst out of the chair standing face to face with Rathkey.

Milo smiled. "This is not the last you're gonna hear from me." He and Sutherland turned to leave. Sutherland was the first to hit the door.

Crandell sat back down and mumbled, "Like your old man—in the way."

As they got back in the Honda, Sutherland asked, "Why is he so angry?"

Milo put both hands on the steering wheel, leaned back, and turned to Sutherland, "Angry or scared?"

§

Sgt. White went back to her desk and called the cellphone number Gramm had given her. Amy answered on the first ring.

"Mrs. Gramm, it's Robin White."

There was a long pause. "Well," Amy said finally, "if you're talking to me, Patsy Rand was murdered."

"Correct," White said.

"How?"

"Aconite poisoning."

"Aconite? Oh, come on! That queen of poisons? It's every old mystery writer's go-to from Agatha Christie on up."

"Also called," White checked her notes, "monkshood, wolfsbane—the list goes on."

"What can I do to help you, Robin?"

"I would like to meet you this afternoon. Milo Rathkey will be with me."

Amy said she would get back to her about the time, but midafternoon seemed to be good.

7

"Really? You've never eaten at Gustafson's? How do you work downtown and not eat at Gustafson's?" Milo asked Sutherland as they approached the restaurant's front door.

"I conduct business at lunch. This place has a reputation for being noisy," Sutherland explained.

Milo shrugged. "Where'd you get that idea?" Milo opened the door to a cacophony of voices, laughter, shouts, and clinking dishes.

Sutherland stepped back as if he had been physically assaulted. "Yeah. I wonder where I got that idea," he shouted.

"Sorry can't hear you," Milo shouted back.

Nick and Nichola—Gustafson's owners—smiled and waved from behind the counter. "Hey, Milo," Nick shouted as he pointed to the back booth knowing Milo would be looking for Gramm and White. The couple's last name was Christos, not Gustafson, but they had owned the place for so long, their customers had forgotten if there ever was a Gustafson.

As Milo and Sutherland made their way to the back, Nick shouted to his wife, "Milo's friend, the one with the suit. I'm thinking hummus."

"Maybe," Nichola shouted back watching Sutherland slide into the booth. "but he looks more like a salad type. No meat on his bones. Not like you."

Nick smiled. Nichola returned to cashing out customers with her usual efficiency.

Gramm, surprised to see Sutherland, looked at Milo for an explanation.

"Sutherland was in the neighborhood and had never been in here. It's part of his education," Milo explained.

"Well, it's not like he hasn't been along on any other police investigations," said Gramm as Sutherland got situated.

"How many of your friends are suspects in this one?" White added to the sarcasm referencing their last case together, the death of a Minneapolis realtor.

"I don't even know who's been murdered. All I know is, once again, I didn't do it," Sutherland said, hands up in mock surrender.

Gramm turned to White. "I don't think he's afraid of us anymore."

The waitress, Pat, slapped down four menus and began explaining the specials.

Gramm put up his hand stopping Pat's monologue. "Wait, last time the specials were clipped to the menu. What happened to that?"

"You and everyone else complained. Apparently, reading the specials on your own was too taxing, so I'm back reciting them. I've got other tables, so be quiet and listen, so I can get through this."

"He's old and doesn't do well with change," Rathkey quipped.

"And you're Mr. Young Jeans? Hardly!" Pat chortled.

"This is fun," Sutherland cracked.

Pat looked at Sutherland and said, "You're new. I'm Pat. As long as you don't waste my time with meatloaf sandwiches, we'll get along fine."

Sutherland looked over the menu, not understanding the meatloaf reference, but figuring it had to do with Milo. "It says hummus here. What kind of hummus?"

"Don't let the name of the place fool you; it's Greek hummus, Greek moussaka, Greek baklava," Pat said. "Don't forget the Greek salad…a customer favorite. Drinks?"

White ordered coffee, Gramm and Sutherland asked for water, and Milo requested his favorite, Diet Coke."

"So," Gramm began, "I've talked to the Deputy Chief. Because Amy is involved, Robin will take the lead. I can consult–I want to be kept up to speed. Milo, we will need you on board. Pretend you're a police detective."

"Amy's involved in a murder? And, by the way, because of you I'm a police consultant. I don't have to pretend anything," Milo complained.

White jumped in hoping to avoid a ridiculous, time-wasting discussion. "Here's what little we know. The victim was a sixty-year-old female from Duluth. Her name was Patsy Rand. She was stricken at a book-club meeting attended by

Amy Gramm last Thursday night, and died on the way to the hospital. Doc Smith declared her death a murder only two hours ago."

"What took him so long?" Milo asked.

White explained Amy's questioning the word 'yellow,' Doc Smith sending samples to a lab in Minneapolis, and the finding of the poison, aconite.

"So, there's been no processing of the scene. No interviews. Nothing for...what...four days?" Milo questioned.

White shook her head. "Nothing."

"What else do you know about this Patsy Rand?" Milo asked.

"Not a thing. We're starting from scratch."

"I'm safe. I don't know her," Sutherland said, "so I have no motive."

"We still think you did it," Gramm charged as Pat returned with drinks and stood waiting for food orders.

Gramm ordered the special: roast beef sandwich with sweet potato fries and a side salad. Robin opted for the moussaka, then turned her attention to her phone. Sutherland decided on the Greek salad with a side of hummus (a tie for Nick and Nicola). Milo asked four questions about various items on the menu before ordering his usual hot meatloaf sandwich, mash potatoes, and green beans, reminding Pat to add extra gravy.

She gave him a disapproving look. "Are you going to eat the green beans or push them to the side like always?"

"I consider them a garnish," Milo said, "like parsley. Who eats parsley?"

"Yeah right. This place is known for its garnishes." Pat grabbed the menus and disappeared into the sea of customers.

White put her phone on the table. "We have another wrinkle. When we went to impound Rand's car from the Johansson's, the driver's-side window had been smashed. We don't know what, if anything, was taken."

"It could be a crime of opportunity," Milo said. "What about where she lives?"

"I'm told nothing out of place. No break-in. Forensics is there now, and…" White was interrupted by another message on her phone. She ended a quick texting session as she accepted her plate of moussaka from Pat. "That text was Amy confirming our three o'clock appointment." Looking at her boss, she said, "Your wife knows how to text."

"Yeah, yeah," Gramm said digging into his sweet potato fries.

Milo cautioned as he moved his green beans off to the side, "I hope I'm not the note taker in our dynamic duo. Nobody will be able to read 'em. Even me."

White looked at Sutherland. "Can you take notes?"

Sutherland stopped in mid-hummus. "What? I'm not a cop. I run a business." Realizing Robin was kidding, he relaxed and added, "Besides, if I was a cop, you'd lose your favorite suspect."

Gramm broke in, "We have a new crop of rookies. Let's find one who can take notes. It'll be good experience for him or her."

"Him or her! You've come a long way," White said. "I'm so proud."

Even Gramm had to laugh.

§

"I have an idea for a note-taker," White said to Gramm as they settled back into the office.

"Who?" Gramm asked.

White read from her note. "Kate Preston. She's a rookie and eager."

Gramm shrugged. "If you like her, go for it."

"We have to get her transferred," White said.

"So, transfer her."

"I can do that?" White questioned.

"With great responsibility, comes great power. Call the desk sergeant and tell him you want her transferred."

White was skeptical until she made the call. Preston was standing at the sergeant's desk ten minutes later where White filled her on her duties.

"Kate is new on the force," White explained to Milo, as he and Kate shook hands. "We've got her for the afternoon." Turning to Preston, White said, "Milo used to be a detective, but now he consults."

"Can you make a living consulting?" Preston asked.

White laughed leaving Preston to wonder why.

The trio arrived at the Gramm household shortly before three o'clock and were greeted by the smell of freshly baked molasses cookies.

"Yesterday I sat out on the deck enjoying the warm sun," Amy said, putting the plate of cookies down on her coffee table. "but today it's too cold, even for me who likes the cold."

"I think I may have to confiscate these cookies to make sure they aren't poison. I mean Amy you are our prime suspect," Milo said biting into his first one.

"Are you going to have them analyzed or just eat them, and we'll see if you die?" White asked.

"Yeah, I like that plan. I'll take one for the team."

Officer Preston took out her Chromebook and set it on her lap.

White gave her a long look. "No notebook?" she asked.

Preston looked surprised. "This is a notebook. It's department issued."

"Ha!" Milo laughed. "Robin you are so yesterday."

"This must be how Gramm feels every day." Realizing Gramm's wife was in the room, White sputtered, "Sorry."

"Mr. Luddite?" Amy questioned. "He hasn't figured out the toaster."

White smiled. She liked Amy. "Before we get into Thursday night, do you know how we can find Patsy Rand's next of kin?"

Amy thought for a minute. "I can tell you what I told the hospital. I remember Patsy mentioned a daughter once, but I don't know where she lives. The hospital social worker might have been able to make contact. I'll email you her info."

White proceeded to the first question. "Besides you, who was at the book club?"

"Let me think. Linda Johansson made the chili. The meeting was at her house. Erin Cohen brought the hotdish. She makes great hotdish."

Milo turned to Preston, "We can rule this Erin person out. Anyone who makes great hotdish cannot be a murderer."

Preston looked puzzled and glanced at White.

"Part of the job is learning when to ignore Milo. It's tricky," White explained.

"I was being serious," Milo complained.

White ignored him urging Amy to continue.

Amy closed her eyes. "Carrots and celery—Dr. Charles Carlson. Vegetable dumplings—Evelyn Chen. Hawaiian rolls—Crystal Bower." Amy opened her eyes and laughed. "I guess you can tell I was handling the food table."

"What did the victim bring?" Milo asked.

"Patsy?" Amy thought for a minute. "Nothing."

"Is that it?" White asked. "Are those all the members of the book club?"

"That were there that night. Not everybody attends every meeting, and I forgot to mention our guest author, Ron Bello. He's a former newspaper reporter who writes excellent crime and mystery fiction.

"Oh, I've read his books!" White exclaimed.

"Then you'll be interested in this. Ron is in town researching a new book. Oh wait," Amy said, "there's one more person, Linda's brother Liam..."

"Same last name?" White asked.

"Yes," Amy said. "Liam was the bartender. He's not a book-club member. He just moved here from California. He's living with Linda, so she put him to work.

White glanced at Preston who had already finished typing.

Amy added, "I know you need contact numbers for everyone. Let me email them to you, Robin."

"Good," White said. "That'll help."

"One stop shop," Milo mumbled. "In my day we wrote on our hands."

Preston turned to White, "Ignore?"

"Yes ignore, however, as we get into this investigation, he'll say something like Heidi somebody went up the hill."

"Heidi Reinakie. Her husband is the Cadillac king," Milo explained.

"That, as it turns out, should not be ignored," White said.

"They didn't teach this at the academy," Preston mumbled.

"You should have all the contacts now," Amy interrupted.

White forwarded the email to Preston.

Amy stood up. "I have coffee to go with these cookies. Let me get the pot. Milo, could you grab the mugs from the counter?"

White glanced at Preston, still uneasy about the note-taking method. "Are you keeping up with everything?"

Preston showed her the notes.

White was impressed. Preston had captured all the information, even the Hawaiian rolls.

Milo came back carrying a tray with four mugs, sweeteners, and creamers, which he set on the coffee table. "I expect a tip," he said as he sat down.

White looked at the creamers. "Pumpkin spice creamer. I love pumpkin spice. Milo, you be quiet."

"What? I didn't say anything. If you want to ruin a perfectly good cup of coffee with pumpkin spice..."

"See. There, you said something."

Amy came in with a carafe of coffee and poured four cups. "Milo, you sound like Ernie. I do love pumpkin spice this time of year. It goes well with my molasses cookies."

White took a sip of her coffee and said, "So, Amy, everyone arrives bringing food except for the victim and that author..." White paused.

"Bello, Ron Bello," Preston said looking at her notes.

White nodded. "You're our best witness Amy. Take us through the evening step by step."

Amy thought for a second. "Well, it was a normal beginning. Everyone but Patsy arrived, dropped their food with me in the dining room, got their drinks from Liam in the office—the two front rooms of the house, and then joined our guest down the hall in the living room. Patsy Rand arrived late with her usual commotion."

"Usual commotion?"

"I've only known her a short time, but she never slips into a room unnoticed—even when late. That night I remember Patsy knocking things down, yelling because she couldn't find us, all the while demanding a drink."

"Who mixed the drink?" Robin asked.

"Liam, I imagine. I don't know. I didn't see him do it. Come to think of it, Patsy didn't get her drink right away and kept yelling about it. After she sat down in the living room, she complained about a stomachache, said she had a horrible dinner, and searched her purse for antacids."

Milo interrupted, "She had a stomachache, was looking for antacids, yet wanted a drink? Alcohol's not much of a stomach soother."

"Actually, it is. Brandy and Whiskey can help in digestion, although I don't think she knew that. I think she needed the drink because she had a bad day—probably got into a fight with somebody."

"Did that happen often?" Milo asked. "The fight I mean."

Amy took a bite of her cookie. "Remember, I didn't know her that well, only at book club, but she seemed to look for arguments."

White took over the questioning, "With other members?"

"Yes. Her arguments often got personal. At one time or another, she was disagreeable with everyone, including me."

"Give me an example of her getting personal," White said.

Amy stirred her coffee. "Well, this was the latest. Evelyn Chen..."

"Vegetable dumplings," Milo added.

"Yes, Milo, vegetable dumplings," Amy agreed. "Evelyn Chen owns an herb shop. A couple of months ago, one of her customers with a heart condition had a heart attack and died. Patsy got it in her head that Evelyn's herbs were responsible. She spread that on her blog and podcast. The man had heart disease—it had nothing to do with Evelyn's herbs. That was personal."

"Are there any others that come to mind?" White asked.

Amy shrugged. "I think Crystal Bowers and Patsy have known each other for a number of years. They would snip at each other from time to time, but then Patsy did that with everybody. Recently, Patsy has been zeroing in on Erin Cohen and her travel agency. I don't know what it's about. You'll enjoy talking to Erin. She sees herself as a young Miss Marple, always the first to suggest a solution to whatever mystery we're reading."

"Is she usually right?" White asked.

"That's the funny part, almost never, but it is amazing how she ignores the obvious and focuses in on the minutia."

Milo thought that she and Sutherland would make an interesting crime fighting duo.

"Anyone else that our victim crossed?" White asked.

"She referred to Dr. Carlson once as a quack and said I was naïve."

"Did you kill her?" Milo asked.

"Because she accused me of being naïve—wouldn't that be overkill?" Amy grinned. "Pardon the pun."

After topping off her coffee with another squirt of pumpkin spice creamer, White asked, "What happened when the victim collapsed?"

"We were all in the dining room preparing to fill our plates. The large jug of water—you know, the kind with a spigot—fell off the dining room table and broke. We were picking up the mess."

"Was the victim there?"

"No. She was in the living room. We heard her fall and rushed to her. I checked for a pulse. It was weak. Dr. Carlson said to call for an ambulance. She died en route to the hospital. Before she got into the ambulance, she said four things to me, 'hurt, yellow,' and later 'the book, why'."

White asked if Amy knew what any of that meant.

"Hurt is self-explanatory; she was in pain. But, as a nurse, I thought yellow was important. I thought it meant she was seeing yellow which could be a clue to several medical issues."

White nodded, "That was a good get on your part, Amy. Without it, we might have missed this murder altogether. What about the other part—the book and why?"

"I don't know. It was a book club. Maybe she was talking about Bello's book."

White was about to wrap up the questioning when Milo interrupted. "Amy, have you ever run into aconite poisoning?"

"Not in the ER, but I've read about it in mystery books. It is usually some old lady growing it in her garden. I have it in mine. It's a pretty purple flower—called wolfsbane or monkshood. It doesn't hurt wildlife and it's deer resistant."

"Are you sure you didn't do it?" Milo kidded.

Amy shook her head, "I think I would have remembered that."

§

Driving back to the station, White asked Preston if she liked this new assignment.

"Oh rats, I haven't blown it already have I? I love this assignment and the pumpkin spice."

White laughed. "I wasn't threatening your job. I was making conversation. So, what was your impression of our first interview?"

"I think we were lucky that Amy Gramm's a nurse and recognized something was off with the victim—that yellow thing. Otherwise, I didn't get much. The victim wasn't a nice person, picked fights, but is that enough to get her murdered?"

"That's pretty much what I got. Now, we're going to go to the gentleman in the backseat, so you can see why we bring him along," White said. "Milo? Whaddaya got?"

Milo cleared his throat. "Where did the victim eat dinner?"

"What?" Preston blurted. "Who mentioned dinner?"

"Amy did. She said the victim indicated she had a horrible dinner. What made it horrible?"

"Crap!" White exclaimed. "I missed that too. Forward your notes to me Preston. I gotta see what else I missed."

"Did you catch the part where the book club had a bartender?" Milo asked.

"Yeah, I caught that," White answered, "And that means what to you?"

"I might want to join that book club."

§

Sutherland hit the lights chasing away the dusky shadows on the basketball half court. Agnes—clad in her neon-green biking outfit and headband—stood out from the dull gray sweat gear the others were wearing.

"You're neon bright this evening," Sutherland cracked.

"I'm a flash on the court. The neon is so you can see me—not that it will do you any good," Agnes joked.

"Trash talking? This is a friendly game to help Jamal," Sutherland complained.

"Let's play!" Martha said. "I'm getting cold!"

Agnes moved to the back of the court, threw the ball to Martha, and the basketball game began. Jamal moved up to defend, but he was too late. Martha dribbled around him, sidestepped Sutherland, tossing an easy layup for the first two points. Agnes rushed over for the celebratory high five.

"It's two points! We just started! A high five for two points?" Sutherland grumbled.

Agnes bumped Sutherland, "Two cold points made in forty degree weather."

Jamal grabbed the ball and threw it to Sutherland in the backcourt. Sutherland dribbled while watching Agnes amble up to defend. A quick pass to Jamal in the right corner caught Martha by surprise and Jamal drained it. "That's a three pointer!" he yelled.

Martha took exception, "Three pointer? Where's the three point line?"

"It's organic," Sutherland offered.

"Vegetables are organic not three point lines," Martha complained, walking the ball back, holding up one finger, and firing the ball to Agnes. Neither Sutherland nor Jamal moved up, figuring she was too far away to make the shot. Agnes smiled and shot a jumper. Swish. "We can be organic too. Three points—us," she boasted. There was another high five.

"Nice shot," Sutherland grudgingly admitted.

Agnes swaggered past him, chiding, "Not bad for gravy," a reference to a comment made by Sutherland last June about her tennis skills.

Sutherland grimaced, wondering if he would ever live down that faux pas. He turned to Jamal. "They have plays?"

"Naw. Martha's faking...I think."

Sutherland held up five fingers. Jamal nodded. Martha laughed. "Oh, now *they* have plays."

"The famous five finger play," Agnes joined in the joke.

Sutherland hurled the ball to Jamal in the corner and charged forward as Jamal threw the ball up toward the basket. Sutherland jumped reaching for the it. Agnes equaled his effort slapping the ball away from his hands out of bounds.

"Great move, Flash!" Martha yelled.

"She fouled you," Jamal charged.

Agnes laughed. "I can't help it if your teammate got outjumped."

Sutherland retrieved the ball and flipped it to Jamal who had out maneuvered Martha. Jamal turned and shot but hit the rim. This time Sutherland got the angle on Agnes, rebounded, and stuffed the ball in the basket in one move. "I out-flashed the Flash."

"In your dreams," Agnes retorted.

Martha held up two fingers. Dribbling around Jamal, she drove to the basket as Sutherland countered. Martha delivered a no-look, behind-the-back, pass to Agnes who hit from the corner—another three points and another celebratory high five.

Sutherland and Jamal regrouped, improvised several plays, but in the end the win went to Agnes and Martha by one point. There was a brief dispute about the score, but Martha and Agnes proved their version correct.

"See, Mr. Fourteen-Year-Old-Basketball-Superstar," Martha chided Jamal. "It's not all shooting. You need to work on your defense."

"No one in ninth grade dribbles like you do," Jamal defended himself.

"They will. Prepare for what is come young Jedi," she joked.

Sutherland offered Agnes a bottle of water from the small refrigerator in the wooden shelter under the bleachers. "You have a refrigerator? A court side refrigerator?" Agnes laughed, shaking her head in disbelief.

Sutherland shrugged. "It beats carrying a cooler down here."

"Who stocks it?" Agnes asked, taking a sip of the water.

"I have a guy…"

"Why don't I ever see that bill?"

"You do. It's the Fraser Supply Company. They stock all the small refrigerators, among other things."

"All the small refrigerators? How many are there?"

"Six. My exercise room, the pool, your office, Milo's office, this one, and the one by the tennis courts."

Agnes looked surprised. "My office? I have a refrigerator? Where?"

"It's…the wainscoting panel behind your desk. Push it and the panel pops out. The refrigerator is behind it."

Agnes put her hands on her hips. "How come I've never seen it being refilled?"

"You never used it. It didn't need refilling."

"How does this Fraser company know that?"

"It's a smart refrigerator…tells them what needs to be refilled."

"I would have used it if you told me it was there!"

"I can't tell you all my secrets at once," Sutherland jested hoping to come off as mysterious.

"Well, one secret's out. Neither you nor Jamal can keep score. You need a scorekeeper," Agnes joked.

"We get caught up in the game. The score isn't all that important. It's about skills, but now that you mention it…"

"I was trash talking!" Agnes laughed.

Martha rolled her eyes and mumbled, "Next spring there will be a scorekeeper."

"Not just a scorekeeper—a scoreboard," Sutherland added.

Agnes shook her head. "There's no one to run it."

"Milo," Sutherland said, "or Darian. I wonder who sells scoreboards? "To get Milo to do it, we'll need a time out horn."

§

Late in the afternoon, White, Milo, and Preston arrived back at the police station gathering in Gramm's office where they updated the Lieutenant on the possible suspects from the book club. Gramm handed White the victim's personal effects.

White introduced Preston to Gramm. "She takes notes on a tablet," White explained.

"Like Moses?" Gramm asked.

White laughed, "Yeah. Just like Moses." White reminded everyone to put on gloves and began to examine the victim's large red Cartier tote. She removed a wallet, a makeup bag, antacids, some cocktail napkins with numbers jotted on them, and several business cards, along with the usual hairbrush, paper clips, safety pins, gas receipts, and dust.

"This purse is beautiful on the outside but a mess on the inside," White noted as she began cataloguing and bagging the contents for the file.

"No phone?" Milo asked.

Gramm handed him the phone which had been bagged separately. "So, what happens next?" he asked the group.

"We start interviewing the people who were at the meeting," White said.

Milo added, "And find out where the victim ate dinner."

Officer Preston looked puzzled. "Can I ask a question?"

"Go for it," Gramm said.

"If the poison was in her drink at the book club, why do you keep mentioning where she ate her last dinner?"

"At this point, all we know is she was poisoned. No one said the poison was in the drink," Milo said.

"I assumed..."

Gramm nodded. "That's where Milo comes in handy. He almost never assumes anything. In cases where we're all wondering who put an axe in the victim's head, Milo questions her choice of shoes. It would be funny if he wasn't right so often. It's annoying."

"Footwear and last meals are important," Milo defended himself.

"How do you do that...find where she ate?" Preston asked.

"The Black Bear Restaurant," Milo said.

"What?" Preston asked.

"She ate at the Black Bear Restaurant," Milo said, holding up her phone. "It's on her calendar."

White took the phone. "Doesn't say who she met with."

"Let's hope they have cameras," Gramm said.

White looked over the napkins, put each in its own clear evidence bag, and handed them to Preston. "Check out these numbers. Let's see who our victim was calling."

"What about the business cards?" Milo asked.

White looked at the cards. "Elliot Addison, Director, Urban Forest Commission, Duluth, Minnesota, and Dr. Charles Carlson, Dermatologist." She turned to Preston. "That sounds familiar, the doctor, not the tree guy."

Preston checked her notes. "Dr. Charles Carlson, celery and carrots, was at the book club and tended to the victim once she was stricken. He rode with her and Amy Gramm in the ambulance."

"They knew each other. Why would she have his card?" White asked.

"I find the forest guy much more interesting," Milo said.

"Of course, you do," Gramm sighed.

"I wonder what kind of shoes he wears," White asked.

Milo nodded. "It makes all the difference."

8

"Nothing is easy," White muttered to herself after a quick Tuesday morning call to the hospital social worker. The social worker had not started the process of locating Rand's daughter because the body had been transferred to Doc Smith.

White's next call was to Kyle—the forensic IT guy who was examining the victim's phone. He answered with his usual cheeriness. "Robin you've got to give me time. I haven't found any contact listed as 'killer' yet."

"What? Kyle, I was counting on you," White said going along with the joke.

"Give me twenty-four hours, and I'll hand you the pestilent poisoner."

"Pestilent?"

"It's my word of the day. I have one of those calendars."

"I'm glad for you, but, for the moment, have you at least gotten into the victim's contact list?"

"Of course. Piece of cake."

"Any mention of a daughter or a lawyer?" White asked.

"Aha, looking for a monetary motive."

"Kyle you're being pestilent…"

"Okay, okay. No mention of a daughter in the contacts, so I've moved on to the emails. There is a lawyer. She needs one. I've gone back about three months and already she's been threatened with three lawsuits."

"And the lawyer's name is?"

"Thomas Howard. He's with—hang on a minute let me call it up—Haney, Jenson, and Hampft."

White checked the time. *Nine o'clock. He should be in his office.* She hung up on Kyle without saying goodbye and called Thomas Howard.

"Howard here," the lawyer answered.

White introduced herself.

"I expected this. I read in the paper Patsy's death was suspicious."

"I need information—next of kin, terms of the will, and any legal problems."

"So, she was murdered."

White decided to give a little to get a little. "We believe she was poisoned. That's all I can say."

"I probably shouldn't say this, but it doesn't surprise me," Howard said.

White grabbed her pen and notepad. "Why doesn't it surprise you?"

"On that podcast of hers, Patsy accused people of horrendous crimes. We were fending off lawsuits all the time. I urged her to tone down her rhetoric especially because she never had proof. It was slander. She didn't care. Several of the threatened lawsuits could have bankrupted her if she lost, and she would have."

"I'm going to need the names of those people, but right now, I need next of kin and terms of the will." White listened to Howard typing on his computer.

"She has a daughter, Valerie Nethercamp, who lives in Orlando."

"Any husband?" White asked.

"Yes. Ex-husband, Neil Nethercamp. He lives in California—Sacramento."

Howard gave White the phone numbers but said neither was interested in attending the funeral. "As the executor, I have contacted the Anderson Funeral Home to handle everything once the body is released," Howard said. "When will that be?"

"I'll let you know." White hung up and dialed Valerie Nethercamp's number, explained who she was, and offered her condolences.

"How did she die?" Valerie asked.

"She was poisoned," White said. "We are trying to eliminate as many people as possible from our inquiries. Can you tell me where you were Thursday night?"

"Me? I was on stage singing at Disney World. A lot of people saw me, but I looked like the Little Mermaid. I'm on stage every Tuesday, Thursday, and Sunday."

"Have you talked to your father since your mother died?" White asked.

"No. He's in California with his second wife and two children. I don't think he cares, and I know I don't. I was an infant when my parents broke up. I lived with my father. Patsy wasn't interested."

"Do you know of anyone who wanted to harm your mother?" White asked.

Not really. She was a stranger to me."

§

Milo spied Annie curled up in her gallery Gianna tree. Attempting stealth, he eased past her to see if it was possible to outsmart the bacon-craving cat. Approaching the hearth-room door, Milo was celebrating success when he heard the thump of cat paws landing on solid ground. A quick sprint and an irritated meow moved Milo to the side with Annie arriving at the breakfast table first.

Milo declared defeat, slumped into his chair, accepted his breakfast from Martha, and began breaking off bits of bacon to feed the champ. Annie meowed one more time before sampling her bacon.

"You're racing the cat?" Sutherland questioned, not looking up from his paper.

"I almost won," Milo said.

"She lets you do that. She has your number." Sutherland winced as he folded his paper.

Milo, noticing the bottles of Turmeric and Ginger on the table, asked who was stiff, sore, achy or all of the above.

Sutherland glanced at Martha as she delivered his breakfast smoothie. She shrugged declaring she felt fine.

Glancing from Martha to Sutherland, Milo asked, "What did I miss?"

"A spirited game of basketball," Sutherland said. "We're getting Jamal's game up to speed."

"And where does Martha come in?"

"Martha and Agnes challenged us. We were um…"

"Set up?" Milo asked.

"That's one way to put it, but Jamal and I held our own. It was almost a tie."

"Like I almost snuck by the cat."

Not willing to admit defeat, Sutherland shifted into planning mode. "We need a scoreboard and someone to operate it. We thought of you."

"Do I get a horn that honks at the end of quarters?"

"Of course."

"I'm in," Milo said.

Back in the kitchen, Martha shook her head and laughed, as she started Milo's eggs. *New rim, new backboard, and now an electronic scoreboard—a simple Lakesong Estate neighborhood pickup game.* She retrieved Milo's breakfast from the warming drawer, adding the scrambled eggs. Milo got up and poured himself a cup of coffee as he looked out at two kayakers in wet suits paddling close to the shore.

"Have you seen those guys, the kayakers? It's gotta be cold out there!"

Sutherland looked up. "Brisk. I envy them. I have to go to work. We have a kayak in the boat house, and you can borrow my wet suit."

Milo looked at Sutherland then himself. "A wet suit from an eight foot skinny giant—should fit just fine."

Sutherland laughed. "You're right. I don't want you stretching it in the middle," he said patting his stomach as Milo dug into his hash browns. "Smoothies make a difference."

"Too high a price to pay," Milo said, feeding a few more small pieces of bacon to the cat.

"How's that other investigation going? You know, the one you get paid for," Sutherland asked.

Milo filled him in on the few book-club attendees he could remember, and then added, "One interesting thing, the victim had business cards from a dermatologist, a Dr. Carlson—who was at the book club—and from the city forest something or other."

"I know Dr. Carlson from the country club. Does the fact that she had his card make him a suspect?" Sutherland asked, drinking his coffee.

"Everybody focuses on the doctor," Milo insisted. "The victim's in her sixties. Consulting a dermatologist is pretty normal. My question is why talk to a tree guy?"

"So why did she talk to the tree guy?"

"Don't have a clue."

Martha came into the morning room. "Gentlemen, as long as you're both here, I have a proposition for you. I've got a fourth grader and ninth grader in the same bedroom. If I don't separate them soon, there will be another murder you can investigate. I would like to add a fourth bedroom to the cottage. I have the money saved."

"Oh, for goodness sakes, we can pay for it," Sutherland said. "It adds to the value of the estate. Right, Milo?"

Milo seemed confused.

"Milo?" Sutherland asked again.

"Sure, we could that," Milo said, "but who's using all the bedrooms?"

Sutherland urged Martha to sit down as this conversation looked as though it was going to take a while.

Sitting down, Martha explained, "I have the front bedroom. Breanna has the small one in the back, and the boys share the middle bedroom."

"So, who's in the attic?" Milo asked.

"Attic? What attic?" Martha questioned.

Sutherland put his head in his hands. "It's happening again," he said in reference to Milo knowing about a forgotten elevator and basement kitchen.

"The attic would make a great bedroom," Milo explained. "Mr. Henderson—the old caretaker—loved astronomy. When I was a kid, he would invite me up there to look through his telescope. Mrs. Henderson brought us hot chocolate in the winter, and Kool-Aid in the summer. I loved it."

"We've lived in that house for five years. There's no stairway…it's not there…you can't get up…"

"It's hidden. It's been years since I have been in there, but I remember Mr. Henderson kicking the bottom of the wall between the living room and kitchen. You know, that wood on the bottom."

"The baseboard?" Sutherland offered.

"I guess."

"I think I would have noticed a door. There has to be a crack, right?"

"Nope. The hallway still has wood panels, right?" Milo asked.

"Yes." Martha agreed.

"Well one of those panels is magic—at least it was to me as a kid," Milo said.

"I've cleaned that hallway. How would I not know this?" Martha questioned.

"Don't feel bad. Sutherland didn't know he had an elevator." Milo fed another piece of bacon to the cat.

§

"I checked on those napkin numbers," Preston said as the trio headed to the Johansson's. Two of them were authors our victim wanted on her podcast and the third was an Instagram influencer."

"I'll bite," Milo said, "who does an influencer influence?"

"Her followers," Preston explained.

"What about the people threatening to sue Rand?" White asked.

"Working on it."

White pulled up to the traditional prewar-gray, two-story house updated in the seventies with aluminum siding and black shutters.

Preston was looking for the house number. "I think this is it. Isn't this close to the Gramm house?"

"Same Observation Hill neighborhood." While White pointed out another update, the pretty carriage lamppost, in the front yard, Milo wondered out loud why a matching storage shed was in the front yard and not in the back.

"They have a great view of the harbor, but it's steep. I bet the back is a drop off," White explained, stepping up onto the front porch. She rang the doorbell. As the door opened, she looked up at an unsmiling sandy haired-man in a green-plaid flannel shirt. White showed her badge, introduced Milo and Officer Preston, and asked if either Linda or Liam Johansson was available.

Without speaking, the man showed them into the office and left. They looked around the small room with a desk, a Queen Anne chair and two straight-backed client chairs. "This isn't going to work," White said looking at the lack of seating.

"I wonder if that was Liam," Preston asked. "Not a friendly sort."

Footsteps could be heard coming down the hall from the kitchen. They stopped short for a brief moment and then continued until a woman with frizzy blond, over-peroxided hair poked her head into the sitting room. Linda Johansson's look was stuck in the eighties. Old girlfriends had told her the hair color complemented her watery blue eyes—a happy time in her life.

"Hello," she said. "I'm sorry; this room is too small. I don't know what my brother was thinking. Let's go into the living room." Linda led the way.

White and Preston sat down on one side of the sectional couch, Linda took the other side, and Milo sat in one of the far chairs. Liam stood and leaned against the archway. White did the introductions, telling Linda and Liam that Patsy Rand had been poisoned.

Linda glanced at Liam and stared at the chair Patsy Rand had occupied Thursday night."

"We are only beginning the investigation," White continued.

"Do you think she was poisoned here?"

"We don't know where she was poisoned. We're creating a timeline—talking to witnesses."

Linda folded her arms. "A timeline of what?"

"Of the victim's movements and interactions," White explained.

Linda again stared at Liam whose face had not changed from the hard-set attitude he had when he opened the door. Linda turned back to White. Liam left the room.

"I understand this is upsetting," White said.

Parroting White, Linda spewed, "You understand it's upsetting? You have no idea!"

Milo shrugged. "Inform us."

Linda took a deep breath and refolded her arms in a protective gesture. "Okay, let's do this! Your victim was responsible for putting my brother in jail for murder twenty-two years ago. That bitch buried evidence that would have proven his innocence. Because of her, Liam—that man who just left the room—spent twelve years of his life behind bars for no reason. Are we sad she's dead? Hell no!"

"Did you kill her?" White asked.

Preston noticed the bluntness of the question.

Linda scoffed, "No, but she deserved death and more."

White sat back in the couch. "Why would you have someone you hated as a guest in your home?"

Linda stared daggers at White. "I didn't know. I knew her as Patsy Rand, pain-in-the-ass blogger. Ron Bello recognized her and told us that Pasty Rand was Patsy Nethercamp."

"How did you not know her?"

"I never met her. I was having my twins and was confined to bedrest during the trial. Liam told me he was innocent and not to worry."

"I'm confused," White said. "Pasty Rand or Nethercamp was a blogger. How does a blogger put your brother in jail?"

"She was a prosecutor until she got disbarred. Don't you know anything about her?"

"We got this case this morning. Anything you can tell us about her is helpful."

"How about this. Patsy Nethercamp railroaded my innocent brother into prison."

"Railroaded how?" Milo asked.

"She hid evidence and intimidated witnesses that would have cleared him, but she was found out."

"Who found her out?" Milo asked.

"Ron Bello of course. He wrote all the newspaper articles that exposed her. You really don't know anything about this do you?" Linda challenged.

"Wait a minute," Milo said. "So, in this book-club meeting you have the man railroaded into prison, the woman who ran the railroad, and the reporter who derailed it."

"Yes! I had that awful woman in my house and didn't know who she was. I thought she had long ago crawled under the dirt and died." Linda smiled for the first time. "And now she has."

White glanced at Preston, hoping she was keeping up. "Are you getting all this?"

Preston nodded as her fingers flew over the keyboard balanced on her lap.

White resumed the questioning. "Give us your version of the events from last Thursday night,"

Linda's version of events was similar to Amy's except she admitted that she and Liam mixed Patsy's drink, but neither of them delivered it. "I thought while we were all in the dining room she got up and got it herself. She certainly wasn't helping us."

"Are you sure she ever got the drink?" White asked.

"Yes. There was a broken amber glass where she fell. She was the only one who wanted a mixed drink and my mixed drink glasses are amber."

"Where is that broken glass now?" Milo asked.

"We threw it out that night before it could hurt anybody. It's gone. The garbage came Friday morning."

"Did she eat anything?" White asked.

"Not that I saw. She was screeching about a stomachache and antacids. She prattled on about a horrible dinner."

Milo perked up. "Who with?"

Linda shrugged.

"Who invited her to join the club?" Milo asked.

Linda startled, thinking of this for the first time. "Crystal Bower. She sold her to us as a blogger who had connections to authors."

"Did she know who the victim was in connection to your brother?" White asked.

Linda eyebrows furrowed. "I don't know, but I'm gonna find out."

"One last question," White said. "The victim was heard saying 'the book' as she was dying. Any idea what that meant?"

Linda shook her head. "Maybe she read Ron's book and figured out it was about her. He kills her in the book. It's gruesome and lovely!"

"Ron's book?" White asked.

"The guest author," Preston advised. "Ron Bello."

Linda agreed. "After he left the newspaper in Minneapolis, he started writing books. *Death Comes to the DA* is his first best seller. That was the book we read for Thursday's book club."

White told Linda that they needed to talk to Liam too—he needed to come back into the room. Linda got up, found her brother, and directed him to the living room. He sat down in the Patsy Rand death chair, used his arm to cross one leg over the other holding on to his ankle. He began by saying the police were not his favorite people.

White nodded. "Your sister explained. Tell us about last Thursday night."

Staring at his shoe, Liam said in a flat tone, "I was the bartender,"

"Did you mix the drink for Patsy Rand?" White began.

"Yes."

"Your sister said she helped you."

"Yes."

"Which is it Mr. Johansson? Did you mix the drink or did you and your sister mix the drink?"

"Both."

Milo tried next. "When you delivered the drink, did Patsy Rand recognize you as the person she put in jail years ago?"

Liam looked up. "I didn't deliver the drink."

"Why?"

"There was an accident in the dining room."

105

"Who delivered the drink?" Milo asked.

"Don't know. I was cleaning up the mess in the dining room."

"When did you get released from prison?" White moved the conversation on.

"2002."

"What did you do then?"

"I took a job in California."

"When did you come back here?" White asked.

"A week ago."

"Why did you come back?"

"I was offered a job here. I missed winter."

White thought he may be the only person to miss a Duluth winter. That in itself could make him a liar. "Didn't you recognize her when she came in the door?"

"No, I was cleaning up at the bar. I heard banging and yelling, but I never saw her."

White wanted to press him. "Do you expect us to believe you didn't know that woman was in this house?"

Liam let go of his ankle, put his foot back down at the ground, and leaned forward, elbows on his knees, staring at the floor. "I will say it again—please listen. I had no idea."

"Did you kill her?" White persisted.

He looked up. His face seemed to harden even more. "I know you want to pin this on me, but I've spent enough time in prison. I'm not about to spend more."

Milo nodded. "Okay, let me get this straight. Both of you mixed the drink, but neither of you delivered it. How does that happen?"

Linda spoke first, "As we both told you, there was an accident in the dining room. A large water urn broke. Both of us were cleaning it up."

"So, you left the drink on the bar?" White asked.

"Yes," Liam said. "I wasn't thinking about it after the water crashed."

"Where was the bar?" Milo asked.

"The office—the room I put you in when you first got here. The drink was on the credenza I set up as a bar," Liam said.

"So, anyone could have grabbed the drink," Milo said.

Liam grunted. "Anyone, including her."

§

"Is the coffee still hot, Martha?" Agnes asked, as she strolled through the Lakesong kitchen into the morning room and poured herself a cup. "I'm a little stiff from reliving my high school basketball glory that never was. How are you doing?"

"I'm good. Bring your coffee and the cart back in here, will you?" When Agnes arrived with the coffee cart, Martha asked, "Are you real busy this morning?"

"Nothing that can't keep. What's up?"

Martha smiled a rare mischievous smile, "Something fun, I think. Keep your jacket on and bring your coffee. You and I are going to look for a hidden staircase in the cottage," she said, explaining the conversation at breakfast and Milo's revelation.

"Oh, that sounds like much more fun than cataloging books. You know, Milo should give us all a guided tour of this estate. He seems to know more about it than Sutherland."

"Upstairs, downstairs." Martha smiled. "Remember Milo was the cook's son."

"You're right! Milo was the cook's son. He knew how the house actually worked," Agnes agreed.

A brisk walk to the cottage later, Martha and Agnes threw their coats on the living room couch, got on their knees, and began pushing on the baseboard between the living room and the kitchen.

"This cottage is cozy," Agnes said. "I've never been inside."

Martha agreed. "I was so lucky to get this gig. This house has been perfect. But now the little people are becoming big people, and it would be nice if we had more space." Standing up, Martha declared, "This isn't working. Milo said the old caretaker kicked the baseboard."

"If I scuff the baseboard, I'm sorry," Agnes said, tapping the wood with her tennis shoe. "This feels so wrong."

Martha laughed. "I know what you mean."

After moving up and down the hall several times, the two met in the middle with no result. "Would Milo do this to us as a joke?" Martha asked.

"Doesn't sound like Milo," Agnes said. "You know, this Mr. Henderson was a caretaker. I bet he had hard soled shoes. Maybe we're not kicking hard enough."

Martha left to find harder shoes and came back with a pair of Jamal's church shoes and some tube socks. "He's outgrown these," she explained, "and they're still too big for

Darian. Put the tube socks in the toe and let's get back to kicking—caretaker style!"

Agnes took the left one, Martha the right. They started laughing as they hobbled down the hall, preparing to boot the baseboards. "I'm going to think of someone I'd like to dropkick into the next county. You know, for motivation," Agnes said.

"Sounds great, as long as it's not me."

"Never you, Martha. Where else could I play basketball one day and kick baseboards the next? This is fun!"

Martha clogged to the living-room end of the wall. Agnes went to the kitchen end. Martha with her left foot, Agnes with her right began walloping the baseboard—with no result. Agnes reached the halfway point first and began working her way back. "Milo has lost his mind," she laughed.

Martha didn't answer. Agnes turned toward her. "Martha?"

"No, he hasn't," Martha whispered.

Martha was standing in front of a wood panel that was now ajar. She pushed it opened with care revealing stairs climbing up into the dark. "There are buttons on the wall. Should I push one of them?"

Agnes came over, poked her head into the space. "Oh yeah, that's an old electric switch. I had to replace those all over my house when I redid the electrical," Agnes said, pushing the upper button. A ceiling light came on exposing the staircase plus twenty years of dust and spiderwebs.

"Do I explore or clean?" Martha asked.

"Oh, we explore!" Agnes declared, dropping Jamal's shoe, replacing it with her own, and sprinting up the steps. Another old-fashioned light switch met her at the top. Pushing the button revealed a gigantic room with one cluttered table, two folding chairs, and several piles of books on the floor.

"Martha, hurry up," Agnes urged. "This is perfect. You could hold a dance up here. It's huge and heated!"

Martha was wary as she entered the room and looked around. "Any critters I should be aware of?"

"None so far," Agnes replied.

Martha moved her hand over the white plaster walls. "This room needs cleaning, but you're right, it's big!"

"Yes and no. The floor area is huge, but the roof slant is steep on all four walls. See? I can't stand up here," Agnes said hunching over by the far wall.

"Yeah, but Darian is still a short guy. He has one big room here," Martha said.

Agnes' eyes followed the slanting roof to the top, which was flat with a hatch door and rope hanging down. "Where do you suppose that leads?"

Martha looked up. "That's a pull-down attic door, but we're in the attic. I thought the cupola on the roof was decorative—apparently not."

" More exploring?"

"Not today," Martha said. "I have some cleaning and thinking to do."

"So, Darian gets this room?" Agnes asked.

"That was the plan, but Jamal may want it."

"How do you resolve that?"

"That's where the cleaning and thinking comes in. They go well together."

§

"This is tucked well out of the way," White said as they pulled up to a small strip mall hidden behind a larger complex off the Miller Trunk Highway. The four-store mall supported a Chinese restaurant, a nail place, a dry cleaner, and Evelyn's Herbal Remedies.

The store was empty of people as they entered. After a few seconds, Evelyn Chen emerged from a backroom taking off a pair of rubber gloves. The place reminded Milo of Ed Patupick's electronics store—no customers.

White introduced herself along with Milo and Preston. "Is there a place where we can talk?" she asked.

"Follow me," Evelyn said, as she turned and walked to the back of the store. A simple red cloth separated the main store from the backroom. Parting the cloth, Evelyn led them into a room with baskets of plants under grow lights, and shelves filled with bottles. "I'm preparing some supplements on that bench by the wall, so let's sit here at the table."

As they sat down, White asked her to describe the events leading up to Patsy Rand's death.

"I don't understand. What events?"

"At the book-club meeting Thursday night."

Evelyn thought for a moment. "I left early—didn't feel well."

"Tell us what happened before you left," White continued.

"I arrived the same time as Crystal Bower. I brought steamed dumplings. Put them in the dining room. I didn't feel well. I took something. It didn't help."

111

White waited for her to continue. She didn't, so White asked, "What happened next?"

"I left."

"Were you there when Patsy Rand arrived?"

"Yes."

"Tell us about that."

"She was shouting," Evelyn rolled her eyes, "always shouting."

"About?"

"She wanted a drink, her stomach hurt. I offered her one of my herbal remedies. She refused. I went into the bathroom. I also didn't feel well. I had the stomach flu."

"We understand a water jug fell on the floor. Where were you when that happened?" White asked.

"In the bathroom."

"Did you see who brought Rand her drink?" Milo asked.

"I was in the bathroom. I told you that."

"What was your relationship with the victim?" White asked.

"She was not a nice woman. She attacked my business."

"How?"

"One of my customers died, and Patsy blogged I killed him—my herbs were responsible."

Milo got up and started looking at the bottles and glass jars on the table.

"Please stay away from there," Evelyn warned. "Some of those mixtures are strong and can be absorbed through the skin."

"I'm looking for something for achy muscles," said Milo. "My friend says I need to take ginger and tammy or something like that."

"Turmeric?" Evelyn asked.

"Yeah that sounds right."

"Good advice. They're in the front of the store, not something I mix."

"He also suggested Aco something. It's made from a plant—Wolfshood."

"If you mean wolfsbane or monkshood, that would be aconite," Evelyn said.

Milo shrugged, "Could be."

"I mix it and sell it, but I wouldn't suggest it for you. Tincture of aconite is good for chronic pain. You lurch when you walk but not as if you are in pain."

White suppressed a smile.

Milo, unfazed, asked, "Can I buy a bottle just to try?"

"No. What I have here is too strong for you. I could mix you a mild tincture. It will be ready in six weeks."

"You're that busy?" Milo asked sitting down once again.

"If I made it today, it would take that long. There's no way to rush it."

9

On the way to lunch at the Chinese Dragon Restaurant, White cracked, "It's scary how well you play dazed-and-confused, Milo. Wolfshood? You do know it's monkshood and wolfsbane, not wolfshood."

"Sure, but I got what I wanted," Milo stated.

"Which was?"

"We learned she makes aconite without telling her it was the poison," Milo said as White parked the car.

"You know, if she's the murderer, she already knows the poison," White said leading the way into the restaurant.

Milo had to admit she had a good point.

"We will now play Milo's Chinese Restaurant Game," White said to Preston who was staring at the oversized gold Buddhas which surrounded the diners.

Preston smiled. "How is that played?"

"Milo will ask for a menu. The owner, his friend, will refuse to give him one because Milo always orders egg foo young *don't skimp on the gravy*—like it's part of the dish."

Preston crinkled her nose. "Never had egg foo young. Isn't that just a loaded omelet?"

"She says that like it's a bad thing," Milo said.

Henry Hun—Hank to his friends—met them at the door. White introduced Preston. Hank grabbed two menus. "Follow me. Lieutenant Gramm is already at his table in the back."

"I want a menu, too," Milo complained.

Hank did not turn around. "No, you don't. You will order egg foo young and accuse me of skimping on the gravy."

Preston whispered, "Oh my God, you're right. Do they do this all the time?"

"It's like *Groundhog Day*, the same thing over and over and over," White said.

"I was thinking of gun pan chicken," Milo retorted.

"There is no such thing as gun pan chicken," Hank said as they arrived at the table.

Lt. Gramm shook his head. "Milo can we order once without you abusing Hank?"

Milo shrugged. "I have no idea what you're talking about."

Hank handed out the menus, skipping Milo.

"I'm serious. I want a menu," Milo said.

Hank ignored him. "The special today is spareribs in black bean sauce."

"No silly name like mofo dufus?" Milo asked.

"Once again, that's mapo doufu. Today's 'silly' name is pai kuat," Hank chided. "Thank you for thinking Szechuan and Cantonese names are silly. By the way, your egg foo young is a 'silly' American dish."

Milo leaned over to a couple sitting at the next table. "This guy won't give me a menu because I was a much better baseball player than he was. I mean he's carried that grudge since high school."

"Please ignore him," Hank pleaded as he left to find another menu. Neither table saw the smile on his face.

Preston was laughing. Gramm asked her not to encourage Milo.

Hank returned, tossed the menu at Milo and said, "Okay, let's dance."

"I just got my menu," Milo complained. "Get their orders while I make my choice."

Gramm ordered the ribs as did Preston. White asked for bok choy with Chinese mushrooms. Everyone looked at Milo. "The broccoli chicken, is that real chicken?"

"No," Hank snarked, "it's duck, but a duck who thought it was a chicken."

Preston laughed.

"You're encouraging them again," Gramm admonished.

Preston defended herself. "They're funny."

Milo handed back his menu saying, "I'll take the chicken egg foo young—don't skimp on the gravy."

Hank yanked the menu away from him, telling the group, "I was a much better baseball player than he was."

"That's why you rode the bench for four years," Milo said.

"Right next to you!" Hank threw back over his shoulder.

As a waiter brought tea, Preston asked Milo, "How is it you're not poisoned?"

"He loves our little game," Milo said. "I'm the highlight of his day."

Gramm interrupted, "I have an idea. Let's stop talking about Milo's order and discuss murder instead."

White filled him in on the morning's interviews.

"Three suspects already, and the day is only half over," Gramm said. "This Chen woman actually makes this poison—can't get better than that."

"Evelyn Chen was right. I googled it in the car," said Milo. "It takes weeks to make aconite."

Gramm added, "Someone thought about killing that woman for a long time."

"Unless they went into Evelyn's store and bought a bunch of it," Preston suggested.

"Did you ask her?" Gramm inquired.

"No, we didn't." White pursed her lips. "I will check with her and other herbal shops to see if anyone has bought any of the strong aconite. Turning to Preston, White added, "When I say *I will*, I mean *you will*."

Preston nodded and typed a reminder note.

"Good for you Robin. Delegate," Gramm said.

"I learned from the master," she quipped.

Gramm added, "Doc Smith called me this morning out of force of habit. Robin, I reminded him to call you on this case from now on. He checked with a toxicologist about dose and delivery of aconite since we still don't know when or where she was poisoned."

Preston continued taking notes.

"I asked him if the effects could be delayed—poison now, die later. He said it could be put in a capsule which takes some time to dissolve."

"How do you get her to take it?" White asked.

Gramm shrugged. "Tell her it's a stomachache remedy—I'm guessing."

"Possible," White said.

"Or," Gramm went on, "she could get one dose at one time and another dose an hour or two later."

"Two people working together?" Milo asked.

"Possible," Gramm answered.

A waiter brought their food. Conversation ceased except for one comment by Milo, "I don't lurch."

§

Following the police interview, Linda called Amy with three words, "I gotta talk."

Recognizing the tone, Amy invited her over and immediately added Erin Cohen, the other member of their small support group. The three old friends settled in at the kitchen table where they had grappled with life's problems for the past twenty years.

"The police interviewed me this morning," Linda said, holding a cup of hot coffee as if her hands were cold.

"It wasn't Ernie was it?" Amy asked.

"No, no it wasn't," Linda said. "It was a couple of young women and an older guy. I'm so upset. I don't even know where to start."

"I can see why," Erin said. "Having someone die in your house is awful."

Linda's hands folded into fists. "Died in my house! If she hadn't died in my house, I would have killed her! She was the monster who put Liam in jail for twelve years!"

Amy was confused. "What are you talking about? What do you mean?"

"Patsy Rand was Patsy Nethercamp, the prosecutor who railroaded Liam into prison. That bitch was sitting in our book club for a year. I've had her in my house twice before!"

"Why did you let her join the book club? I'm also confused," Erin said.

"I didn't know who she was. I found out the night of her murder. In fact, Ron Bello told Liam and me who she was seconds before that water jug broke. By the time we cleaned it up, Rand was all but dead. I don't know what upsets me more, the fact that woman was allowed to touch my life again, or that now both Liam and I are suspects. I'm afraid I lost it all over the police."

"I'm sure you're not a suspect." Erin tried to console her.

Amy shook her head, "We are all suspects, Erin. I'm a cop's wife. I know that. This is upsetting Linda, and I know you're scared and angry, but don't ever say, 'I would have killed her' to the police."

"I may have already. I told you—I lost it. I don't remember what I said. Maybe I'll be the second Johansson to go to prison. They interviewed Liam too. He's gone into prison-shutdown mode. It's scary. He sounds so hollow."

Amy and Erin let Linda rant and cry for the next twenty minutes, filling her coffee cup, and feeding her chocolate cookies until she ran herself down.

Amy put her arm around Linda. "You know, Patsy was already sick when she came to the book club. She could have been poisoned somewhere else. She said she had an awful dinner. My cop-wife radar says they're checking out who she ate with. That's their prime suspect."

Linda sat back and stared at Amy. "Are you being nice, or is this real?"

"I wouldn't lie to you. The police interviewed me yesterday, and I mentioned Patsy's dinner and how she was feeling. That's where I'd start looking."

"Makes sense," Erin said, "I'm sorry all this is happening, Linda. My bump in the road seems pretty tame."

"What bump?" Linda asked.

Erin accepted a refill from Amy. "We need to sell the travel agency. It's a bump, but it's so small compared to what's happened to you and Liam."

"I thought you were doing well," Linda said.

"We were, but in the last year Barry's dad came to live with us—Alzheimer's. While I was busy with his dad, Barry insisted on running the agency and he's wasn't up to it. I'm still crunching numbers to see how much trouble we're in. To begin with, we're closing the office and working out of the house. Barry's not pleased. I don't care."

Amy refilled the plate of cookies and the support continued.

§

White, Rathkey, and Preston met Ron Bello at the Harbor Six Resort Hotel on the waterfront. The restaurant was emptying fast, as the post-lunch tourists were scattering for a chilly afternoon of spectacular fall color up the North Shore. Preston scanned the room looking for an author type. She asked if they had a description of Belo. White, who had asked Bello what he looked like when she set up the interview, marched past Preston to a six-foot-three African American man with black horned-rimmed glasses and a friendly face.

"Mr. Bello?" she asked.

He stood and shook White's hand. "Officer White?"

"Sergeant White," she corrected and introduced Officer Preston and Milo. Bello seemed almost shocked at hearing Milo's name. "Milo Rathkey? You're a cop?" he asked.

"Used to be; consultant now," Milo said.

The group sat down as Bello began flipping pages over on a yellow legal pad. "Milo Rathkey. I have you down as a private investigator."

"Why do you have me down at all?" Milo asked.

Bello's full-throated laugh caused several people to look in their direction. "I'm researching my next book, a fictional account of the Jessica Vogel murder. I need to talk to you—so when you've finished interrogating me, can I interrogate you?"

White interrupted, "That's yesterday's murder. I have a fresh one. Patsy Rand. Tell me about her."

"Ahhh, so that's what this is about. I read the article in the Sunday Duluth paper. So, did someone dispatch dear Patsy?"

White nodded.

"Can I ask how?"

White ignored the question. "We know you have a history with her. Please tell us about it."

"Indeed, I do." Bello sat back thinking of how to begin. "Back in 2008, a friend—a lawyer in the DA's office in Minneapolis—asked me to investigate what she thought were questionable prosecutions in her office. She thought evidence was being withheld. She had proof that at least two witnesses had been hidden from defense attorneys. She wanted me to check if there were others."

"Why you? Why didn't she do it herself?" White asked.

"Politics. It was her office, and she didn't know how far the malfeasance went."

"What did you discover?" White asked.

"Plenty. Within six months I wrote a three-part investigative series in the Minneapolis Tribune that led to Patsy Rand—then known as Patsy Nethercamp—being fired and disbarred. Several convictions were overturned by the State Supreme Court."

"Does your history end there?" White asked.

Bello laughed again. "No. After she was disbarred, Patsy reinvented herself as a blogger. She accused me of letting criminals walk the streets and advised that no one should buy my books because I shouldn't be rewarded for corrupting the criminal justice system. That was one of her favorite lines. She was a freak show."

"I bet you didn't like that," Milo said.

"I was okay with it. Sure, she may have cost me some readers, but I was a new author who needed to get my name out there. Patsy got my name out there. Several people told me they bought my book to see if I was as bad as she said I was." He laughed again. "In a twisted way, I'm gonna miss her."

"I read your latest book," White said. "It's about the death of an incompetent DA. From what I now know of Patsy Rand, you hardly disguised her. You also shot her nine times on the steps of the courthouse. That doesn't seem like a person you're going to miss."

"Fiction, Sgt. White, fiction. Authors get to kill any number of people without recrimination. Which is why I always include the author's disclaimer: any resemblance to actual persons, living or dead is purely coincidental." Bello gave a sly smile.

"Did you interview her anytime during your expose' back in 2008?"

"I tried," Bello said.

"Did she ever admit or explain why she withheld witnesses?" White asked. "She had to know she would be disbarred if caught."

Bello folded his hands and leaned forward. "You don't know her yet, do you? The Patsy Nethercamp I came to know convicted people in her mind. Facts were irrelevant in that decision—the end justified the means."

"Give me an example," Milo said.

"I'll give you one close to home—Liam Johansson. She interviewed a witness who saw the altercation and said Liam was not the murderer—had a completely different description of the killer. Liam should have walked. She hid that witness statement. She later testified she knew the witness was lying. The state supreme court informed her that juries determine truthfulness, not prosecutors."

"Do you think either of the Johanssons killed her?" White asked.

Bello shrugged. "I don't think so—unless I've been conned. They didn't seem to know their Patsy Rand was the infamous Patsy Nethercamp. I had to tell them."

White asked Bello to describe the events of Thursday night. His narrative was similar to others they heard. Bello said he was in the dining room, people watching, when Patsy was stricken. He did not see who brought her the drink.

"You said Liam, not Mr. Johansson," Milo said. "are you friends?"

"I suppose. We spent a lot of time together through two or three extensive interviews. When you do this kind of story, a bond forms between the reporter and the subject. It may not be a friendship, but it's a bond."

White thanked him for his time and asked him how long he'd be in town.

Bello stood. "At least a week. Mr. Rathkey, when can I interview you?"

"Let's say tonight, my place, dinner?" Milo offered hoping he could pass Bello's questions off on Sutherland.

"Sure. Where do you live?"

"I've got a place by the lake."

"Nice."

White laughed. "You have no idea."

Grabbing a few minutes between interviews, Milo called Martha giving her a heads up on the dinner guest. To Milo's surprise, Martha knew Ron Bello from her days in Minneapolis.

§

Crown Dermatology Center occupied a suite of offices in a modern two-story building over the hill off Arrowhead Road. Dr. Charles Carlson was the Medical Director and one of three partners in this robust practice. Carlson, clad in a crisp white coat over his shirt and tie, was waiting for the investigating trio in his office.

"We could smooth out that lumpy complexion," Carlson said after being introduced to Milo.

"Lumps? What lumps?" Milo asked, almost commenting on Carlson's tiny, diamond stud embedded in his huge, lumpy earlobe.

Carlson laughed. "It's one of my best opening lines for getting new business."

Milo wasn't having a good week. One suspect called him a lurcher, and this clown wanted to smooth out his lumps.

"So," Carlson said, sitting back in his expensive leather chair, "I suppose you are here about Patsy Rand."

"You suppose correctly," White said, sitting down in one of two patient chairs. Milo motioned to Preston to take the other while he grabbed a chair against the side wall and brought it to the desk watching Dr. Carlson close his laptop.

Milo wondered how a busy doctor, ridding the world of lumps, would have time for on-line poker.

Carlson began. "That night it was clear she was having a heart problem of some sort. I don't understand why the paper said it was suspicious."

White ignored his complaint. "Tell us about that night."

"Patsy was griping about stomach upset when she arrived. I was milling around the living room, chatting with that author fellow. When we were called to the dining room to eat, Erin Cohen knocked over the water jug. While dealing with that mess, I heard a thud from the living room and rushed back in there. Patsy was on the floor. She had hit her head—a rather serious gash. I think I asked someone to get a cold compress. Amy was tending to her, and quite frankly, her experience in the emergency room made her much better equipped to deal with Patsy."

"Before all that, I understand the victim wanted a drink. Did she get it?" Milo asked.

Dr. Carlson thought for a second. "I couldn't tell you. Wait. There was broken glass on the floor. Maybe it was hers. I was dealing with the emergency. Someone called 911, and I went out to meet the EMTs to fill them in on the situation. Amy took over. Unfortunately, there was little we could do. Patsy coded on the way to the hospital—efforts to revive her failed."

Milo continued the questioning. "I want to get this clear. When the victim fell, were you in the dining room?"

"Yes, but first I fetched an antiseptic sample to patch up Erin Cohen."

"Patch up?" Milo asked.

"She cut herself when the glass water-jug broke."

"Where was the antiseptic?"

"In my coat, in the office."

"Erin Cohen was in the dining room?" Milo asked.

"No, in the kitchen, running cold water over the cut," Carlson said.

Milo tilted his head and stared at Dr. Carlson. "The dining room, the office, the kitchen, where were you when the victim hit the floor?"

"In the dining room. Erin cut her arm. I sent her to run cold water over it. I got the antiseptic, patched her up in the kitchen and went back to the dining room. I was hungry. Then Patsy fell."

"Why did the victim have your card in her purse?" Milo asked.

"I don't know. I'm a dermatologist. We have a frown-line treatment she could have benefitted from—you could too." Carlson's too-broad smile irritated Milo.

"Did you hear the victim say anything before the ambulance arrived?" White asked.

"I was outside directing the EMTs." Carlson shrugged. "Was she even conscious?"

"We know she first said, 'hurt yellow,' and then she said, 'the book why.'"

"If you say so. I didn't hear anything."

"What do you suppose the book reference was all about?" White asked.

Carlson leaned back in his chair and began bouncing his fingertips together. "If those were her last words, I assume they were important." The bouncing fingertips continued for a while and then stopped. "I have no idea."

What a putz, thought Milo.

"Did you like Patsy Rand?" White asked.

Carlson smiled. "I may have been the only one in the room who found her amusing, although I think Crystal Bowers was a friend of hers."

"Amusing?" White asked.

"I know why you'd question that. She angered almost everyone. Her picking away at people kept the book club meetings lively. You may want to talk to Evelyn Chen. She told Patsy to go to hell right before Patsy collapsed."

"In those words?" White questioned. "Go to hell."

"Well, it was in Mandarin."

"You understand Mandarin?" Milo asked.

"Some. I spent time in Taiwan when I was in the Air Force."

Preston summoned her courage to weigh in on something that bothered her. "Why are you the only male member of the book club?"

Carlson laughed. "There are two other men who didn't attend this meeting. We all like mysteries, suspense, and murder—fictional murder that is. Now, if that's all, I have patients."

As they left, Milo wondered if 'patients' was code for poker.

"I hope you didn't mind my question," Preston said as the three stepped out into the September cold.

"It was a good question," White said.

"What's next?" Milo asked.

"Kate is going to the Black Bear Restaurant to find out who our victim had dinner with Thursday night," White said as Preston nodded. "Then she's going to check on sales of aconite while I read over her notes. And you, Milo are preparing to be interviewed by Ron Bello."

"Good plan. I'm going to take my lurching, lumpy body home. I've taken enough ego blows today."

"Don't forget frown lines," Preston said without thinking.

White laughed. "You're getting it."

10

Milo arrived back at Lakesong in the late afternoon. Martha was working on dinner; Agnes was taking a break from cataloging.

"What's new?" he asked as he came in from the garage.

"I didn't know one house could have so many books," Agnes said. "They are everywhere! Including..." Agnes looked at Martha who looked up from her work.

"Oh yes. There are astronomy books in the attic of the cottage," Martha said.

"So, you found the staircase?" Milo asked, as he help himself to a Diet Coke.

"I'm glad there weren't any hidden cameras," Martha said, laughing, "We were quite a sight."

"Let's say it involved a pair of Jamal's old shoes and tube socks," Agnes said.

Milo admitted he would love to see the attic again, and Agnes offered to show him, if it was all right with Martha.

"Go! I can get my work done if you're both gone," Martha said.

"Do I have to borrow Jamal's magic shoes?" Milo asked.

"Go!" Martha said. "Or there will be no dinner for you or your guest. The cottage is empty. Jamal is at basketball practice, and Darian is at Science Club."

Taking the tunnel route to the cottage, Agnes asked about the guest and Milo filled her in on Ron Bello, including the fact that Martha knew him when she lived in Minneapolis.

"Is he married? Is he cute?" Agnes asked.

"I don't know, and I don't know…besides aren't you and Sutherland…"

"…yeeaah, but I'm not asking for me, I'm asking for Martha," Agnes explained.

"He's a suspect in a murder investigation—forgive me if I didn't go right to cute."

Agnes opened the door that led from the tunnel to Martha's cottage. The stairway climbed up to Martha's back hall off of the kitchen. Milo follow Agnes to the secret door. He kicked where she pointed and the door cracked open.

"Like I remember. Mr. Henderson's magic door," Milo said opening the door further.

As they walked up the attic stairs, Agnes asked why a staircase would be hidden. Milo explained that Mrs. Henderson thought it was drafty, so Mr. Henderson put in a door like the ones in the main house.

Agnes stopped halfway up the stairs, turned around, and looked down on Milo. "Say that again?"

"Mrs. Henderson thought it was drafty?"

"No. The thing about the main house."

Milo shrugged. "He told me he copied doors in the main house."

"So, there are doors in the main house that are hidden like this one?" Agnes asked.

"I don't know. I don't look at doors. I just open and close them."

Agnes persisted. "Maybe he was talking about the design for hiding doors,"

"Could be. Cut me some slack. I was only eight," Milo said.

Agnes continued walking up the stairs to the attic. "I believe there may be secret doors in the main house like this one," she ventured.

Milo was used to Sutherland taking insufficient information and developing elaborate but incorrect theories. Agnes and Sutherland had that in common. Of course, unlike Sutherland, Agnes could be right.

"Tomorrow, I'll wear my hard shoes, and I'll be kicking a few baseboards on my breaks," she joked.

Milo gazed at Mr. Henderson's astronomy room for the first time in thirty some years. "Hasn't changed."

Agnes walked over to the piles of books. "So, Henderson was into astronomy?"

Milo looked toward the ceiling. "He had a telescope up there in that little room. The trapdoor is still there."

"We didn't go up into the cupola this morning," Agnes said. "Let's go exploring and report back to Martha."

Milo pulled the rope, the trap door opened, and the fold-up ladder descended. He moved up the rungs. The small clapboard room was cold and cramped. But both Agnes and Milo stared at the large refracting telescope and tripod connected to the platform.

"It's still here!" Milo exclaimed. "Mr. Henderson was serious about astronomy, but it was my fun. If it still works, this platform lifts up, and the roof opens."

"The roof opens? How?"

Crawling around on the floor Milo said, "I have no clue how it works. I was eight, remember." Opening a compartment in the floor of the platform, Milo produced a black iron crank and inserted it into an opening in the floor. "Hang on to the telescope," he told Agnes. "I always did."

Agnes felt a jerk, heard squeaking, and then the platform began to rise as the roof opened. The telescope, Milo, and Agnes came to a stop at the top of the cupola.

"I guess it needs some grease, but it still works!" Milo beamed, standing up.

Agnes clung to the tripod. Mr. Henderson had not bothered to add guard rails. One misstep would mean a bad trip down the cottage roof.

"This thing is not safe!" Agnes complained.

"Dangerous as hell," Milo said.

"He brought you up here when you were a child? Was he crazy?"

"It was a different time. I loved it!"

"Right now is right now, and I don't! People die falling from great heights. Take me down please!"

Milo obliged, cranking the platform back into its resting place.

Descending the ladder, Agnes said, "Martha is not going to like this."

Once they were both safely on the attic floor, Milo said, "You have to understand, when you're a kid looking at Jupiter through that telescope, you tend to not notice the danger."

"He brought you up there at night?" Agnes was wide eyed.

"Well, telescopes don't work well during the day."

Agnes' phone rang. "Oh crap! It's Martha. Hi Martha." Agnes said in her best pleasant, sing-song voice.

Holding the phone away from her ear, both she and Milo could hear Martha's raised voice.

"What are you two doing to my house? I saw you and Milo ascend from the top of my roof with a large pipe-like object. I assume you two were not on your way to heaven!"

Agnes handed him the phone. "It's for you."

He mouthed the word 'coward.' Agnes shook her head in the affirmative.

"Hi there, Martha. Guess what we found," Milo said with great cheer.

In measured words, Martha asked, "What did you find?"

"You are the proud owner of an expensive telescope and a somewhat dangerous viewing platform."

"I don't own it. You own it. I don't want it!"

"I understand. We'll put everything back, close it up, and no one will know it's here."

"I will know," Martha said as she hung up.

Agnes noticed that Milo was holding the crank. "Why do you have that?" she asked.

"I am keeping it from the kids. No crank, no lift, no trips to the emergency room."

Agnes added, "I am sure Martha will get someone to hide the trapdoor."

"Oh, cover it up. And people wonder how Sutherland lived in a house with an elevator but never knew it."

§

Sutherland arrived home to unusual aromas coming from the kitchen. He peeked in to find Martha hard at work stuffing wonton wrappers.

"What are we having?" he asked.

Martha looked up, "A guest."

Sutherland laughed. "We have to stop cooking guests. People are beginning to talk."

Martha gave him a hard look. "Mr. Rathkey's humor is rubbing off on you."

Sutherland searched for a tidbit of food to scavenge. "I don't remember inviting a guest."

"Mr. Rathkey invited him, and there's nothing here to pick at until dinner. I could cut you some celery."

Sutherland spotted cut English cucumbers. Martha, following his gaze, said they were for dinner, but she had cut extra. Chewing away, he asked, "Does this guest run a mob family, or is he a run-of-the-mill extortionist?" Sutherland referenced Milo's only other guest, gangster Morrie Wolf.

Martha looked at her prized Japanese knife, a present from Wolf after Martha catered his granddaughter's wedding.

"Back to my first question," Sutherland said. "What are you making?"

"Japanese bento boxes, with sashimi, gyoza, chicken karaage, among other choices."

"Wonderful! Does Milo know?" Sutherland smirked.

"I have options for Mr. Rathkey."

"I'm going up to bike," Sutherland said. "It's the virtual California Coastline tonight."

"Watch out for virtual traffic," Martha shouted at his retreating figure, "also, virtual rockslides."

Sutherland waved as he headed for the front stairs.

§

Agnes suggested slipping into the house through the gallery doors to avoid Martha's wrath or questions.

"I hope you have a key, because I don't," Milo said.

"Of course, you do," Agnes said, removing her phone from her pocket. "It's an app."

Milo stared at her phone. "Just kill me now."

"I bet Sutherland showed you this when you moved in," Agnes said. "He said he put all of the house apps on your phone. They're in a folder labeled 'Lakesong'.

"I was feeding the cat. I must have missed it. Open the door."

Agnes complied. All the gallery doors unlocked with an audible click.

"What are you going to do with the crank?" Agnes whispered.

"I have a closet. It has a ladder," Milo explained. "The ladder leads up to boxy shelves that—I'm told—once upon a time, gentlemen stored their many shoes."

"Do you have a lot of shoes?"

"No, but I have a lot of empty boxy shelves that are perfect for hiding cranks. Besides, I get to use the ladder. It's on wheels."

"Like the one in the library?" Agnes asked.

Milo thought for a second, "Yes, exactly like that, except the library ladder makes sense. My closet ladder is silly."

"Buy more shoes," Agnes suggested, as she headed for her office.

Having ridden the ladder and deposited the crank, Milo settled into the library to read. Annie the cat strolled in, looked at the empty fireplace and registered her complaint. With a sigh Milo got up, bowed, and said, "Your wish is my command." He grabbed several small logs near the fireplace, some kindling, and a propane fire starter. Before long, Annie was basking in the heat from the fire wondering what else she could get this human to do.

An hour later the intercom announced a car at the gate. Along with adding a voice, Ed Patupick had converted all the intercoms in Lakesong, so that they now displayed real-time video of people at the front gate. Milo saw it was Bello. "I'll buzz you in, Ron. Park by the front steps."

Milo made his way to the foyer. Moments later Ron Bello rang the doorbell. "Welcome to Lakesong," Milo said, as he guided Ron into the gallery. "What would you like to drink?"

"Scotch if you have it," Bello said, looking around the park-like room.

Milo smiled, remembering the rare Scotch he and Sutherland found in a smuggler's tunnel this past summer. "Oh, we have Scotch."

"I have to warn you, I'm somewhat fussy about my Scotch." Bello smiled.

"Hold that thought," Milo said, going into the billiard room for the bottle of Macallan single malt. Having poured two fingers of the amber liquid into a glass, Milo handed it to Bello who began to swirl it appreciating the aromas.

Bello sat down and took a sip. "My God man, what is this?"

"It's was on sale at Walmart," Milo said. "Five bucks a bottle."

"Hardly," Bello laughed. "You're a strange guy."

"You have no idea," Sutherland said, as he entered the seating area in the gallery. Shaking Bello's hand, he said, "I'm Sutherland McKnight the sane co-owner of Lakesong."

"Good to meet you. I'm Ron Bello, author and Scotch lover."

""That's a good Scotch to love," Sutherland said. "Macallan 1937."

"Maybe we got the gin at Walmart," Milo mused. "I get confused."

Ignoring Milo's mumblings, Sutherland asked Bello his reason for being in town. He was surprised to discover that Bello was an author, and that his next book would be based on the death of Jessica Vogel which had occurred at the beginning of summer.

"Why would you want to write about that?" Sutherland asked.

"I like to wrap fiction around real life events. I guess it's the reporter in me," Bello said. "Of course, in fiction, I can give it whatever outcome I please."

"Where did you get my name?" Milo asked.

"I read about the murder in the Minneapolis paper. It intrigued me, so I called a buddy in the St. Paul PD asking for more particulars. He called the Duluth PD, and your name came back as one of the particulars."

"I don't know why. I didn't do much," Milo protested.

Sutherland glanced at Milo and was about to protest when Milo cut him off.

"I think it's time for dinner; let's go into the family room." Milo led the way.

Martha, wearing her red chef's coat, was filling water glasses as they entered. She gave their guest a smile. "Hello Ron."

"Martha!" Bello stopped, closed the gap between them, and gave her a big bear hug.

Milo, in awe, watched Martha keep the water pitcher upright while greeting her old friend.

"Glad to see you're still a hugger, Ron," Martha joked as the hug ended.

"He didn't hug me," Milo complained.

"Per usual, I have no idea what's happening," Sutherland mused.

"What are you doing here?" Bello asked Martha.

"I'm working."

"Martha, since you and our guest are old friends, why don't you join us for dinner," Sutherland suggested.

Martha declined, "I'm working."

"Let's grab lunch tomorrow," Ron offered.

Martha accepted.

The trio sat down as Sutherland asked how Bello knew Martha. He explained that when he was a struggling reporter, he and Martha had friends in common. Because of that, he was invited to one of Martha's informal popup dinners. Bello confessed he was a foodie, and after the first dinner, he was hooked. For fifteen dollars, he would get a mouthwatering, multi-cultural gourmet meal."

Martha returned from the kitchen pushing a cart with three black-lacquered bento boxes, giving one to each diner. "I remembered you love Japanese cuisine Ron, so I have prepared bento box delicacies."

Before Bello could respond, Milo said, "If I get raw fish, you aren't coming back, Ron."

Martha sighed. "No, Mr. Rathkey, your delicacies are fully cooked, and all things green have been avoided."

Each diner was given a choice of chopsticks or a fork. Bello and Sutherland pick up their chopsticks expecting Milo to opt for the fork. He didn't. Instead he picked up the chopsticks and began sampling his version of the bento box. "Coleslaw, pickles, and fried chicken—I love it."

"Chicken Karaage," Martha corrected.

"It's as delicious as I remember, Martha," Bello added as Martha left for the kitchen.

Milo looked at Sutherland who was staring at him. "What?" Milo asked.

"Since when do you use chopsticks?" Sutherland asked.

"Since always. I'm pretty good with them."

"There has to be a back story," Sutherland suggested.

"In my highly successful life as a private detective, I had one fork in my apartment, and it disappeared. Most of my suppers were take-out from the Chinese Dragon. Hank gave me chopsticks. It was learn how to use them or starve."

"Why didn't you buy another fork?" Bello asked.

"Who buys one fork? I don't even know where to buy one fork," Milo explained.

"How did you solve your forkless situation," Bello quipped, "besides the use of chopsticks?

"I came to live here. The place came with forks."

Sutherland agreed. "Lakesong doesn't offer much, but it does come with forks."

Bello was filled with questions about Milo and this massive house, but he thought it prudent to wait until he could get the background information from Martha. He spent the next fifteen minutes pumping Milo and Sutherland concerning the Vogel murder. Milo underplayed his involvement. Sutherland chatted without restraint.

Eventually, Milo turned the conversation around to Patsy Rand. "Tell me about her," Milo asked.

Martha had delivered desert—Japanese Castella cake, and Bello finished his first bite before answering. "I told you everything in the police interview this afternoon."

"I was in one of those once," Sutherland said. "They're no fun."

"Yeah, but you were guilty," Milo lied. "Back to Patsy Rand. I want to know about her. Tell me something I don't know."

"She hated my books."

"You mentioned that."

"Well, I did blow the whistle on her, got her fired, and disbarred. Of course, she brought that on herself, but she never saw it that way."

"You mentioned that too. Is there something more you can tell me about her?"

"I assume you know about her personal life—married, divorced, one child."

Milo nodded. White had filled him in on her phone calls that morning.

Bello crossed his arms over his broad chest, closed his eyes, and thought for a while. "I was told, years ago, she wrote a book."

Milo perked up.

Bello continued, "I never read it, but I was told that she pulled it."

"What was it about?" Milo asked.

"It was about the death of Harper Gain's partner."

"Who's Harper Gain?"

Sutherland gaped at Milo wondering if he was kidding. "He's famous. Harper Gain is a cult figure, Milo. He owned Tettegouch Software, beat Hodgkin's lymphoma using herb supplements, and wrote numerous books on health and life-style. I've read all of his books. That's why I drink smoothies."

Milo turned to Bello. "Who's the dead partner and what happened to him?"

"I never investigated. I only know the pop version. When Gain and his partner, whose name I don't remember, were in their twenties they developed a video game that made a fortune. The partner died young in a rock-climbing acci-dent. Knowing Patsy, she accused Gain of murder. I'm only guessing. I never read her book. I tried to find it years ago, part of my investigative series, but as I said, she pulled it."

"What's the title?"

"I remember it was over the top—melodramatic. Empire.. blood...something, something." Bello said.

"Why didn't you ask her for a copy?" Milo asked.

"I never—let me emphasize that—never had a civil conversation with her. I called her when she was a prosecutor to get her side before I published my articles condemning her, but she swore at me and hung up. After the series started, she tried to get me fired," Bello grinned. "She failed."

"Where is Harper Gain now? He could be a suspect in Patsy Rand's death," Milo said.

"Not likely. He died last year," Sutherland explained.

"Getting back to Rand's book, are you thinking she accused this Harper Grain..."

"Gain," Sutherland corrected.

"...this Harper Gain of murder with no proof?"

"Patsy didn't think she needed proof. If she thought a person guilty, they were guilty and that was that—sharp, swift, over-eager justice. Crazy town. You know, there were a lot of people who hated her enough to want her dead."

Milo took a bite of his cake. From the look on his face, he enjoyed it. "A lot of people wanted her dead for twenty, thirty years, but the question is..."

"...who did it?" Sutherland interrupted.

"No," Milo corrected, "why kill her now?"

11

A gentle but firm paw in his face and a silent meow was Milo's reminder that Annie's bacon time was nonnegotiable. Throwing on a pair of old pants and a Metallica t-shirt, he followed the cat into the morning room.

"Going casual this morning?" Sutherland asked.

"I was sleeping in, but the cat was starving to death—on the verge of passing out—so I had to respond," Milo explained.

Sutherland looked down at Annie who was still complaining about the lack of bacon. "I would have thought those extra pounds around her middle would have staved off starvation for another month."

"She doesn't see it that way."

Martha arrived with Milo's breakfast. Unlike a dog—who would have been grateful for a few pieces of bacon—Annie, being a cat, meowed with attitude as if to say, 'about time' and waited for more.

Looking up, Sutherland said, "Martha was worried you'd want some sashimi from last night, but Ron and I ate it all."

Milo put down his fork. "Sashimi and bacon—my favorite. All my hopes and dreams—crushed."

Sutherland went back to his Wall Street Journal.

Milo was going to say more, but his phone rang. The caller ID was the Duluth Police Department but the ring was not Ernie's 'da dunk' sound from Law and Order. He pushed the answer button, and he heard White. "Milo? Hello?"

"Robin?"

"Gramm doesn't say goodbye and you don't say hello."

"I didn't know who you were. I gotta get a ring sound for you."

"Pharrell Williams—the chorus from Happy."

"I don't know what that is," Milo complained.

"Google it."

"Is it going to embarrass me when it goes off?"

"Can you be embarrassed?" White asked.

"Let me think."

"Think about this instead. A waiter at the Black Bear Restaurant remembered Patsy Rand from last Thursday night because she was such a problem—returned her drink twice."

"Did he remember her companion?" Milo asked.

"Companion? Who says companion?"

"I think I did."

"Okay. Yes. Her *companion*, who paid with plastic and tipped generously, was Peter Gain."

"Peter Gain?"

Sutherland looked up. "I know him."

"Of course, you do," Milo said. "He belongs to the country club doesn't he?"

"As do you," Sutherland said, going back to his paper.

"What's going on? Who is that?" White asked.

"Sutherland informs me he knows Peter Gain. Why were those two having dinner?"

"You can ask Gain. I've set up an interview at three today at his home. I am texting you the address. You do text don't you?"

"I'm a texting fool," Milo said.

"I'm saying goodbye now."

Milo refilled his coffee cup. "So, Sutherland, what do you know about our country club buddy, Peter Gain."

"I think he's a scientist or something, but I'm sure you know about his father," Sutherland said, taking a sip of his smoothie.

"Oh sure, Clancy Gain. Who doesn't know about Clancy Gain?" Milo snarked.

"Harper, not Clancy. Ron told you about him last night."

"Aren't you late for work?"

Sutherland checked his phone. "Yikes! You're right." He gulped down the rest of his blue smoothie, put on his suitcoat, and headed for the garage. Great breakfast Martha! Thank you!"

Martha laughed. "My blender skills are magnificent."

As Sutherland left, Agnes entered the kitchen from her office. "Morning Martha."

"Good morning," Martha said. "More book cataloging today?"

"Yup. Doing the books in the upstairs library. I'm also going to do a little baseboard kicking." Agnes laughed.

"Speaking of that," Martha said, leaving Agnes for the morning room, "Mr. Rathkey, I've talked with Mr. McKnight about doing some remodeling of the attic room at the cottage."

"Like a bathroom?" Milo asked.

"When I can afford it," Martha said.

"No, no, no. Have it all done now. Clue in Agnes. She'll pay for it out of the house fund."

Hearing her name, Agnes ambled into the morning room.

Martha sighed. "That's what Mr. McKnight said, but I'm not comfortable with that. The room is for Darian, I should pay for it."

"It's not your house," Milo said, shocking Agnes. "It's my house. If my house needs renovation, I pay for it."

Martha began to clear the breakfast dishes. "As much as you're rubbing off on Mr. McKnight, he's doing the same to you. Okay, you pay for it."

"There is a difference between me and Sutherland," Milo said.

"Such as?" Martha asked.

"I'm not doing the bathroom in marble and equipping it with a sauna."

"Darian will be so disappointed," Martha smiled.

"So, the room is definitely Darian's?" Agnes asked.

"I took them both up there last night. Jamal hit his head three times, once going up, once walking to the window, and once going down. Nursing lumps on his head, he signed away all rights to the attic. *Darian the Short* loves it."

Milo's phone buzzed again, this time with an unknown number. He answered, expecting a robocall. An electronically disguised voice said, "I know who killed you father...old steel plant access road in an hour."

Milo stayed silent. The phone went dead.

§

"Have you reached Patsy's daughter yet?" Amy asked as Ernie sat down to breakfast.

"Robin is handling that. I think she has. I'll ask her this morning," Ernie said.

"If Robin is handling the case, what are you doing?"

"Not much."

Amy put two pieces of toast on his plate. "Are you upset you're not in charge?"

Gramm smiled. "No, not upset, but it's different. In the future, try to stay away from murders during your social engagements."

"No promises," Amy said, spreading jam on her toast. "So, what are you doing with all your spare time—long lunches, massages?"

"Hardly. I'm consulting. Milo and I have changed jobs."

§

Before leaving to meet the voice on the phone, Milo stopped by Agnes' office to ask her to pick up Ron Bello's book, something about death and a DA. "I need it today," Milo said with unaccustomed abruptness.

Agnes nodded and noticed a bulge under Milo's wind breaker as he turned and walked away. He didn't anticipate a gun battle, but unearthing secrets, long-packed-away, was tricky. His nine millimeter was holstered but handy.

The Duluth steel plant—a silent relic of a bygone era—was an abandoned hulk of rusting buildings, overgrown railroad tracks, and red dirt. The lone road into the plant had been chained off, but the chain now lay on the ground—random vandals or opened deliberately? Milo stopped, unzipped his jacket, pulled his gun out of the holster, and set it in easy reach on the front seat. The Honda thumped over the chain and began to climb the hill up to a small, multicolored wooden structure that used to be the official guard house—now an unofficial paint-ball-target, its windows blown out.

As he got closer, Milo could feel his heartbeat. *This is stupid,* he thought. *A guy in that guardhouse could pick me off before I had a chance to react.* He slammed on the brakes and jammed the car into park. Grabbing his gun, Milo scrambled out of the Honda and took cover behind the trunk. In the distance to his left stood the scrap heap of the old plant. His caller could be hiding in the twisted metal and mounds of broken bricks. The area was perfect for a sniper, but Milo's attention kept darting back to the guard shack. The treeless expanse did nothing to stop the cold wind that rolled over him as he waited. A swamp sparrow glided overhead using the wind gusts to stay aloft. In front of him, the slow climbing road remained empty; no one was approaching. Was he being watched? The cold was taking its toll. He hadn't dressed for a long standoff.

Milo crept back into the Honda, upped the heat, and shifted into drive. Staying low was tough. He had to slump down enough to keep from getting his head shot off yet be upright enough to stay on the narrow ribbon of road avoiding the overgrown gullies on either side. As he inched the car closer to the guard shack, the shattering of the front windshield and the force of the bullet hitting the passenger seat forced him to fall across the console. He jerked the wheel full to the left while his right foot slammed the gas pedal to the floor. The Honda responded, spinning around in place. A second bullet shattered the back window. Milo swerved as he sped down the access road and out of the old plant. There were no more shots.

His heart still racing, Milo considered lying in wait for the sniper to come out of the plant, but his nine millimeter was no match for a rifle. Continuing to drive, *a let's meet and chat* coffee house came up on his right. Wrenching the steering wheel, his tire's squealed into the only open parking space—the van-handicapped spot right in front. Several patrons stared at him as Milo exited the wounded Honda and called Gramm.

"*Yeah! Gawk you double latte, mocha chais,*" he thought. *I always drive with two shot-out windows.* Milo's adrenalin was fueling his anger and the coffee gawkers were catching it in his mind.

Running his hand through his hair, Milo took a deep breath. Small pieces of glass stuck to his fingers. Some fell to the ground. He was still brushing glass from his hair and his clothes when Gramm and two cop cars pulled on either side of him in the parking lot. The coffee patrons were getting a show.

Glad to see Milo was uninjured, Gramm snarked, "Did your barista blast you?"

"Very funny," Milo said. "He tried to kill the Honda."

"He who? Somebody here?"

"No, over at the old steel plant," Milo said.

"What the hell were you doing there?"

"Got a call...said to meet there for information...about you know, my other investigation." Patting his reholstered gun, he added, "I thought I came prepared."

"Did you discharge your weapon?" Gramm asked.

"Nope. I brought a pistol to a rifle fight, so I got the hell out of there."

Gramm surveyed the damage to the Honda. "Both front and back. This guy was serious. Any idea who?"

"My best bet is a former cop named Josh Crandell. He lives out here, Morgan Park."

"I remember him—not fondly. How does he play into any of this?"

"He and his partner investigated the original scene of my dad's death."

"Partner's name?"

"Prepinski."

Gramm shrugged "Before my time." He looked at an approaching officer who said, "Forensics are on their way. They're sending a tow truck."

"Whoa, sounds expensive. I can drive it," Milo protested.

"In your dreams. The windshield is shattered and there's glass everywhere. Besides we need to find those bullets."

"What am I going to drive?"

"You're kidding, right? Rent one! Or perhaps you can motor in the Bentley. And by the way, you're parked in a handicapped spot."

"The Honda is currently handicapped!" Milo protested, patting the hood. "Sorry old friend."

12

Cataloging Lakesong's books gave Agnes a legitimate excuse to explore the second floor of the mansion. The grand, white marble, double staircase led to the upstairs library plus unused bedrooms on the left, and Sutherland's suite of rooms to the right. Agnes stared at Sutherland's closed door. Her curiosity was piqued. A person's home says a lot about who they are, and the rooms beyond the closed door were Sutherland's home within Lakesong. He had yet to invite her into Chez Sutherland even though they had spent a lot of time at her house. She wondered why. *Maybe he's really a secret slob that pretends to be neat, clean, and fastidious. No,* she thought. *He has housekeepers! At times he is obtuse. I have evidence of that! Maybe I'm not important enough?* That was one of her buttons. She and her sister carried that thought in their heads as foster children—never feeling important to anyone except each other.

"Stop!" Agnes scolded herself. Since Barbara's death almost a year ago, Agnes had been working to rewrite that message. She was special to herself and her friends and that was enough.

She turned on her heel, declaring Sutherland obtuse. Agnes walked over to the far rail and looked down at the parklike gallery which dominated the entire center of the house. Annie, in her Guiana chestnut tree, looked up and gave Agnes her famous silent meow. "I bet you've never been invited into Sutherland rooms either," Agnes said. Annie yawned and laid back down. "Oh, I see," Agnes said. "We are pretending we don't care. I can do that."

Consulting Milo's crude map of the second floor Agnes turned left, opened the first door and entered what Milo described as the 'small' upstairs library. "Oh, come on! Milo, you and I have to discuss the meaning of small and large," Agnes said to no one. While smaller than the main library, this extensive room and its wall-to-wall books were not what she was expecting.

Agnes sat down at one of three long, glossy, wooden tables and looked around. An upstairs library, in her mind, was an old-fashioned, pre-television, way to provide overnight guests with a small selection of books to enjoy before falling asleep. This room looked like a reference library.

"Who built this?" she asked the room. "And why?" The room did not respond.

As she unpacked her computer, barcode scanner, rubber gloves, and disposable mask, Agnes became conscious of the lack of dust. The table shone. She pulled out a chair—no dust. Walking over to one of the bookshelves, she inspected several books, all dust free. *This room is not on the cleaning schedule, but where's the dust? Something to ask Milo.*

Agnes expected cataloging books would be easier than cataloging art as most books have a barcode that can be scanned and entered into a database. When Agnes came across a book without a barcode, she put it on its spine so she could come back and manually enter what she called her *problem* children. As the morning wore on, book zapping was proving to be more tedious than cataloging Lakesong's art. The upstairs library had more than its share of problem children.

After several hours, Agnes put down her scanner, did a couple of yoga stretches, gave a mischievous look to the baseboards and began kicking. She was startled when a section of one bookcase inched forward, mirroring the movement of the panel in Martha's cottage.

Agnes looked around, wishing Martha was here as her partner in crime. "Did I break it?" she asked out loud. The panel in the cottage was on hinges and swung out. This did the same, but this was a heavy bookcase full of books. Slipping her fingers into the gap, she tugged hard. The bookcase door swung open slamming into the bookcase behind it. "Oh my God, I've broken something," she said covering her mouth with her closed fists.

Nothing fell down. Nothing cracked. After her heart returned to its normal rhythm, she ran her hand over the mahogany bookcases checking to be sure she hadn't broken anything. Her attention was drawn to the dark chasm behind the open door. Fumbling with her phone, Agnes accessed the flashlight app, and shined the beam into the dark space. On the left, two cloth-encased wires led to a strange device with a small bar and a ball on top, like a mini joystick. It was electrical but looked dangerous. Agnes did not want to die while not cataloging books. She avoided it.

Agnes moved her light around, illuminating a small landing and descending stairs. *Do I tell somebody? Who would I tell? I'm in this house alone!* In her mind she could hear a horror-movie audience yelling, "Go back! Go back! Close the door!" At the same time another voice was whispering, "Be brave, Agnes. You can do this."

Inching her way down the stairs, Agnes used only her right foot to feel her way. With each step, she turned to see the illumination from the upstairs library checking that the bookcase door did not slam shut, sealing her inside. Her imagination grew. She was sure one of the steps would trigger the door and entomb her forever.

Dust clogged her nostrils forcing her to stop and cough. This was worse than Martha's stairs. Whatever kept dust out of the library had no effect here. Lifting her fleece over her nose in an attempt to provide a filter, she chastised herself for not bringing her mask. She was midway down the stairs—decision time. Should she continue down or retreat. "Stop it Agnes!" she shouted at herself and coughed again. What followed was a troublesome trek down the stairs to the sounds of coughing, a mythical horror-movie audience screaming, "Go back, go back!" and the voice of her therapist whispering, "Be brave, be brave."

Agnes reached the bottom of the stairs only to face a blank wall. She took one last look up the stairs. The light from the upstairs library was still shining—escape was still available. Moving the light around the wall in a grid-like pattern, she searched for a crack, a handle, a lever—something that would open a door. *Could these mysterious stairs have been walled up? The secret door on the first floor lost to history.* Turning the light to the left, she began to check the other wall. At the bottom of the wall, inches above the floor, Agnes found a brass pedal, similar to the pedals of a piano.

"It opens another door. Right?" she asked herself. *"Or does it close the one upstairs. Come on Agnes. Why would it close the one upstairs? Gees."* She shined her phone light around the space again, hoping for written instructions. None. There was only the pedal. Holding her breath, she lifted her foot, lowered it onto the pedal, and leaned her full weight on it. She heard a click. Agnes' heart did a flip when the wall moved forward. Agnes pushed it out with less force this time. She knew this room—the main library. The middle bookcase now sat ajar as she walked into the room. Agnes looked around and smiled.

Now the size of the upstairs library made sense. This was all one library. As she contemplated how the secret of the library might have been lost, her mischievous nature began to make plans. "This will be fun."

§

When will they be done with the Honda?" Milo asked, as he sat down in front of Gramm's desk.

"You were shot at. Shouldn't you be more upset about *that*?" Gramm asked.

"Maybe. But I figure if the guy wanted to hit me, he would have," Milo said, not admitting he was a little shook.

Through the years, he had been beaten, kicked, and kidnapped but never shot at. While fleeing this latest assault, he kept thinking he had a good life and this was no time to die.

"He shot at you twice. I think he wanted you dead," Gramm said.

"So, your theory is he was a bad shot?" Milo asked.

"Exactly."

Milo thought about his number-one-suspect, Josh Crandell—not at the top of his game, possible stroke victim. Gramm could be right and he was lucky.

"Any clue as to the weapon?" Asked Milo.

"No shell casings recovered, but forensics is digging the bullets out of your car as we speak."

"Tell them to be careful," Milo admonished.

"It's a car Milo. It can be repaired." Gramm reached into his lower-right desk drawer and pulled out a bottle of brandy and two mismatched glasses. He poured two healthy portions, handing one to Milo. "This will steady your nerves."

Milo didn't argue. He offered a toast to bad shots and drank the brandy in two gulps.

"Have you overturned the wrong rock?" Gramm asked.

"Crandell so far. He's a slimy SOB," Milo said.

"And dumber than a rock," Gramm added. "He takes two shots at you in his own backyard. Did he tell you anything he might regret now?"

Milo filled him in on the Wills brothers.

Gramm thought for a while as Milo poured himself an uncharacteristic second shot. "Not much there. When you left Crandell was he angry?"

"Oh yeah, but there's more," Milo said. "He was scared."

"Of what?"

"I don't know."

Gramm gave Milo his stern look. "In the future, why don't you let the rest of us know what you're up to rather than going off by yourself, like an idiot, getting yourself shot at...twice!"

Milo shrugged, "I've made better decisions."

"Agreed. And for your punishment, we need you to type up a statement. You'll find the form in the computer. You know the drill."

As Milo was finishing his paperwork, White came up to him and asked if he was okay.

"I'm fine," Milo said.

"Still up for Peter Gain this afternoon?"

"Sure."

"When we catch this guy who shot at you, I'm gonna slug him!" White exclaimed.

Milo laughed. "You don't have to hurt your knuckles for me."

"Not about you. I'm upset he didn't take a shot at me. I'm the lead in this case. You would think the shooter would have known that. I hate sexist shooters."

"Wrong case." Milo filled White in on Josh Crandell and his other investigation. "I think I should drive myself to Gain."

"With what?"

"Oh yeah. I forgot."

"Hide in the backseat," White joked as she handed him a sandwich. "I took a guess—ham and cheese."

"Good guess," Milo said. "How much do I owe you?"

"Gramm already paid for it. He doesn't know it and won't until he gets my expense account."

Gramm came out of his office and walked over to Milo. "The forensics guys…"

"…and gals," White added.

Gramm sighed. "And gals have dug out the bullets. They're seven millimeter Remington Magnum."

"Oh great, the favorite of deer hunters everywhere," Milo complained.

"Yeah. And we've checked Crandell. He has a deer license. I'm sending a couple of guys over there to find out what ammo he uses," Gramm said.

White rolled her eyes over the term 'guys' but said, "I know that bullet; it's got a flat trajectory and powerful muzzle velocity

"Perfect for long distances," Milo said, thinking about where Crandell could have been hiding.

Gramm asked, "When they're done with your car, where do you want us to tow it?"

Milo indicated he wanted to ask Sutherland's advice, hoping that this was something Mr. Anderson could put right. Milo trusted Mr. Anderson. Gramm went back to his office.

After five minutes of bad music, Sutherland finally came on the line. "Milo? Why don't you call my cell phone?"

Milo ignored the question. "Can Mr. Anderson fix two smashed windows and a couple of holes in the Honda's passenger seat?"

"Did you pick up a boulder from a passing dump truck?"

"More like a couple of bullets from a hiding sniper," Milo countered.

There was a brief silence on the other end. "Are you okay?"

"No. I died. Now, can Mr. Anderson fix my car?"

"Yes, he can. Have the car towed to the Lakesong garage. Call Agnes so she knows to expect it."

"Thanks," Milo said and hung up. Milo told Gramm to tow the car to Lakesong, and he gave Agnes a call. "My car is being towed back to Lakesong. I had a little accident."

"Are you okay?" She asked.

"I died, but I'm feeling better," he quipped. "I forgot to tell you this morning, I need another book. A woman named Patsy Rand wrote a book a long time ago. Could you find the title and get your hands on a copy?"

"What's this one about?"

"Some guy named Harper Gain."

"Some guy named Harper Gain? You mean Harper Gain the software giant and lifestyle guru?"

"Yeah, him."

"I take it this book is nonfiction."

"I think so."

"Sweet. I loved Harper Gain. I have all his books," Agnes said hanging up.

"Sweet?" Milo mocked. "Who says 'sweet'?"

§

After finishing his statement, sated by Gramm's calming brandy and White's filling ham-and-cheese sandwich, Milo began Googling Harper Gain. Most of the thousands of articles were on the benefits of clean living. Milo didn't care.

Wikipedia had all the information Milo needed. Grabbing a legal pad, he began to take notes.

— *Harper Gain born 1958*
— *Partner, Mark Carlson (Dr. Charles Carlson?)*
— *Tettegouch Software formed*
— *Gain gets Hodgkin's Lymphoma*
— *Mark Carlson dies in a climbing accident at Tettegouche state park. (Local)*
— *Gain becomes a health nut after being cured of Hodgkin's*
— *Gain dies of a heart attack. (kale?) 2018*

White walked over to see what Milo was doing. Glancing at his notes, she asked, "What's this?"

Milo looked up. "Everyone seems to know about this Harper Gain guy but me. I wanted a little information before we talk to his kid."

"Why do you care about…" she looked closer at the pad trying to read Milo's writing, "Mark Carlson?"

"He was Gain's partner who died in a climbing accident. According to Bello, Patsy Rand wrote a book years ago that may accuse Harper Gain of killing Carlson. I'm trying to find that book. Also, I'm wondering if the murdered Mark Carlson was any relation to Dr. Charles Carlson."

"Somebody named *Carlson* in Minnesota. Good luck with that. There must be a million of 'em."

"We could ask the kid," Milo said.

"The kid?" White asked.

"Peter Gain."

"Hardly a kid."

"He's Harper Gain's kid. It's the way I'm going to remember who's who."

"We have time, if you have more research," White said.

Milo turned off the computer. "I would like to check out the victim's house if that's okay with you. Where did she live?"

"In Congdon Park on East Superior Street."

"Congdon Park? Isn't that pricy?"

"Could be."

Milo stood and grabbed his coat. "We can stop by Rand's house and then go to Peter Gain," Milo said.

White rounded up Preston who said she checked on aconite sales with the few shops that sold it—no unusual purchases. As they headed out to the east end of Duluth. White couldn't resist a little fun at Milo's expense. "Scrunch down back there. We don't want anyone taking pot shots at us."

"Nice," Milo said, but he did slump down.

"Too soon?" White asked.

"I was wondering what took you so long," Milo said.

Preston looked at White. "What's going on?"

"Milo got shot at this morning," White told her.

Preston laughed thinking White was kidding.

§

Martha was the first to arrive at Va Vena's Italian Restaurant and asked for a table by the massive windowed back wall. She caught the reflection of her new black blazer—nipped in at the waist—that complemented and updated her tried-and-true gray sweater dress. Martha was pleased. It wasn't a look she got to wear often. She was glad she could still pull it off.

A few minutes later, Martha saw Ron waiting at the hostess stand. She waved to him, catching his attention. He smiled, and being such a tall man, seemed to promenade through the restaurant. She stood—Martha barely coming up to his shoulders. As they hugged again, she remembered how comforting a Ron-Bello-bear-hug could be.

"It's so good to see you again, Ron," she said as they sat down in the minimalist, Scandinavian-like restaurant with blond wood chairs and tables, lit by as much sunshine as Duluth in September could provide.

In a delaying motion, Ron put his napkin on his lap, wondering how to begin. He decided to charge ahead. "What happened to you? You disappeared. None of our friends knew where you went, or why."

Martha told him about her parents' accident, her emergency parenthood, and landing this perfect personal-chef's job that combined cooking and a place for her siblings. "We live in a cottage on the estate," she said. "It has given the kids stability and a trust that life continues. Plus, I'm still a chef, if only for two mismatched gentlemen."

"And an even better chef if last night's dinner was any indication. You have skills, Martha dear," Ron added with a slight bow.

Martha laughed. It was what Ron always said to her even when her experimental recipes didn't always work. "Those were fun times," Martha said.

A waitress came over with water and menus and took their drink orders. Martha asked if her friend Gabby was the chef today. Assured that Gabby was in the kitchen, Martha told Ron he was in for a treat. The waitress indicated that pappardelle ai funghi was the special today. She explained it was house-made pappardelle tossed in a mushroom-and-thyme sauce with crispy prosciutto.

After the waitress left, Martha asked, "Getting back to the gourmet group, where is everybody?"

"We all grew up, although none of us had to do it as quickly as you did." Bello detailed the whereabouts of the various characters with the exception of one or two people whose fate he didn't know. "Now you're off the *disappeared* list. How did you get the job at…what's the name of the place?"

"Lakesong. I got the job through my old boss at the restaurant in Minneapolis. When I told him why I needed to quit and move back to Duluth, he told me he had a friend of a friend in Duluth who was looking for a personal chef. I drove up the next day and got the job, and the cottage. It was perfect—the kids didn't even have to change schools."

"But you had to give up your experiments in cooking."

"Yes and no. Sutherland McKnight loves unusual foods as long as they're healthy. His father, John, wanted meat and potatoes, and an iceberg-lettuce salad."

"I didn't meet John," Ron said.

"Unfortunately, John passed away last year."

"Sorry. So, where does this Milo Rathkey fit in?"

Martha smiled. "After John died, I was afraid Sutherland was going to sell the place and my perfect situation would disappear. However, John had a plan. He left half the estate to Sutherland and the other half to Milo."

"Who was Milo to him?"

"He was the son of a former cook. From what I was told, Milo grew up in Lakesong, and he and John were close. I see a lot of John in Milo, especially the meat, potatoes, and those iceberg-lettuce salads."

Ron laughed. "So, Sutherland and Milo are like brothers from different mothers, if you excuse the cliché."

"And fathers. In fact. they never met each other until Milo moved in last December."

"You can't make this stuff up. That's a plot of a book," Ron said, looking at the menu. "I missed breakfast, so I'm hungry. I'm thinking of the Bistecca. How about you?"

"It's wonderful, but I'm going with the special."

The waitress came back with their drinks and took their orders.

"We've talked about everybody," Martha said, "except you. Bring me up to date on you, Ron."

Ron smiled. "I gave up journalism—too many hours and not enough money. I write books now, primarily fiction. Oh, and I think I'm a suspect in a murder case."

Martha laughed. "That doesn't make you special, at least not since Mr. Rathkey moved into Lakesong. He attracts murder suspects. That's why he invited you to dinner."

"I think he invited me to ask me about the murdered woman. I accepted because my next book will be a fiction-alized account of the Jessica Vogel murder. It fascinates me."

"You should talk to..." Martha was going to say Agnes Larson but thought better of it. She did a speedy recovery. "...Sutherland McKnight. Oh, but you already did."

"He gave me all kinds of insights."

"He is a talker," Martha said wondering if her recovery was natural. Ron was sharp at reading people.

§

Patsy Rand's house did not match the pricy neighborhood. The Georgian-Style house was small, and red-bricked, with a flat front accented by a one-step porch. From the street, Milo, White, and Preston could see that the front door was open.

"What the hell?" White said, as she braked the car hard and jumped out. Milo was right behind her, followed by Preston.

The door had been forced. Splinters of wood from the door jamb littered the front hallway. White pulled back her jacket, showing her gun to Milo, questioning if he was also armed. He nodded. His heart was still recovering from this morning's gun play.

Here we go again, Milo thought.

White and Preston drew their weapons. Milo kept his holstered. White pointed to the stairway and with practiced caution, back against the wall, moved up the stairs.

Milo and Preston searched the first floor but found no intruder. The basement was also cleared. Preston climbed back up to the first floor, White was on her way down from the second floor.

"Clear upstairs," she said.

"No one on the first floor or in the basement," Preston said. Except Milo. He's lingering.

"I didn't notice anything disturbed upstairs. There looks to be some pretty expensive jewelry up there," White said, as she called in the B&E on her phone.

Preston asked, "Why do a break and enter and not take anything?"

Milo joined them from the basement and disappeared again.

"Milo?" White yelled.

"In the office," he yelled back.

Preston and White followed the voice into the office and found Milo crouching behind Patsy's desk chair. White checked out the room which was surrounded by floor-to-ceiling bookcases. In the center of the room, Patsy had a large table with a mounted microphone and a small audio console—equipment for her podcast.

"On Monday, forensics took a computer that was part of this setup. They found audio files for her podcast but no book," White explained.

Milo was still behind the chair.

"Seeing anything, Milo?"

Milo stood up. "Look at the shelves in this room. Wherever there's an empty space on the shelf there's decorative bookend holding the books up straight. Our victim liked tidy bookshelves." Rolling the chair to the side of the desk, Milo continued. "Down here, the books are falling over; at least one book is missing. It seems out of place... out of character."

White walked over to look. "Someone broke in to steal a book?" she asked.

"Maybe I'm not the only one interested in our victim's book."

"That's a stretch," White said. "We don't know what book filled that space, and maybe, she ran out of bookends."

"You're right," Milo admitted. "We also don't know why or when a whole box of books was taken from the basement."

Preston looked at Milo. "I didn't see missing books." Realizing the absurdity of what she said, Preston tried to recover but was interrupted.

"Milo seeing missing books is so Milo," White explained.

"Come, you two; see for yourselves."

Arriving in the basement, White checked the area. To the left of the steps, boxes of books were piled three high. Milo moved his hand over one of the boxes and showed the dust collection to White. One set was only two boxes high. Milo was about to move his hand over it when White said, "I get it. No dust. Someone removed a box of books recently, but it's still a stretch to think it was a box of her books. Even if it was, she could have moved the box herself in the last few days."

"I doubt she moved the box, her being dead for six days and all," Milo snarked.

"Point in your favor," White admitted, checking the remaining box for dust. "Pristine. No dust at all. The box on top of it was moved in the last day or two."

"I...I...didn't notice 'no dust' either," Preston lamented.

"Again, don't beat yourself up," White said. "Milo looks at the world a little differently. You were looking for an intruder. He was looking for dust. Go through the rest of these boxes. I want to know what's in them."

As Preston was cutting packing tape and ripping box flaps open, White asked Milo, "Wouldn't the intruder have to look through all the boxes in the basement like we are?"

"Not if the person already knew how many books the victim had and where they were stored."

Milo and White waited while Preston finished opening the boxes and looking at their contents. "These are all random books. No Patsy Rand books here," Preston reported.

White turned to Milo. "Okay, let's go with your theory. Why is Rand's book worth stealing?"

"Don't have a clue, but we gotta find a copy of that book."

§

After picking up Ron Bello's book for Milo, Agnes asked the young man at the information section of the bookstore to search *Books in Print* for Patsy Rand's book. He found no listing for the book but suggested trying the US Copywrite Office database. That search also failed.

13

Peter Gain lived with his wife and three children in a custom-built, Mediterranean-style house on the shores of Island Lake—a reservoir twenty-three miles north of Duluth. The brown, brick-paved road leading to the house reflected the copper and crimson fall foliage which lined both sides of the quarter-mile-long driveway. Milo, whose mind still counted the cost of almost everything, wondered how much was spent maintaining the brick, especially after a tough winter.

Driving past the four-car garage, White parked by the front door. Summer flowers were gone, but both sides of the walkway were lined with welcoming fall mums, asters, and goldenrod. "Well, if you have to live somewhere, I guess this place is as good as any," White said.

"Certainly private," Milo said.

"Says the guy who lives behind a gate," White chided, as she rang the doorbell.

A short man with uncombed, receding brown hair dressed in a University-of-Minnesota sweatshirt and jeans answered the door. "I don't have much time," he said without humor. "I have an appointment."

"Nice place," White said looking at the dark carved woodwork and the multitude of arches.

"We like it," Gain said, leading the troop past the formal living room into a rustic, Mediterranean-style kitchen.

"We could have met you at your office," White said, after making the introductions.

"I took the day off. So, what is this about?" he asked, grabbing his coffee cup from the kitchen island. Gain sat down at the head of a long, wooden, hand-crafted table that accommodated his family of five plus at least five more.

White sat down on his left side with Preston next to her. Milo wandered around the kitchen, enjoying the lake view out the dark, wood-framed French doors, before choosing the seat opposite Gain at the far end of the table.

White began, "We know you had dinner with Patsy Rand the night she died."

Gain ran his fingers through his hair. "Dinner? I did?"

"You did."

Gain played with his coffee cup. "What night are we talking about?"

White shifted in her chair. "Last Thursday, six days ago."

"I was at the Black Bear Thursday."

"With Patsy Rand. We have your receipt. Let's drop this confused act, Mr. Gain."

"Is her name on my receipt?" Gain argued.

White opened a folder and pulled out a still from the restaurant security camera. "No, but your face is on this picture and that's Patsy Rand at your table."

Gain took a drink from his cup. He knew it wasn't going well. "Okay, yes. I met her Thursday night against my lawyer's advice."

"Why?"

"I wanted to see if she was as crazy as I was told. I heard about her from my father over the years, and I was curious. Big mistake."

"Fill us in on the history between Ms. Rand and your family," White prodded.

Gain took another sip of coffee. "I only know what my father told me. He insisted he didn't know her, yet Rand claimed she knew him and his partner in college."

"Why are your lawyers involved?" White asked.

"Lawyers? What lawyers?"

White pointed to Preston. "Did he say anything about lawyers?"

Preston scrolled back. "He said 'I met her Thursday night against my lawyer's advice.'"

Gain got up and poured himself another cup of coffee. *I'm really not good at this.* Returning to the counter, he said, "Look, my dad died last year. No one is supposed to know this, but I'm in the process of selling his company. There are a lot of moving pieces to this process. I'm not a corporate mogul. I'm a chemist. The lawyers have advised against talking to anybody. So, I shouldn't be talking to you."

"Mr. Gain, this is a murder investigation. If you refuse talk to us, you'll need those lawyers," White insisted.

"Did you read her book?" Milo asked.

"What book?"

"The one where Patsy Rand accused your father of murdering his partner," Milo responded—turning Bello's earlier conjecture into fact—to see Gain's response.

White, stone faced, not knowing where Milo was going with this, continued to stare at Gain.

Gain leaned back and folded his arms. "As I said, I'm trying to sell my father's company. Any crazies that come out from the woodwork could cost me millions—and there have been crazies. So far, the army of lawyers have either bought them off or sued them away. Rand was a crazy. She mentioned a book, but I've never seen it."

White stood up. "Peter Gain, I'm arresting you for obstruction of justice."

Gain's eyes opened wide, and he felt his heart beat faster. "Whoa! Why?"

White, still standing, pushed the restaurant picture back to Gain. "Look at the table. That's a book. And that's a picture of Patsy Rand on the cover."

"I'm going out on a limb here," Milo said, "but I would guess that's her book and you just lied to us."

Gain put up his hands in mock surrender. "Okay, okay." White sat back down. "She sent the book to me. I read part of it. It was filled with cruel lies. I returned the book to her at dinner that night."

"That was easy. Why did you lie?" White asked.

Gain pushed the picture away. "I don't know what I'm doing half the time. I shouldn't be talking to you about anything without the lawyers here. This was my father's world.

I'm so out of my league. The lawyers keep lecturing me that this deal is precarious. That's all I know."

White saw a motive for Gain to eliminate Rand but needed to know more. "Why?"

"Tettegouch is not a butcher shop. The company's value is wrapped up in my father's image. If that image gets tarnished, the price goes down or buyers don't buy."

"You said Rand's book was filled with cruel lies—about what?"

"She claimed my father pushed his friend and partner down a cliff when they were rock climbing. That infuriates me. He was a man who spent his life helping people. He wasn't a murderer. She was counting on a payday from me but was facing another lawsuit instead."

"Another?" White asked.

Gain threaded his fingers through his hair and began to massage his temples. "I'm always on these calls. The lawyers tell me things I only half understand." Gain looked up in panic. "You people need to leave. I'm saying too much. I can hear the lawyers screaming at me now."

White told him to calm down, "If you want a personal lawyer, that's fine, we can continue this interview at the police station. However, corporate lawyers have no place here. I don't care about your business deal. This is a murder investigation. For the last time, when did you sue Patsy Rand before?"

Gain sighed. "Father told me he sued her years ago and got the book removed from the shelves. In my hubris, I thought I could deal with her."

"Did you deal with her?" White asked.

"What do you mean?"

"Did you kill her?"

"Me? No!"

White stood up and gathered the pictures into the file. "I'm going to forget about your obstruction for now, Mr. Gain, but when we talk to you again, and we will, don't waste our time with lies."

Milo asked one last question as Gain was showing them to the door. "Was Patsy Rand sick that night?"

"Sick?"

"Like a stomachache."

Gain shook his head. "I don't know."

"So, she ate?"

"I guess. She had a drink and ordered a steak. I left. I didn't watch her eat."

"At any time did she take an antacid?"

"I don't know," he said as his smart watch buzzed. "Look, I gotta go."

"Pressing engagement?" Milo asked.

"Haircut," Gain said. "Wife's rule...my hair is below my ears...haircut time."

Once outside, White asked Preston her thoughts about Peter Gain. "He has billions of dollars of motive," Preston said.

Milo weighed in. "Also, Peter Gain is trying to protect his father's image. Powerful stuff. He had opportunity, two motives, and he's a chemist. He could make that poison."

Preston turned to Milo. "Can I ask a question?"

"Always," Milo said.

"You asked about the antacids. Do you think the poison was in the antacids?"

"I want to know when she became sick," Milo said. "If it was at dinner, we should check her activity before dinner."

"Well, Gain's a liar. He was lying before Sgt. White pulled her bad-ass move and threatened to arrest him," Preston said.

White laughed. "I did my best Gramm imitation."

Getting into the car, Milo said, "Everyone lies but only one lies because they're the murderer. Of course, none of us have asked the real question."

White turned to look over her shoulder. "You're doing that *Milo thing* aren't you. What's the question?" White asked. "The color of his socks? Why the coffee pot was half full? Have any of his kids been arrested? What?"

"Where's the book?"

"Book?" Preston asked.

"If Gain gave it back to her, where is it?" Milo asked.

"Umm, I give up," Preston said.

Milo speculated, "If she had it with her when she went to the book club…"

White laid her head on the steering wheel, "Augh! She left the book in the car!"

Milo smiled. "The same car that later suffered a break in."

White lifted her head and looked straight ahead. "Okay, it's not a stretch—someone is collecting her books!"

"I got my assistant looking for a copy," Milo said.

"Don't tell me. The 'present-at-every-murder', Agnes Larson," White chided as she started the car and began the trek back to the station.

Preston looked as if she was going to ask who Agnes Larson was. White stopped her. "Long story; don't ask."

"Actually," Preston began, "I was going to ask about that house—Gain's house. What style is that? French? Italian?"

"Expensive," Milo said.

White ignored him. "Definitely Mediterranean, maybe more Italian. Why?"

"I was trying to picture my great-great-grandmother in that house."

"She was Italian?" White asked.

"No. She was French until she became Italian."

"You're taking lessons from Milo, aren't you?" White accused.

Preston laughed. "No. Mine makes sense."

"I'm in the car you know," Milo complained.

"Explain," White said, ignoring Milo.

"My new thing is DNA testing. You know, the heritage stuff. My cousin and I thought it would be fun if I sent my test to one company, and Angie sent hers to another. Our mothers are sisters so our DNA should be pretty close. We're Scotch and Irish like I figured, but there was one problem—At every family reunion on my mom's side, there was a story told about a French great-great-grandmother. She threw knives at her husband. I was always compared to her. I guess I threw my toys at my sister when I got mad."

"So?" White interrupted.

Before you ask, no one ever knew if they were sharp knives or butter knives. Anyway, now I don't know if she was real. It's silly but upsetting. What I thought was real, isn't. What else isn't real and why?"

White wasn't getting the point. "I don't understand."

"Oh yeah, I left a part out," Preston said. "Everyone said she was French, but according to the test, I don't have any French DNA. Neither does my cousin. We're two percent Italian! If it's from her, she was Italian, and not French. If it's not, she never existed, and the story is a lie."

White smiled. "Well, all you Europeans look alike to me. Is there a difference between French and Italian?"

Milo sitting in the back seat laughed. He enjoyed Preston's monologue.

Preston thought about White's question. "Well, I had a picture of this lady in my mind throwing knives, and now it's gone! I have to create a new picture. I could put her in Gain's house if it's Italian like you say."

"Family secrets," Milo mused.

White shook her head. "Oh, come on—someone in the retelling made a mistake."

"Or," Milo said, "for some reason, lost to time, Great-great-grandma had a country change because someone thought French was better."

§

Milo's old job—following wayward spouses—had not brought him to the new townhouse complex built on the shore of Lake Superior in the east end of the city. "I didn't even know this place was here. When was it built?" he asked White as she knocked on the door.

"Ten years ago. You should try to get out more," White quipped.

"Ten years ago. I was moving here from Brainerd, and you were in what, fifth grade?"

White flashed her best disdainful look at him as Crystal Bower came to the door and invited them upstairs to the living area of the townhouse. Crystal pointed to a plate of macaroons, a silver coffee carafe, and orange mugs on a round, black, coffee table as she sat down on a contemporary couch with wooden sides.

Crystal was approaching sixty as if it was the new forty. She moved with a smooth, no-hitch motion as she folded her long legs under her and settled into the plush white pillow filling the corner of the couch. "Come sit down. I assume this is about Patsy," she said, brushing off imaginary lint from her black leggings.

The group spread out. White and Officer Preston sat down in two matching orange chairs opposite the couch. A large Afghan Hound joined Crystal on the couch, tucking her legs under herself in a similar fashion to her mistress. Milo—trying hard not to comment on the physical similarities between the dog and his host—was left standing.

"There are chairs in the dining room," Crystal said. "I didn't know there would be so many of you."

As he lifted the chair, Milo looked out the window. The condo complex had been built right over the lake. *One good November storm and these people will be living in the ice cold water,* he thought. Milo brought the chair from the dining room and asked the dog's name.

"Her name is Azin. It means *decoration* in Persian. I'd move her, but this is her spot. If you sit here, she'll sit on top of you." Crystal petted Azin.

"Tell me what you remember about last Thursday night," White began.

Despite the warming fire in the fireplace, Crystal reached behind her for a black sweater that was lying on the top of the couch, pulling it over her turquoise t-shirt. "Maybe it's living this close to the lake, but I always feel a chill around this time of day," she said explaining the sweater.

"Thursday night?" White questioned again.

"I knew I would be asked, so I've made notes," she said, reaching for a spiral notebook on the coffee table. "Please take some coffee while I refresh my memory."

Milo complied. White and Preston did not.

Reading from her notes, Crystal said, "First, Patsy came in late complaining of an upset stomach. She's had an ulcer for years, so I gave her a sample of one of our new strong bismuth subsalicylates."

"When you say *our* what do you mean?"

"I'm a sales rep for a large pharmaceutical company—soon to be vice president, I hope."

"What's bismuth submarine?" Milo asked.

Crystal laughed. "Bismuth subsalicylates—Pepto-Bismol on crack. Evelyn offered her some godawful potion from her weed store."

White interrupted, "Did she take either?"

"I don't really know, although I assume she would have preferred mine to Evelyn's. For as long as I've known her, Patsy has never accused me of killing anyone, unlike Evelyn."

"How long have you known her?" White said.

"Oh, years. I don't want to tell you how many, but we shared an apartment in college." Crystal pulled her long, wavy, blond hair back, twisted it around her finger, and watched as the curl fell on her right shoulder.

Milo thought that Crystal did not look to be a contemporary of Patsy Rand.

Crystal continued reading from her notes, "I was in the dining room when Erin Cohen's klutziness sent the water container crashing to the floor. I helped clean it up. Then Patsy collapsed in the living room and the rest you know."

White backtracked. "I understand she ordered a drink."

"At the top of her lungs."

"Who brought it to her?" White asked.

"Not me! I didn't do Patsy's fetch-and-carry work. Linda's brother was the bartender. Ask him."

"Did he bring you a drink?" White asked.

"No. I got mine at the bar."

"Tell me about everyone's movements after the water jug fell," White said.

Crystal grabbed her pencil and notebook. "I think better when I write. Let me take some notes. Look, you people have to eat these macaroons," she said pointing at untouched cookies.

Milo looked at Azin who was eyeing him and the cookies. He wondered if the dog was clued in on the invitation. She didn't seem to mind his pouring coffee. Preston braved the challenge, grabbing a macaroon. Azin didn't move a muscle. Feeling safe, Milo reached in. The dog jumped up and barked, never losing sight of the plate.

"Azin!" Crystal scolded. "Let the man have a macaroon."

Azin whined, looked at Crystal, and folded herself back onto the couch. Milo snatched the closest cookie. It was blue. *Who has blue cookies?* He was hoping it wasn't Azin's favorite.

"She doesn't like men," Crystal said. "I tend to agree with her most of the time." She petted Azin's snout. "Don't I baby."

The dog didn't answer but enjoyed the attention..

"I'm ready," Crystal announced. "I've got more notes."

White glanced over at Preston who was ready to take her own notes.

"Like I said, I was helping to clean up. Amy was there and so was Linda who sent Liam to the shed for paper towels. I don't know where Evelyn was."

"What about Erin Cohen?" White asked.

"Her arm was bleeding. When I went to the kitchen…"

White stopped her, "Why did you go to the kitchen?"

"Liam was taking forever, and I wanted to wipe the water off my leggings."

"Where was Ron Bello?" White continued.

"I don't know."

"When you were in the kitchen did you see anyone go into the living room?"

"No. I was blotting water."

"Okay, you're in the kitchen, then what?"

"Erin was at the sink. When my leggings were dry, I went back to the dining room through the butler's pantry."

"Dr. Carlson?"

"As I was leaving the kitchen, he was coming in with something for Erin's arm. I didn't see him; I only heard him."

Milo looked at White and waited. White nodded at him to begin. "I understand Patsy wrote a book about Harper Gain. Did you ever read it?"

The question took Crystal by surprise. "That old thing? Is that why Patsy was murdered?"

"We're exploring all avenues," White said, shuttering at a Gramm cliché.

"So, you read it?" Milo asked again.

Crystal smiled. "I think she sent me a copy. I can't remember if I read it or not."

"Do you still have it?" Milo asked.

"If I did, I tossed it years ago. It was awful."

"I thought you said you didn't read it," White charged.

"Oh, right," she laughed. "I guess I must have read some of it. From what I remember, it was fantasy—a typical Patsy fairytale."

"What do you mean by fantasy or fairytale?" White asked.

"Let me see if I can remember a few of them. I didn't write them down." She took a sip of her coffee. "Well, the big one was that she and Harper were an item in college. I went with Harper, not her. She did that all the time. She would take other people's experiences and make them hers. One of our friends went to Europe the summer of our junior year. Recently, right in front of me, Patsy talked about her fabulous European trip while in college. She never went to Europe— couldn't afford it. She spent that summer waiting tables with me. Isn't that some sort of a neurosis or something?"

White, refraining from mental illness diagnosis, brought the subject back to the book. "Any other things you remember from the book?"

"I remember some of the pictures because they were mine. She stole them! Of course, half of them were mislabeled because she didn't know what was going on in them."

"So, you're saying the book was untrue?"

"Total hogwash. What I remember was mistakes and lies. She even misspelled the name of Harper's and Mark's company! I was there when they gave it that name, Tetegouch—like the state park only no 'e' on the end. They debated that for days," Crystal laughed as she unfolded her legs, smoothed down her leggings, and tucked her legs back under her. "Both Harper and Mark were friends of mine and like brothers to each other. I resented what Patsy's fairytales insinuated. Lying about going to Europe was one thing but lying about murdering a friend..." Crystal shook her head.

"Were you going with Harper Gain when Mark Carlson died?" Milo asked.

"No. We broke up two or three years before that. To be honest, I didn't want to come in second place to a video game. When Harper was code writing, bringing Mark's ideas to life, I was an afterthought. Before all that game stuff, Harper was a lot of fun—a wild child. In my youth I liked bad boys, and Harper was bad."

"How bad?" asked White.

"Well, he didn't rob banks, but he drove like a maniac. It seemed like he lost his license every other day. No Uber back then. The cops on the late shift knew Harper well. They'd either arrest him or drive him home. It was fun, but, in the end, he just didn't have time for me."

"Did you and Harper Gain keep in touch?" Milo asked.

"No. I waited for him to come after me, but he never did." Azin laid her long snout on Crystal's leg. "But you do, don't you Azin?"

Smart dog, Milo thought.

"Also, I heard Harper stopped being a wild child. I don't know if he was too busy or if he could no longer drink because of the cancer. Being a drug rep, I now know that some people with Hodgkin's experience severe pain when they drink alcohol. I guess Harper was one of those people."

"You don't know for sure?" Milo asked.

"No, I never talked to Harper again."

"I did some research," Milo said. "Gain told people he cured himself of cancer through herbs and exercise."

"I never read his books. I reached out to him, but he never got in touch. When I knew him, he was never health conscious, but life experience changes people. Look at me, I used to have a great memory, now I have to make lists."

"Did you know Patsy Rand was going to republish her book?" Milo asked.

Crystal rolled her eyes. "She told me she was. We had a fight about it. I also told her I wanted my pictures back, and if she got sued, I'd testify against her. I told her to rename it Nethercamp's Never-Never Land."

"How did she take that?" White asked.

"Not well. She screamed at me. I put her on my loony list again."

"So that was the end of your friendship?" Milo asked.

Crystal sighed. "No. She's gone on and off my loony list over the years. Besides, for Patsy, it was me or nobody. After the fight, we were still...how shall I put it...long-armed friends. In fact, the day after the fight she told me about some people who were going to help her republish her book. Apparently publishing lies cost thousands."

Milo was still confused. "We think she still had copies of the original book. What was wrong with those?"

"There was the name thing," Crystal said.

"Name thing?" White asked.

Crystal nodded. "When she first wrote it, she published the book under her married name, Nethercamp—That's why I suggested Nethercamp's Never-Never Land. Like most things Patsy touched, that marriage was a train wreck. When her husband dumped her, she dumped his name."

While White was asking about the husband, Milo was texting Agnes with the name Patsy Nethercamp, not Patsy Rand.

14

"I'll be glad when these preliminary interviews are over," White said as the trio pulled up in front of Erin Cohen's Lester Park split-level. "This would have been a lot easier had Patsy Rand been shot."

"Stabbed would have been better because the perp would have been bathed in blood," Milo added. "Read 'em their rights and out the door."

Preston was still unused to the dark humor.

White mounted the one-step porch and rang the doorbell. "Instead, we're doing a real estate tour of the city and we don't where or when the victim was poisoned," she complained.

Erin Cohen came to the door and invited them in. Where Crystal Bower was tall and angular, Erin Cohen was short and soft. "I've got it, Dad!" she yelled down to the lower level. Leading the police and Milo upstairs, she said, "I've got to be by the phone and intercom, so let's talk in my office."

"What do you do?" White asked.

"My husband Barry and I are travel agents. He is at the office. We're closing it and going to work out of the house. His father has dementia and needs care. In-house nursing is not in our budget."

Erin rolled her desk chair over, while Milo and Robin sat in nearby chairs with Officer Preston on a loveseat. "I didn't knock over the water as a diversion. I'm not in collusion with anyone. It was an accident," she blurted. Noticing the surprised look on White's face, she added, "Look, we read mysteries all the time. We're all pretty savvy on this stuff."

"To be honest, it did cross our minds," White said.

"Of course, it would. Ever since Amy told me Patsy was poisoned, I've been trying to figure out who did it and how."

Where Ernie Gramm would never let a witness lead the interview, White was intrigued. "What did you come up with?"

"Well, there are three possibilities. The first is she was being poisoned by someone close to her over time, little by little, like in her morning coffee." Erin's eyes glowed as she retold her theories. Moving closer to the group, she added, "Patsy came from a dinner and was already in dire pain. She was the walking dead! That's my second theory."

"Walking dead. Dire?" Milo questioned.

"Well, maybe not dire, but she was uncomfortable. She was looking for an antacid...oh wait, I almost forgot both Evelyn and Crystal offered her medicine."

"Did she take any of it?" White asked.

Erin looked disappointed. "I'm afraid I don't know. I think the truth is always in the details, but, in this case, it's not coming to me."

The comment amused Milo. Erin and Sutherland would make a dynamic crime fighting duo. "Number three?" he asked.

"Three?" Erin questioned.

"You said there were three possibilities."

"Oh, yeah. The third is she was poisoned at the book club."

"By whom?"

Erin smiled, "That is the question isn't it. I'm working it out. I think it was a matter of opportunity. I always come up with good theories. It takes me a while. I'll let you know when I work it all out."

"You mentioned two people who offered her medicine. Is that what you're working out?" Milo asked.

"I guess," Erin said, "but Patsy arrived already in pain. Who did she have dinner with? That could be the perp… so to speak."

Erin theories were stating the obvious, and White was no longer intrigued. "Tell me about spilling the water."

"Not much to tell. As I said, I didn't do it on purpose. It was one of those spigot thingies on a stand. When I went to get a drink, the stand broke and the water went all over. It was a mess."

"Who brought the spigot thingy?" White asked.

"No one. It was Linda's. She's had it for years."

"Could the leg have been loosened for, as you said, a diversion?"

"Ooooh, never thought of that," Erin admitted. "So, I was the dupe in the diversion? That's not very nice!"

"Neither is murder," White said, sounding more like Gramm than she cared to admit. "Who helped you clean it up?"

Erin looked up at the ceiling trying to recall the scene. "Ms. Cohen?"

"I'm trying to see the picture in my mind. Amy...Amy Gramm, Linda and Liam Johansson." Erin continued to close her eyes. White waited. Erin opened her eyes but said nothing.

"What about the others?" White asked.

"Well, it was so chaotic, I don't remember. The others were fading shadows. I like that line—fading shadows. Do you like it?"

White ignored the question. "A number of people we talked to disliked the victim; how about you?"

"She was despicable," Erin announced without skipping a beat.

Once again, White was shocked at the bluntness. "Tell us why."

"She used that podcast of hers as a weapon. She had the nerve to ask us for travel discounts or she would bad mouth our agency."

"Did you give her discounts?"

"I told her to go to hell."

"Did she 'bad mouth' you?"

"I don't know. I never listened."

"Let's go back to the chaos for a second," Milo said. "The water spills, did you stay in the dining room?"

"No. I cut my arm." She showed her bandage. "Charles, Dr. Carlson, told me to run cold water over it while he went to get me something to help."

"So, you went to the bathroom?" Milo continued.

"I tried, but the door was closed. I knocked, but no one answered. I went to the kitchen. Crystal Bower came in complaining about her wet leggings, like I cared—I was bleeding. She left and Charles arrived with his medicine."

"Where was the medicine?" Milo asked.

"He said it was in his coat."

"Do you remember where Ron Bello, the author, was during all of this?" White asked.

"Standing in the corner of the dining room, watching. I guess that's what authors do."

"Could you see the living room from the kitchen?" Milo asked.

"Well, yes, but I was busy washing blood off my arm, trying to stop the bleeding."

"Did you see anyone go in there?"

Erin tilted her head. "Not really."

White glanced at Milo who put down his cup, stood up, and said, "Mrs. Cohen, this is a murder, a real murder. Please don't treat it like a mystery book. Murderers are dangerous. Did you see anyone go in there?"

"No."

White thanked Erin and the trio stepped out into the late gray afternoon. "What happened to the sun?" White asked, as she buttoned up her trench coat.

Preston was doing the same with her officer's jacket. "I read there's a storm moving in—could be a good night to stay in and binge watch Netflix."

Milo didn't bother to zip his jacket. "Robin, can you drop me off?"

As they got in the car, Preston asked Milo if he lived on this side of town. Milo said he did and she asked, "In a house or an apartment?"

"A house," Milo said.

White laughed.

"What's so funny?" Preston questioned.

White pulled into the Lakesong driveway far enough for Milo to use the security keypad from the backseat. As the gates opened, she said to a surprised Preston, "His *house* has a name."

"Welcome to Lakesong," Milo said, as White drove up the circular drive to the front steps. "Thanks for the lift."

As Milo left the car, he was greeted by the storm's first rain drops.

White pulled away and drove back through the iron gates.

"Why did you drop him off at the main house?" Preston asked.

"Because he lives there," White said.

"Does he work security as a second job?"

White turned onto London Road, no mean feat at this time of day. "That's his house. He owns it."

"How much does the department pay a consultant?" Preston asked.

"Not that much. I haven't gotten the whole story, but that's Lakesong and that's Milo's house."

Standing in the rain on the front porch Milo tried the front door. It was locked. *I haven't gone through the front door since I came to live here,* he thought. The rain was coming faster, pelting sideways onto the back of his jacket. He tried and failed to find the app on his phone. Feeling the rain soak through, he pressed the intercom button.

"Mr. Rathkey?" Martha asked.

"Yeah, I don't have a key or a car and I'm getting wet. Can you buzz me in?"

The buzzer sounded. Milo pushed one of the two leaded glass, mahogany front doors and slipped inside. "Gotta get a front door key," he mumbled, as he shed his wet jacket and walked to his bedroom.

§

Dylan's *Blood on the Tracks* album was playing through the sound system as Sutherland watched the rain pelt the doors and windows of the gallery. Lightning and thunder had joined the party. Three quick strikes on the dark lake gave Sutherland a light show illuminating the back lawn. For a second, Sutherland thought he saw movement. He opened one of the doors to get a clearer look but the rain drove him back. He thought he had secured the door.

Milo mixed a second pre-dinner gimlet before joining Sutherland in the gallery. "It's a good night for a second gimlet," he said as thunder cracked overhead. Milo hoped Sutherland didn't notice his flinch.

"Milo, if I got shot at, I think I'd have six drinks all lined up in a row."

Milo looked at him. "I'm not that thirsty."

"Oh, come on! You got shot at. At least I think you got shot at. I don't really know. All I got was a terse phone call."

"Terse?" Milo questioned.

"Brusque? Cryptic? Those work for you?"

Milo took a healthy swallow of his gimlet. "Let's stick to terse until I have more drinks, then we can branch out."

"Are you going to expand on what happened to your beloved Honda?" Sutherland asked.

Milo sat down, swung his feet up on a rattan ottoman and detailed the weird phone call that led him to the old steel plant.

"Why didn't you call me?" Sutherland asked. "We could have gone together."

"I thought it might be dangerous," Milo said. "Besides, if you were in the car, I'd be planning your funeral right now—the first bullet went through windshield and into the passenger seat."

Sutherland blanched. "That's grim. Wait! You said 'first bullet.' How many bullets were there?"

"Well, a second one went through the back window, but I sped away after making a terrific one-eighty turn."

The lights flickered and went out. Sutherland counted to three and the lights came back on.

"Love that generator," Milo said.

"Should we stop doing this investigation?" Sutherland asked.

"Just cause the lights went out? We should find the son of a bitch who wounded my Honda!" Milo said with force.

"Well, that's the other option," Sutherland said, pouring a second martini from his shaker. "We could hire a security firm, you know, to guard the grounds in case this lunatic follows you here. My God, we need to let Martha know—the kids play on the grounds!"

"I think we should hunker down in the wine cellar. You get the dynamite; I'll put my howitzer on Goliath," Milo said, referring to the halftrack snowplow used to clear Lakesong's estate roads after a heavy snowfall.

"You have a howitzer?"

"You have dynamite?"

Sutherland laughed. "Okay, I could be a little over the top, but is this guy going to try again?"

"I think we both know who 'this guy' is, and Gramm is going to rattle his cage tomorrow."

"Morrie Wolf?" Sutherland asked.

"No. Not Morrie. Why would you think Morrie? Helping his granddaughter get married is not a shooting offense. Morrie loves us."

"I don't know. He's a gangster. I figured…"

"Josh Crandell, the ex-cop," Milo said.

"The pathetic old man who had trouble getting out of his chair?"

"No, the rude, angry, frightened old man who threatened both of us, and shot at me twice, " Milo said. "We see things differently."

"What's our next move?" Sutherland asked.

"I think the next move is up to Gramm—calling Crandell in for a chat."

"Speaking of Crandall and sneak attacks, I don't want to scare you, but I saw something moving out on the back lawn before you came into the gallery," Sutherland explained.

Lakesong shook as lightning struck nearby, followed by a quick thunderclap. Rain and wind battered against the gallery windows. The two men jumped up as a rush of wind blew open the unlatched gallery door, and in the doorway, silhouetted by the lightning, stood an intruder, yellow eyes, white teeth, coal black fur. "Squeak."

"What is it?" Sutherland yelled.

"Did it squeak?" Milo asked.

The creature walked into the room and once again squeaked. Neither man moved, but Annie the cat hustled down from her Guiana tree to confront the intruder. Her tail puffed, a sign that she was about to fight, but the intruder rolled on its back and squeaked once again. Annie sniffed it, meowed once, and went back to her tree.

"It's a cat!" Milo said.

"A black cat," Sutherland added. He maneuvered around the side wall of the gallery to close the door latching it securely this time.

Milo inched his way to the cat.

"Hold out your hand, so it can smell you," Sutherland suggested.

"It's not a dog."

"You still let it smell you."

Milo ignored him and scritched the cat on its head. It rolled over again, so Milo could pet its wet tummy.

Martha announced dinner. The intruder cat followed Milo and Sutherland into the family room. Martha watched with amusement as the unknown cat slinked under the table and laid down on Milo's feet.

"Who's your new friend?" Martha asked—looking at the newcomer—knowing she wouldn't get an explanation unless she asked.

"Sutherland? He's lived here for a while," Milo said. "Sutherland, you don't make much of an impression."

Martha laughed, but asked again about the identity of the jet black furball.

"Don't know," Milo said. "The door blew open and there he was."

"He's gotta be a Dylan fan," Sutherland mused.

Both Milo and Martha looked at Sutherland."

"It's the lyric! He was seeking shelter from the storm." He began playing air guitar doing his best imitation of Bob Dylan. "You know, a creature from the wilderness, la la la, shelter from the storm."

From under the table, they heard a single squeak.

"He thinks Dylan did it better," Milo snarked, "and he knows the words."

Sutherland checked the strings on his air guitar and let it disappear.

"Dylan sounds hungry," Martha said, as she left in search of cat food.

"Milo sounds hungry too," Milo said, digging into his iceberg, bleu-cheese-dressing salad.

Hearing the sound of a cat-food pull top, the visitor abandoned Milo's toes and dashed into the hallway where Martha was waiting with a dish of ocean fish cat food.

"How do you even know who Bob Dylan is?" Milo asked Sutherland.

"I'm a musician. I've played in bands. Everyone knows Bob Dylan songs. They're iconic. Besides, my dad was huge Dylan fan. How is it you're a Dylan fan?"

Milo stopped eating and looked at Sutherland. "How do you think?"

"Of course," Sutherland said, smiling. "Dad was a huge Dylan fan."

Milo nodded.

§

Milo lit a one-log fire in the library, preparing to begin Ron Bello's book which Agnes had left for him on the side table. Annie, as was her custom, came down from her tree and laid by the fire. Milo saw a small movement in the doorway followed by a squeak.

"Why do you squeak? I thought cats meowed," Milo asked.

The black shadow with yellow eyes moved closer but did not squeak or meow. Annie rose from her place by the fire, stretched, and sat, a clear sign to the new cat that the fireplace position was hers.

"Have you dried off yet?" Milo asked. As if to answer, the fury lump of coal walked over to Milo, falling over on its back exposing its tummy yet again.

"Oh my! Am I supposed to pet that, or is that a tummy trap where I pet you, and you bite me? That's your trick, isn't it Annie?"

Annie gave Milo one of her silent meows as she waited to see how this was going to play out.

The slate-colored fluff stretched and wriggled on his back like a snake. "Okay, you get one shot at this," Milo told him. "You bite me, no more pets. We talk only."

The purring was hesitant then grew to a full throated quaver. After a few minutes of tummy scritching, Milo picked up his book from the table at which time the still-purring cat claimed the table as its own. Annie laid back down by the fire. The library had been reset. The fire was Annie's. The chair was Milo's, and the table now belonged to the dark stranger who came in from the storm.

15

Milo awoke to a *whoosh*, and a trickle of light. A second *whoosh* and the light was gone. It happened again, and then again. *Am I having a seizure?* he wondered, as he rolled and squinted at the bedside clock. It was six thirty.

Another *whoosh*. Milo turned toward the sound. His drapes had opened by themselves. *The remote control must have lost its mind,* Milo thought, remembering his first night in Lakesong when he discovered the remote control not only operated the television and the lights but the drapes as well.

The faint sound of a squeak coming from the foot of the bed told Milo he was not alone. The onyx feline stared at him, his paw still resting on the remote control. As if inviting Milo to the game, the cat's paw came down on the close button once again and the drapes obeyed, closing with a *whoosh*.

"I'm not going to ask how you figured that out," Milo told the cat.

In response the cat came up from the bottom of the bed to Milo, advanced up his chest, and sat down for morning pets. Milo obliged. "You are such a handsome fellow," Milo said.

The cat squeaked.

After Milo dressed, the storm-driven furry addition to the household jumped down and joined in behind Milo until they arrived at the gallery. Annie's hiss and puffed up tail greeted them as she staked out the bacon as hers. She led the way, followed by Milo and the cat Milo now called Squeak.

Martha delivered Milo's breakfast to the morning room with one hand and swooped up Squeak with the other. "Come on Dylan, your food is in here."

"Dylan? His name is Squeak. It's all he does," Milo protested.

Sutherland took a sip of his smoothie. "Are we sure Dylan Squeak is a he?"

"Good point," Milo said."

Martha checked. "He's a he."

"So, I was right. He's such a handsome fellow."

An assertive meow and a tug on Milo's pant leg told him that Annie didn't care if the new cat was from Mars. She wanted her bacon.

After complying with Annie's request, Milo dug into his breakfast. Getting shot at made him extra hungry. "I read about half of Ron Bello's book last night."

Sutherland looked down at the bacon-eating cat. "Did Annie join you?"

"She laid by the fire. I don't like it when she reads— she moves her lips."

Watching Milo feed Annie, Sutherland mentioned her pending visit to the veterinarian, indicating it was Milo's job. "You can also bring that new cat and get it checked out."

"Me? Why me?" Milo said, allowing as to how he had not been to a doctor himself for more than a decade.

"The cat is much more health conscious than you are," Sutherland said, returning to his paper. "After her checkup, she can take you to your doctor."

Milo, feeling out of his comfort zone, was not pleased. "How did I get this job?"

"It's in the will—all that stuff you didn't want to read."

"Why don't we have a guy? You have a guy for everything. Why don't we have a 'take-the-cat-to-the-vet' guy?" Milo asked, finishing off his hash browns.

"Every time Dad took the cat to the vet he received a lecture about giving her bacon. You should hear the same lecture," Sutherland said. not looking up.

"Did John stop feeding her bacon?"

Sutherland thought for a second. "No. He ignored the advice. The Annie before this Annie lived nineteen years. He figured he knew more about feline physiology than the twenty-five-year-old vet."

"Then why do I have to hear the bacon lecture?"

"It's a household tradition. Besides, it's in the will."

"Can I see the will?"

"Annie has it." Sutherland took a sip of his smoothie.

"Where?"

"How do I know. Ask Annie."

Milo's phone did the Ernie-Gramm-da-dunk-Law-and-Order sound. "Ernie. What's new?"

"Not much that's helpful. Thought you'd want to know we couldn't get a search warrant for Crandell's deer rifle, and forensics tells me the bullets were too damaged to get an exact match," Gramm said with his usual gruffness.

"Wonderful."

"But we've invited Mr. Crandell to the station for a little chat. I thought you'd like to observe."

"He agreed?" Milo was surprised.

"He did. I think he's playing the I-have-nothing-to-hide card."

"What time?"

"Around noon." The phone went dead.

"What was that about?" Sutherland asked.

"Crandell."

"What about him?"

"He's coming to have that chat with Gramm."

"Just a chat?"

"At this point. Meanwhile, I've got a full day," Milo said. "First on my agenda is the Honda. When will Mr. Anderson get here?"

"Martha said someone opened the gate early this morning. We assumed it was Mr. Anderson. Not many people have the gate code," Sutherland said, returning to his paper. "

Milo was out of his chair and heading for the garage. "I gotta talk to Mr. Anderson. My car is in serious condition. It's been shot—twice."

Sutherland laughed. Martha came in to clear Milo's dishes. "Does he know?" She asked.

Sutherland shook his head. "Nope."

As he entered the garage, Milo heard the sound of a power drill. He walked over to his car and saw someone in the front seat doing something with suction cups, fishing line, and a drill. At last he was going to meet the legendary Mr. Anderson who, earlier, had revived Milo's beloved Honda from years of neglect due to the owner's poverty.

Opening the driver side door, he asked, "Mr. Anderson?" The figure turned toward him. Milo stepped back, confused. He expected a grizzled, grease-spotted, old guy. Instead he was looking at a young woman with no grease stains and an ungrizzled face.

"Give me a second," she said returning to the power drill that was attached to an orange spool that held what appeared to be fishing line. She pressed the trigger of the drill, drawing the line up under the broken windshield of Milo's Honda. Once done, she pushed the windshield out to a waiting stand that held it up with suction cups.

Milo was impressed. After a few minutes, the woman slipped out of the Honda, took off a glove, and said, "I'm Mister Anderson. Who are you?"

"You're Mr. Anderson?" Milo questioned.

She laughed. "Well, my dad is Mr. Anderson. Our company is *Mister Anderson Automotive Repair*. Dad retired a couple of years ago so I took over. I'm Lilly."

"So, you're the one who fixed the Honda?" Milo asked.

"That would be me. I really enjoyed it. It was in horrible shape. Usually my repairs at Lakesong are routine maintenance—dusting and replacing belts and fluids. This car needed everything. I mean everything."

"I own it. I'm Milo Rathkey." They shook hands.

Lilly smiled. "Do you plan on getting shot at a lot? I need to know if I should stock more windshields."

"This was a first. I'm not planning on a second. Can you fix the seat?"

"You have three choices: We can repair it, but you'll still see where the holes were. We can reupholster the injured seat or we can replace it. It's up to you."

"Can you make the repair look like bullet holes? I'm looking for street cred."

She looked at him, not knowing if he was kidding. "You mean that, don't you?"

"Of course. It's my work car. It keeps me grounded. My fantasy car is that Mercedes over there."

Lilly nodded. "I assumed the Honda took priority. The Mercedes is routine maintenance."

He shook her hand again and turned to leave the garage.

"Can I ask what you do for a living?" She shouted.

"I'm a philosopher," Milo joked, as he left Mr. Anderson to her work.

"Philosophy must be a tough field," Lilly said to Milo's broken windshield.

§

Yesterday was a long day, and White needed a strong cup of coffee. She admired how Gramm made being chief investigator look easy. White added a little cream and a long dribble of honey to her tall mug of coffee.

Weaving through the various officers filling out reports, talking to civilians, and dealing with arrests, she arrived at her desk only to see Gramm standing in his doorway. White smiled. "Want a briefing on the case?"

"I was thinking about a second cup of coffee, but coffee and a briefing is good too."

"There's still some in the pot," White said, grabbing Preston's notes, stepping past Gramm, and making herself comfortable in one of Gramm's office chairs.

Gramm laughed. His new sergeant was no longer new—he had to get his own coffee.

"Where's Milo?" Gramm asked, as he sat down with his freshly poured cup.

"Don't know. He did get shot at yesterday. Maybe he's recovering," White said.

Preston appeared at the door. "Should I be in here?"

"Yes. I read your notes. They're good," White said.

"Thank you. I'm waiting on a new pot of coffee. Someone drained the pot and didn't make a new batch," Preston said, as she went in search of her computer tablet.

Gramm, wanting to avoid any discussion about the empty coffee pot, asked White, "Do you want to keep her?"

"Yes. How do I do that?"

"I have to do it if you want to keep her for the entire investigation."

"Can I listen?"

"Sure, this requires an easy touch—there are fragile egos, schedules have to be redone, it's a big deal."

White watched as Gramm called the desk sergeant.

"Hey, it's Ernie. That Officer Preston person. Yeah, that's the one. We're keeping her until this investigation is over." He hung up.

"Easy touch," White said. "I like your technique."

Gramm's phone rang. He ignored it. "So, how do you like your new role?"

"These first interviews were time consuming," White said.

"Tell me about the poisoning," Gramm asked.

"I don't know much. All evidence from the book club—with its cast of thousands—was thrown out by Linda and Liam Johansson the next day."

Gramm's bushy eyebrows rose up. "Suspicious?"

"Not really. Three days passed before we declared it a murder. I can't see them leaving broken glass on the floor, and the garbage pickup was scheduled," White said.

"How many of the cast of thousands could have made this poison?"

"Four, if you count Amy, have some scientific background. Milo looked aconite up while in the backseat of the car. He now knows how to make it. Wolfsbane is common. Amy told us you have it in your own backyard—so any of them could have made it."

"Okay, that's disturbing," Gramm said. "Do we know *where* she was poisoned yet?"

White smiled and shook her head. "No. That would be too easy. The night she died the victim had dinner with a man named Peter Gain—Harper Gain's son. Do you know who Harper Gain was?"

"Who doesn't?"

"Milo."

"Not surprised. Motives?"

White filled him in on the people at the meeting and the fact that many of them had a personal dislike for Patsy

Rand. She added that Peter Gain had financial motive and that he's a chemist.

Gramm's eyebrows did another jump. White told him not to get too excited. "The restaurant camera takes a still every minute. It does not show Gain touching her drink, but then there is a minute between pictures."

"Let's say she was poisoned at the meeting," Gramm said. "How could that have been done?"

"It could have been in her drink, but this was not a simple, quiet meeting where people sit down and talk about a book. There were food accidents, people were bleeding and getting sick—comings and goings having nothing to do with the victim, and that was before the meeting which never did get started."

Gramm thought for a minute. "Let's say the poison was in the drink. Who delivered it?"

"The Johanssons admitted to mixing it but not delivering it. No one else admits to delivering it or seeing anyone do the same. In order for the drink to be delivered, the murderer would have had to pick it up in the office, take it down a hallway, passing the dining room and the guest bathroom before turning into the living room where the victim sat."

"Who could do that?"

"Hard to tell. Like I said, people were everywhere. I need to draw a diagram of everyone's movements."

Gramm nodded. "I've done that before. It helps. Let's get back to Peter Gain. What's your gut say?"

"Gain lied when asked about knowledge of the victim's book—suspicious."

"I hate liars. Tell me about this book."

White detailed Patsy Rand's book and her accusation that Harper Gain had murdered his partner years ago. She added that the book was squelched by Harper Gain when it first appeared thirty years ago, but Rand was determined to publish it again now that Harper Gain was dead.

"Why would his son lie about the book?" Gramm asked.

"He said it could complicate the sale of his father's business and his dad's image could be harmed."

Preston came back, coffee and tablet in hand, followed by Milo.

"Good of you to join us, Milo," Gramm chided. "We usually come to work around nine."

"I went to visit the wounded Honda. Did you know Mr. Anderson is Lilly Anderson, his daughter," Milo said without explanation.

"Do I need to take a note?" Preston asked. "I don't remember a Mr. Anderson."

Both Robin and Gramm chorused a resounding "NO!"

Milo pulled in a chair from the bullpen and sat down.

"I'll bite," Gramm said. "Who or what is a Mr. Anderson?"

"Lilly," Milo corrected.

Gramm began twirling his eyebrows, a sign he was tiring of this exchange.

Milo explained his discovery.

"Let me get this straight," Gramm said, "you're upset because your mechanic is a woman."

"No. She's a great mechanic. That's not the problem. She wasn't what I expected," Milo said.

Preston added, "Like my French great-great-grand-mother—it throws you off."

"As I was saying," White asserted, "the initial interviews are done."

Milo interrupted, "What about the forestry guy?"

"The forestry guy wasn't at the dinner or the meeting," White challenged.

"The victim had his card. Everyone who knew the victim is a suspect," Milo said.

White looked at Gramm who shrugged. "It's Milo's mind lint but go talk to that forestry guy."

White nodded.

Preston added that Rand's lawyer finally got back to her with the people who were threatening Patsy Rand. There were three of them—all had alibis.

"Do you know about Rand's book?" Milo asked Gramm.

"White filled me in on what you got, but it's all second hand."

"I've got my assistant looking for a copy of the book," Milo said.

Gramm almost spit out his coffee. "Assistant?"

White beat Milo to the name. "Agnes Larson. No murder investigation would be complete without her."

Milo smiled.

Gramm was confused. "I thought she was your house manager. I have time. Explain it to me."

"She was house manager, but then she wasn't. It was Mary Alice's idea."

"Mary Alice Bonner? I lied," Gramm said. "I don't have this much time."

§

Josh Crandell felt uncomfortable as Gramm led him through the bullpen area to the interview rooms. Nothing was familiar in this new cop shop. Young faces, bright colors, nothing like the way Crandell remembered it. "This place is going soft," Crandell complained.

"New times—adapt or retire," Gramm shot back, opening the door to Interview Room A, sitting down, and starting the official recording.

Crandell looked around the stark room with one long table and four chairs. "We can't do this in your office? I'm a cop."

"Sit down! You have the right to remain silent."

"Why the hell are you sayin' that to me?"

"You're being charged with endangerment," Gramm said, continuing to Mirandize Crandell.

"Endangerment? Kinda strong. What about simple assault?"

"Assault? You didn't punch Milo. You shot at him!" Gramm shouted, confused as to why Crandell was admitting to anything.

Crandell was silent.

"You want a lawyer?" Gramm asked.

"Not yet."

"Are you admitting to shooting at Rathkey?"

Behind the one-way glass, Milo was unsettled as he watched the man who tried to kill him. Crandell began to rub the top of his head, the same move he made when Milo and Sutherland asked him about the night Karl Rathkey was shot. It was a definite tell.

"Hey Gramm, do they make you water those potted plants in the bullpen?" Crandell spat.

Gramm ignored the diversion. "Where were you yesterday from noon on?"

"Don't remember. I'm gettin' old."

Gramm was confused. Crandell seemed willing to admit the shooting as long as the charge was assault. He wondered why Crandell would admit to it at all. *This all started with Milo asking questions about his father. I'm gonna try the same thing.* "Tell me about the murder of Karl Rathkey,"

Crandell twitched. "Jesus! What is with you guys? Let it go!"

"You seem to care a lot about *it*," Gramm goaded him on.

"I care crap about Karl Rathkey. What I care about is his kid goin' around askin' questions."

"Why does that matter? What are you afraid of?"

Crandell ran his hand over his hair again and cupped his fingers under his arm pits. "Morrie Wolf—that's what I'm afraid of."

The name jarred Gramm. He glanced at the one way mirror.

Behind the glass, Milo leaned forward, as puzzled as Gramm.

"So, I got your attention?" Crandell asked.

Gramm nodded.

Crandell folded his right hand over his left, elbows on the table. "I always thought the way that night went down wasn't right, but I was the rookie. You know what it's like. I did what Prepinski told me to do."

"What did he tell you to do?"

"To go off and check for perps on the site. Rod stayed with the body and called for an ambulance."

Gramm spent a career trying to find something on Morrie Wolf that would stick. He wasn't going to let the reference to Wolf pass. "Why would Wolf care about any of this?"

Crandell began drumming on the table with the fingers of his right hand.

"You brought him up," Gramm said, noticing that Crandell's left hand remained quiet with fingers curled under. "How does Morrie Wolf figure in this?"

Milo didn't like where this was going. Unlike Gramm, he had gotten attached to Morrie's plaid coats and skinny ties.

Crandell's drumming stopped as he pulled his left hand close to his body. "All I know is after Rod retired, he would get in these moods and give me a call to meet him for some beers. He'd keep talkin' 'til they closed the bar about how Morrie Wolf was gunnin' for him. He was buyin' so I was listenin'. Then one day I hear he gets beat to death, and shoved in the trunk of a car, and the car ends up in the lake. Now who does that?"

Gramm was silent, hoping Crandell would say more. He did.

"It was like those two brothers back in the day."

"Brothers?" Gramm asked.

"Yeah brothers…the Wills brothers, fightin' young Wolf for control of the rackets—baseball bats, car trunk, lake. Same MO…I don't wanna end up that way."

Gramm sat back. "Let me get this straight. You're afraid Milo's questions will remind Wolf that you're still alive, so you tried to kill him."

213

"I didn't try to kill nobody—just scare him so he'd shut the hell up."

Gramm took a deep breath. "I'm going to drop the endangerment charge for now. Go home, but know Rathkey's kid is listening to this interview, and he and Wolf are friends."

What little blood was in Crandell's wrinkled face, drained.

"If Wolf didn't know you were still around before, he will now. If Wolf does kill you, I might be able to nail him for it—so thanks." Gramm got up to leave.

"Wait! You're signing my death warrant."

Gramm shrugged. "What do you want me to do?"

Crandell rubbed his head again. "You owe me protection."

"Don't have the budget."

"I shot at your boy! You gotta hold me! Assault takes me off the street for a month or two 'til this dies down."

Gramm left the room. Seconds later two officers arrived to cuff and escort Crandell to the bullpen area for booking.

Milo sat back in his chair. Crandell had told him and Sutherland that the Wills brothers had disappeared. He hadn't said anything about a car trunk or the lake—Morrie's urban legend. *Killing the Wills Brothers made sense. They were rivals. But why would Morrie kill a retired cop that way? Revenge? Revenge for what? The killing of Karl Rathkey? What's under this rock?*

§

White expected to meet the head of Duluth's urban forest, Elliot Addison, in his office. That was not the case.

Instead, Addison directed her to the Fond du Lac area of west Duluth where he was working. After driving for a half hour, Robin followed her GPS to a muddy dirt road and pulled up behind a Duluth forestry truck.

"This area used to be an Ojibway settlement," White informed Preston.

"Why did your people leave?" Preston asked.

"I don't think it was our choice."

The two left their vehicle, avoiding puddles from last night's rain, and went looking for any sign of life. "Elliot Addison!" White yelled.

"Hello!" The voice came from above their heads. "Up here in the trees."

White looked up to see an orange figure maneuvering in a tree by a series of ropes. Pulling on a rope, the man glided down to the ground, and removed his hard hat and protective eyewear. White was surprised to see that he was far from young—pushing sixty—but lean and hard. He yanked off his gloves and held out his hand. "I'm Elliot. You must be Sgt. White."

White shook his hand and introduced Preston. "I didn't expect you to be in the trees."

"Most people don't. How can I help you?"

"What are you doing in the trees?" Preston asked.

"Checking on our favorite anomaly. There are Elm trees in this forest that seem immune to Dutch Elm Disease." He patted the tree that still held his ropes. "This beauty is my favorite. She tells me everything."

"I didn't know there were elms that are immune," White stated.

"There are," Addison said, adjusting his glasses. "We find them all around Minnesota. We hope to plant the saplings of these trees around town replacing the elms we've lost."

"Interesting," Preston said.

"I imagine you did not come out here for a lecture on trees."

Robin took a picture of Patsy Rand from her folder. "We think this woman may have talked to you recently. She had your card in her purse."

Addison adjusted his glasses and looked at the picture. "I remember her. I think she got my card from the office. She came out here wearing high heels, yelling at me because the ground was soft, and I wasn't in the office where she thought I belonged. I didn't invite her out here."

"What did she want with you?" White asked.

Addison took off his glasses and wiped them with a blue handkerchief. "She wanted me to fire one of my staff members."

"Who?"

"Liam Johansson—somebody I was pleased to get—lot of experience and not an office guy."

"Did she give a reason?"

"She told me he was an ex-con and a murderer. I know all about Liam and his incarceration. I told her to leave."

"Did Johansson know she had been out here?" Robin asked.

"Sure. He was up in the tree. The way she was screeching, he heard the whole thing. I was surprised he didn't drop a pole saw on her."

White look up at three men in the trees. "Is he up there now?"

"No, he's working Lester Park today."

16

Milo looked at the wood box next to the library fireplace. It was full, as was the kindling box. It wasn't full yesterday. "Who gets the wood?" he said out loud. Annie, anticipating a fire, joined him, but did not divulge the secret of the wood delivery. Milo shrugged and went about building and lighting his fire. Annie seemed pleased and curled up to absorb the warmth. The new cat—now dubbed Dylan Squeak—took his place on Milo's end table.

Milo hated late afternoons, especially on dark, cloudy days. Firelight, which reminded him of reading in this library as a boy with John McKnight, lifted his mood. He picked up Ron Bello's book and reflected on what he had read so far. Someone shot the villainous DA nine times on the courthouse steps and Bello's book centered on three possible suspects including one that mirrored Liam Johansson.

So far Bello's writing was clever. Shade was thrown on each suspect, but nuances hidden in narration cleared each one. It was going to be a two-log fire to finish Bello's book. Reaching the last chapter, Milo explained the book to the sleeping feline gathering. "Either Bello was going to bring in a new guilty character at the end—something Milo hated—or there would be only one conclusion. It would be ballsy, but fun."

Annie didn't see the act of reading doing anything for her or cats in general, except for the lighting of the fire, so she ignored Milo's dissertation. She did manage a stretch and yawn as she changed positions to allow her other side access to the heat. Dylan, being the new cat in the house, stood up and looked at Milo as if he comprehended it all.

Milo finished the book, stretched out his legs, and leaned back, hands behind his head. "Cats, Ron Bello does not disappoint. Clever. The narrator, a journalist, did it."

Annie meowed. Dylan squeaked.

"You're both right," Milo said. "Would he dare to commit a murder in fiction that he later commits in reality? He could have thought none of us were going to read his book, or he wrote it so we would dismiss him as a suspect."

Annie was asleep. Dylan was licking his paw.

§

Sutherland arrived home and found Milo and cats in the library. "Did you light the fire for yourself or the clowder?" He asked.

Milo looked up. "Clowder?"

"Exactly. A group of cats is a clowder."

"Who gets the firewood?"

"What? What does that have to do with a clowder?" Sutherland was lost.

"I wasn't talking about a clowder. You learned a new word. Congratulations. I'm interested in the firewood. It was half full yesterday. Today it's full."

"We got a guy who comes once a week. He adds to the wood box in the maintenance shed, fills the wood boxes in the hearth room, and here in the library, various bedrooms— wherever there's a fireplace."

"Now I know," Milo said. "I thank you and the clowder thanks you."

Annie gave Sutherland one of her silent meows.

"What happened with Crandell?" Sutherland asked.

"He admitted to shooting at me...says he was afraid of our stirring things up again. Gramm charged him with aggravated assault."

"Assault? That was attempted murder!" Sutherland was outraged.

"It's enough to hold him. The guy is frightened."

"Frightened of what? You?"

"No...you, Sutherland. He's frightened of you."

Sutherland straightened his tie. "I do have that corporate assassin look."

"Well, it was either you or Morrie Wolf. I'll leave you to guess which one."

"Not Morrie Wolf again!" Sutherland sat down opposite Milo. "How is Morrie Wolf going to affect my life this time?"

"Don't know. It will require a trip to the Rasa Bar. Wanna come along."

"Gee, I'd love to meet Morrie again because, you know, gangsters and I get along so well, but I'm busy all month. Sorry."

Milo laughed.

"Where's Agnes?" Sutherland asked.

"I haven't seen her. She's been working in the upstairs library."

"Did she tell you she won't be here tomorrow?"

"No. Where will she be?" Milo asked.

"We're going to the Cities for the weekend. The Walker Arts Center has a limited exhibit, and I scored tickets for a preview tomorrow," Sutherland said, beaming. "Then Saturday night, we're going to a Katy Perry concert." Reacting to a Milo double take, Sutherland admitted, "Yeah I know. But she puts on a great show and Agnes loves her. It's a surprise."

"Nice," Milo said, wondering if Mary Alice enjoyed limited exhibits. *How do I keep track of special exhibits? That's a question for Jules, Mary Alice's art dealer.*

Sutherland found Agnes at her laptop in the upstairs library. She smiled at him. "Did you bring your suitcase?" He asked.

She knew Sutherland's question was really asking, 'Do we have to stop at your house first'? "It's in my office."

"I'll put it in the car," Sutherland said. "I told Milo you aren't going to be here tomorrow," Sutherland said. "He didn't seem to know about our trip."

"Oh, is he home?" Agnes asked. "I need to tell him about a book he wanted me to find."

"Work, work, work," Sutherland teased. "You finish up here. I'll go back to the library and tell Milo you have information about the book he wanted"

This was the moment Agnes had been waiting for. Grabbing her laptop and kicking the baseboard by the secret door, she raced down the steps, sprung out of the bookcase, closed it, gave a shocked Milo the sign to remain silent, and sat down.

Sutherland came into the room, saying, "Milo, Agnes has found…" He noticed her sitting in the room staring at her computer screen. "How are you…here?"

Agnes looked up. "Talking to me?"

Sutherland blinked and stared. "Yes, I'm talking to you. You were upstairs."

"Are you okay to drive?" asked Agnes with mock concern.

"She's been here for hours," Milo said.

"Okay, I don't know what's going on here, but Agnes was not in the room when you and I talked."

"I don't remember us talking," Milo said.

Sutherland knew he was being put on, but how? Without a sound, he turned and, with his long legs flying, raced up the front staircase. Agnes, with longer legs, was quicker up the secret staircase. Sutherland arrived in the upstairs library to find Agnes sitting where he had left her.

"I should have told Milo about tomorrow. Thanks for taking care of that," she said, trying to stifle her laugh.

Sutherland took a deep breath. "You're playing with me."

"Me? Never."

"I give up. How did you do that."

"Seriously, Sutherland, are you all right?" Agnes laughed.

"Look, you're out of breath too. You ran up here like I did, but how? Where?"

Agnes stood up laughing. "How long have you lived in this house?"

"All my life, why?"

"And you never once decided to kick a baseboard?"

Sutherland stared in disbelief. Even as a child he didn't kick the woodwork. "Why would I kick a baseboard?"

Agnes walked up to the middle bookshelf. "For magic to happen." She gave the baseboard a kick and the bookshelf clicked open.

Sutherland's eyes grew wider as Agnes pulled the bookshelf back. She held out her hand as if giving an introduction "Mr. Sutherland McKnight, Lakesong. Lakesong, Mr. Sutherland McKnight."

"Why do I never know these things? This is my house!"

"Come on, let's play with your house," Agnes said, leading him down the stairs and through the library bookcase.

Milo turned to see them coming. "Aw! You told him. I would have gone at least a day."

"You knew about this!" Sutherland charged.

Milo looked up from his book. "I didn't know about this one, only the one in the cottage."

"There are more?" Sutherland asked Agnes.

"I don't know...yet," she laughed. "I think this wonderful old house only reveals her secrets one at a time."

§

Amy Gramm made a quick stop at the grocery store for pasta, ricotta, mozzarella, and spinach. Her daughter Julie and family were coming over on Sunday. It was time for family-sized lasagna, a rarity these days now that she and Ernie were empty nesters. Amy was making the trek from the garage to her back door with her three bags of groceries when her phone vibrated. Not wanting to drop her groceries she let it go to voice mail.

Once inside, the grocery bags on the table, she took out her phone and saw the caller was Crystal Bower. "That's odd," She said to herself. Amy and Crystal were friendly but not friends.

Amy hit call back.

"Thanks for returning my call, Amy," Crystal said.

"What's up?" Amy asked.

"I think we should have a memorial service for Patsy."

Amy hesitated. "Shouldn't that be up to her family."

"It should be, but it won't be. I found her daughter, but neither she nor Patsy's ex-husband are interested in any kind of service."

"Wow. How did you do that? Find her daughter I mean."

"Patsy told me she had a daughter in Orlando. I searched Linkedin and found a Valerie Nethercamp in Orlando. Bingo!"

"I'm impressed."

"I called. She's not interested in any kind of a service, but I got all the information. The Anderson Funeral Home is handling the cremation, and they will rent us a small room for next to nothing. I was thinking Monday; the room is cheaper during the week. I'll put a notice in tomorrow's paper."

Crystal was moving too fast for Amy. "Wait! Are you sure this is a good idea? I mean Patsy wasn't well liked," Amy noted.

"Well, not in the book club, but who knows. She may have had friends from other parts of her life," Crystal said.

Amy thought this could be true. "I thought you were her friend."

"Let's not get carried away. We've known each other a long time. I wouldn't go right to friend."

Amy checked her calendar. She was on the mid-shift in the ER on Monday. She could attend though she'd rather not. *What's the worst that could happen?* she thought. *Nobody shows. Patsy's dead. She won't mind.* "What do you need me to do?"

"E-mail the book club members. I'll take care of the rest."

"Should we do some food afterward?" Amy asked, while putting away her groceries

"No. We only have the room for an hour and no idea if anyone will come."

Amy said goodbye and hung up, thinking Monday morning could be pretty gruesome. She heard Ernie's Jeep Wrangler pull into the driveway. A few minutes later she heard the familiar, "Did anyone here call for a police officer?"

"Only one," she said, giving him a peck on the cheek.

"Lucky for me," he said, hanging up his jacket in the back hallway.

"Oh, I didn't say it was you," Amy kidded, "but I guess you'll do. We're having one of your July-fishing-trip walleyes tonight."

"Good times," Ernie said.

"And fancier times—fishing from the back of Milo's yacht," Amy kidded.

"Beats a rowboat and an outboard motor."

"I know you love to grill the fish. It's already in foil. Grab your jacket and start the grill."

"I caught it; now I have to cook it?" Ernie complained.

"Life's tough. Get over it."

Ernie laughed, having heard that phrase all his married life. Putting on his jacket, he headed to the back deck, shivered a bit, and lit the grill.

When Ernie Re-entered the house, Amy filled him in on the memorial service for Patsy Rand as she chopped tomatoes and cucumbers for the salad. "Crystal and I could be the only ones to show up."

"Cops love funerals, so I'll be there as your escort. Of course, Robin and Milo will show up along with the murderer—you know, visiting the result of his or her handiwork."

Amy closed her eyes and exhaled. "I hadn't thought of that."

"I was kidding." Ernie kicked himself.

No, you weren't, Amy thought.

§

"She's been here for hours! Traitor!" Sutherland admonished Milo as he emerged from the hidden staircase.

Still in his chair by the fireplace, Milo smiled. "That woman can walk through walls. I was afraid."

Sutherland leaned against the chair opposite Milo. "Yeah, she can be scary when she gets mad."

"I have a question to ask her before you guys leave," Milo said.

As if on cue, Agnes entered the library after retrieving her impractical ivory-tapestry roller bag. "Looking for me?" she asked Milo.

"I was wondering how you're doing tracking down that book?" Milo asked.

Agnes smiled. "Oh, I found the book this morning. Patsy Nethercamp, *Empire Built On Blood: The True Story of Harper Gain.*

"That's great! Can I get my hands on a copy? Somebody else seems to be collecting all of them."

"You have a copy," Agnes said.

"I do? Where?"

"It's upstairs by the computer. It's one of my problem children—books without barcodes. I meant to bring it down but Sutherland distracted me."

Milo looked at Sutherland. "Your dad bought that book?"

Sutherland shrugged. "Don't look at me. I know he liked to support regional authors. He may have bought it and forgot about it."

Agnes offered to go get it, but Milo said he'd do it. He needed the exercise. Annie the cat looked up and yawned. She did not need the exercise. She climbed up her Gianna chestnut tree several times a day.

"Use my secret stairway. It's the direct route." Agnes laughed as she and Sutherland headed to the garage.

Milo got up, walked over to the moveable bookcase, kicked the baseboard, heard the click, and pulled it out. *Did John know about this? Naw. He would have told me or at least*

Sutherland, Milo thought, wondering if these secret spaces were on the blueprints Sutherland found in the vault this past summer. *It did show that tunnel to the lake.*

Milo's curiosity was aroused, but a session with the blueprints would have to wait. He had urgent business with the writings of Patsy Nethercamp Rand.

§

Evelyn Chen looked at her phone in disbelief. Amy Gramm had sent a group message to the book club members advising them of an upcoming memorial service for Patsy Rand. "I can't believe it!" she said to her employee Jay.

"Believe what?" he asked.

"They are going hold a memorial service for Patsy Rand on Monday morning."

Jay continued stocking the shelves. "You hated her. Don't go."

Evelyn put her hands on her hips. "I'm going."

Jay turned around. "What time and where? I can't miss this."

"You have to stay here and tend to the shop," Evelyn said.

"Rats. Can you stream it?"

"I don't know what that means, but no."

§

Dr. Charles Carlson saw the text from Amy Gramm and texted back, *Of course I'll be there.* Sitting at his desk he thought, *let the fireworks begin.*

§

Linda Johansson thought the idea of a memorial service for that woman was hideous. When her brother arrived home from work she told him about it. Liam was stunned. "Why!"

"It's Amy Gramm. She sees the good in everybody."

"There was no good in Patsy Nethercamp. No good at all."

"Are you going to go?" Linda asked.

"Me? I wasn't invited. Besides I'm working on Monday. Don't tell me you're going?"

"I don't want to, but I worry if I don't, I'll look guilty, like I'm trying to hide something."

"Oh," Liam said, "should I go?"

Linda sighed. "I don't know."

§

"Remember that awful woman that tried to extort travel discounts from us?" Erin Cohen asked her husband, as she shut down the business computer for the night.

"The blog lady?" Barry Cohen responded.

"Yeah. Patsy Rand. They are holding a memorial service for her on Monday."

"She died?"

"Oh gees, Barry. She was murdered at my book club meeting last Thursday. I told you all about it."

"You said there was a murder, but you're always talking about a murder. It's a murder book club."

"She's a real person, and she was poisoned at the book club."

"Did you do it?" Barry asked.

"Not funny, Barry."

§

Milo, who had eaten solitary dinners for ten years, found eating alone in the Lakesong family room to be disquieting. Martha had served dinner but left for Jamal's basketball game.

"You were right, John," Milo said to the ether. "Lakesong is kinda creepy when no one else is here." He felt something rub up against his leg followed by a squeak. Looking down, he saw two, wide, yellow eyes looking back.

"Well, Squeak, I guess I'm not alone," Milo said, as the cat rolled over for a tummy pet. "Did John send you?"

The cat was noncommittal.

Milo put his dishes in the dishwasher, grabbed a Diet Coke, and retired to the library to read *Empire Built On Blood: The True Story of Harper Gain.* After lighting the fire, Milo sat down and was joined by Annie and Squeak. He managed to grab his drink before the black cat knocked it off the side table. Annie gave a loud meow as if to say, "That kitten has no manners."

17

Milo yawned as he made his way to breakfast. Martha greeted him from the kitchen. He attempted a half-hearted wave, grabbed a large mug, and filled it with much-needed coffee.

"If you would like breakfast later, especially on days Mr. McKnight is not here, let me know."

Milo yawned again. "No. I was up half the night forcing myself to read."

"That doesn't sound right, bad book?" Martha asked.

"A really bad book, and it kept getting worse." Milo broke off small pieces of bacon and dropped them for the cat.

"Why waste your time?"

"Evidence."

"Well, you have murderers to catch and my contractors are here." Martha rushed back to the kitchen. Milo got up and refilled his coffee.

Sutherland was not there to rattle his Wall Street Journal and prattle on about financial items. Annie curled up by the fire in the hearth room, leaving Milo alone to eat his breakfast. With Annie's departure, Squeak thought it safe to appear and rub against Milo's leg.

"This cat knows how to keep me company!" Milo yelled at Annie.

A loud, disagreeing meow from the hearth room told Milo what Annie thought of that comment.

As she ran through the tunnel to the cottage, Martha thought, *It's not that he talks to the cat that's disturbing. It's the fact that the cat talks back.*

Milo's phone vibrated. It was White who filled Milo in on the interview with Elliot Addison, the urban tree guy. "Throws more shade on Liam," White said.

"Not if the guy wasn't going to fire him."

"What's to say Rand wasn't going to go over Addison's head? Liam decided to eliminate that possibility."

"Does Liam know poisons?" Milo asked.

"Prisons have libraries. Plus, he is a tree person. His education had to include the study of plants—including poisonous plants."

"Good point. FYI, Agnes found Patsy Rand's book, the one about Harper Gain. I read it last night."

"Really? Where?"

"In the Lakesong library."

"No, not where you *read* it. Where did she *find* it?" White laughed.

"In the upstairs library. John McKnight bought it in the brief time it was for sale," Milo explained.

"So, what did you find out?" White asked.

"It's a book that preaches and rambles. It was hard to read—past and present get confused."

"Other than the literary critique, what did you find out?"

"Rand claims that what the world saw—Mark Carlson and Harper Gain being friends, almost brothers—was false. She claims they hated each other, fought all the time, and were jealous of each other. Carlson had the ideas. Gain had the money," Milo explained.

"Does Rand's book claim Gain killed Carlson?"

"Oh yes! She insists Gain killed Carlson because Carlson was about to leave the company."

"Why kill him?"

"She paints Gain as an egomaniac control freak. You know, 'If I can't have your ideas no one can.' According to the book, Gain pulled Carlson to his death while they were climbing the cliffs at Tettegouche State Park."

"Proof?"

"None."

"Any Milo mind lint?"

"Well, since you asked, there's a hodge-podge of pictures in no apparent order. One picture of Gain shows him celebrating a company success with employees. Rand's caption says the picture was taken after Mark Carlson died. That picture bothers me."

"Why?"

"I asked myself the same question. The obvious thing is he's toasting the company's success with what appears to be a beer."

"So?"

"Remember Crystal Bower said he couldn't drink."

"Are you sure it's a beer? I drink ginger ale, looks like beer," White said.

"Could be tea for all I know."

"So that's what bothers you?"

"I don't know. That's a question I have to clear up. I have no idea what bothers me."

White sighed. "I guess we'll have to wait for the back of your brain to talk to the front of your brain, as Gramm says. In the meantime, what do the other pictures show?"

"There are quite a few of them. One picture—Rand says supports her theory—shows the two of them in a heated argument, or they could have been mugging for the camera. They were young, long-haired, techy types posing for a picture. One other tidbit for you to think about," Milo added. "the book mentions that Harper Gain dumped his college girlfriend because of her cocaine habit and started going out with Rand."

"Does she mention the name of the girlfriend?" White asked.

"Not there, but she slips it in later, in the picture area. There is a picture of Gain and that girlfriend—none other than Afghan-Hound-Lady and drug rep, Crystal Bower."

"Cocaine habit? Not good for a drug rep. I wonder if she's our break-in book collector?" White mused.

"She and the victim were friendly. I bet she knew where all those books were stored."

"Crystal has won a second interview. She can tell us why the victim thought she could publish that book now. If there's an injunction against it, she can't publish it—period."

"My day is open. Let me look into the lawsuit," Milo offered.

"Be my guest. If we ask the DA to do it, it'll take a week."

§

Ron Bello was finishing his second cup of coffee when he found the notice for Patsy Rand's memorial service in the paper. He checked his calendar, entering the time and place. *Cops always suspect no-shows.*

§

Seeing Rand's memorial notice in the paper, Peter Gain shuddered with a sense of dread. Patsy Rand's death should have been the end of her and her book. He put Patsy Rand's memorial service on his calendar.

§

Still unwilling to give up on summer, Milo threw on a green t-shirt even though it was only forty five degrees outside. He rationalized his decision by foregoing shorts for jeans. With his hair still damp from swimming, he headed into his office and turned on the computer and the gas fireplace. He stared at the fire until the computer finished its bootup.

After fifteen minutes on his legal software, Milo was puzzled. He couldn't find a lawsuit between Harper Gain and Patsy Rand or Patsy Nethercamp—not back in the eighties, not now. Thinking he was doing something wrong, he called

Saul Feinberg—former client and long-time poker buddy—hoping to catch him in his mobile legal office.

"Saul, I'm on Lexis..."

Feinberg interrupted, "I'm impressed."

"I'm a detective. I have subscriptions to lots of things." Why do you think I was broke all the time?"

"I have a half hour. What's your problem?"

"I've looked for a lawsuit between Patsy Rand or Nethercamp and Harper Gain or his company Tettegouch Software—*Tettegouch* with an 'e' on the end and without. Nothing."

"I have a couple of other databases—which court?" Feinberg asked.

"What?"

"Where was the lawsuit filed?"

"Crap. I don't know," Milo said.

"Let's assume it was filed in Minnesota. I'll start with the Twin Cities because that's where Harper Gain lived, and that's where Tettegouch Software is headquartered."

"Why does everyone know so much about this guy but me?" Milo complained.

"Because most people haven't lived in a small cave for the past ten years—this year not included," Feinberg said, putting Milo on hold. After about five minutes of *Stairway to Heaven*, Feinberg came back on the line.

"'Stairway to Heaven'? Really?" Milo complained.

"It's soothing. Classic and edgy. It tells the client who I am. Are you interested in what I found?"

"Yes, my classic, edgy friend," Milo snarked.

"No lawsuit with those principals."

"Are you sure? Harper Gain's kid thinks there was." Milo was puzzled.

"The lawsuit could have been a threat, and this Rand person folded. The suit was never filed. It happens all the time."

"Thanks Saul."

"Is the card game at your place on Sunday?" Saul asked.

"Nope. Creedence's."

"Great. Gotta go."

Squeak, announcing his approach with a trill, jumped up on Milo's desk using Milo's lap as a launching pad. This was new. The sleek, shiny, fur ball settled between the edge of the desk and the keyboard forcing Milo to reach over the purring cat to continue his research. Milo backspaced over Patsy Rand's name, erasing it as Squeak got up, stretched, and stepped on the enter key.

"Doing your own research, Mr. Cat?" Milo asked. The cat sniffed Milo's nose, squeaked, and stretched out on the desk. His work here was finished.

Milo looked at the screen to assess the damage. It now contained all of the lawsuits filed against Harper Gain since the early eighties. One name stood out.

"Son of a bitch," Milo said to himself before saying, "Good job Squeak!" Milo downloaded the lawsuits and emailed them to White under the heading, *GET A LOAD OF THESE!*.

His phone began playing 'Uptown Girl.' Milo smiled. It was the ringtone he reserved for Mary Alice Bonner. "Hey. What's up?"

"I need an escort."

"I can be an escort," Milo joked.

Mary Alice laughed. "There's a fall festival tomorrow at Chester Bowl, and I'm the head of the Chester Bowl Citizen's Committee. The fall festival is our major fundraiser to pay for outdoor sports equipment for kids. In the past, I've gone with Richard, but he just told me he'll be out of town."

"So, the part of Richard will be played by Milo Rathkey?"

"You catch on fast. Pick me up at eleven."

"Yes ma'am."

"One other thing. For a part of the time I will be glad-handing with politicos and the wealthy."

"I get it. I need to amuse myself."

"This is working so well."

"You *will* have to talk to me though—I'm wealthy."

"So you are. I keep forgetting."

Milo wasn't sure if that was good or not. Mary Alice was always a puzzle.

"See you at eleven. Bring that Mercedes and think about how much you're going to donate," Mary Alice said, as she hung up.

A cloud came over Milo's mood. He remembered another fete, the Paul Bunyan Festival in Brainerd more than ten years ago. A major miscommunication between him and his ex-wife, Jen, had led to their final fight—an uncomfortable silence. She was looking forward to him taking her to the festival—as if it was a date—but he didn't get it. He had signed up to work the festival as security, thinking she would like the extra cash. He had left the check on their kitchen table. She never touched it. Several weeks later Jen announced she was leaving him. Milo took a deep breath. He would like to think that he was smarter now.

18

White finished the lawsuits Milo had sent to her, sat back, shook her head, and called Milo. "You were right. I never would have thought Dr. Charles Carlson was the cousin of Gain's dead partner Mark Carlson. But according to these lawsuits you sent me, he sued Harper Gain for a share of the company. Good work."

"I can't take credit. Squeak the cat did it," Milo said.

"Your cat does your research?"

"Cats—Annie did the same thing nine months ago. I turn on the computer and let them go to work."

"Well, those kittens on the keys can't do all your work. Tomorrow we are going to do second interviews with both Gain and Carlson," White directed.

"On Sunday?"

White had already hung up.

§

The gate was open. Milo was expected. The Mercedes cruised under the portico to a waiting figure in a bright red sweater. *Mary Alice wouldn't get lost in any crowd.*

"I love this car!" Mary Alice said, slipping into the leather seat opposite Milo.

"I was going to open the door for you," Milo complained.

Mary Alice smiled and touched his arm. "You can be chivalrous later. Right now, I need to get to the festival."

Milo headed out of the estate. "I practiced putting the top up in case it rained."

Mary Alice looked up at the cloudless blue sky. "Glad you came prepared, but I think we're safe for now. So, anything new at Lakesong? I like to keep track of the neighborhood."

"We have another cat," Milo said.

"You bought a cat? What happened to Annie?"

"Oh, she's still there, and we didn't *buy* the cat. He came in from the storm the other night. The door blew open, and all we saw were yellow eyes."

Mary Alice turned toward him. "A black cat?"

"Yeah. All he does is squeak, so that's what I call him. Sutherland calls him Dylan because Bob Dylan's song was playing during the storm," Milo explained.

"That's a story I want to hear, but your new cat's name is Jet. I'm glad you found him," Mary Alice said without further explanation.

"How do you know that?"

"I keep track of the neighborhood. A black cat named Jet belonged to Emma Worthington. She was eighty three when she adopted Jet as a kitten—optimistic, I know. She lived on the Hawthorn estate up the shore from Lakesong."

"Lived?"

"Her death surprised us all. In all of comings and goings, Jet wandered out. We were all worried about him. He would have been a tasty morsel during the gathering of hawks and falcons over Hawk Ridge. I'm glad he has a home again."

"We gave him shelter from the storm." Milo glanced at Mary Alice.

Turing her blue eyes him, and she nodded. "I get it. That was the song that was playing. Spooky—in a good way."

"Sutherland mentioned something about a chip and finding his owner. I'm sure the relatives will want him."

Mary Alice patted his hand. "The relatives are gone. The estate is up for sale. I'm sure Jet is all yours." As Milo was digesting this news, Mary Alice interrupted with practical information. "We're getting close. I have a pass so we can park in the Chester Bowl parking lot."

Milo gunned the Mercedes up 21st Avenue East before cutting across Woodland. Mary Alice directed him to the tiny parking lot in Chester Park. An attendant stopped them until she flashed her parking pass. Milo, still unused to being a VIP, had to admit it beat walking from the university parking lot or waiting for a shuttle.

As they got out and started hiking toward the festival, Mary Alice explained how the day was going to work. "I need to go greet people, hug, shake hands, pave the way for donations. Here are your options: You can stay with me or go enjoy the festival and check in from time to time—your choice."

Milo decided to start with Mary Alice and see how it went. Some of the people from the Country Club knew Milo as Mary Alice's tennis partner, but eyebrows raised to see him with her sans racket. After a couple of these interactions, he opted to enjoy the festival on his own and check in with the lady-in-red from time to time. Wandering through the tented tables, his eyes skimmed over the many handmade crafts, pumpkin patches, and face painters creating sparkling rainbows or ferocious daggers. Wanting neither, Milo parked himself on a bale of hay near a maple-cotton-candy stand. He sat enjoying the crisp temperatures, cloudless blue skies, and bluegrass band playing in the background. Unaware of the possible damage bailed hay could be doing to his seldom-worn N&J slacks, he watched Mary Alice work the crowd. This was the Mary Alice—minus the Vera Wang gown—he first met nine months ago at her New Year's Eve party. Of course, her black slacks and long red cardigan sweater set could have been Vera Wang. Milo had no idea.

Finishing his snack, he returned to her side between donor handshakes—checking in as he promised. She smiled her 'you're-the-most important-person-in-the-world' smile. "Well, Mr. Milo Rathkey, have you decided how much you are going to pledge?"

"Me?" he asked.

"Yes. I told you I'd ask."

"Okay, you tell me. How much am I going to pledge?" Milo knew she said something, but he was lost again in the blue eyes. All he could muster was, "I didn't bring my checkbook."

Mary Alice laughed. "That's okay. I know where you live." Taking his arm, she continued, "Walk me around so we can see if I missed anybody."

"I can't identify donor types, but I have scoped out the festival and found the following: maple cotton candy—five stars; chili dogs and candied apples—definitely worth trying; oatmeal-lavender soap and tree stumps with clocks in the center—not my style; six ears of corn for a buck-and-a-quarter. So far no pickpockets."

She stared at him.

"It's what I used to do at festivals when I was a cop."

"How do you spot a pickpocket?"

"I'm not telling. You could become a pickpocket I can't spot."

Mary Alice smiled as she directed Milo to an eccentric-looking older woman in a straw hat and overalls. Mary Alice introduced her as Mille Greysolon. "Mille, you and Milo are neighbors."

"Neighbors?" Mille asked.

"Milo inherited half of Lakesong not quite a year ago," Mary Alice explained.

"Oh, only a year? It's an old money neighborhood. Contact me again in fifty years," Mille said.

"Don't I get any credit for the time the McKnights have lived there?" Milo asked.

"John McKnight moved in only forty-some years ago—practically a newbie. As Sutherland was born there, we give him a pass."

Milo decided he liked Mille and thought he would like talking to her over the fence—if Lakesong had a mutual fence, and if he could even see her house from his. He couldn't. Leaving Mary Alice to her fundraising, Milo headed to the coffee booth.

Avoiding the pumpkin-spiced lattes and honeybun espressos, Milo ordered his plain, medium coffee with cream. He found a corn-cob-decorated wooden box to sit on and proceeded to people watch—family groups with kids pulling in opposite directions, strollers with fall souvenirs, and couples walking hand in hand. Two familiar faces caught his eye.

Taking a sip of coffee, he watched Erin Cohn and Liam Johansson in mid hug. Their animated conversation included several ever-so-slight touches Erin placed on Liam's arm. *These two are more than passing friends,* Milo thought. He was wondering if he was looking at a current affair or a past relationship. Erin and Liam began walking through the crowd. Intrigued, Milo got up and followed. At the south entrance they stopped, linked hands for a moment, and then parted. Milo could see Erin walking toward her travel-agency booth and her husband. Liam made a sharp left. Milo followed. Liam wound his way to the Duluth Forestry Department booth. Milo doubled back in search of Mary Alice.

He found her poised on a bench, chatting with her former tennis partner Brad Nelson. Seeing Milo, she smiled, stood up, and put her arm through his. "I would like that chili dog," she said.

"I know where that is. Follow me," Milo said, leading Mary Alice away from tall, handsome, Nelson who stared at the retreating couple in disbelief.

Mary Alice's dog was smothered in chili, onions, and cheese. Milo, being cautious, opted for a plain dog with a splash of ketchup and mustard. They sat down at a nearby picnic table.

"Kind of a naked dog you have there," Mary Alice joked.

"I'm hoping to not wear the ketchup and mustard. If I had what you're having, I'd need a hazmat suit." Milo looked down at his charcoal V-neck sweater.

"It's all in the wrist," she joked, taking a bite of her chili dog and dabbing the corners of her mouth with her napkin. "See? No dripping."

"I'm impressed," Milo said, as, on cue, a small drip of mustard left his hotdog and fell onto his slacks. Laughing as hard as he had ever seen her laugh, Mary Alice handed Milo a napkin. "Dab away Milo, dab away."

"I'm a pro dabber."

Without further incident, they finished their food and walked the grounds. Mary Alice bought a few items from longtime vendors whom she conversed with as friends—no donor talk. After paying for two bars of honey-lavender soap, Milo stopped and asked Mary Alice to wait for a second. Stepping in front of a young man dressed in a long-sleeved, white polo shirt and tan slacks, Milo said, smiling, "You need to give that man back his wallet in five seconds, or I'm going to arrest you."

Mary Alice was stunned. She wondered if Milo had lost his mind. She hadn't seen anything amiss.

"I don't know what you're talking about, Dude," the young man sputtered.

"Three...two..."

"Stop!" the man, said producing a wallet from his front pocket. "All I did was pick this up off the ground."

"Then return it to the man standing over there."

Turning to his mark, the young man shouted, "Sir, I think you dropped your wallet."

After the wallet was returned Milo said, "Now get out of here and don't come back. This is your only free pass. I have your picture; it can become your mug shot."

The young man careened through the crowd toward the exit.

Mary Alice caught up to Milo. "Old habits?" she questioned.

"It's in the DNA."

Milo felt a hand on his shoulder and heard a familiar voice say, "The man was trying to make a living." Turning he saw Saul Feinberg with an attractive brunette.

"Saul, Kim how are you?" Mary Alice said, hugging them both.

"I'm Milo Rathkey," Milo extended his hand to Kim. "I save Saul's failing law practice almost every week."

Kim laughed. "I knew someone had to."

"I'm sorry," Mary Alice said. "I thought you two knew each other."

"Have the maple cotton candy. It's delicious," Milo advised.

At Saul's insistence Mary Alice and Milo agreed to meet them later that evening for dinner at J J Astor, the revolving restaurant at the top of the Radisson Hotel.

On the way home, Milo asked, "Should I have known Kim?"

Mary Alice said, "My New Year's Eve party—Kim and Saul were dancing partners."

"Oh! The backless-dress lady!"

Mary Alice looked at him. "Men have the strangest way of remembering women. Although backless-dress-lady is charming, her real name is Kimberly McKenna. Rather pretty, don't you think?"

"I didn't notice." Milo sensed a trap.

Mary Alice tilted her head and smiled. "The man who sees a pickpocket in a crowd doesn't notice a pretty woman in front of him. Nice try. She's one of the best defense attorneys in the state. I wonder why she's in town."

"Where does she live?"

"Minneapolis? St. Paul? I'm not sure."

19

A myriad of thoughts drifted through Milo's brain as he floated in Lakesong's swimming pool staring through the pool's glass dome at the gray, hazy sky: thoughts about whether this fog would burn off and break into a beautiful fall day; amusement at Brad Nelson's shocked faced yesterday when Mary Alice made it clear she was with Milo; perplexity over the fact that Squeak, aka Dylan, is in fact named Jet, and according to Mary Alice, is now a permanent resident of Lakesong.

Milo flipped over and began a lazy breaststroke. Midway through the third lap, his thoughts turned to lawsuits. Searching only Harper Gain, he found Dr. Carlson. What would he find out searching only Patsy Nethercamp nèe Rand?

Leaving the pool and heading upstairs, Milo wanted nothing more than to spend the day in an old shirt and jeans but this was a murder investigation. Robin had scheduled second interviews with Peter Gain and Dr. Carlson about the lawsuits. Remembering his go-to dress slacks were in the dirty-laundry hamper soiled with mustard stains, he explored the N&J portion of his gentleman's closet and found two never-worn pairs of slacks hidden in a garment bag.

Neither Annie nor Jet joined Milo at the computer this morning. Annie knew it was Sunday—no Martha—no bacon. Jet experienced his first generous Sunday morning feed at the hands of young Darian who did his job well. Both cats were snoozing.

Using the cat's technique, Milo entered only Patsy's name and came up with many lawsuits—only two interested him. Patsy Nethercamp vs Ron Bello for libel, and a more recent lawsuit Ron Bello vs Patsy Rand for slander. The first—filed in 1997—was thrown out for lack of evidence. The second was still ongoing. He sent the file to Robin.

§

White took a sip of her Sunday treat—store bought-car-amel-latte macchiato. She needed the espresso rush this morning. Through force of habit, her glance shot to Gramm's office, waiting to hear him call her in at any moment. His office was dark, a reminder that she was in charge.

"Hi Boss!" Preston said, as she arrived and sat down at her desk.

White didn't respond at first, unused to being called boss. "Oh hey. I'm going over these *Carlson vs Gain* lawsuits Milo sent me. Interesting reading."

"Thanks for sending them to me," Preston said. "I read them last night. I wonder why these weren't mentioned when we interviewed these guys?"

"That's exactly what we're going to find out today," White said.

Preston looked around the bullpen area. "Is Mr. Rathkey joining us?"

White smiled. "He is. He sent me another lawsuit to read. He's stopping off at Ilene's bakery. I told him to pick up some goodies."

"I like Ilene's!" Preston said.

"Don't we all."

"Now I'm glad I didn't have time to grab a gas-station donut." Preston said.

White laughed. She too had been running a little late but still stopped off and got her coffee. Sometimes it's good to be the boss.

§

Milo pulled the repaired Honda up to Ilene's. Ilene got the late-Sunday-morning church crowd and then closed at one o'clock. Beating the church crowd was a must or all of the cream puffs would be gone.

"My favorite private detective!" Ilene shouted as Milo walked in. It was fall and Ilene's hair streaks had gone from summer white to fall orange.

"I need a cup of coffee and a cream puff," Milo said, sitting down at his preferred table near the back.

Ilene came over with two cups of coffee and Milo's cream puff.

"I need a to-go box with four cream puffs, two apple strudels, and two bear claws."

"That's only eight. You get a deal with twelve."

"A couple of cinnamon rolls and eclairs."

"You know those cream puffs need to be refrigerated unless they're eaten right away," Ilene advised.

Milo looked up from his coffee.

"Sorry. I forgot who I was talking to. Of course, they'll be eaten right away," Ilene said, adding, "This to-go box is not usual cop donuts."

"I'm not a cop; I'm a consultant. This is a box of consultant donuts."

"I miss your fuzzy thinking."

"How's the guy who took over my old place?" Milo asked, referring to the new tenant who rented his old office and living space that he leased from Ilene for ten years before moving to Lakesong.

"He pays for his pastries, gets the rent in on time, and never complains."

"Sounds like a gem."

"If you must know, it's creepy."

"Well, you told me he did remodel on his dime."

"Yeah, and that's even creepier. I miss you Milo."

§

Milo arrived at the cop shop, pastries in hand. One bear claw went to the desk sergeant. The rest he dropped on an empty desk near White with the instruction to go easy on the cream puffs.

"In case you didn't know," White said to Preston, "Milo is cream-puff fueled."

"That's okay," Preston said, looking over the choices. "I'm cinnamon-rolled fueled."

Milo saw White studying the twenty-or-so pages of the Bello-Rand lawsuits. "Find anything?"

"Is that all these suspects do is sue each other?" White asked.

"More popular than poker," Milo said, remembering it was Sunday—poker night at Creedence Durant's. Milo saw a diagram of Linda Johansson's house on White's desk. He picked it up. Each person was color coded and his or her movements were detailed on the diagram.

Noticing Milo staring at her work, White explained, "I wanted to see who could have picked up the drink and taken it to the victim."

"And?"

White sighed. "I've eliminated Amy and Linda Johansson because they didn't leave the dining room. Everyone else had an opportunity to travel from the bar to the victim unseen."

"Well, you eliminated two. Congratulations," Milo said.

"I wish. If there was a conspiracy, Linda Johansson could be working with Liam. The water jug break could have been a purposeful diversion."

"Let's arrest Amy," Milo joked. "What's on tap for today?"

"Carlson will be in at eleven. Peter Gain has requested that his lawyer be present. His lawyer is not local so we won't talk to him until Monday."

"Lawyering up? Already?" Milo asked.

White shrugged. "He's rich. The rich do stuff like that—present company excluded."

Preston finished her cinnamon roll as White continued the day's dance card. "Crystal Bower will be coming by at one. That should do it. Tomorrow we have the Rand Memorial Service at the Anderson Funeral home. After that Peter Gain said he and his lawyer will be available."

"I got two more," Milo said.

"Two more what?"

"People to talk to?"

White listened.

"I was at the Chester Bowl Fall Festival yesterday..."

"Excuse me!" White interrupted. "For a second, I thought you said you were at a fall festival yesterday."

"I had a hunger for cheese on a stick. Anyway, I saw Liam Johansson walking with Erin Cohen."

"To grab a Gramm word, were they canoodling?"

Preston grabbed her phone and Googled the word *canoodle*.

"They were chummy," Milo said.

White sighed. "Tomorrow will be busy."

§

Dr. Carlson arrived on time and already wanted to leave. "Will this take long? I have a two o'clock tee time."

White gave him no assurances as she guided him into an interview room. He looked around at the plain surroundings.

253

"I've seen places like this on television. Are you going to beat a confession out of me?"

White smiled. "If you would like to confess, go right ahead."

"I'll pass," Carlson said as he carefully removed his golfing hat and threw it on the table. "What can I clear up?"

Milo ran his fingers through his thick curly hair. *I may have lumps buddy, but at least I don't need hair plugs.*

White slid the two lawsuits over to him. "You sued Harper Gain twice. Once in 1990 and again recently. In both suits you state Gain's late partner, Mark Carlson, was your cousin. Care to explain?"

Carlson twisted his diamond stud earring as he looked through the papers and then at White and Milo. "This has nothing to do with Patsy Rand's death. Why do you care about these lawsuits, both of which I dropped?"

Milo slid his copy of Patsy Rand's book across the table to Carlson, waiting for a reaction.

"Where did you get that?" Carlson asked, again pulling on his earlobe.

"You recognize it?" Milo asked.

"No, but I can read. It's some book Patsy Rand wrote."

White jumped in. "Patsy Rand? The cover says Patsy Nethercamp."

Carlson leaned back. "I made an assumption."

White stared at Carlson for several seconds before challenging, "You know about this book."

"Okay, okay. Patsy showed me her book several months ago. She thought it would help in my lawsuit against Harper Gain," he said, shoving the papers back to White. "I told her she was too late. Peter Gain and I were coming to a mutual agreement. We did. Everything is being settled out of court. I didn't need her help." Carlson smiled at the thought of his windfall.

"From what we know about the victim, altruism was not her strong suit. When she offered to help you, what did she want in return?" White asked.

"Money! Money to republish this book," he said, rapping on the cover with his knuckles. "But, like I said, she was too late. I didn't need her or her book. Peter Gain and I reached an understanding."

"Understanding? Agreement? What are we talking about here?" White asked.

"Settlement. Money."

"How much?" Milo asked.

"I'm not at liberty to say, but I can tell you it's substantial. Peter had the good sense to sit down and talk to me. We quickly worked out an agreement. His father, Harper, never came down from his ivory tower to meet with me or my lawyers."

"You lied to us about your card being in Rand's purse. She wasn't seeking Botox," White said.

Dr. Carlson drew himself up. "I didn't lie. She saw me professionally."

"What for?" White asked.

"HIPPA rules. I can't tell you. Are we done here?"

White stood, said they were done for now, but cautioned Carlson to remain available. Milo wished him a good golf game.

"No motive there," Preston said as they returned the bullpen area.

"Early yet," Milo corrected. "Remember the break-ins at Rand's house and car. Someone is collecting this book. He was surprised we had a copy."

"But why would he care?" Preston persisted.

"Just because we don't know, doesn't mean there isn't a reason."

§

Crystal Bower was a half-hour late. As she strode into the cop shop, Milo thought she looked incomplete without her long, lanky dog. Pushing her hair off of her face, Bower said, "Sorry I'm late. Azin was feeling frisky today—long run by the lake."

Remembering the dog's lazy attitude, Milo doubted the story.

White showed little interest in her excuses and led Bower into the interview room. "This room needs work," Bower said, looking at the industrial gray walls. "An accent here or there would improve the ambiance of this room."

"It works for us," White said.

Milo put the book on the table.

Bower almost jumped out of her seat. "Oh my God! Where did you get that?"

"Surprised to see it?" Milo asked.

"Yes! It's been ages." She took the book and fanned through it stopping on the pictures. Milo noticed she lingered on the photo of her and Harper Gain.

White—who had not yet read through the book—asked about the picture.

Bower smiled sadly and moved her hand over the picture. "It's been so long since I've seen these pictures. This one of me and Harper back in college was mine. One that Patsy stole."

"She did more than that," Milo persisted, "but you know that."

Bower looked up at him wondering how to respond. "I don't know what you're talking about."

Milo took the book, turned back several chapters and read, "Gain split up from his girlfriend because of her dependence on cocaine..."

"That doesn't say it's me."

"Is it you?" White asked,

Milo added, "Rand does label you as Harper Gain's girlfriend in the picture."

Bower pursed her lips. "I wasn't dependent on cocaine. It was the eighties. Cocaine was a party drug. I told you Harper and I split up because I came in second to the video games."

"Your current employer may not approve of your party-drug past," White persisted.

"Do you think I would kill her because thirty years ago I used a party drug? No! I'm up for a promotion—VP of Sales—and I've already cleared a background check."

"Would you have cleared that background check if Rand's book had been published?"

Bower laughed. "Of course. Even if my bosses read the book and made the connection, no one cares what happened at parties thirty years ago, unless I killed a somebody."

"Did you kill her?" White asked.

"No!"

After Bower left, Milo gave White his copy of the book. "Enjoy Rand's rantings."

§

"What the hell is this?" Gramm asked, looking at a minuscule white-something framed, hung, and top-lit above Creedence Durant's fireplace mantle. He moved closer and squinted, but it didn't help identify the object.

With pride, Creedence gushed, "That is my copy of the toe bone of a small raptor dinosaur found this summer in Montana." Being an amateur paleontologist, Creedence had numerous artifacts that he collected on his digs over years, but this small bone had a place of prominence.

"Why don't we have the toe bone of a limping dinosaur over our fireplace?" Milo asked Sutherland.

"What makes you think he's limping?" Sutherland questioned.

"Because we have one of his toes," Milo explained.

"Okay funny guys," Creedence said. "This toe belongs to a small, foot-high raptor named Duranticus, after its discoverer."

"Duranticus? As in Creedence Durant—icus?" Feinberg asked.

Creedence's cherub face beamed.

"I'm impressed. You found a new species?"

"Yes, I did," Creedence bragged.

"A foot high?" Gramm questioned. "With all those big dinosaurs walking around, you should have named this one squashedasouras."

"Ha ha," Creedence mocked. "He may be small, but if you went back to his time, he and his buddies would gnaw you down to bones before any of the big guys even knew you were in the neighborhood."

"Could be a she," Gramm said, proud of the gender-neutrality training he was getting from Robin.

"With dinosaurs that's a tricky question. We don't have their DNA, and even if we did, unlike mammals they…"

"Let's play cards," Milo suggested. As they all moved to the dining room, Creedence continued to explain dinosaur genetic sexual traits, though no one was listening.

Creedence's 1890s, three-story barn-like house featured original tall wainscoting in the dining room that complemented the round oak pedestal table. Creedence had placed tonight's snacks on a matching oak sideboard.

"Gentlemen," Creedence said, "as long as no one cares about the sex-life of Montana dinosaurs, let me introduce you to the poker snacks from Montana."

"You have our attention," Milo said.

"We have bison and elk sliders with swiss cheese, caramelized onions, and bacon jam; huckleberry squares, garlic cheese curds…"

"How do we know these aren't Wisconsin cheese curds and you're lying?" Feinberg asked.

"I hate when people lie," Gramm grumbled.

Milo joined in. "They do look like Wisconsin curds."

Creedence ignored them. "We also have Montana beef jerky. All of these foods kept me going on the dig where I found my dinosaur, Duranticus, which, by the way, a finding that has failed to gain the proper group adulation with the exception of Saul."

"Congratulations," Sutherland said.

"Way to go," Feinberg chimed in.

"Nice toe," Milo added.

They all looked at Milo. "What? Whaddaya you say when someone finds a toe?"

Creedence sighed. "I have a book of congratulatory telegrams from around the world."

"Did the dinosaur send one?" Milo asked.

"Let's play cards," Creedence suggested, admitting defeat but enjoying the chiding.

Sitting down, Gramm began his usual finger-stretching exercises. "I'm well-rested. I've got my lucky socks. I fear no evil and I'm eating elk sliders, which are good by the way."

The huckleberry squares met with equal appreciation.

Before dealing, Creedence pointed out that he had chokecherry wine, and he offered to make chokecherry spritzers. Milo set the tone by saying he was going to stick to his Guinness. Sutherland—ever the gentleman—tried the spritzer, but only one, before switching to Chardonnay. Creedence shuffled the cards and called seven card stud, duces wild.

Gramm groaned. "Why must we have wild cards? I hate wild cards."

"Then don't call any when you deal," Milo chided.

Sutherland, just back from his trip to the Cities, looked a little blurry eyed while Saul Feinberg speared a fork full of cheese curds.

Gramm had a deuce up. Checking his down cards, he found one more. Suddenly, wild cards weren't so bad.

"So how was the Katy Perry concert?" Milo asked Sutherland, drawing stares from the others.

"Excellent. How was your trip to the Chester Park Fall Festival?" Sutherland countered.

"I was at the Chester Park Festival," Feinberg said.

"Anybody else see Katy Perry?" Milo quizzed.

Ernie chimed in, "Look, if it's not Taylor Swift, I'm not going."

The room fell silent as everyone now stared at Gramm, shocked he knew Taylor Swift.

"What? I've got grandchildren. They educate me," Gramm said, as he bid twenty-five cents which sent up a howl from the group."

"A bluff? Already? We just sat down," Creedence complained, pushing his glasses up the bridge of his nose. Milo had decided that this repetitive movement wasn't a tell—it was a nervous habit.

"It will cost you twenty five cents to find out." Gramm smiled.

Sutherland threw in a quarter chip as did Creedence, Feinberg, and Rathkey.

Creedence dealt another card up.

"A dime," Gramm said dropping his chip into the pot.

"The big spender has settled on down," Milo joked.

Gramm began his usual oh-poor-me rant. "With all you millionaires at the table, I have to employ strategy."

"I'm not a millionaire," Creedence protested.

Gramm looked at the other three. "Anyone else? Anyone? Nobody? I rest my case. With the exception of poverty-stricken Duranticus here, I'm at a table of millionaires. Could someone pass one of the bison sliders?"

Saul pointed out that if Milo had not become a millionaire by accident, they'd be up in that collective clutter of crap he called an apartment."

"By accident?" Milo complained. He was ignored.

"Good point, Saul," Ernie agreed. "Instead of this delicious bison slider, we'd be eating Milo's four-week-old generic chips."

"And listeria-laden dip," Feinberg added.

"Oh my God, and to think you all survived. It was a miracle. Sutherland, do you want to complain about my folding chairs? No one has done that yet."

Sutherland took the diplomatic route." I did not experience them, so I cannot speak to the issue."

The comment took Milo by surprise. He had forgotten that Sutherland was not part of the game at this time last year.

Everyone kicked in a dime and received his next card. Ernie got another deuce. He was not pleased. It showed his hand to be powerful with two wildcards showing. His next bid of a dime was met with stony silence.

"The pot is yours," Milo said.

"Oh, come on. One of you millionaires can take a chance."

Feinberg shook his head. "You've got two wildcards up. I'm not contributing to the Gramm retirement fund."

"I hate these wildcard games!" Ernie said pulling in his winnings.

"Ernie, I've never known you to be well rested," Creedence said as Feinberg dealt the cards and called Wild Widow.

"What?"

"You said you were well rested. Why?"

"Oh yeah. I don't have any cases at the moment, unless you consider Milo getting shot at a case," Ernie cracked.

"What?" Creedence and Feinberg exclaimed at the same time.

"It's a long story," Milo said, shooting Ernie a nasty look. "A retired cop shot up the Honda."

"While you were in it?" Creedence asked.

"Yeah, I was driving."

Ernie jumped back in, "We are only going to charge the guy with jay-walking or loitering."

Feinberg laughed. "He tried to take out Milo's Honda? I'd let him walk."

"Yeah, we see it as public beautification," Ernie joked.

"Ha ha," Milo feigned. "He failed. My Honda has been fixed—as beautiful as ever."

Feinberg had dealt the first four cards to each player and then a single card up. It was the four of spades.

"What the hell are you doing?" Ernie demanded.

"It's Wild Widow. Five card draw, but after I deal the fourth card, the next one up is the wild card. It's a four, so the remaining fours are wild," Feinberg explained.

Everyone looked again at his hand. Feinberg dealt each player one more card. Milo started the first round of bids at a dime.

Feinberg asked the particulars of the cop and his motive for shooting at Milo. Both Milo and Ernie filled him in on the real story. By the time the bid got around the table, Gramm was looking at a quarter and folded. The remaining four players dropped cards and were dealt new ones.

"How come you're not investigating the death of that blog woman, Patsy Rand?" Feinberg asked Gramm.

Gramm arranged his chips. "Amy was there when the woman died. My partner, Sergeant White, is handling the investigation along with some minor department consultants."

Feinberg sorted his new cards, trying to hide the fact that he filled an inside straight. "By minor, you must mean Milo."

"He does," Milo said, trying to hide the fact that his hand sucked. A new round of bidding began. Feinberg did not pursue the matter of Patsy Rand any further which surprised Milo. Saul was always curious, especially about murder.

Saul's straight took the hand.

Milo grabbed the cards, shuffled and called five card stud, one-eyed royals wild. Gramm groaned. Creedence looked confused.

Sutherland explained, "Three face cards show only one eye: Jack of Spades , Jack of Hearts, and King of Diamonds. They're wild."

"Why not cards that Milo has spilled mustard on?" Gramm cracked.

Milo looked down at his shirt. He had done it again.

20

Sutherland did a double take as Milo sat down to breakfast. "Coat and tie—what's the occasion?"

"I'm working a funeral," Milo said, pouring his coffee as a steady rain was plinking against the windows of the morning room. "Kind of a perfect day for it."

Martha came over with his breakfast, offering him an extra cloth napkin to put over the front of his shirt. "In case you spill," she said.

"Spill? Me?" Milo joked, knowing full well that the napkin was necessary.

Annie ate her offering of Milo's bacon and headed to the hearth room where Martha had lit a fire to take the dampness out of the kitchen. Jet had gobbled down his cat food and squeaked at Martha for more. He was ignored.

"Why do the police go to those things?" Sutherland asked. "What do you expect to happen?"

"Full confession every time."

"So, it's going to be that kind of a morning. Fine," Sutherland sighed.

Martha came back into the morning room handing both Milo and Sutherland three estimates for remodeling the cottage attic. "They're all pretty close in price," she said.

"Whichever one you prefer," Sutherland said. "Tell Agnes."

"You can't tell her to tell Agnes. I have to tell her to tell Agnes. Agnes works for me. She just goes to random art galleries with you," Milo said.

Sutherland smiled. "My mistake. You tell her to tell Agnes."

Milo looked over the bids. "I don't see adding an overhead electric train track anywhere on these bids."

Martha shook her head. "No, you won't. This is for walls, floors, bathrooms, closets, and paint, not electric trains!"

Milo looked up. "Darian's a growing boy. He needs a suspended electric train."

"I agree." Sutherland said.

"Growing boys need nutrition and boundaries."

Milo and Sutherland looked at each other and shook their heads.

"This will be me heading back to the kitchen," Martha said. Next you'll get him a chemistry set and we'll all go up in flames."

"Not a bad idea!" Milo shouted. "Sutherland write down chemistry set—not the flames part."

Martha came back into the morning room. "Speaking of boys and their toys. Agnes tells me we now have a scoreboard for the basketball court."

"Oh yeah, Ed Patupick, our electronics go-to guy, installed it," Sutherland acknowledged. "Give me your phone, Milo."

"Why?"

"I need to install the scoreboard app. It works on Bluetooth. You get to be our scorekeeper."

"I'm in," said Milo, handing Sutherland his phone. "When's the next game?"

"How about tonight? Martha?"

Martha laughed. "I'll check with Agnes' and Jamal's schedule."

"I saw Jamal when I came home yesterday," Sutherland said. "He said he's clear."

"I'll double check the real schedule, not Jamal's fourteen-year-old brain," Martha said, returning again to the kitchen.

Milo was pushing the horn button on his new app.

"You have to marry it to the scoreboard, and right now you're too far away."

"I knew that," Milo said, pushing the horn button one last time.

§

White closed her umbrella as she and Preston prepared to enter the Anderson Funeral Home, an old Victorian house complete with turrets, towers, and wrap-around porches. Looking at the building, Preston asked, "Are we going to a funeral or high tea?"

White decided that Preston and her sarcasm were fitting in.

The first floor had been broken up into several viewing-rooms and offices. White and Preston were directed into one of the smaller viewing rooms. The two walked in and slipped into chairs at the back, saving one for Milo.

Preston began to identify some of the arrivals typing their names into her notes. Leaning over to White she whispered, "I don't know half these people."

"They're gawkers," White said.

Amy Gramm was surprised as the room began to fill up. Funeral-home staff scurried for more chairs.

Milo was one of the last to arrive, sliding in next to White. He took in the crowd and the single picture of Patsy Rand propped up on an easel at the front of the room. Crystal, who was sitting next to Amy, asked about the picture. Amy leaned over and whispered, "Downloaded from her webpage." Amy stood up and walked to the podium. The room fell silent.

"Welcome. We are here today to remember Patsy Rand. I didn't know Patsy well, but I know she loved to read and was an active contributor to our book club. I appreciated her contributions to our discussions. As many of you know Patsy was also an active blogger and book critic." Amy cleared her throat. "None of us are perfect people, including Patsy. I'm hoping we can remember Patsy's positive contributions to our lives. I would like to start our remembrances with Patsy's longtime friend, Crystal Bower."

Crystal nodded at Amy as she took her place at the podium. "Patsy and I were friends in college, and we remained friends off and on." She turned to the picture of Pasty. "I don't regret meeting you. I regret trusting you and thinking you were someone different." Crystal turned back to address the gathering. "Whatever we thought of her, she didn't deserve to die the way she did."

White whispered to Milo, "So sweet."

Milo whispered back, "Sugared aconite, perhaps?"

Dr. Charles Carlson came up next. Taking a few moments to look over the crowd, he placed his hands on the side of the podium. "I agree with my fellow book-club member, Crystal. Patsy deserved better. In our years on this Earth, we all try to do the best we can. I like to think that Patsy was trying her best too. As Amy said, let's all remember her in a positive light today, as we would all want to be remembered."

Preston whispered to White, "Are we getting anything?"

White whispered back, "It's still early." *Good God, I'm uttering Grammisms. I wonder if my eyebrows are getting bushy?* she thought, running a finger over both of them.

Evelyn Chen marched up to the front of the room before Dr. Carlson finished. She took his place at the podium and announced, "Patsy Rand was a nasty, vindictive person for all of the years I knew her. Let's hope she had time to repent before she left this Earth. That's as positive and I can get." With murmurs from the crowd, her small frame sped toward the back and out the door. She had said what she came to say.

Ron Bello ambled up next. "Patsy Rand, former prosecutor, blogger, and failed author was murdered at a local book club meeting last week. The world is a better place without her." With that he took his seat.

No one followed Bello for a few minutes. Amy was about to wrap up when a red-headed woman dressed in bold, houndstooth leggings and matching jacket came to the podium. Preston asked White if she recognized her. White shook her head.

"Hi," she waved. "I'm Arial Jenkins. I'm usually at all the book club meetings, but this month it fell on my new exercise night. I love book club meetings, but I also love yoga. The doctor says it's good for me, but if I had known there was going to be a murder I would have skipped yoga."

Amy groaned.

Arial thanked the group. No one was sure why.

Several other members of the book club came up to the podium to speak before Milo stood up and walked to the front of the room. Preston glanced at White who shrugged.

Adjusting the microphone and his tie, Milo began, "I never met Patsy Rand, but having just read her book, I can't help but feel hers was a scattered, tortured mind. I'm part of the team that is trying to find her killer, and I can assure you we will succeed. Thank you." Milo stepped away from the podium and retook his seat.

White looked at him.

Milo said, "Tie-clip-camera—got everyone but Evelyn."

Amy asked Ernie what that was about.

"I hope you smiled," Ernie said, "I think Milo was taking our picture with one of his toys."

After waiting a few more minutes, Amy got up and thanked everyone for coming. A few people remained to chat. Most got up and got on with their Monday. The rain had stopped. White, Milo, and Preston lingered in the parking lot. Peter Gain, who had attended, but did not speak, walked up to Dr. Carlson who was leaning against his car. They seemed surprisingly cordial. White expected animosity or at least distance between the two given the lawsuits. She nudged Milo. "Get a picture of this."

Milo again straightened his tie and pressed the button in his pocket capturing the two shaking hands and smiling.

Gramm stopped next to Milo and said, "I hope you got my good side."

"Sorry Ernie, I could only get you from the front, but Amy looked as beautiful as ever." Milo traversed the puddles as he moved toward the Honda wondering what about the memorial service bothered him other than Arial Jenkins preferring murder to yoga.

§

"What took you so long," Barry Cohen whined. "I'm hungry."

Erin defended herself. "You could see I was in a conversation. I was checking out my theory."

Barry emitted an exasperated huff. "What theory?"

"I told you. You never listen." She looked around then whispered, "It's my theory about who killed Patsy Rand. I told you about this person who was encamped across from the living room. If I'm right, my suspect could have gone across the hall to the living room any time, poisoned Patsy's drink, and sought refuge back in the bathroom. Right after Patsy was stricken, this person left the scene."

"So, who were you talking to?"

"I wanted to see if I was right. That night, I saw someone else go into the living room. I wanted to know if Patsy was okay at that time. I was assured she was. My theory is correct."

"Maybe that person did it," Barry conjectured.

Erin sighed. "Never! Even when you listen, you get it wrong."

"Tell the police after we go to lunch," he said.

Erin balked. "We don't have money for lunches, Barry!"

Barry bristled but said nothing.

Erin continued as she got behind the wheel of the two-payments-overdue car, "But we may have money for lunches soon. The friend I was talking to about my theory is looking for investments and wanted to know if we were interested in a partner. That's what took so long."

"An investor? Why would someone invest in a travel business going nowhere?" Barry rolled his eyes at his grim humor.

"People invest for all kinds of reasons. We were talking about Patsy and the conversation turned to investment. I've a meeting planned."

"Great! When?"

"I'm doing this on my own Barry. You don't need to know"

§

"How are we going to get your bow tie pictures?" White asked, as she and Milo sat down in Gramm's office.

Milo looked down, "Am I wearing a bow tie?"

White rolled her eyes, "Tie-clip pictures. Excuse me."

"They're on a computer gizmo. I handed it to one of the IT guys when I came in."

"By gizmo you mean memory card?" White questioned.

"Sure. Why not."

White changed the subject. "You know, we never considered book club members who were not at the meeting where Rand died."

Gramm was sitting behind his desk. "How could they have poisoned her?"

"Yeah, it makes no sense, but when that woman stood up and made her yoga excuse, I had a moment of panic," White said.

Gramm noticed that Milo seemed to be zoned out. "Milo?"

"Something's bothering me," Milo said.

Gramm's eyebrows arched upward. "Oh boy, here we go. I ask this knowing you don't know. What bothers you?"

Milo shrugged. "Something in the service bothers me. I don't know what."

"Was it the yoga lady?" White asked. "I enjoyed her, but should she be a suspect?"

"I have no idea," Milo insisted.

"Don't waste your time, Robin. It's stuck in the back of his brain. It'll worm it's way to the front soon enough."

"Did anyone count the cars in the parking lot, like Milo did up at Enger Tower?" White kidded referring to the Jessica Vogel murder from last summer.

"Cars! Parking!" Milo exclaimed, "Oh my God! That's... not it!"

Preston came in with the GrubHub-delivered lunches. "Let's see, a Cobb salad—that has to be Milo's."

Milo was about to protest when Preston started to laugh.

"She's not afraid of you anymore," Gramm said to Milo.

Preston handed the salad to White, a French dip to Gramm, a Croque Monsieur to Milo, and she sat down with a Monte Cristo. Gramm looked at Milo.

"What?"

"Is that a sandwich with a French name?"

"Forget the name, it's a ham and cheese."

"How do you know that?" Gramm wondered.

"I've fallen in with a bad crowd," Milo said.

"I don't want to discuss Milo's food," White said. "I want to talk murder."

Gramm shrugged, dipping his sandwich in the au jus. "So, talk."

"Peter Gain is the number-one suspect in my book. He's hyper about his father's image and the sale of his late father's company. I think Rand's book—which labels his father a murderer—is more threatening than he lets on."

"How did he poison her?" Gramm asked.

"Remember, the victim told Crystal Bower and Evelyn Chen that she took an antacid earlier, but it wasn't working. Peter Gain could have given her that antacid when they met at the restaurant," White said. "Doc Smith told me about slow-dissolving capsules which puts Peter Gain in the picture."

"Possible," Gramm said, "but, there's a lot of supposition there. From what you've told me, Liam Johansson should be the number-one suspect. I see a straight line from him to the victim. He hated her with good reason. He mixed the drink and disappeared. He could have been bringing her the drink, not getting paper towels. Motive, means, and opportunity."

"Means could be the problem," White argued. "We have less proof that Liam knew how to make aconite. Peter Gain is a chemist."

Preston, gaining more confidence by the day, offered her number-one suspect, "Crystal Bower had a clear motive to keep Rand's book from being published. She's up for a big promotion and a close reading of the book paints her as a cocaine user. I don't know a lot about big pharma, but I bet being accused of drug addiction doesn't move you up to the C-suite."

"If we're talking means, don't forget about the herb lady," Milo reminded the group.

Preston checked her notes. "Evelyn Chen. She does make tincture of aconite on a regular basis and she spent some time in the bathroom across from the victim. She could have delivered the poison or made it for someone else."

"Oh crap! Conspiracy?" Gramm asked.

Milo sighed. "Speaking of conspiracy, remember I saw Liam Johansson and Erin Cohen looking chummy at Chester Bowl on Saturday. They could be in it together. Cohen knocked over the water which could have diverted attention from Liam delivering the poison drink."

Gramm shook his head. "A fancy French sandwich and you went to the family friendly Chester Bowl Festival? You have fallen in with a bad crowd!"

"Does this bad crowd include a lying widow with blue eyes that make men swoon?" White asked.

"Swoon? Who says swoon?" Milo asked.

White, checking the definition of 'swoon' on her phone, said, "Hysterical rapture or ecstasy. Yeah that nails it from what I've seen."

"Lying widow?" Preston asked.

"Mary Alice Bonner. It's before your time," White said. "Okay once again getting back on track, Liam has a great motive, so does his sister, but why would Erin Cohen help either of them?"

"We'll have to ask her, and Liam," Milo said.

Gramm's eyebrows shot up. "Well, now we've got at least three people involved in your conspiracies."

"As long as we're including everyone as our number-one suspect," White said, "Ron Bello brushed aside any animosity toward the victim in our interview, but Milo found a lawsuit he filed against Rand accusing her of slander. He also shot her nine times in his book. That's a bit of overkill."

"And his eulogy this morning was far from indifferent… the world will be a better place…," Preston added.

White continued, "Dr. Charles Carlson says he and the victim were friendly, but he did not tell us that Patsy Rand showed him her book and wanted him to back it. He also didn't tell us that he had filed a major lawsuit against Peter Gain's father."

Gramm shrugged. "What does that have to do with anything?"

"Nothing, but why keep it secret?"

"You wanted me to take their picture at the memorial service this morning," Milo said. "Why?"

"Yeah, I don't know why. It seemed odd," White said.

Gramm pounced on that. "Another conspiracy? I hate conspiracies."

White shook her head,. "I don't know about that, but way too friendly."

Milo looked out into the bullpen and saw Peter Gain arrive with a familiar person in tow. *Small world.*

"What about Amy?" Gramm asked. "She was there, and while we've tried to keep her from poisoning people, several of our neighbors have disappeared over the years."

"Cut her some slack," White said. "She may have been having a few bad days."

"I think Gain and his lawyer are here," Milo said.

The three left Gramm and walked out into the bullpen. Gain introduced his lawyer as Kimberly McKenna. Before White could make any introduction, Kimberly smiled at Milo and said, "Milo. We meet again."

They shook hands. White shot Milo a look and introduced herself and Preston.

Preston led Peter Gain and Kim McKenna to the interview room. White held back for a second, blocking Milo's way. With her hands on her hips, looking more serious than usual, she growled, "Okay, before we go in there, how do you know his attorney, and what don't I know?"

Milo shrugged, "She's a friend of Saul Feinberg, and Mary Alice knows her. I met her for the first time on Saturday. The four of us had dinner."

"Did she mention Gain was her client?"

"No, but she did say she was in town on business."

"In town? Where is she from?"

"Minneapolis."

"Anything else I should know?"

"No."

Once inside the interview room, McKenna began the conversation, "Exactly why are we here?"

White responded, "Your client is here to answer a few follow-up questions. You are here at his request."

"My client tells me your initial interview was confrontational and that you threatened to arrest him. That's why I am here."

Ignoring McKenna's accusation, White opened her file. "Mr. Gain, you indicated that your father and his company sued Patsy Rand to prevent her from selling her book."

Gain nodded.

"We can't find a record of that lawsuit. Can you enlighten us?"

McKenna jumped in. "I don't understand what that has to do with Ms. Rand's death."

"Mr. Gain told us Ms. Rand's book was not a threat because he could sue to stop its publication, like his father had done. So, back to the original question. Why can't we find a record of your father's lawsuit?"

Gain and McKenna had a brief whispered exchange before he said, "I was told there was a lawsuit and that's why the book was never published. I told you what I thought to be true."

"In many libel cases, the threat of a lawsuit is enough," McKenna advised. "Perhaps, that's what happened in this case. Are we done here?"

"Not quite," White said, pulling out another piece of paper from her file. "Mr. Gain, we did find this lawsuit—actually two lawsuits—filed by Dr. Charles Carlson against your father and his company. Are you aware of these lawsuits? I ask because you never mentioned them when we talked before?"

"You never asked. Yes, I'm aware of them, but they are old news. Charles and I have come to an agreement—he drops the lawsuits; we give him a substantial payday."

"Did you offer Patsy Rand the same deal?" Milo asked.

Gain looked angry. McKenna put her hand on his arm and whispered in his ear. Gain calmed down and said, "There was no way I was going to give that woman a dime."

"Why? You paid off Carlson. Why not her?" Milo continued.

"My father considered Mark Carlson a friend. They were partners, and Mark contributed to the initial success of the company. His cousin's claim would never have gone to court if he had asked for a reasonable amount of money the first time. My father felt his suit had some merit, but the money Charles was seeking was ridiculous. It was half the company and, at that time, he would not negotiate."

"Why is Carlson willing to settle now?" White asked.

He looked at McKenna, and she nodded her head. "You should ask him, but I do know he likes to gamble. The amount we are offering will go a long way to solve any financial difficulties he may have."

"And Patsy Rand?"

Gain set his jaw. "Her book was a vindictive work of fiction. I was not going to give her one goddamn dime."

"So, you killed her instead?" White pushed.

McKenna stopped Gain from answering. "Come on detective. That's a stupid question."

21

Agnes spread the three construction estimates out on the kitchen island and flipped through them, comparing plans and prices. "All three of these are pretty similar—insulation throughout, build bedroom, closet, bathroom, and storage room."

"I can't wait for that storage room," Martha said, sipping her new favorite, peppermint rosemary tea. "I still have my things from Minneapolis in one of those pods."

Agnes held up one of the estimates. "This one, Ray's Construction, is suggesting built-ins set into the closet. What do you think about that?"

Martha shook her head. "Too expensive. I told him no. I've shopped around and we can get nice closet organizers at half the price."

"It would add value to the place," Agnes said, thinking of her Lakeside bungalow.

Martha laughed, "I have the master and I don't have built-ins. Why would an attic bedroom have built-ins?"

Agnes leaned on the island. "Taking out the built-ins, all three estimates are in the same ballpark. Who'd you like the best?"

"I want this done as soon as possible and Ray can start immediately—besides, other than the fancy closet, we were talking the same language," Martha explained.

"I don't see anything in here about Milo's telescope room," Agnes said.

"Yes, there is. Notice the trap door is now in the storage room which will be padlocked."

"Ray it is. I will call him this afternoon and get you on his schedule," Agnes said.

"Now to new business," Martha declared. "Mr. McKnight wants a basketball rematch tonight even though the temperature is expected to be in the forties."

"Yeah, he mentioned it. I'm debating between wearing gloves or mittens," Agnes joked. "You know this is all about that scoreboard."

"I knew that toy was going to be trouble."

§

Milo stood by White's desk as she called up the photos from his tie-clip camera. The last picture—Dr. Carlson and Peter Gain shaking hands in the parking lot—stayed up on her screen. Milo looked at it for a long time. "It's this scene that bothers me."

White shrugged. "I see two guys who shouldn't be that friendly, smiling at each other. What do you see?"

"Well, Gain has gotten a haircut since we saw him last."

"And we care...why?"

"It's not over his big ears. He looks kinda goofy."

"What about the fact that they look so friendly?" White asked again.

"I agree it's odd, but…" Milo said.

Officer Preston interrupted, "Sergeant my cousin Angie's in town and has never seen a police station. Can I show her around tomorrow morning?"

"Sure," White said. "Make sure you sign her in, and she gets a visitor's badge."

"If this cousin shares your French-Italian grandmother, how do we know she won't throw knives?" Milo asked.

Preston shrugged. "You don't."

"Let me print the picture of Carlson and Gain. Look at it early and often, Milo," White said, setting the printer in motion.

"You know it doesn't work that way," Milo protested, but he was cut off by a phone call to White telling that her Liam Johansson was in the lobby.

Milo questioned, "If we suspect them of conspiracy, don't we want to talk to Cohen first? She'd be easier to crack."

"In a perfect world, but Cohen begged off today. She said that she had to go out of town. We'll talk to her tomorrow." White stood up, walked to the lobby, and led Liam into an interview room.

"I need water," Liam said.

Preston left the room and came back with a bottle of water handing it to Liam. He took out a pill, put it in his mouth, and washed it down.

"What did you take?" White asked.

"Xanax," Liam said.

"Feeling anxious?" White asked.

"I was in prison for twelve years for a crime I didn't commit. It all started in a room like this. What do you think!" Liam charged, twisting the bottle in his hands.

"Answer our questions, and you'll be out of here."

"Ask." Liam shifted in his chair.

"I understand you and Erin Cohen are close."

Liam narrowed his eyes, "Why would you ask that?"

White sat back in her chair. "Ms. Cohen knocked over a pitcher of water. What a great diversion for someone else to give Patsy Rand a poisoned drink without being noticed."

Liam began massaging the back of his neck and mumbled, "You're trying to pin this on me like before."

"Convince me otherwise."

Taking a deep breath, he began. "Before I went to prison, Erin and I were a couple. I'm twelve years behind bars, ten years a free man in California. That's twenty-two years ago. Erin is married. Now we're just friends. When that jug broke, I rushed into the room and helped to clean up. I want a lawyer."

§

Erin Cohen had never heard of Mama's Fish Grill in Fond du Lac. One step inside and she knew why. Faded, blue-checked tablecloths masked cheap wooden tables. Old neon beer signs littered the walls, some working, some not.

To her shock, a woman in curlers and a washed-out flowered housecoat came from a back room to wait on her. "Are you Mama," Erin asked, "as in Mama's Fish Grill?"

"No honey," the woman said. "Mama's my cat. She comes and goes, keeps the rodents away."

Erin shuddered and pick up the menu encased in a sticky plastic. "I'm expecting a friend. Could I have a cup of coffee while I wait?"

"Sure honey," the woman said, leaving to get the coffee.

Erin was excited as she thought about what an investor could do to revive her floundering business. She wouldn't need much. She would get rid of Barry, if not from her life, at least from the business. It was his mismanagement that led to their current short fall.

The waitress returned with her coffee which, against all odds, was savory. She didn't need a second cup, but her investor was late. Erin was getting nervous. She checked her phone—no messages.

After an hour, she paid for the coffee, mumbled something about getting the day wrong, and left.

"Sorry you got stood up honey!" The waitress yelled as Erin held the door for a well-fed tortoiseshell cat who slinked into the empty restaurant. Walking to her car, Erin heard something behind her. Before she could turn, the lights went out. Darkness.

§

Jamal raced into the Lakesong kitchen, papers in hand. "Martha I made the team! I made the team!"

Martha gave him a high five, looked over the papers Jamal handed her, and said, "Sit down. Here's a pen. Fill these out and I'll call Dr. Bergstrom to schedule your physical."

Jamal went from excited child to sulky teen. "Couldn't you fill these out and get Doctor Bergstrom to say I'm fine?"

"I didn't make the team, you did. It's your name on these papers—they say a 'physical,' so you're getting a physical," Martha said, as she called the doctor's office, hoping to get the appointment desk before the office closed.

Jamal looked over the papers. "I don't know all this stuff," he whined.

"You know your name, age, and address, start there," Martha said.

Jamal began, stopping from time to time to ask a question. "It's asking for a parent's name. What do I put?"

Martha looked over his shoulder as she was on hold with Dr. Bergstrom's office. "It says parent or guardian. That guardian person would be me."

Jamal was still whining about having to take a physical. Understanding that teens are large toddlers, Martha diverted Jamal's attention. "Your Lakesong teammate wants a rematch tonight."

"Sutherland?"

"That's 'Mr. McKnight' to you."

"He told me to call him Sutherland. We're teammates."

Martha did an eye-roll and muttered, "It's interesting raising teenagers when the people who own this house resemble teenagers themselves."

A voice from the hallway inquired, "Are you referring to Milo?"

Martha whirled around, but before she could apologize to Sutherland, Jamal bounded out of the chair and ran over to him. "I made the freshman team, Mr. McKnight!"

Sutherland offered him a high five. "Continuing in the proud Lakesong tradition!"

Martha loved the way Sutherland carried on John McKnight's manner of including the children in the history of the house. He made them feel a part of Lakesong, not just short people who belonged to the help.

Martha had a brief conversation with the receptionist who had come back on the line. "Jamal, your physical is Wednesday after school. I'll pick you up."

Jamal rolled his eyes, looked at Sutherland for help, but got nothing.

The intercom announced that the front gate was opening.

Sutherland looked at the app on his phone, "Good. Our score keeper has arrived. Let's meet at the basketball court in fifteen."

Martha went to the intercom to let Agnes know the game was on as Milo walked in from the garage.

"Basketball in fifteen. Don't take off your coat," Sutherland said, running up to change clothes.

Milo was pleased. "Oh, the horn! I'm ready!"

Fifteen minutes later, Sutherland was regretting letting Milo become the scorekeeper. He kept hitting the horn button, and the game hadn't even begun yet. Jamal couldn't believe they had a scoreboard and a scorekeeper.

Agnes, dressed in sweatpants and a red hooded fleece, asked how the scoreboard would fare in a Duluth winter.

"It comes off the pole and goes into the maintenance shed with Goliath," Sutherland explained, jogging in place to keep warm.

"Goliath?" Agnes questioned.

"Our snowplow."

Jamal jumped in. "It's awesome! It's not just a snowplow. It's a tank!"

"Halftrack," Milo corrected. "Jamal and I will give you a ride this winter." He hit the horn button one more time. "Go play, I'm freezing. Shouldn't the score keeper have a heated hut?"

Sutherland began to think about it when Agnes came over to him and said, "No."

Having won the last game, Martha, toasty in her new purple track suit, white jogging-hat, and new basketball shoes, threw the ball in to Agnes. Martha raced to the basket in time to collect Agnes' bounce pass and score. Sutherland collected the ball and moved to the backcourt with Jamal who had donned shorts and his practice jersey.

"You're gonna need that doctor's appointment for pneumonia," Martha shouted.

"I'm young," Jamal answered. "I don't get cold like old people."

Sutherland tossed the ball to Jamal. Martha moved up to defend but was too late. Jamal hit a three pointer. They knew it was a three pointer because Sutherland had his handyman paint a three point line on the court.

Milo put up two points, and Sutherland yelled at him. "I can't be expected to know that," Milo complained. Darian came out to watch, and Milo showed him how the scoreboard app worked.

The score bounced back and forth until Milo, growing bored, blew the horn in the middle of a play. Everyone stopped and looked at him. "Technical foul on that tall guy in the baggy sweatpants and puffy vest," he said, pointing to Sutherland.

"Me?" Sutherland asked.

"You need jerseys. I can't be expected to remember names," Milo complained.

"No jerseys!" Agnes shouted.

"You can't call a technical. You're the scorekeeper, not the ref," Sutherland admonished. "Besides, what did I do wrong?"

"You dribble funny," Milo explained.

"You do dribble funny, baggy man," Agnes laughed as she moved past Sutherland.

Sutherland turned to Jamal. "Do I dribble funny?"

"It's trash talk. Don't let them get in your head. Coach says that all the time."

Throughout the game, Martha and Agnes commented about how much better Jamal's ball-handling skills had gotten with only a handful of school practices. "We could be in real trouble by next year," Martha said.

"Don't worry about it. As Jamal gets better, Sutherland will get worse." Agnes laughed.

Sometime during the fourth quarter the players noticed that Darian was running the scoreboard and Milo was leaning back, arms folded over his body for warmth.

With the score tied and two seconds to go, Jamal hit from the corner. Darian hit the horn button. The game was over. Jamal and Sutherland did a high five as did Milo and Darian.

"We've each taken a game," Sutherland said. "When's the tie breaker?"

Agnes shivered. "I'm thinking June, you know, spring. I'm cold and hungry."

"You can eat here. I'm sure Martha has made enough," Sutherland offered.

"Thanks, but I have a roast in the crockpot."

Martha told Jamal and Darian that beef stew was waiting for them in the cottage. They had to heat it up. As the adults walked back to the house, Martha whispered to Agnes, "Sooner or later you are going to be eating at Lakesong."

"I know," Agnes sighed, "but I feel weird having you serve me dinner. We're friends."

Martha laughed. "Get over yourself. You do things for me all the time. I'm a personal chef. I cook and serve food. Do you really have a roast in the crockpot?"

"Half a tuna fish sandwich in the refrigerator and some coleslaw."

"Agnes has changed her mind," Martha yelled. "She realized she doesn't own a crockpot."

Sutherland, who was walking behind them, smiled.

22

The smell of old wood, disinfectant, and stale beer reminded Milo of good times as a teen in a pool hall attached to a bar. Milo stood in the doorway for a minute, letting his eyes adjust from the early morning sun to the low light of the near-empty Rasa bar.

"Hey Milo, Morrie's in his booth," Benny called as he wiped down the bar. "You want a beer?"

Benny was one of Milo's kidnappers this past summer. Apparently Benny thought that put them on a first name basis. "Got coffee?" Milo asked.

Benny poured him a cup. "It's on the house," he said

Taking his coffee, Milo tracked his course around the tables to the back booth. Melosh, Morrie's bodyguard—also known as Mike—nodded as he lumbered out of the booth to let Milo sit down opposite Morrie. As always, Morrie Wolf was dressed in his signature striped sports coat and skinny tie, calculating the numbers on the daily betting sheets.

"I've got nothing to tell you, Milo," Morrie said, not looking up.

"I haven't asked anything yet," Milo replied.

"You want to know about your father."

Milo smiled. Why was he surprised. "How do you know?"

Morrie looked up." You've been disturbing calm waters, causing shots to be fired. That's a sign you should go off and live your life."

Milo took a drink of his coffee. Talking to Morrie was a chess match. The secret of survival was knowing how long to play the game. One move was showing up. Milo figured he had one more move. "I'm told two brothers were responsible, and those two brothers ended up in the trunk of a car in the middle of the lake."

The door of the back room burst open. Leroy Thompson—former adult bookstore owner—strutted into the bar. "Hey Boss, I'm back. I dropped the bag in the…"

Mike lunged blocking Leroy from going any further. "The boss is busy."

Leroy looked up and took a step back. "My bad." He disappeared into the back room.

"I see Leroy is still sporting that *Miami Vice* look," Milo said, referring to Leroy's white suit and purple shirt, complete with eighties style sunglasses and goatee.

"Thanks for stopping in Milo. It's always nice to see you looking healthy." Morrie went back to his betting sheet.

Milo felt Mike's large hand on his shoulder. Morrie had made his move. It was time to leave.

§

"We have a problem," White said, as she stepped into Gramm's office.

Gramm looked up from the papers on his desk. "Do tell."

"Erin Cohen is a no-show for a second interview. I called her home. Her husband says she is missing—hasn't been home all night."

"Do you believe him?"

White sat down. "He sounded worried. I want to issue a BOLO for her," White said, referring to the term 'Be on the lookout'."

Gramm thought for a minute. "Officially, she hasn't been missing long enough, but skipping the interview lets us jump ahead—go for it."

§

Milo was signing in at the front desk as Preston handed a visitor's pass to her cousin Angie. They looked so much alike that he did a double take. "Are you cousins or sisters?" he asked.

Both women smiled. "We get that all the time," Preston said.

"I guess the family is short on genes, so we use the same ones over and over," Angie added.

The three walked into the bullpen. Preston introduced Angie to White who was polite but busy.

"When should I be back for our first interview?" Preston asked.

White explained that the first interview had been delayed. "I'll text you when you're needed."

As the two women walked to Preston's desk, Milo questioned the delay. "What gives? Where is Erin Cohen?"

"Erin Cohen is a no-show," White explained.

Milo was staring at Preston and her cousin.

"Milo?"

He didn't seem to hear.

"Milo!" White shouted.

Milo flinched as people turned to look.

"I said Erin Cohen is a no-show," White repeated.

"Son of a bitch," Milo said more to himself than White.

Gramm yelled from his office, "MIND LINT! I recognize it from here!"

White laughed. "No one would believe my life. Do you want to be alone or do you want to join me quizzing Barry Cohen as to the whereabouts of his wife?"

"You go. I need to do some research. I need all the pictures in Rand's book blown up, plus copies of the shots I took at the memorial service."

"Anything you want to share with the class?" White asked.

"Not yet," Milo said as White ordered up the pictures.

Milo sat down at an unused desk, logged into the system, and began searching for articles about the climbing accident that took the life of Mark Carlson. He found a small report in a Two Harbors newspaper, but that was all. *I guess Harper Gain wasn't a big deal back then*, Milo thought.

Getting up from his desk, Milo walked over to Gramm's office. "I need something."

"Yeah?" Gramm said, looking up from his desk. "What's up?"

"I'm not sure yet," Milo mumbled, telling Gramm his request.

Gramm looked at him. "I have a couple of friends in the Lake County Sheriff's Office. I'll ask them to look. Where are you going with this?"

"Family secrets. French women are Italian," Milo muttered going back to his desk. An hour later, a technician dropped off the photos he had requested from White. Milo spread them out on a nearby table. As he examined them, all but three ended up in a discard pile. Pushing that pile to the side, he re-laid the three remaining pictures in chronological order: A shot of young Harper Gain and Mark Carlson either fighting or playing around, a copy of a Polaroid of Harper Gain after the accident celebrating with company employees, and finally, Milo's picture of Dr. Carlson and Peter Gain shaking hands this morning after the memorial service.

Milo took a deep breath. There wasn't anything in these pictures to say his theory was wrong. Looking at the Polaroid his attention centered on the employees. Milo picked up Rand's book from White's desk and found the picture which had a credit: *Picture By Chris Rivard*. Milo wished he was at home with his software, but he gave Google a shot. It worked. Chris Rivard was a noted computer-code writer who had worked for Tettegouch Software, Atari, Microsoft and a number of other companies.

Milo accessed his online-search software. After fifteen minutes, he had narrowed Rivard's phone number down to three possibilities. Calling the first one, he got a young guy who laughed when Milo said he was looking for a Chris Rivard who wrote computer code. The guy said he had trouble turning on his computer. Milo hit pay dirt on the second call.

"How did you get this number?" the man asked.

"I'm working with the Duluth, Minnesota Police Department," Milo said. "I need to know a few facts about Tettegouch Software."

"Boy, that goes back a few years."

"Let me narrow it down. I'm looking at an old Polaroid picture of Harper Gain celebrating the success of a new video game," Milo explained. "There are nine people in the photo counting Gain."

"I took a lot of Polaroids during that time. Can you email it to me?"

"Sure. Hang on. Let me get someone who knows how to do all this." Milo waved to the IT guy who talked techy-talk with Rivard while Milo waited. Five minutes later, Rivard had the picture.

"Yeah, I remember that picture. Harper almost fired me for taking it." He tore up what he thought was the only copy, but I took two."

"Was Gain camera shy?"

"He had scars on his face. I guess he was self-conscious. Why do you want to know about it?"

"The woman who bought the picture from you was murdered. We are working that case. Tell me, what did you and the other people in the picture do for Tettegouch?"

"Murdered? Why?"

"That's what we are trying to find out."

"Do you think it has something to do with that picture? My picture?"

"We don't know. We're only asking questions."

"Those were good times. We were all so young."

"So, what did you guys do for the company?" Milo re-asked.

"The guy with the long hair pulled into ponytail—I think his real name was Dean—he was an animator. We called him Dufus the Dog-Faced Boy. The guy next to him was a sound guru. I don't remember his name. The rest of us wrote code. It was a great team."

"Who thought up the idea for the game?" Milo asked.

"Harper of course. The man was a genius."

"Thanks for your help." Milo said.

"I don't know how much help that could be."

Milo hung up. His theory had yet to be disproven.

23

As Milo backed into an unexpected parking spot in front of Ilene's bakery, with nothing on his mind but delicious, sweet cream puffs until the passenger-seat door opened and Milosh lunged into the car.

"Milosh? Again?" Milo asked.

"Stop whining. Not a kidnapping this time—drive," Milosh barked, trying to find room for his legs and shoulders.

"Where to?" Milo asked.

Milosh couldn't find shoulder room to point, so he used his head. "Go to that pretty highway up the shore for a while! I'm gonna tell you a story; then you're gonna stop asking questions."

"Can't you tell me here? I got a parking space in front of Ilene's. That never happens."

"Drive!"

Milo eased out of his prized parking space, drove down Lake Avenue, and turned left on Superior Street. It was busy.

Milosh moved the seat back, but his knees still hit the dashboard. "This car sucks," he said, appraising the Honda. "No leg room."

A number of snarky remarks ran through Milo's head, but he quashed them thinking Milosh was not a fellow who appreciated amusing repartee. "What's the story?" Milo asked.

"First we go up the shore then you get the story."

After a silent drive out of the city, Milo veered onto the scenic highway. On the left, a pine forest stretched for miles, the dense woods broken from time to time by small cabins. On the right, the now-tranquil gray water of Lake Superior stretched to the horizon. "Nice day for a drive," Milo said, breaking the silence.

"Okay, here's your story," Milosh began. "A long time ago, there was a young, skinny guy stirring up a little shit. Nothin' big—some theft, fencing, a little sports betting—you know, working. One day this cop pulls him over—speeding—a couple of warrants out. Bad luck cuz this young guy was speeding to the hospital. Word got to him his ma had a stroke—a bad one. Mothers are important, so he tells the cop."

As Milosh paused to ponder motherhood, Milo wondered if this story was going to take them all the way to the Canadian border.

"Anyways, this cop believes this young guy and agrees to let him go see his ma, and even gives him an escort to the hospital. He gets to see his ma before she passes. Now he owes this cop a favor. You know. Time goes by and the young guy gets older, advances in his chosen profession, but finds competition. Two brothers are kinda in the way, and they have cops on the take."

Milo was getting the drift of the story. He was guessing, so far, his dad was the good guy.

"Pull over here at the scenic overlook," Milosh ordered.

Milo did as directed, and the two got out. After Milosh stretched his back and legs, the two sat down on a bench.

"I love lookin' at the lake, don't you?" Milosh asked. "So calming."

Milo didn't find the lake particularly calming today but figured Milosh calm was better than the alternative.

"Anyways, this guy tells his friend, the cop, that some of his associates are on the take to the two brothers, figuring he was paying the cop back for the favor." Milosh stood up and walked to the edge of the overlook. Milo didn't follow.

Milosh turned. "Get over here! I'm not gonna throw you off."

Milo obeyed but stayed at arms distance from the rail.

"Anyways, while investigating that information, the cop gets shot and killed. This angers the guy I'm talking about, and he lets the two brothers know he's not pleased and they go away."

Milo's mind was swimming trying to visualize a young Morrie Wolf and Milo's father, Karl Rathkey.

"Are you getting' this?" Milosh asked.

"Yeah, I'm getting it, but these guys were competition and needed to go away anyway, regardless of what happened to my...the cop."

Milosh smiled. "There's going way, and then there's going away. Get my drift?"

Milo wanted as much detail on the story as possible, "Not really."

"A bullet is business—a beating is personal—a beating and a drowning is personal with a message to everybody. Now do you get it?"

"And the message was?"

"Don't kill my friends."

Milo couldn't decide which was more bizarre, that Karl Rathkey and a young Morrie Wolf were friends, or that Morrie Wolf loved his mother—that Morrie Wolf *had* a mother. He decided not to vocalize any of his thoughts but did push Milosh about Prepinski. "One retired cop met a personal-with-a-message end."

"That cop knew what was going to happen to the kid's friend and was part of it. He covered it up for the brothers. He got personal-with-a-message payback," Milosh said.

"So just the one cop."

"Just one."

Milo thought about Josh Crandell living his adult life waiting for an attack that would never come. He smiled.

"Are we good?" Milosh asked.

"We're good."

"Good. We're not too far from Betty's Pies. Mr. Wolf likes the cherry pie." As they walked back to the car Milosh gave Milo a final piece of advice: "You heard the story, now drop it. No more questions. Got it?"

"Got it. Don't buy all the cherry pies," Milo requested. "I like cherry pies too."

"No promises," Milosh said, "and this car does suck."

§

The excursion to Betty's Pies having been successful, Milo dropped Milosh down the street from Ilene's Bakery, the only parking space available. "Thank Morrie for me," Milo said, as they exited the Honda.

Milosh turned and slapped the hood of the Honda. Milo flinched. Milosh's easy-going, story-telling tone was gone. "I didn't mention Mr. Wolf. I like to take scenic drives, get pies, and tell stories. That's all this was. Got it?"

"Got it," Milo whispered, closing the driver's door and inching toward the back of the Honda.

"Where are you going?" Milosh asked.

Milo pointed to the down the street to the bakery door. "Ilene's...morning cream puff...coffee."

Milosh stared at him. "You have three cherry pies."

"For later."

Morrie's old Lincoln pulled up and screeched to a halt. Milo watched Milosh lumber stretch his legs into the Lincoln which disappeared at a high rate of speed.

Milo took a deep breath, checked to make sure Milosh had not doubled back, and quick-stepped into his safe place—cream puffs, coffee, and Ilene's. She looked up from behind the counter, gave him a wave, and headed for the cream puffs in the display case.

Milo grabbed two coffee cups and filled them from the pot Ilene kept on the back counter and sat down.

"I saw you drive up, but then you drove away. Did you get kidnapped again?" Ilene asked, as she sat down with the cream puff.

"Yup. Like a couple of months ago. This is a bad neighborhood," Milo said, biting into a cream puff, filling his brain with endorphins.

"Neighborhood's fine—it's you. No one else gets kidnapped. I thought moving to that mansion would give you a better class of friends." Ilene tapped three sugar packets on the table, a habit that used to drive Milo crazy. This morning, it was a welcomed idiosyncrasy.

Milo drank his coffee, ate his cream puff, and listened to Ilene talk about the bakery and her husband Vern's seasonal return from the boats.

"Oh wait," Ilene said, getting up. "I have pasztecikis."

"You should get a shot or something. Can I catch it?" Milo asked.

Ilene shot him a look, went behind the counter, and came back with two little square meat pies. "These are pasztecikis. If they were round they would be called pierogis. I'm adding them to the lunch menu for fall and winter. Try one."

Milo bit into one, his mouth filling with the taste of onions, meat, and mushrooms. "These are great!" he said. "I always thought you should have added pasterninies years ago. I think I mentioned it several times."

Ilene scoffed. "Paszteciki not pasterninis. I got a good customer who gave me an old family recipe for a Christmas version with mushrooms. I made them for him last Christmas. I did some research, found out there are meat versions. I thought they'd bring in more lunch customers."

"Give me a two dozen. I'm going to the cop shop," Milo said, taking out his wallet and finding his credit card.

Taking the card, Ilene cracked, "I still can't get used to Milo Rathkey using a credit card."

§

"You're late!" Observed White as Milo walked into the bullpen area with his pasztecikis.

"I brought pasterninies," Milo said, holding up a small, white box.

"Pasterninies?" White asked. "What's a pasterninie?"

Milo stopped at her desk and opened the box. He noticed that there was a note inside. White grabbed the note and read, "Milo is going to call these some silly-ass name. These are pasztecikis, polish meat pies." It was signed *Ilene.*

"She knows me too well," Milo complained.

White took one and bit into it. "Yum! There's a whole meal in one bite."

Gramm's gruff voice ordered Milo and White into his office. "We have a development."

Milo sat down and said, "Amy confessed. I knew it was her." He was about to make another Amy joke but noticed the eyebrows were drawn together; Gramm was not in the mood.

Directing his comments to White, Gramm said, "Your case just took a left turn. Ever hear of Mama's Fish Grill in Fond du Lac?"

White looked at Milo who shook his head. "I guess we haven't," she said. "Why?"

"Erin Cohen was found in the parking lot last night. She's in the hospital in a coma."

"Accident?" White asked.

"Not unless she hit herself in the back of the head," Gramm answered. "Thoughts?"

"If Erin and Liam conspired to kill Patsy Rand, and Erin was getting cold feet, it gives Liam motive," White said

Milo was silent.

"Milo?" Gramm asked.

"I kinda doubt it," Milo said, "but we have to talk to him."

"Who else had a motive to try to silence a travel agent that wasn't a threat to anybody?" White asked.

"She could have been playing amateur detective and blundered into the real killer, assuming it isn't Liam," Milo guessed.

Gramm disagreed. "Would she really be stupid enough to meet a killer in that secluded restaurant? I doubt it. But she would meet an ex-lover, like Liam, even if she thought he did it."

White texted Preston to come in with her computer tablet. Preston was there within seconds with two pasztecikis in hand.

"Tell us what Erin Cohen said about the dining room scene after she spilled the water dispenser," White ordered.

Receiving his permission with a nod, Preston put her plate on Gramm's desk, opened the Erin Cohen file on her pad, and read, "Amy Gramm, Linda Johansson, were the only ones she could vouch for, but that was before she went to the kitchen."

"Milo may be right," White said. "I diagrammed everyone's movements, and for a significant amount of time Cohen was in the kitchen, in partial view of the living room. She could have seen who brought the drink to the victim."

"So, we're sure Rand was poisoned at the book club?" Preston asked. "Does that get Peter Gain off the hook?"

White sighed. "No, we're not sure. Right now, we don't know when or where Rand was poisoned. We have no connection between Erin Cohen and Peter Gain yet, but then we had no connection between Erin Cohen and Liam Johansson until Milo saw them at the festival."

"How about a domestic," Preston added. "What do we know about the husband?"

White looked at her. "Interesting, but why would they be at that restaurant? Was she there eating with her husband?"

"Nope," Gramm said. "The officer who responded to the call last night interviewed Mama..."

"Mama?" Preston blurted.

"Mama's Fish Grill—the name of the restaurant," White said, not realizing Mama was the cat.

Gramm continued, "Mama said Cohen was there alone waiting for someone who didn't show."

"I have a theory," Preston said. "The Big Bear Casino is up there. Could Mr. Cohen be a gambler? She said they were in money trouble—fits a gambler. Is there an insurance policy?"

Gramm began twisting a bushy eyebrow. "Nice theory. Do you have any evidence of this?"

"None whatsoever, Sir."

White tightened up her ponytail. "We have to talk to Erin's husband anyway. It's worth pursuing."

"That Casino is near the Fond du Lac woods," Gramm said. "Check with the casino."

White nodded to Preston. "Get on that."

"Does Amy know?" Milo asked.

Gramm nodded before changing the subject by handing Milo several pieces of paper. "Here's the Lake County stuff you wanted. Not much there. Both Gain and Carlson fell. Some hikers found them, called an ambulance."

"Are you asking about that Harper Gain climbing accident?" White questioned.

"Background. Patsy Rand said it was murder. What if she was right?" Milo speculated.

"There's nothing to indicate it was anything but an accident," Gramm said.

Looking at the report, Milo asked, "Does it say how the cops got into the car?"

"The car?" Gramm was puzzled.

"It says the deputies found their wallets in a locked car. I'm wondering how they got into the car. Did they break in?"

"No. It's further down. Gain had the key in his pocket."

"Oh yeah, I see it," Milo said. "He drove a Ferrari? A college kid drove a Ferrari?"

"Yup," Gramm said.

"In 1984 I took the bus," Milo complained.

"Should I tell them I wasn't born yet?" Preston whispered to White.

"Best not to."

§

White called Erin's husband who said he was at the hospital. White and Milo joined him.

"Not her best look," Barry, a bulldog of a man with heavy jowls and deep-set eyes, blurted as they all stared at Erin who was hooked up to every machine the hospital could muster.

Milo chalked the comment up to shock. He had seen it before.

"Mr. Cohen," White began, "why was your wife at Mama's Fish Grill in Fond du Lac, and who was she waiting for?"

Barry played with the knot on his tie. "She told me she was going to meet a potential investor in our travel agency."

"Alone? Why didn't you go with her?" White asked.

"My father has dementia. One of us has to look after him. I've got a neighbor doing it now."

"Did she say the investor was a man or a woman?" White asked.

Barry thought for a minute. "No, I don't think she said one way or another."

"Do you have an insurance policy on your wife?"

Barry didn't flinch. "We cashed in our policies. We needed the money,"

Milo remained silent and waited for the usual objection—none came. He wondered if Barry was this dense. Did he not get it? White was accusing him of attacking his wife.

"What did she tell you about the murder of Patsy Rand at her book club meeting about two weeks ago?" Milo asked.

"I don't know if she mentioned it until she said she had to go to a memorial service."

"Oh, come on, Mr. Cohen," White said, "a woman is murdered in front of your wife, and she doesn't mention it?"

"Well, she might have mentioned it—something about spilling water and prattling on about some of her theories. I thought she was talking about the book they were reading. Quite frankly, I didn't care, so I didn't listen. I do that a lot, and she gets mad at me, so when we were leaving that memorial service, she mentioned her theory again and I paid attention. It was about the real murder, not the one in the book they were reading."

White straightened up. "What was her theory?"

"Something about the bathroom, and someone leaving. She saw someone go into the living room. I didn't know what that meant; she always had theories. I told her to talk to you people. I was hungry. My blood sugar was falling."

"Did she mention any names?" White asked.

Barry thought for a second. "I don't think so."

Milo jumped in. "Did your wife ever mention the name Peter Gain?"

"Peter Gain? I don't think so. Is that who she was meeting?"

"We don't know," White admitted as she got up to leave. "We'll be in touch. If you think of anything more, please contact us."

"Where's the car? It's our good car," Barry asked.

"I don't know, but I'll check," White said.

Barry nodded. "I had to drive our old Honda over here."

Milo tried not to take offense.

§

"I'm hungry. Let's hit the vending machines," Milo said when he and White returned to the station.

White opened her app. "I'm going to order healthy. Do you want something?"

"Two vending-machine burritos, nuked in the industrial microwave, and a Diet Coke," Milo said. "I'm running low on preservatives and trans fats, whatever those are."

White shook her head.

Twenty minutes later, Milo started on his second burrito while White was unpacking her Thai salad. "Before any more people are hurt or killed," White said, "if you have any idea—crazy or not—this would be a perfect time to voice it."

"I have been thinking about one. It's about family secrets," Milo said, explaining his theory to her.

She ate her lunch in silence, saying only, "How can you prove any of that?"

"That's a problem. I can't prove it, but there's nothing to disprove it, and I've been looking."

"How do we proceed?" White asked.

"We have to spook the murderer."

White continued listening."

"I think Erin Cohen did that, which got her hurt. We can do the same."

"I don't want anyone else hurt," White insisted.

"I agree. It's got to be controlled." Milo took a long breath. "I have a hokey idea that might work. We gather all the suspects and let loose with my wild, unprovable theory," Milo smiled. "Then we see what happens."

"You may enjoy seeing what happens, but if it fails, I can tell you what'll happen—I'll be writing parking tickets for the rest of my life!" White pointed out.

Milo nodded, "You're right. Let's get Gramm in on this. He hasn't had a fiasco in years."

The two filed into Gramm's office and sat down. Gramm looked up. "Is this an intervention? I'm not making coffee, even if the pot is empty."

"I have a great idea," Milo said, "but it needs to be your great idea."

"Because?"

"Because," Milo said, "Robin doesn't want to write parking tickets. I don't know why, but there it is."

"And you figure I do?" Gramm countered.

"Milo says you haven't had a fiasco in years," White said. "He wants to gather all the suspects together and smoke out the killer."

Gramm looked at Milo. "There has to be more. Why do you want to do this now?"

Milo explained his theory and what he wanted to do.

Gramm sat back. "Are you kidding me? You think any of this is true?"

"I have nothing to disprove it. Let's give it a shot."

Gramm picked up the phone and dialed the deputy chief. He explained Milo's theory, the difficulties with this case, and the recent attack on Erin Cohen. There was a pause, and then Gramm explained what Milo wanted to do. Another pause. Gramm said, "Heidi Reinakie went up the hill." Everyone in the room heard the deputy chief say, "That Rathkey is an odd duck with a peculiar track record. Sure, let him do it, but, in the future, could we get a normal murder?" The phone went dead.

"Odd duck? Peculiar?" Milo asked.

"He sized you up and yet has never eaten with you at the Chinese Dragon. But let's get serious for a minute," Gramm said. "We—all of us—are about to blow up the image of a national icon. There's no coming back from that."

"That's true," Milo said, not caring about national icons, "but the real problem is do we serve tea or sherry?"

Gramm groaned, but was relieved that Milo was joking—a sign his consultant was certain of his peculiar theory.

White said, "Okay, Hercule, where do we do this?"

"Where it all ended, Linda Johansson's house. Let's do it tomorrow night."

"Why would anybody come?" White wondered out loud,

"We ask for help in recreating the timeline—bland, boring, regular police work. The killer won't suspect we figured it out. Curiosity will pull in the rest."

Preston poked her head into the office, "I've checked with the casino. Barry Cohen is not a high roller, but I asked about our other suspects."

"And?" White asked.

"Dr. Carlson is a favorite—gambles and loses on a regular basis, but…"

"There's always a *but*," Gramm complained.

"He pays his debt on time," Preston added.

"That's a dead end," White sighed. "Good job."

§

Peter Gain took the call on his cell. "I wasn't there that night. I don't belong to any book club," he told White. He listened to her explanation as to why his presence was important in establishing the victim's movements and said, "I'm bringing my lawyer."

"What was that about?" Dr. Carlson asked.

Gain got up and freshened his drink, "If you don't know, you're about to find out."

Gain, Carlson and several lawyers were sitting in Gain's living room finalizing financial details when Carlson's phone rang.

Carlson told White he wouldn't miss it for the world and hung up. "Why were you invited?" he asked Gain.

"I had dinner with her the night she died."

Carlson smirked, "So they think you poisoned her before she got to us?"

"Not funny," Gain said, as he sat down.

§

"A death revisited? I'm all in," Ron Bello told White. "I shot her multiple times in my book, and I loved every single shot, so going through her actual death one more time will be equally satisfying." *Too eager?* he wondered as he hung up.

§

"Rather ghoulish." Crystal Bower said as White explained the reason for the gathering.

"Routine police work," White said.

"Who is going to play the part of poor Erin? Somebody has to knock over the water."

White assured her that they had that covered.

"That's even more ghoulish," Crystal said, as she hung up.

§

Evelyn Chen put the gathering at the Johansson's into her calendar even as she debated whether or not to attend. A reenactment would be annoying, but she needed to accuse Crystal before Crystal accused her.

§

"I'm home," Liam said, removing his boots and coat putting them in the back hallway.

"Did the police call you today," Linda asked.

He stopped dead. "Why?"

"Well, that policewoman called me. She wants everyone here tomorrow night."

Liam walked into the kitchen. "Who's everyone?"

"Everyone who was here the night Patsy died."

"They're trying to pin this on me. I know it." Liam sat down at the kitchen table.

"We don't know that. She said they only want to go over everyone's movements before the murder."

"A reenactment?"

"She said *movements*."

§

"Do you know about tomorrow night?" Amy asked Ernie as he took off his coat and hung it up in the front closet.

"Milo's gathering of suspects?" Gramm asked.

"Is that what it is? Robin called earlier today and said they wanted to go over our movements before Patsy was stricken."

"It's Milo's idea," Ernie said. "He thinks he knows who did it."

"Why doesn't he make an arrest?"

Ernie drew in a long breath; a habit that Amy knew meant that he couldn't talk about it.

§

Milo handed Martha the cherry pies explaining that they came from Betty's Pies in Two Harbors. Martha questioned the need for three pies. Milo explained one was for him and Sutherland and the rest were for Martha and the sibs. Martha thanked him, noting that she and Darian would share one while Jamal was sure to eat a whole pie by himself.

"He's a growing boy and they're small pies," Milo said, looking around the kitchen. "I supposed Sutherland is doing his bike thing upstairs."

"I believe it's the virtual Adirondacks today," Martha said, going back to her dinner preparations.

"I'm going to take a second swim," Milo announced. "I was exhausted after pushing that horn button on the scoreboard yesterday. I need to train."

"I could tell. You were wilting at the end. Darian had to sub in."

"Young thumbs," Milo said, as he took off for the indoor saltwater pool.

As Milo dove into the pool, a rain began to fall—a cold, wind-driven rain on a dark afternoon. Flipping on his back, he watched the drops pelt the glass dome of the pool enclosure and thought about his discussion with Milosh. He now knew how his father died and why. It was not the story his mother told him. Did she know the real story? Milo flipped over and began a breaststroke. The rain had stopped for now.

By the time Milo arrived for dinner, Sutherland was sitting in the gallery looking out at the lake. Another storm was moving in with flashes of lightning and thunder but as yet no precipitation. With each flash, Sutherland could see the gray, white, windblown waves gaining height as they crashed down on the black basalt rocks he had installed to prevent beach erosion. The last storm forced water up and over their boat house and took out a portion of the touristy beach walk close to the Aerial Lift Bridge. Sutherland loved the power and fierceness of the storm but complained about the damage afterward—his love-hate relationship with Lake Superior.

Milo, carrying his predinner gimlet, joined Sutherland in the gallery. "Are we on generator yet?"

"The wind isn't strong enough, but the lightening show is fantastic," Sutherland marveled taking a sip of his martini.

As the two moved to the family room table and sat down, Milo asked, "Remember Milosh, Morrie's guy they call Mike?"

"The huge, tough guy who delivered the liquor before Morrie's granddaughter's wedding?"

"Yup. He and I took a drive up the shore today."

Sutherland closed his eyes and took a deep breath wondering if his life would ever return to those halcyon times before he knew gangsters and their henchmen. "He took you for a drive, and yet you're not garroted."

"You've watched *The Godfather* too many times."

"Well, did he kidnap you again?" Sutherland asked.

"No, this time I drove. He told me a story, and we went to get pie."

"What?" Sutherland interrupted.

Milo launched into a fifteen minute monologue detailing Milosh's story about a skinny criminal and the cop who did him a favor.

Martha delivered Sutherland's mixed green salad and Milo's usual blue-cheesed wedge of iceberg lettuce. She also left a bottle of chardonnay on the table.

"Of course, names were never used," Milo said, cutting his iceberg lettuce with his fork. "Milosh admitted that one of the cops suffered the same personal-message fate as the brothers."

Martha returned with a cut loaf of warm sourdough bread, followed by two steaming bowls of what she called *Lakesong Chowder*.

Sutherland rubbed his hands together. "You read my mind, Martha. Chowder on a cold, rainy night, perfect."

As if on cue, the wind picked up driving the rain against the family room windows. Three quick flashes of lightning were followed by close, resounding thunder.

Milo looked toward the window. "Have the storms of November come early?"

"They seem to have," Sutherland answered, taking a piece of bread and a slab of butter.

Milo did the same. They ate in silence for a few minutes before Milo asked, "Have you thought about the question I asked a couple of days ago?"

"Question?" Sutherland was puzzled.

"When we discovered my dad was shot on your dad's property, I asked if that's why I'm here."

"I don't think there's a connection. It's not the story my dad told me."

"Why would he have told you any story?" Milo was puzzled.

"You sent him a Christmas card…"

"I sent one every year."

"Oh, I didn't know that. Anyway, getting to the point, I think this was about five years ago. I was looking at the Christmas cards and Dad was in a chatty mood, reminiscing. I knew who you were. Dad had mentioned you before, and I had seen pictures—the ones I put in your room. Anyway, that Christmas he talked about when you and your mom came to Lakesong and how much he loved your mom's cooking. At that time, we were again looking for a cook, and I asked how he happened to hire your mom. He said a close friend recommended her."

"What friend? My mom hadn't been a cook for anyone except my dad and me."

"What were you told about coming to Lakesong?" Sutherland asked.

Milo thought about that bad time after his father died. "Mom said we couldn't afford to stay in our house anymore. So, she had taken a job at a big mansion on London Road, and we were going to go live there. I guess, at some point, I asked how she got the job, and she said she saw an ad in the paper."

Sutherland shook his head. "We don't advertise in the paper. We've never advertised. We go through an agency." Sutherland jumped up and took off running.

"Where are you going?" Milo shouted after him.

"I have proof," Sutherland yelled, disappearing up the steps. He was back a short time later with a file in his hand. "My dad's papers. All the dealings with that agency."

"What does it say?"

Sutherland opened it up, arranged the papers, read over it for a few seconds, and handed it to Milo.

Milo looked at the top paper. The agency had found two cooks for John McKnight in the sixties and the seventies. Then nothing until after Milo's mother's death in 1988. Milo looked up. "This agency didn't find my mother."

"Not according to these records," Sutherland said, "and this is the only agency we ever used. We can go with your mom's story about an ad in the paper or my dad's story about a friend's recommendation."

"In his story, Milosh went out of his way to say mothers are important. If your dad's story is true, and a friend recommended that John hire my mother, could that friend be Morrie Wolf?"

Both Milo and Sutherland continued eating in silence. Neither could contemplate a conversation between Morrie Wolf and John McKnight.

§

On Wednesdays, sixty-year-old Larry Embers swept the hallways of the old, two-story, red-brick shop building in the central hillside. His building—now used for storage—once received boys who were bused in from the all over the city to learn woodworking, metal work, and electricity. The boys were paired up, never two from the same school. Exceptional work was put on display in glass-enclosed shelves which lined the main hallway. Though the boys were long gone, the projects remained, viewed only by Larry Embers who, for thirty years, pushed his broom down the long corridor of winning projects: electric motors, bird houses, hot dog roasters, and cribbage boards. He always stopped at what he thought was the most unique among the displays: an electric gun with relays and electromagnets mounted on a plywood platform. And every Wednesday Larry mumbled, "They wouldn't let kids build that now days." Then Embers would move on, pushing his broom past the faded picture of two smiling boys—arms around each other's shoulders– and the caption which read, *Best Project 1958, John McKnight and Morris Wolf.*

24

"Do you have any bottles of sherry?" Milo asked Sutherland as the two sat down at breakfast. "I've been told sherry doesn't go with eggs and bacon."

"It goes with unmasking a killer."

"It does? What killer?"

"The person who poisoned Patsy Rand—the other case I've been working on." Milo explained his murder theory. Sutherland started shaking his head before Milo was half through. "What?" Sutherland exclaimed. "I can't believe this!"

"Let me ask this again, do you have any bottles of sherry?"

"We, I emphasize *we*, have numerous bottles of sherry."

"Good," Milo said. "Bring several tonight. You are the official sherry pourer."

"Wait, the last time you dragged me into one of your murders we all got shot at," Sutherland complained.

"You didn't get shot at. You and your cycling crew were off to the side. Besides, this murderer poisons people."

"Ignoring all that's wrong with that statement," Sutherland said, "why sherry?"

"All 'gatherings of suspects' have sherry or tea. It's tradition," Milo said.

"Do you like sherry?"

"Don't know—never had it."

§

Linda Johansson's decorative yard light made hiding a police presence difficult. The officers were staying out of sight, hiding in unmarked cars, until all of the suspects arrived at the ordinary gray house in the Observation Hill neighborhood. No one attending would know that the police had more in mind than a routine police procedure.

Amy, bundled against the cutting wind, didn't see anything out of place. Ernie, offering Amy his arm, did notice the unmarked cars but said nothing. Milo and Sutherland rushed up the path to join them.

"Milo, gathering all the suspects together," Amy said on her way in, "is a cliché."

"We can avoid all this if you confess, Amy," Milo said once again.

"Not until I get my little glass of sherry," Amy answered, echoing Milo's attempt at humor.

Gramm questioned the sherry, "I thought they all drank tea."

"We're upper-crust criminals," Amy joked. "In the evening, after supper, sherry is fictionally correct." Amy, Ernie, and Sutherland proceeded into the living room where all the chairs were set in a semi-circle filled in by the sectional. Milo stayed by the door. The humor stopped.

"I was told to arrange the furniture this way. Please sit anywhere in this room," Linda Johansson told them, as Liam inched his chair out of the circle.

Milo greeted Ron Bello at the door.

"You know, Milo, if I wrote this corny gathering into one of my books, my editors would red line it."

"Oh, come on, you love it," Milo said as Crystal Bower scurried up to the front door hurrying to get out of the cold wind.

"Macabre!" she said, as she entered.

"Welcome," Milo said with no apology.

Peter Gain arrived with Kimberly McKenna. "I told Sgt. White, and I'll tell you," she said to Milo, "my client is here as a courtesy. We reserve the right to leave at any time."

Milo nodded, gesturing toward the back of the house. They moved past him down the hall into the living room.

Milo caught sight of Evelyn Chen and Dr. Carlson conversing on the street before they approached the house. The two took the remaining places in Linda Johansson's living room.

White entered the living room with Preston and welcomed everyone, thanking them for coming. Several mumbled 'as if we had a choice' when Ron Bello spoke up. "If you are going to reenact Patsy's demise, I'm afraid you've screwed up. This misshapen semi-circle wasn't here that night. And where's the death chair?"

"Gone," Linda said looking at Liam, whose dining room chair occupied the same spot.

White stood facing the semi-circle said, "In our investigation of the Patsy Rand murder, we've found almost everyone here had a motive."

Some agreed while others expressed concern.

White asked for silence so she could continue. "All of you had the opportunity to poison her as you had contact with her that evening and had the ability to make the aconite or obtain it."

"So, you're arresting all of us," Crystal shouted, "like *Murder on the Orient Express.*"

"No, Ms. Bowers. I said *almost* everyone. So far, we cannot find a motive for Amy Gramm or Dr. Carlson."

"The fix is in!" Evelyn shouted. "You're going to say I did it! I told you, Charles."

"So, you did," Carlson agreed.

White walked over to Evelyn Chen. "Ms. Chen, you make aconite, and Rand was maligning your business and reputation, accusing you of murder. It would have been easy for you to drop the poison in her drink or hide it in the stomach medicine you gave her that evening."

Evelyn shook her head. "I'm innocent! Patsy would never touch my herbs. Not a chance. When I…"

White held up her hand to stop Evelyn from continuing. "Ms. Chen, you may be correct."

"Wait, she's off the hook? She makes that poison! That makes her a suspect! That wouldn't fly in any of my books!" Bello blustered.

White moved to face Ron Bello. "Mr. Bello, after you ruined her legal career, Rand went after you with a vengeance, costing you money and readers. I'm sure in all your research you could figure out how to make aconite."

Bello smiled, "Oh, if only I did. It might have almost been worth going to prison."

"No, it wouldn't," Liam mumbled.

White moved to him next. "Mr. Johansson, you are my prime suspect," she said. "You had the most powerful motive. The woman cost you twelve years of your life." Turning to Linda Johansson, she added, "Or did your sister do it for you?"

Linda was going to protest, but Liam put his hand on her arm and whispered something to her. Neither of them said another word.

Next, White moved to Peter Gain. His lawyer, Ms. McKenna, appeared ready to pounce. "Mr. Gain, the victim's book accused your father of murder which caused you personal pain and could cause you financial pain. The sale of your father's company seems to be consuming your every move. We have evidence someone tried to collect all of those books after Rand's murder; was it you?"

"I thought we were here for a reenactment of a meeting my client did not attend. Now you are accusing my client of theft or murder or both. Let me remind you, Mr. Gain is here voluntarily."

"As are the rest of us," Crystal's pointed out, which was followed by general grumbling.

White was worried she was losing them. Milo's soiree would be a bust, and she would be a meter maid for life. "Ms. McKenna, no one is being accused of anything. There are several people, besides your client, who wouldn't have wanted the contents of Patsy Rand's book revealed." Pivoting over to Crystal Bower, White asked, "Are you our book collector Ms. Bower? You would not have wanted Rand's college reminiscences getting in the way of your career advancement."

Crystal shrugged, crossed her long, lanky legs, and rolled her eyes. "Spare me. This doesn't seem much like a reenactment."

Evelyn piped up, "I don't want a reenactment. I was in the bathroom all night. I was sick."

White nodded. "You say you were in the bathroom all night, but it would have been a quick trip from the bathroom across the hall to the living room where you could have delivered the poisoned drink."

"I didn't!"

"I'm not saying you did, only that you had the opportunity. Now, everybody, Mr. Rathkey needs your input."

As Milo took White's place, Ron Bello began to clap. "Are we doing good cop, bad cop? A definite upturn in dramatic intensity—nicely done." Bellow applauded again.

Amy, feeling unnerved, asked when they were going to get the sherry which caused Ernie to laugh.

"Okay with me," Milo said. "Sutherland, would you please hand out the sherry?"

Sutherland picked up Linda's silver tray, offering a glass of sherry to each person.

"How do we know there isn't aconite in the sherry?" Dr. Carlson asked, looking at his glass.

"Bad joke," Evelyn said.

"I'm not joking."

Sutherland raised his hand. "It's my bottle of sherry. I didn't know the victim. I have no motive. I don't even know why I'm here."

"You're here to pour the sherry," Milo answered, before beginning his theory. "Most of you suffered abuse from Patsy Rand—years in some cases—all motives for murder. But I wondered—why kill her now?" Milo held up Rand's book. "It's all about this book, a book the murderer could not allow to be published. It answers the question, 'Why now?'" Milo was unhurried as he showed each person his copy.

"I've never seen that book!" Evelyn shouted. "I'm innocent!"

Milo continued, "Peter Gain claims he gave Rand's book back to her the night she was murdered. We only have his word for that."

Gain stood up to protest. As Milo gestured him down, McKenna reached out to keep her client seated.

"If we believe him, that copy of this book was stolen out of Rand's car. Also, her house was broken into where other copies were stolen. This book so frightened someone in this room, they murdered the author and stole all the copies."

Kimberly McKenna jumped in. "Mr. Rathkey, if the murderer stole all of the copies of that book, what book do you have in your hand? Is it a prop?"

Milo showed her the book. "No prop. It's the real deal. I happened to have a copy."

Sutherland cleared his throat.

Milo corrected himself, "The house I live in happened to have a copy."

Inching to the edge of his chair, Peter Gain interrupted, "Unlike Ms. Chen, I've known about that vile book all my life. It's nothing but lies. Nothing in that book is worth murdering for."

"Mr. Gain, you say the words may be lies, but the truth is in the pictures. Did you look at the pictures?" Milo asked. "There are two pages of pictures."

"I'm in a picture. So what?" Crystal blurted. "I was young. It was the eighties. Big deal! I've told you all this before."

Milo turned toward the unexpected outburst, "You say you don't care about the picture, but it seems to upset you."

Crystal held up her hand as if to block Milo's words. "You say it's all about the pictures. Well, I'm the only one in this room that's in one of those pictures, but I didn't kill her!"

Milo walked over to her. "There are many pictures, but I'm only interested in three." He asked Sutherland to give each person a copy of picture number one. "This is one that I found interesting. Ms. Bower, would you tell me what you see in this picture?"

Crystal snatched her copy of the picture from Sutherland, expecting to find an image of her younger self. "Oh, I'm not in this one. That's Harper and Mark fooling around—pretending to fight. They did that a lot. They thought it was funny."

"How old are they here?" Milo asked.

Crystal tilted her head as she looked at the picture. "Young, maybe sophomores…nineteen, twenty…it was before Tettegouch was founded."

"You told me they were like brothers."

"They were," Crystal said. "They did everything together. They worked together. They played together. Look, both in jeans and t-shirts, and shoulder length hair." She laughed. "They both had a fear of barbers."

Milo nodded and asked Sutherland to hand out the second picture. "This one is a blow-up of a Polaroid taken by a Tettegouch employee. When this picture was taken, Mark Carlson was already dead. Harper Gain is celebrating the success of the company's second video game."

Evelyn Chen again demanded to know why she was here, "I don't know about any book or any of these people."

"I don't know these people either, but I'm in," Bello said, leaning forward in his chair. "This is great!"

Milo approached Dr. Carlson. "Tell me about picture number two."

Dr. Carlson stared at the picture and shrugged. "It's Harper Gain becoming successful, and my dead cousin's family not getting a dime. That's why I sued many years ago." He nodded at Peter Gain. "We're correcting that oversight now."

"Harper Gain? How do you know that's Harper Gain?"

Dr. Carlson glanced at Milo and then reviewed the picture again. "Well, I remember the caption. I saw this picture in Patsy's book, and she labeled it. It was... Harper Gain Celebrates...or something like that. Look, he has scars on his face, I assume caused by the fall down the cliff."

Crystal laughed and began to speak. Milo stopped her. "I'll get to you in a minute."

"Is that all you see, Dr. Carlson?"

"There are other people in the picture, but I don't know who they are."

Milo walked back to Gain. "Tell me what you see in this picture."

"Dr. Carlson is correct. It's my father after his accident. He hadn't grown his beard yet. I think it was because he was still getting his face fixed."

"Notice the other people in the picture. They are employees of Tettegouch Software. I talked to the guy who took this picture, Chris Rivard," Milo explained. "He said most of them were coders—they wrote computer code." Pivoting back to Crystal, Milo said, "You told us that Harper wrote code."

"That's right," Crystal agreed. "Harper was the coder and Mark was the idea guy."

Milo once again referenced the picture. "So, Mr. Gain, why would your father hire all these people to write his code?"

"He didn't have time?" Peter Gain guessed. "He was running a growing company."

Milo left Gain and joined Crystal. "Now, it's your turn. You laughed when you saw this picture. Why?"

Crystal, who had put on a pair of seldom-used glasses laughed again.

"Fill us all in on the joke," Milo suggested, feeling more confident in his theory.

"That's Patsy—sloppy. She mislabeled this picture. This isn't Harper, it's Mark!"

"Ridiculous!" Peter Gain shouted, rising from his chair. McKenna grabbed him for a third time.

"I agree. It's ridiculous," Dr. Carlson said. "I would know my own cousin."

"I went with Harper for two years. I knew him—intimately!" Crystal insisted. "That's not Harper. That's Mark! This picture must have been taken before Mark fell down the cliff, but how's that possible?"

Most of the circle was staring at Crystal. Ron Bello looked again at his copy of the picture. "I should have recorded this entire event. This is a best-seller in the making."

Evelyn muttered, "I still don't know anyone."

"You read the book years ago Crystal, why didn't you notice this mislabeled picture before?" Milo asked.

"I could say I wasn't wearing my glasses, but the truth is, I didn't want to look closely at some of the pictures back then—brought back too many memories."

Milo moved back to Gain. "Again, let's look at the employees in the background—coders. I checked. The second game was labeled by reviewers as brilliant. Tettegouch never suffered a lack of creativity. Why?"

Peter Gain was becoming even more agitated, "I have no idea."

"Oh...my...God!" Crystal blurted. Her eyes teared up.

"Ms. Bower gets it. Care to enlighten us Crystal?" Milo asked.

"That's Mark in the picture! Mark was alive! Harper died on that cliff!"

Milo smiled, "We have a winner! You are correct! Mark Carlson never died! Harper Gain died."

Gain shot up out of his chair. "I'm Peter Gain! My father was Harper Gain!"

Crystal was looking at the picture. She said softly, "I am positive this is Mark Carlson. He had huge ears, especially the lobes. You're Peter Carlson."

"How?" Bello asked.

"Glad you asked," Milo said. "Two guys who look alike fall down a cliff. One of them has the key to a car—the car that belonged to Harper Gain. On the strength of that, and that alone, the hospital misidentified the two men."

"Why would Mark Carlson have Harper Gain's key?" McKenna asked.

"I know," Crystal shouted. "I told you. Harper was a crazy driver, drove too fast, got into accidents. He lost his license all the time. When they were together Mark insisted on driving."

"This is nuts," Peter Gain said.

Milo continued, "Not nuts at all. Harper Gain died in the fall from the cliff, and Mark Carlson took his place. Gain had no family, only inherited money. No one would miss him, and his money was needed to fund the company. The mix up began at the accident scene, and Carlson never corrected it."

"Mark became Harper," Crystal whispered. "Harper died forty years ago."

"Yes. Tettegouch needed Gain's money. Carlson allowed his name to die to keep Tettegouch and Harper Gain's memory alive." Milo again picked up the book. "Patsy Rand's attempt to revive her long-dead book threatened to reveal this monster of all family secrets."

Peter Gain looked at his lawyer who whispered, "Let's see where Milo's going."

Evelyn Chen jumped up. "What are you waiting for? Arrest him!" She pointed at Peter Gain. "He did it! He murdered Patsy to keep his family from shame!"

Milo cleared his throat. "Not that family member, Evelyn," Milo said, turning to point at Dr. Carlson. "this family member."

Dr. Carlson scoffed. "Me? That's crazy. Remember, I'm the one with no motive." Pointing at Peter Gain, he added, "He's the one with the secret."

Milo asked Sutherland to pass out the third picture. "This picture was taken at Patsy Rand's memorial, and something bothered me about it. You and Peter Gain have the same receding hair line, same earlobes, same everything."

Everyone stared at the two men. There was a murmur of acceptance of what Milo said.

"I don't see it," Dr. Carlson protested.

"Not a problem. Let's compare DNA samples. Mr. Gain would you give us a sample of your DNA?"

Peter Gain glanced at his lawyer who nodded.

"Dr. Carlso…"

Carlson leapt towards Milo, pushing him down hard, his back hitting the edge of a chair. The pain was sharp. Milo struggled to get up. Before anyone could react, Carlson was out the door and running toward his car. As White and Gramm rushed outside, they heard Officer Hughes shout, "Tricksie, Fass!" That command was followed by a growl, a thump, and a howl of pain.

Milo winced as he sat down in a chair. "Anyone got Excedrin?"

Evelyn reached in her purse and took out a small bottle of murky liquid. "Turmeric and Ginger suspended in liquid form. Drink it."

Sutherland laughed.

Crystal tossed Milo a small bottle of Excedrin. "Here."

Gramm strutted into the room. "A running suspect! Milo it worked! Now we can get a court ordered DNA test to prove your wacky theory which seems to be correct."

"The back kinda hurts, but I'm fine. Thanks for asking."

Amy stood up and said, "I don't know about anybody else, but I need another glass of sherry, and somebody has to tell me what the hell just happened. Why did he hurt Erin? I still don't get it."

Nobody moved except Amy who grabbed the bottle of sherry from Sutherland, filled her glass, and handed off the bottle to others in the group. Everyone turned to Milo. Ron Bello agreed with Amy, "It's a great plot, but I'm not following it either. Why would that guy kill Patsy? It makes no sense. She was his friend."

Milo stretched his back. "She appeared to be. I suspect Carlson offered to back her book at one time. I also suspect that was a lie to delay her. Patsy was tired of waiting and told him she got other backers. That was her fatal mistake. He couldn't allow that picture to get out. Crystal knew immediately, or at least when she put on her glasses; others would too."

White came back in and told everyone that Carlson was on his way to jail.

Evelyn stood up once again. "I don't get it. Peter Gain loses everything. I think you're wrong."

"Thank you, Ms. Chen, but he doesn't lose much," Milo said. "Dr. Carlson loses everything. His claim to money was based on his cousin Mark Carlson being dead. He wasn't. That mislabeled picture in Patsy Rand's book showed Mark to be alive. Carlson's claim to any part of the company evaporated when Mark, his own cousin, died last year and left Dr. Carlson nothing."

Peter Gain shook his head, "I saw that picture when Patsy let me read the book. It didn't register with me."

"Charles wasn't worried about you," Milo said. "He was worried about people like Crystal who knew both men back then. That's why he collected what he thought were all the books."

"I could have been his next victim!" Crystal shouted.

"And you might have been had the book been published," Milo agreed.

"You didn't answer my question, Milo. Why did he attack Erin? She didn't know anything about those pictures," Amy said.

"I don't know. I hope he will tell us."

"I don't know how you figured this out Milo," Amy said, "but I have a headache."

Gramm nodded, "Welcome to the club."

25

Knowing today was going to be another long one, White stopped to get a double shot of espresso on her way into the cop shop. She arrived shortly after nine—late—but she was still in charge, at least for today. Gramm motioned her to come into his office as soon as she put her coat on the back of her chair.

He didn't shout for me to come in, she thought. *That's a good sign.*

As she sat down, Gramm reached for his phone. "Sanders has been wanting to talk to you. He and I had a conversation this morning."

"The deputy chief? What's he want with me?"

"This is the part of the job you never see. The deputy chief needs to know the details as soon as possible after we make an arrest. I filled him in and now he wants to talk to you."

"This is the politics part of the job, isn't it?"

Gramm looked at her, his bushy eyebrows lowering. "It's all political."

"Got it. Should I do a mea culpa?" White asked.

"I got an idea—let's we call him and find out." Gramm hit a button on his speed dial.

"Sanders," a gruff voice answered.

"Jerry, it's Ernie. I got Sgt. White here with me."

Before White could comment, the deputy chief launched into a rapid-fire praise of her work ending with, "Great Job!"

She began to explain that it wasn't she but Milo. Gramm cut her off. "Jerry, Robin has to finish paperwork, tie up loose ends, and interview the perp."

"Go to it. Again, Sgt. White, great job!" The phone went dead.

White stared at Gramm. "I can't take complete credit for this. It wasn't…"

Gramm held up his hand. "Stop it! Milo doesn't need the credit; he doesn't want it. You deserve the credit because you let him do what he does. Another person in your place might have been so insecure that either we would have arrested the wrong person, or the case would never have be solved. Besides when you're in charge you'll be blamed for every screwup. Take the praise. It doesn't happen often, and you made Sanders look good too."

§

"Charles Carlson," Liam said, as he sat down at the kitchen table. "Go figure."

His sister Linda handed him a cup of coffee and sat down next to him. "In a sea of enemies, Patsy gets murdered by a friend."

"Beware of friends bearing aconite." Liam laughed.

Linda knew the laugh was masking fear. This had been a close call. On this cold but sunny morning, Liam could have been on his way back to prison.

§

Evelyn Chen labeled her medicinal bottles of aconite along with several other compounds and brought them into the front of her store. Jay took them from her and began stocking the shelves.

"I understand that you are not the murderer," Jay said with disappointment in his voice.

"How do you know that?" Evelyn asked.

"The radio this morning said they arrested some doctor."

Evelyn began telling Jay about the meeting last night and couldn't stop.

"I'm glad he didn't have a gun," Evelyn said. "He could have killed us all!"

§

Azin laid her head on Crystal Bower's arm. She petted her head and played with the long floppy ears. Turning the pages of an old photo album, she whispered, "All these years, Harper...all these years."

§

Ron Bello smiled as he finished his morning call to his agent. His publisher wanted a Harper Gain book and wanted it yesterday. He had to get busy. The first call would be to Milo Rathkey—more research, different book.

§

Dr. Charles Carlson sat in the stark, gray-walled interview room confident that a good criminal attorney could fix this problem. His left leg burned as he picked at the bandage applied after the dog attack. *I was assaulted. That attorney can start by filing that lawsuit.*

White, carrying a large file, entered the room followed by Gramm and began the official recording of the interview by announcing date and time and identifying the people in the room.

"I want an attorney!" Carlson shouted.

White shrugged, "We offered to get you a public defender last night. You declined."

Carlson pounded his fist on the table. "I don't want a goddamn public defender. I'm not charged with stealing a car! I get a top-class criminal attorney!"

White plugged a land-line into the wall jack and handed the phone to Carlson. "Call one."

"I don't have their numbers! I'm calling my wife."

"You called her last night," White said, "but call again."

After several rings, Wendy answered. "Hello?"

"It's me. I need that lawyer—now. Did you call Pat Waukin?" Charles demanded.

"Well, sweetie, this is awkward. I decided to use him for my divorce. You'll need to find someone else. Bye-bye." The phone went dead.

"Wendy! Wendy!" Charles shouted, but she was already gone. "I'll call my office," he said to White. She nodded her approval.

"Crown Dermatology Center," answered the receptionist.

"This is Dr. Carlson. I need to talk to Aditya or Howard."

"Which one, Dr. Carlson?"

"I don't give a damn!" he shouted. "Either of them."

Gramm played with his eyebrows as they waited for Carlson to finish. From the look on the doctor's face, this conversation was also not going in his favor.

Carlson slammed the phone down hard. "Idiots!"

"Go easy on that," Gramm said. "It's city property."

"So?" White asked.

"They are not going to help. It seems that I'm a liability."

Unfazed, White again made an offer for a public defender.

"I want the best!" he demanded.

"You get the next one up," Gramm said.

"That's not acceptable. People of my status do not get the next-one-up!"

"Your status has changed."

White added, "The clock is ticking. Do you want the public defender or not?"

"All right, I'll play this game for a while—but you'll all be sorry."

§

"What do you have on tap for today?" Sutherland asked Milo.

"All my murders have been solved, so I'm going to light a fire in the library and read with my two feline companions."

"What do they read?" Sutherland joked.

"Jet reads *Cat in the Hat*—he's young—and Annie is working her way through *Old Possum's book of Practical Cats.*"

"Impressive."

"What are you doing today?"

"Agnes and I attended the *Light Duluth Teal* kickoff at the Aerial Bridge earlier this week. It's a part of a fund raiser for MOCA, Minnesota Ovarian Cancer Alliance. Tonight, we're going to the gala at the convention center. Are you and Mary Alice going?"

"She's out of town, and I'm afraid galas are not on my bucket list."

"You did fine at Mary Alice's New Year's Eve gala," Sutherland chided.

"I wouldn't go right to fine," said Milo, sipping his coffee. "I talked to a dead-guy-walking."

"There's a golf scramble on Sunday," Sutherland added.

"Do you not know me? I don't even own golf clubs."

"I can give them your check," Sutherland persisted.

"Is this charity important to Agnes?" Milo asked.

"No, it's important to me. My mother was a victim of ovarian cancer," Sutherland said.

"Laura? I didn't know. Sorry. How much do I give?"

"Whatever you want."

Milo glared at him. "Give me a number. I knew Laura before you did. She was a friend of mine."

"You know, this arrangement is so strange." Sutherland smiled. "I never referred to my mother as Laura. It's disconcerting hearing it from you."

"Give me a number," Milo insisted.

"If I asked you at this time last year, how much could you have given?" Sutherland asked.

"Five bucks."

"Add three zeros."

"Okay," Milo said, getting up to get his check book.

"Sit down and give me your phone. You can donate online."

"Good! I could pass out writing a five thousand dollar check."

§

Cody Cookson, a twenty-seven-year-old attorney in a stiff, dark, polyester suit, presented himself to White as Carlson's attorney. "I know it's late in the day, but I'm here to talk to..." he said consulting his file, "a Dr. Charles Carlson who is charged with...well, well, murder and assault."

Overhearing the conversation, Gramm came out of his office. "I'm Lieutenant Gramm. You're new."

"I've been on the job for a year now, but this is my first time talking to homicide detectives." Cookson raked his sandy brown hair off his forehead with his fingers

Preston was enlisted to show him into the interview room where he was greeted by a less-than-thrilled client. As

Preston left, she heard Carlson complain, "Are you even old enough to drive?"

The boyish-looking Cookson was used to such attacks on his credibility. "Tell me why we're here."

Carlson explained the murder of Patsy Rand. "I'm totally innocent. She was a friend of mine for years. The cops even said I didn't have a motive. I'm suing for false arrest."

Cookson looked at his paper. "You are also charged with assaulting an Erin Cohen."

"I know her of course, but I didn't assault her. There is no proof of any of this. They grabbed me because after their dog-and-pony show last night, I chose to leave. They set the hounds on me!" Carlson showed his bandaged leg.

"Why did you choose to leave?"

"It was all so ridiculous. They're going to say I ran. I simply walked fast. They said at the beginning we could leave at any time, so I left. I'm a well-respected dermatologist. I shouldn't be treated like this."

"Their case sounds weak. I think you will be out of here soon," Cookson said, wondering why a well-respected dermatologist would need a public defender.

Dr. Carlson sat back thinking perhaps this kid could do the job.

Cookson let the guard outside the room know that he was ready to discuss the charges against his client with the arresting officers. White entered the room carrying the same large manila folder. Gramm followed. They sat down opposite Cookson and his client. White started the recording again.

"From what my client tells me, you have no case," Cookson stated.

"Hold that thought," Gramm said, sitting back, folding his arms.

"Dr. Carlson," White began, "we have executed search warrants for your office, car, house, and a storage unit we discovered while searching your papers." She handed Cookson copies of the search warrants.

"You have no right!" Carlson blurted, rising out of his chair.

Cookson eased him back down. After a quick review of the warrants, Cookson said, "These warrants indicate that you told the judge that my client attempted to flee after being accused of the murder of..." he looked at the warrants again, "a Ms. Patsy Rand. My client denies that action...fleeing."

"We have about ten witnesses that say otherwise," White said, "which is why the judge signed the warrants." White spent the next ten minutes filling Cookson in on the complicated case and the reason Dr. Carlson killed Patsy Rand.

"Are we talking about *the* Harper Gain?" Cookson asked. White nodded.

"Assuming for now that what you say is true, none of that proves my client is guilty of anything other than losing a fortune," Cookson countered. "He could have been so overcome by the loss of that money, he left the room. You misinterpreted his quick leave-taking as fleeing."

White took a series of papers from her folder and spread them on the table. "These are balance sheets of gambling debts that your client has run up at the Big Bear Casino. This morning, when we executed the search warrant on Dr. Carlson's offices, we learned his partners have discovered a cash shortfall. We think that your client covered his gambling loses with money from his medical practice, money that had to be restored—and would have been had the agreement with Peter Gain gone through."

"You only 'think' he took money from his practice?" Cookson jumped on the word.

"His partners are auditing the books as we speak," White said

"All that proves is that my client is a bad gambler," the lawyer said, tapping the papers.

Dr. Carlson smiled. *This is going well,* he thought.

Undeterred, White next produced a picture of books. "These are copies of the victim's book found in Dr. Carlson's storage locker."

"She gave those to me!" Carlson insisted.

White smiled. "We doubt that, but let's move on to the single book on the floor of the storage unit next to the box. That book was taken from the victim's car sometime after she was killed. We know that because it has small shards of window glass from the victim's car between the pages..."

Cookson was about to object, but White held up her hand to stop him. "I'm not finished. There are three sets of fingerprints on the cover. The victim's, your client's, and Peter Gain's. Gain is set to testify that he gave that book back to Patsy Rand only hours before she died."

"We confess," Cookson mocked. "You have my client on breaking into a car."

White continued with another picture. "This workbench is also in the storage unit. Our forensic people tell us that Dr. Carlson was making aconite. Two jars of the substance were found along with roots of the wolfsbane plant. Patsy Rand was killed with aconite."

"I'm not the only one making aconite. Evelyn Chen also makes it. I use it for back pain," Dr. Carlson said.

"Our forensic people say that this strength of aconite would be fatal," White countered.

"I dilute it of course."

"All this is circumstantial," Cookson said.

"Let's move on to the assault on Erin Cohen. She was struck on the head with a blunt instrument. The night Patsy Rand died, Ms. Cohen was in the kitchen and could have seen the defendant go into the living room with a drink that he poisoned."

Cookson sighed. "Again circumstantial."

Gramm was impressed with the young lawyer in the cheap suit, but he knew the best was yet to come.

White dropped the last picture. "This is a tire iron taken from Dr. Carlson's car. How are you going to explain away Dr. Carlson's fingerprints along with Erin Cohen's blood?"

"Someone took it and used it," Carlson said.

"Then put it back?" White asked.

"Yeah, to frame me."

"Someone without fingerprints who did not smudge your fingerprints?"

"I had to change my tire," Carlson said.

"Well, that's not true," White declared. "There are no fingerprints on the jack, nor on the spare tire."

"I need to confer with my client," Cookson said.

Gramm pushed his chair back and looked at Carlson. "While you two are having a chat, consider this: we've talked to the DA. He is willing to reduce the charges to second degree murder giving you a chance of parole in twenty-five years if you confess today."

"What?" Carlson yelled. "Prison? That's unacceptable! I don't go to prison!"

Gramm shrugged. "Well, the alternative is first-degree-murder which puts you in prison for life without parole. Prisoners need dermatologists too. Your choice. Oh, by the way, Erin Cohen is conscious and talking."

"Before we forget," White said, handing the lawyer a piece of paper, "a court-ordered DNA test for your client." With that, she turned off the recorder and followed Gramm out of the interview room.

§

Milo was sitting by the library fire reading when his phone began playing "Happy." Both cats were lying by the fire. Since neither made a move to answer nor even acknowledge the disturbance, Milo sat up and swiped the green button. "Hello, Robin. What now?"

"I thought you'd like to know Dr. Carlson confessed to murder, robbery, and assault."

"I smell a deal. What'd he get?"

"Second degree murder, twenty-five-to-life, a chance of parole."

"It was a slam dunk," Milo said.

"Not quite. His lawyer made good arguments up until the Erin Cohen evidence."

Milo was taken aback, "What Erin Cohen evidence?"

"Oh yeah, I forgot to mention that we found the weapon—a bloody tire iron complete with fingerprints—in Carlson's car. It appears her assault and attempted murder was a miscommunication."

Milo shook his head. "I don't get it."

"Dr. Carlson said he thought he was being blackmailed. Erin told us this morning that she saw him go into the living room, but she didn't grasp the significance of it. She pegged Evelyn Chen as the murderer, but Carlson didn't know that. So, when Erin asked him if Patsy was okay when he went into the living room, he assumed she was being coy, and he was being blackmailed. That's why he made his offer to invest in her company, mollifying her until he could deal with her."

"Interesting. Was I right about his motive to kill Rand?" Milo asked.

"You were right; he needed that money—gambling debts."

"Debts? The casino said he always paid up,"

"Ha! We learned he borrowed, and I use that term loosely, from his practice. That money needed to be paid back."

"Wait a minute! With Carlson going to the slammer, what happens to my bumps?" Milo asked.

The phone went dead.

Milo looked at it for a second before saying to the cats, "She's learning."

§

Kimberly McKenna decided to go old-school and picked up a paper-copy of the Minneapolis Tribune on her way to the hotel restaurant. This was a free day. Her work as Peter Gain's personal attorney was finished for now. He was no longer under suspicion for murder. Sitting down in the half-empty café, she unfolded the newspaper and immediately pulled out her phone and dialed Peter's number.

"Kimberly?" Peter Gain answered.

"Have you seen the paper?"

"I'm looking at it—still no mention of my father, thank goodness," Gain said.

"Maybe not the Duluth paper, but it's all over the Minneapolis Tribune. The headline is 'Harper Gain Unmasked!'"

Gain groaned. "How the hell did they get the story?"

Kimberly glanced at the story's byline, "Aah, Ron Bello wrote it. He was there last night. You better alert your corporate lawyers ASAP."

"Thanks Kim," Gain said. Another call was coming in. It was the head of his corporate legal team. This was going to be a long day.

McKenna ordered smoked salmon and avocado toast before calling Saul Feinberg.

"Feinberg," he answered on the first ring.

"So officious. Don't you look at your caller ID?"

"Sorry Kim. I'm in lawyer mode."

"I'm in play mode since my client is no longer under suspicion. Your friend, Milo Rathkey, put on the performance of a lifetime last night." She laughed.

"Performance? Did he sing and dance?"

"In a way. It was quite entertaining. I'll tell you all about it over lunch if you're free."

"I'm doing some prep for next week, but it can wait," Feinberg said. I'll pick you up. What time?"

"Are you going to pick me up with your office van?"

Feinberg laughed. "What? Never been picked up by a law office?"

"Never. Where's the Maserati?"

"At home."

"The law office it is. Pick me up at one." McKenna said hanging up and turning back to the Minneapolis Tribune.

26

"I'm going over to Lakesong this morning," Ernie said, as he poured himself a cup of coffee and buttered a piece of toast.

Amy was surprised. "Why?"

"It's a thing. After Milo does his Milo, we go over to Lakesong so one of us can ask, 'WHAT?'"

"Does he even know?"

"It's usually something small that triggers it. Last time a woman went up a hill. I suppose this time it's his creampuff looked like an ore boat."

"Sure he wasn't eating an éclair?"

Ernie laughed. "I'm not sure of anything with Milo."

§

"Oh, it is Monsieur Poirot, and cat, but where are the moustaches?" Sutherland kidded.

Milo poured himself a cup of coffee and sat down. "The cat has the moustaches, and you have been caught. You know Agatha Christie."

Martha set Milo's plate on the table. "I hope you don't mind. I opened the side gate for the contractors. They are starting work in the attic."

"Fine," Sutherland said. Holding up his blue smoothie he asked Martha, "Is this the last of Milo's blueberry contribution to my smoothies?"

"One or two more and then the blue fades away," Martha said, returning to the kitchen.

"What's the next color?" Milo asked.

"Depends on what you pick next."

"Winter's coming. You're gonna starve."

Annie, having eaten her fill of Milo's bacon, headed back to the gallery. Jet watched her go and with great care edged into the morning room to sit by Milo's chair. Milo looked down and Jet rolled on his back, exposing his tummy. Milo petted the soft fur as the cat stretched out. "He's so long," Milo said, placing a piece of bacon on the floor as he did for Annie.

Jet sniffed it and started to bat it around.

"Bacon hockey," Sutherland said. "I love it."

"Please don't make bacon hockey a habit," Martha said from the kitchen. "I don't clean these floors, but I have to walk on them."

"He needs toys," Sutherland said. "I'll stop at the pet store today and pick some up."

"He could use a kitty scoreboard," Martha chided.

"Good idea…"

The discussion was cut short by the intercom, "Someone is at the front gate."

Sutherland looked at the app on his phone. "It's Ernie, Robin, and the young officer from last night," he said, pushing the talk button. "Can I help you?"

"Open up, it's the police!" Ernie commanded.

"I didn't do it," Sutherland joked. "It was a dermatologist." He pressed the gate-open button and left to let them in the front door.

Ernie and Robin? John, your son is on a first name basis with the homicide division—whaddaya think? I guess Sutherland's uneventful life is picking up. Milo thought as he looked around the morning room and at his personal chef in the well-appointed kitchen. *And I guess my chaotic life has settled a bit, and it hasn't even been a year.*

Sutherland returned with Ernie, Robin, and Kate. Gramm grabbed a piece of Milo's toast as they all settled in around the table.

"Between the cats and the cops, it's lucky I don't starve to death," Milo complained.

"Milo," Kate interrupted, "do you know you have a park in the middle of your house?"

"It's not a park, it's the gallery," Sutherland answered. "Home of our cat, Annie."

"You built an indoor park for your cat?"

"My mother had it built; the cat took ownership."

"Enough with the cats!" Gramm barked as Jet rubbed up against his pant leg. "We know the big chunks, but Robin is going to have to write this crazy case up. For that report we need to go over this step by step."

"We investigated this case together. I thought the murderer was Liam Johansson," Robin said. "You, looking at the same evidence, decided Harper Gain wasn't Harper Gain and that's why Patsy Rand died. How did you do that?"

Martha returned. "This sounds like it might take a while, what would you like for breakfast? We have coffee and juice on the cart."

"Robin and Kate declined food but headed to the coffee. Gramm looked at Milo's plate of half-eaten eggs, bacon, and toast. "I could be convinced to try a little of what Milo's eating."

"Comin up!" Martha said.

"As long as you're still cooking," Milo said, "I could use some more bacon. I donated my last piece to the final game of the cat hockey league."

On her way back to the table, Robin felt soft fur against her leg. "Oh! Hello there! Who are you?"

"That's Jet. He's such a handsome fellow," Milo explained. "He walked in, and he's planning to stay."

Jet squeaked.

"Did no one hear me say enough with the cats?" Ernie complained. "Milo, explain yourself."

Milo took a sip of coffee. "It all started with Officer Preston and her family story about a French ancestor who threw knives."

Preston was pleased but confused. "How did that help?"

Robin nodded. "I heard that story, but I didn't go right to Harper Gain died and Mark Carlson lived."

"I've been thinking about family secrets and thought it was a funny story," Milo said, "but then Preston introduced her cousin."

"Oh yeah that made all the difference," Robin mocked.

"I was trying to figure out the picture I took of Dr. Carlson and Peter Gain. It bothered me, but I didn't know why until I saw Preston and her cousin. They looked so much alike. It made me realize Gain and Carlson also looked alike. One was older and trying to hide his receding hairline, but the resemblance was still there, even the big ears. The idea of one huge family secret popped into my brain and would not go away. I tried to disprove my idea, but it kept holding up."

"How do you disprove something like that?" Preston asked.

"First, I went back forty years to the original accident. Two men fell. Neither had ID on them. No one at the scene knew who they were. The cops found their wallets in the car. The car at the scene was registered to Harper Gain. The car key was found in the pocket of one of the climbers. The assumption was made that the climber with the key in his pocket was the owner of the car—not unreasonable. Both had extensive facial damage. When Carlson regained consciousness, they assumed he was Harper Gain. Apparently, he went along."

"Wait a minute," Robin challenged, "if they had their driver's licenses, didn't they also have their pictures?"

"I assume they did, but this is 1982, the pictures weren't great, these two guys had long black hair, and both of them had suffered facial damage. Remember, Crystal said they looked alike."

"What about fingerprints or DNA?" Preston asked.

Gramm scoffed, "No DNA in 1982 and why take prints after an accident?"

"Ernie's right," Milo said. "This wasn't a crime. No one thought a mistake had been made. No need for fingerprints."

"But who does that—switch identities for life?" Preston asked. "Mark Carlson wakes up in the hospital. Someone calls him Harper and he thinks, *that's a good thing, I'll go along with it.* Why?"

"Like I said, Tettegouch needed Gain's money, and maybe he wanted to keep his friend's memory alive. But those are only guesses. We'll never know. That's the tough part of family secrets, everybody's dead, there's no one to ask."

"How did you come up with Dr. Carlson's motive?" Robin asked.

"It helps to have friends in low places. I checked with Feinberg, talked him through my idea and asked who loses. He said Peter Gain could lose some money because the legend of Harper Gain was built on a lie, but the big loser was Dr. Carlson who hadn't yet settled his lawsuit."

"Well your gathering-all-the-suspects stunt worked."

"I have a question," Sutherland broke in.

Everyone turned to look in his direction.

"How could Dr. Carlson know that the water would spill, and that he'd have a chance to put the poison in Patsy Rand's drink?"

"I think he made the poison and waited for a chance to use it. The water-bottle breaking gave him that chance."

§

355

Peter Gain was still trying to grasp all that he learned in the last forty-eight hours when his lawyer, Kim McKenna, called again.

"Peter, I'm putting on an agent's hat. We have an interesting offer on the table."

"Offer?"

"A publishing house would like you to write a book about your father and, of course, the identity switch."

"How did they know to reach you?"

"I guess they called Tettegouch. When this first started, I left word there that any inquiries about you, not the company, should go through me. I hope you don't mind."

"Why would I write a book?"

"To give your father's side of the story. You must know that there will be a flood of books. I suspect Bello is already at his computer. I don't think his book is going to be a hatchet job but be prepared for the less scrupulous."

"I guess...I don't know. I have bigger things to worry about."

"Such as?"

"What do I call myself? Am I still my father's heir?"

"Your birth certificate says Peter Gain, so you're Peter Gain and you are still your father's heir."

"I'm torn. Am I disrespecting my father if I don't change my name to Carlson?"

"That's personal. I only do legal but keep in mind that your nearest Carlson relative is going to jail."

"Kim, you're not helping, but in the face of indecision, I'll do nothing."

"That's a choice."

§

Arial Jenkins, who had earlier lamented her lack of attendance at this month's ill-fated book club meeting, said the obvious as club members left Erin Cohen's hospital room. "We need a new person for the book club to replace Patsy."

Amy Gramm and Crystal Bower stared at her in disbelief. Linda Johansson told her she was being insensitive.

Arial shrugged. "I'm not wrong."

Evelyn Chen shook her head. "You are wrong. We need two new members. I don't think Dr. Carlson will be attending anytime soon."

Amy sighed. "I don't think anyone will want to join—we took murder off the printed page."

"Are you kidding me?" Arial exclaimed. "People will be demanding a seat. By the way, I may have been telling people that I was there that night rather than at yoga. It's a teeny-tiny little white lie. I expect you people to back me up."

"Expect?" Evelyn asked. "Or what? You'll poison us?"

"Not funny," Amy said.

"I know one thing," Arial proclaimed, "no more yoga on book club night."

27

Milo looked out the dining room's leaded-glass windows at the light snow falling on Lakesong's front lawn. December was only days away and Lakesong was taking on its winter look. The dining room, with its grand table bracketed by two massive fireplaces, dwarfed the small gathering, but Sutherland had insisted they use this room. He thought Lakesong should start celebrating again as it had when his parents held their holiday parties here—parties described by Milo who had attended as a child.

Mary Alice watched as Milo's head moved slightly from side to side then up and down. "Having fun?" she asked.

"I am. I forgot how I liked to look through these windows. Everything is misshapen, and if you move your head the shapes change. I haven't done this since I was a kid," Milo said, continuing to move his head. "Try it."

Mary Alice gave it a go. "I see what you mean. Like a kaleidoscope—no colors but sparkles."

"What are you doing?" Sutherland demanded of Milo.

Milo explained. Soon the entire gathering was enjoying the light show provided by the translucent glass with its beveled edges.

"Welcome to a new Lakesong tradition," Sutherland joked. "Personal kaleidoscope viewing." Sutherland offered a toast. "This dinner party is a celebration of friendship and life—a baby step toward the revival of celebrations at Lakesong. Milo, you started it this summer with the wedding of the granddaughter of *He who shall not be named*."

"What's his name?" Ron Bello asked.

Sutherland held up his hand, "Best you don't know. That way your kneecaps stay on your knees."

"Oh! Good old what's-his-name!" Bello proclaimed. "I've known a few of those in my day."

Martha jumped in, "I like good old what's-his-name—he tips well!"

"I agree!" Agnes said.

"Tip?" Bello asked.

"An exquisite Japanese knife," Martha explained.

"And a painting," Agnes added. "One I could never afford."

Sutherland, still holding up his glass, cleared his throat. "Continuing the world's longest toast, I think we need to address the elephant in the room. Last year was difficult. Agnes lost her sister. I lost my father. From what Agnes has told me about Barbara, and what I know about my father, John, they would want us to get on with life—enjoying every moment. So that's what we're doing. To Barbara Cook and John McKnight, tonight we celebrate their lives."

A chorus of here-here's preceded the draining of the wine glasses.

"I think you will all be pleased with the caterers, Alpha-Omega," Martha said. "I know I am. They've shown me a half-dozen authentic Greek recipes."

As if on cue, Pat, the waitress from Gustafson's, entered the room with a tray of Greek country-salads. Pat saw Milo and stopped in her tracks.

"You?"

Every head turned to Milo.

"Hello Pat," Milo said.

"Do we have to make a meatloaf sandwich?" she asked.

"Alpha-Omega is Nick and Nicola?" Milo questioned.

"It is," Pat said.

"It seems that I've picked a caterer with history," Martha said.

Pat put a salad in front of Milo.

"Why doesn't this salad doesn't have any lettuce?" Milo complained.

Pat served the rest of the company before answering him, "It's Greek—feta cheese, kalamata olives, and somethings that you're better off not knowing. Eat it. You'll like it."

Mary Alice couldn't contain her laughter. "Milo Rathkey, extreme foodie."

"Greek country-salad is hardly extreme," Sutherland declared.

Martha decided to weigh in. "So, Mr. Rathkey, would you prefer mixed greens, or no lettuce? I'm asking for a friend."

Milo took several cautious bites. "This is delicious," he proclaimed.

Martha turned to Agnes. "Mixed greens are still out."

Agnes agreed.

Pointing to one corner of the room, Milo said, "The dining room Christmas tree goes there. I remember that from the parties John and Laura held here."

Sutherland disagreed. "No, it went over there, the opposite corner."

Milo was about to object when Mary Alice said, "Buy two Christmas trees, put one in each corner."

"Tell us about the parties," Agnes urged.

Both Sutherland and Milo began then stopped. The whole group started to laugh.

"Do you want the older version or the younger version?" Sutherland quipped.

"Let's start with the older version," Agnes said, squeezing Sutherland's hand.

Milo began. "John and Laura had two holiday parties, an afternoon one for the children of employees, clients, and friends. That included me. It was spectacular. There was a tree in every room, Santa showed up along with a fleet of elves, and each kid got a present. Then we had cake and ice cream here in the dining room. A few days later, there was an adult party. In my teenage years I helped out at both parties until I left for the Navy."

"Your turn," Agnes said to Sutherland.

Someone is at the gate, the intercom announced.

Sutherland looked at his phone, telling the gathering that he had an app for the intercom and the front gate. "It's a woman...in a car," Sutherland said, as he pushed the talk button and asked if he could help her.

"Yes. I may be in the wrong place. I'm looking for Milo, Milo Rathkey. I was given this address."

Sutherland had his phone on speaker. He handed it to Milo. "You can take it off speaker by pressing the speaker icon."

Milo didn't bother. He recognized the woman in the car. "You're in the right place, Jen, just a day early."

"Milo? Sorry, but I couldn't wait."

Mary Alice leaned over to see the live video from the front gate. Milo handed the phone back to Sutherland and asked him to buzz in the visitor. Turning to Mary Alice he said, "My ex-wife."

Milo got up and went to the front door.

Ron Bello said, "A visit from the ex-wife comes with the salad. What will the entrée bring? Someone in this house must adopt me."

Milo opened the door, and Jen walked up the step in bewilderment. "Do you work here Milo? Are you like the security guy?"

Jen looked tired and worried. "I live here. Come in."

Mary Alice came up behind him, followed by Sutherland and the rest of the party. Agnes had said their presence was inappropriate, but Sutherland whispered that this was the woman who ran off with the dog catcher. No one understood Sutherland's reference.

"Oh, I'm interrupting a party. I'm so sorry," Jen said.

"That's fine," Mary Alice said, putting her hand on Milo's shoulder. "You're in distress. We can continue without Milo for a bit. Can we get you something?"

Milo recognized that Mary Alice had switched into hostess mode.

Jen noticed Mary Alice's gesture for what it was—a claim on Milo. This woman was more than Milo's guest.

Jen said, "Lars is missing."

Milo led her into his office, the others went back to the table and waited for Milo to return. Nick gave each a glass of ouzo. "This will help the time pass," he said.

Fifteen minutes later, Milo walked Jen to her car. She turned and said, "Your girl is lovely, Hubble."

"What? Who's Hubble?" Milo was confused.

Jen shook her head. "*The Way We We*re. Barbara Streisand and Robert Redford?. I only rented it at least six times and forced you watch it twice. How can you be so good at what you do and not…never mind."

"I'll find him," Milo said. Despite Jen's distress she was still the black-haired beauty he married so many years ago. But now, however, the ache of loss in the pit of his stomach was gone.

As Jen got into her car, she said, "Thank you, Milo."

Milo watched her drive away and couldn't help remembering her car disappearing in the distance ten years ago when she left him. Even that memory no longer brought any pain.

Returning to the party, Milo said, "Jen and I were married but divorced ten years ago."

"I hope you don't mind," Sutherland said, "but I filled everyone in on the fact that she left you for the dog catcher. You told it as a funny story."

Milo sat down. Mary Alice put her hand on his. "That's fine. She came to tell me Lars is missing, and she wants my help finding him," Milo said.

"Is Lars the dog?" Sutherland asked.

"No. Lars is the dog catcher."

Missed The Murder Went to Yoga

*If you wish to contact the authors, email us at
authors@dbelrogg.com or leave a message at
www.dbelrogg.com.*

If you enjoyed this book please leave a review on Amazon.

BOOKS BY D.B. ELROGG

GREAT PARTY! SORRY ABOUT THE MURDER

FUN REUNION! MEET, GREET, MURDER

MISSED THE MURDER. WENT TO YOGA

Made in the USA
Las Vegas, NV
20 February 2023

67826624R00215